North of Watford

Lynn Phillips

Pen Press Publishers Ltd

First published in Great Britain by
Pen Press Publishers Ltd
25 Eastern Place
Brighton BN2 1GJ

ISBN13: 978-1-906206-85-7

Printed and bound in the UK

A catalogue record of this book is available from
the British Library

Cover design by Jacqueline Abromeit

Author's website: www.lynnphillips.co.uk

Praise for *MOON OVER WATFORD*

Second in a series of novels by Lynn Phillips

'Wow, Lynn Phillips has done it again! Hot on the heels of her award winning novel, Watford under Wood, Moon over Watford continues following the life of Sergeant Greta Pusey.... Lynn Philips is a master, or rather a mistress, of the crime novel....I can't wait for the next one, knowing it will definitely be as good as its predecessors.'

Jules Lancaster, Milton Keynes Writing Group

'Lynn Phillips' second crime novel is written in her distinctive fast-moving style with a full cast of diverse yet credible characters....Lynn succeeds in cleverly weaving Greta's and her colleagues' personal lives in with their working lives. These sound like `real' police officers - i.e. human. But does Greta get her man? I recommend you read this gripping novel to find out.'

'De ma tante', reader's review on Amazon's website

'Greta Pusey does it again! (or rather Lynn Phillips does it again.) Grabs you by the shirt tails and hauls you along on another rattling tale of life at Shady Lane Police Station.... MOON OVER WATFORD is fast paced and full of humour and keeps you turning the pages. Lynn Phillips has created a crime series which is definitely different.'

Bertha Newbery, Chairman, Belmont Writers' Circle

'In her second book featuring the police station in Shady Lane, Watford, Lynn Phillips once more has us turning the pages long after we should have put out the light and gone to sleep. Recently promoted to Detective Sergeant, feisty Greta Pusey proves that she is up to the job by sorting out the intricate plots within plots of her first case as a Scene of Crime Officer (SOCO).'

Brenda Bowley, Northwood Golf Club

In another tale tale of complexity and unexpected twists, Lynn Phillips' portrayal of newly promoted Detective Sergeant Greta Pusey and her colleagues captures many characteristics of officers I have known in over 29 years of service.'

Neil Collin, MPS Inspector –
Commanding Officer of Ruislip Police Station

Praise for *WATFORD UNDER WOOD*

First in a series of novels by Lynn Phillips

'I just finished 'Watford' and was more than suitably impressed. Normally I don't care for 'detective novels' but this one was a jolly good read! (I couldn't resist this bit of English.) I am so impressed that you could put it all together and tie all the loose ends up in such a tidy manner at the end without getting obvious , silly or outlandish. We are looking forward to great things for you in your literary future.'

Bebe Zigman

'The Watford portrayed in her novel Watford under Wood is in many respects a familiar one, but with the sort of intrigue that would have local newspaper journalists salivating. There is murder, sex, corruption, cover-ups and more . . .'

Martin Booth, Watford Observer

'Greta Pusey is the plausible and determined young detective assigned to investigate this truly complex case. In Watford under Wood, Lynn Phillips has accurately captured many of the frailties that Police officers experience.
This an interesting "warts and all" tale.

Inspector Neil Collin,
Officer Commanding Ruislip Police Station,

'Readers who relish the combination of a gripping detective story with a wealth of recognisable geographic details have a new location to savour. To Morse's Oxford and Rebus's Edinburgh is now added - Greta Pusey's Watford.'

Northwood Residents Association Newsletter

'I just finished "Watford" and was more than suitably impressed. Normally I don't care for "detective novels" but this one was a "jolly good read". I am so impressed that you could put it all together and tie all the loose ends up in such a tidy manner at the end without getting obvious, silly or outlandish. We are looking forward to great things for you in your literary future. Let us know as soon as you receive your first invitation to Buckingham (Palace) or anything else that would excite envy in the hearts of lesser mortals.'

San Diego Book Club, California, USA

'I've just finished reading your book and was highly entertained. Many congratulations. When's the next one coming out?'
PS Is the Watford police station really in Shady Lane?'

London reader

'This is a great book, compelling and intriguing. Lynn Phillips has the ability to keep the reader hooked until the very end.
An excellent read.'

Reader's review on Waterstone's/Amazon's website

Chapter 1

I tapped his shoulder and he jumped a foot in the air.

'Ho, ees the lady detective sergeant! What you doing here?'

'I might ask you the same, Juan Garcia. When did you get out? And why haven't you gone back to Colombia?'

His swarthy skin had turned the nasty greenish colour it always went when he was scared. He tried to smile. The effect wasn't pretty. The warm summer's day didn't account for his sudden outflow of sweat, either. But then at his best this second-rate crook had never been much in the looks department. Nor noted for his cool.

'Nobody is sending me back to Colombia,' he explained. 'I was model in prison, so they send me out. But nobody is saying not to stay here. You wooden send me back, Sergeant dear? Is dangerous there.'

'Better here,' I suggested, and he nodded so hard I thought he'd dislocate his neck. 'So what's with the silver, Juan? Where did you get it? Not up to your old tricks, I hope?' I watched him, thinking hard what to say next.

I'd wandered in past the sign that said GIANT BOOT SALE, in a dozy state, ready to be amused. I certainly didn't have murder on my mind, or anything else to do with work. The nearest I'd got to using my brain was wondering what all those super-clever fictional American lady detectives would make of GIANT BOOT SALE. They'd probably think it was a special for people with huge feet, I sniggered to myself.

Or the FBI HQ at Quantico, would they read sinister codes into it?

I didn't really expect to find what I'd come for, but it was worth a try. My buddy Detective Sergeant Alfie Partridge had told me this was a good place. I was after some of those old 78s of opera singers warbling the stuff that our boss, Detective Inspector Derek Michaelson, thought was so wonderful. I was keen enough on him to try to learn to like the noise they made. Or maybe kid him that I shared his interest. My real aim was to get him to fancy me.

I'd mooched around, peering at some of the rubbish this rabble was trying to sell. Amazing that people were actually buying broken vacuum cleaners, dusty cushions, moth-eaten toys and some iffy-looking hot dogs.

Then I'd stopped at a hatch-back with its back door open and a surprising array of really authentic-looking silverware on show.

The owner was still arranging his display, but something about his back had looked familiar. It was Juan Garcia alright, not gone back to Colombia.

'See, Sergeant, am helping a fren,' he offered. 'No tricks, see?'

I waited. I knew if I just stood and looked at him with that hard look I'd learned from Alfie Partridge he'd have to say more. I stepped closer and looked down at him. Juan cowered in my shadow. It worked. It always does with these little nervous types. Words came gushing out, and I remembered enough of his weird accent to be able to understand most of them.

'Am meeting a lot of nice maties inside, Sergeant, you wooden believe. Prison here not like at home, here is all frens and telling to each other help thins. So then I got especial matey, he esplain thins to me I diden knowing before thees.

He tole me fencies is no good. You got stuff, you bring it here to sell from boot. So he give me, I bring it. See, Sarge, is all above wood.'

Up to then I'd followed his tale of meeting helpful fellow-criminals in prison who told him how things worked here in England. I had my doubts about it being wiser to sell burglary proceeds at a car boot sale rather than through the usual channels. Still, Juan had never been a good judge. But what was clear to me was that most likely we had here somebody's missing goods, and Juan was handling them. Maybe his 'matey' had thought there was little chance of the police checking up on a boot sale. And he'd played it safe by getting Juan to do his dirty work anyway.

'OK, Juan,' I said, 'you're coming along with me. You're nicked.'

And I grabbed him. Of course he wriggled and fussed and yelled for help. But it didn't do him any good, and he should have known that from experience. He'd suffered enough at my hands in the past, although maybe he'd forgotten about my Black Belt in karate.

Previously, he'd been involved in drug smuggling, using counterfeit credit cards, and had almost got himself done for the gruesome murder of the boss of a big criminal operation. But it seemed his luckiest break was in not being deported back to Colombia. As he said, the pokey there was not a patch on ours, and sooner or later he was bound to have ended up inside. He must have been the most hopeless villain I'd ever met, and obviously he hadn't come by any brains since our last get-together. Hadn't he just as good as told me he was disposing of stolen goods for a friend?

Holding him firmly with one arm under his chin, I used the other hand to call to my home base, Shady Lane Police Station in Watford, for backup. Not that I needed help with little

Juan Garcia, but there was the stuff to bring in. I spoke to my darling boss, the handsome DI Derek Michaelson. I always tried not to give away how mushy I felt about him, although Alfie Partridge had sussed it out ages ago.

As briskly as I could I outlined the situation to Derek, and then was flattened by his reaction. His first words told me there was something bad coming.

'Detective Sergeant Pusey, are you mad!' he barked. Not 'Greta', you notice. Oh no, if he spoke to me like that it meant Trouble. 'What possible reason do you think you have for arresting this fellow?' he went on. 'He's served his sentence for past wrongdoing, you said so yourself. Selling silverware at a car boot sale is certainly not against the law. You have no grounds for suspecting that it's stolen property. Let him go immediately, Sergeant, before he decides to accuse you of assault and threatening behaviour!'

'But sir–' I bleated, but he'd hung up.

I let go of Juan, brushed him down and wandered off. I didn't bother to explain to him, and he was only too glad to get away from me, so there was no more conversation. I knew damn well that the stuff was stolen, but if Derek said let him go…

I went home. I'd lost interest in the rotten car boot sale anyway. I would have liked to lose interest in Dearest Derek too, but unhappily for me I'd fallen for him the first moment I'd seen him, and nothing seemed to help me to become unfallen.

A while back he'd managed to get a transfer to Watford from Durham, just to be nearer the current love of his life at the time. Then when she'd dumped him I thought my blessed hour had struck, even though there was the slight problem that he was my superior officer. And some might think it a snag that he was a few inches shorter than me, though I certainly didn't.

Well, with a lot of encouragement, Derek had got to the point of giving me a lovely snog every now and again. But I couldn't seem to get him any further. Very frustrating.

When I got home there was an unusual sight on my doorstep. Standing there with his back to me was a uniformed plod. What? I'd committed no traffic violations, and I couldn't think of any other reason for a visit from a uniform. Then he turned round and gave me a big beaming smile.

'Hallo, lovely girl,' he said.

It was Aristotle Anapolis, who I hadn't seen since he'd told me I broke his heart by refusing to marry him. He'd said that he was going to give up the private investigation business to go back into the Met, but I didn't know if he'd got fit enough to be accepted again. When I'd last seen him his health had been pretty broken up from being left tied up alone in an empty house for a week.

I positively leapt up the path into his arms. I couldn't help it. I knew at the time I shouldn't have done it, but what with being so pleased to see him again and feeling a bit sore at the telling-off I'd just had from Delectable Derek – and well, anyway, I knew right away that I still fancied him as strongly as ever.

Things had been very complicated at the time that Ari and I had become sort of more than friendly. I'd had a long-standing ongoing bunk-up arrangement with Jim the Long-distance Lorry Driver, I was madly and hopelessly in love with Derek, and yet I kept finding myself in bed with Ari. So I couldn't blame him for being put out when I wouldn't consider marrying him, and as far as I knew he'd gone off on the rebound with a dainty little blonde. It was the contrast, probably, me being five-ten, well built and mousy-haired.

Of course I shouldn't have given Ari such an ecstatic

welcome, whatever the current situation might be. It was open to all kinds of misunderstanding. Anyway, I thought the least I could do was invite him in for a cup of tea. Another mistake. When we'd got over our greetings and exclamations, he said, 'I've been waiting for you to change your mind, lovely girl.'

It wasn't fair. He knew very well that being called lovely girl always softened me up. I tried to explain about really being madly in love with my boss, DI Derek Michaelson, and while being fond of Ari himself, not actually *in love* with him. But he started kissing me. I didn't mind that. It was nice. Extremely nice. And I didn't have to bend my knees to make it easier for him, either. We fitted together excellently. Of course the other difference between Dear Derek and Ari was that with Ari my heart wasn't involved, just the rest of me.

So one thing led to another, and it was bed in the afternoon in the home of DS Greta Pusey, Watford CID, who should have known better.

Ari wanted to take me out to dinner afterwards, but I said I'd rather have a pizza delivered so that we could sit around and tell each other all our news in private. After all, we hadn't seen each other for a year, and there was a lot to catch up on.

'Right,' Ari said, 'just as well, innit. I shouldn't really have come out in uniform on my day off duty, but I wanted to show you. You've never seen me in the gear before, and I thought you'd like it. It looks good on me, dunnit? And I've got to get back to South London later on, to be on early call in the morning.'

'South London? That's a long way away,' I said with mixed feelings. Maybe it was just as well that Ari wouldn't be too near. My life was scrambled enough, without the complication of frequent calls from him. Not that I didn't want to see him, but his visits always seemed to end the same way. Nice, but not part of the DS Greta Pusey life plan.

'I tried for Harrow and Stanmore and Hendon,' Ari told me earnestly, 'but Brixton was the nearest I could get. You wouldn't think they're short of bodies in the Met, they're that choosy.

'Mind you, talking about me looking good in my uniform, lovely girl,' he went on after munching at his pizza for a while, 'you've put on a bit here and there. Looks good on you, mind, and doesn't show so much when you're dressed, but maybe you should go easy on the grub for a bit.'

He was probably right, and if anyone else had said that to me they would have got a rusty answer. But Ari was always so straight, I couldn't be put out. I must have started putting on a bit of weight when I bought DC Dusty Miller's car just before she went inside. That was when I stopped getting about by bike or roller-blades. I'd better start getting more exercise, I thought, taking another slice of pizza.

'What's that funny picture on top of your TV?' Ari asked me. 'Looks like some sort of animal.'

I'd forgotten how much of my recent history he didn't know. Probably just as well. There were a few things I wouldn't want to tell him.

'That's Felix,' I told him. 'He was a lovely little ferret that Jim gave me after I got shot. Course, you didn't know about that, either, did you. Anyway, you remember Jim, the Long-distance Lorry Driver? I was very fond of him–'

'What, Jim?'

'No, course not, Felix. But I couldn't look after him properly. While I was out at work I had to keep him in a cage all the time, otherwise he kept eating the furniture, and it wasn't fair. He wasn't happy being locked up, so I had to find him another home.'

'I never knew you was so fond of animals, Greta. Just

shows, you can always learn more about people. What happened to Jim, anyway?'

'Oh, well, when I found out how upset his wife was about him bunking up here every couple of weeks, I just blew him out. He was a bit choked at the time, but I expect he got over it.'

'I know how he must have felt, lovely girl.'

And before I knew where I was, we were at it again, while the rest of the pizza got cold. No more conversational catching-up for a while, then.

So we were still up to our elbows in cold pizza and warm lager and chat and so on when the phone went. I almost let the machine answer, then changed my mind at the last minute. Sorry I did. It was Derek, in his worst growly mood, but still, trying to get round me by using my first name.

'I know you're off duty officially, but I need you right now, Greta,' he barked. 'There's a body in the field you called from earlier, where the car boot sale was. And you won't be Scene of Crime Officer. But perhaps you'll be able to identify the body. I think it might be your little friend, Juan Garcia.'

'Course you have to run when he calls,' Ari grumbled as we were scrambling into our clothes, 'he's your boss and you're mad about him. I'm just here for fun, ain't I.'

It wasn't like Ari to be so sarcastic and bitter. One of the things I've always liked about him is his sweet nature. Still, I suppose it's a bit upsetting if the woman you love keeps telling you she's madly in love with another man every time she goes to bed with you. So I gave him a big smacking kiss and a hug and a front door key and told him to lock up after himself when he left and that I was looking forward to seeing him again. It was only partly true, but you have to think of other people's feelings sometimes.

When I got to the field entrance, Alfie Partridge greeted

me with, 'What were you up to when the Guv phoned, Greta? You look as if you've just got up.'

He couldn't have meant anything by it, but I was glad it was too dark for him to see if I was blushing.

'I was just pigging out in my pyjamas, eating pizza and watching telly,' I told him. 'What's occurring?'

'Doesn't look like that Garcia chap to me,' he said, 'from what I remember of him. But if you saw him earlier today, you'll have a better idea.'

I went over to where they'd rigged up some lights. I was surprised how glad I was when I finally got to the body and saw it wasn't Juan Garcia after all. Why should I care if that little no-good idiot got himself killed? Another of life's little mysteries. But it certainly was murder, no question. Nobody could hit themselves on the head like that, however intent they may have been on suicide. And there was no way it could have been an accident, either.

I could see why Derek might have thought it was Garcia, though. It was a little swarthy man, about Juan's build and colouring, and since I'd seen him in this very field on this same day, it was reasonable to think it was the same person. And he had no identification on him. I didn't tell Derek my first thought, because he would have said I was jumping to conclusions again. But I was afraid that if Juan Garcia wasn't the victim, maybe he was the perp. Or, as Ari would have said, he dunnit. No, couldn't be. He didn't have the guts for it.

'Who found the vic?' I asked, and Derek pointed to a figure standing next to DC Fred Archer.

'You're in for a surprise there,' he warned me, but even that didn't prepare me for the shock I got. I could hardly believe my eyes. At first I thought it was just the dim light that made me think I knew her. But no mistake.

'Dusty Miller!' I exclaimed. 'What are you doing here? I didn't know you were out!'

I got the feeling that I'd said that to somebody else recently, but in that action-packed day I'd lost track of who and what.

'Well,' she said, in her same old surly grudging way, 'I've got to make a living somehow, haven't I. So I organise these boot sales. Couldn't expect my old job back, could I.'

That was a sure thing. After even the light sentence the beak had given her, she positively couldn't get back into the police. And that gave me no regret. She'd always been a cow to me, from my first day in CID.

On the other hand, her life was in bits; her old dad had died while she was inside, and she certainly couldn't get any work where appearance counted for anything. She'd never been much in the looks department, and her time in Holloway hadn't improved matters. So I made up my mind the time for revenge had gone, and decided to be nice to her.

As kindly as I could, I asked her, 'Tell me what you know, Dusty.'

'It's not Dusty any more, it's Dorothy,' she snapped back, so I could tell we were back on our old terms. 'All I can tell you is that earlier on I saw this geezer and his mate that was doing the selling having a big argument. And when I came back to make sure there was nothing left in the field, I found him. So I phoned Shady Lane, didn't I. That's it. Fred's got my address, in case you've forgotten it, so can I go now?'

'I don't know,' I barked. 'Ask DI Michaelson.'

And I stamped over to the body and started the usual routine, wondering who else was going to come popping back into my life from the past.

What with all the people who'd been tramping around the field, and the vehicles driving in and out, there was no chance of picking up much in the vicinity except litter. Still, routine had to be followed, so after the doc had certified that the dead body was a dead body and it had been taken away, I got the immediate area where it had been found covered up with plastic sheeting, and the field cordoned off with a plod minding the entrance, and we all went home.

Time enough for forensics to do their stuff and uniforms to do an inch-by-inch search of the whole field the next day when it was light. Not that we could expect anything useful to be found, but we have to stick to the regulations, even when we think it's daft.

As it happened, I was wrong. Practically the minute we all got there at daybreak next morning, Fred Archer found what was obviously the murder weapon.

I nearly said 'How corny!' because it's what you see all the time when it's murder stories on TV.

It was a tyre lever.

Somehow, I don't know why, I was prepared for the report later on that there was a clear set of fingerprints on it, matching the records for one Juan Garcia. There was a kind of pattern here. Knowing that the poor little bugger had been stitched up in the past was no help. But I just couldn't see him as a murderer. He was too nervous, too squeamish, too feeble. None of which was a legal defence. So I reckoned I'd just have to do some serious sleuthing for my own satisfaction. Nobody else would have any doubts about this seemingly cut and dried case.

'How did they match up Garcia's fingerprints so quickly with the ones on the tyre lever, Alfie?' I asked, trying to sound off-hand.

'Obvious,' he said. 'He was prime suspect right from the start, so they just got out his record, and there it was.'

'Do you believe he did it?'

'Well, he's a right little tyke, so he's up for anything. But now you mention it, maybe he hasn't got the nerve or the, what do you call it, you know, bad temper or guts…'

'So you agree with me. He's been framed.'

'Now then, young Greta. Stop that. Didn't you get yourself in enough trouble in the past deciding you were going unofficial. I've told you, if you want to get on in this job, you've got to go with the flow. Stop trying to solve everything on your tod.'

'But Alfie–'

He went dark red. A bad sign. I know he's fond of me in his funny way, but I do seem to make him a bit testy sometimes.

'Don't you dare start on at me about justice, Sergeant Pusey,' was all he said, but I could tell the conversation was closed. It wasn't just his colour or the tone of his voice, but him saying Sergeant Pusey was a real danger sign.

He never called me that, except when he'd congratulated me on my promotion.

Not that I had a clue what to do about poor little Juan, anyway.

*

A few days after Ari's remarks about my body, I decided to take more exercise. I've never been one of those women who spring out of bed before daylight, go for a five-mile run, then a couple of hours work-out in the gym before starting the day. I don't know if they even exist, except in feminist American crime novels. On the other hand, I've got nothing against exercise as such. I didn't get my karate Black Belt for being a slug.

So I'd taken to leaving the car at home and walking to and from Shady Lane. And then I dug out the old roller-blades and thought I'd go for a spin on them late at night when the streets of Watford are pretty empty and I'm not likely to meet any colleagues who might have a bit of a laugh at my expense. Before I'd acquired Dusty Miller's car, I'd gone everywhere on foot, or by bike or on roller-blades. I'd almost forgotten how much I love Watford on warm summer nights when there's nobody around. And blading around late at night sometimes helped me think things through. Perhaps that way I'd get an inspiration what to do about Juan Garcia and his murdered buddy.

Needless to say, it didn't work. But I did get a different sort of surprise.

I like Watford. I was born and brought up there, and all my career so far had been there. But I've got to admit that we have our problems with the homeless, just like other places. Of course, nothing like the scale of London itself, where I believe you can hardly walk the streets, specially at night, without tripping over bodies kipping here and there. But some of our benches and doorways are occupied by dossers, and our plods don't give them a hard time.

On the other hand, when I go past one of those shadowy bundles in a doorway and it gives a loud groan, I have to investigate. Turned out it was a tiny woman, in an advanced state of pregnancy. In fact, I was horrified to see that she seemed to have started giving birth already. Well, we've been trained to deal with this sort of thing. But the trouble was, she was Chinese, and couldn't speak a word of English. And I was on roller-blades. And I hate babies.

That about sums it up.

I 999'd for an ambulance, took off the blades and hung them round my neck, and started praying that help would arrive before the baby. As my old Gran would have said, my god was with me, and I didn't have to deliver. I'd assumed that once the ambulance came and I showed them my warrant card, I'd be off the hook. I would have been, except that the mother-to-be kept a tight Chinese grip on my hand, and I couldn't summon up enough heartlessness to prise her off. Also, except for an occasional groan, she was so silent that her bravery got to me. So I went with her to the hospital in my socks and hung around, trying to hide my roller-blades from prying eyes.

By the time the babe arrived it was morning. Then they asked me to wait until they found a translator to question the little woman, who looked to me like a kid of about twelve, but might have been forty for all I know about what Chinese people are supposed to look like.

I called in to Shady Lane and when I tried to explain my absence, got it in the neck again from my gorgeous boss.

'What the devil do you think you're doing, Pusey?' he yelled. 'Don't tell me you've forgotten we're on a murder case! What's all this nonsense about Chinese babies, anyway?'

'I thought the murder was solved, Guv,' I stammered. 'Once we've found Juan Garcia all we've got to do is charge him – open and shut, isn't it?'

'I see, Pusey, you think finding him is the easy bit, do you?'

'No, Guv, but–'

'Oh, well, you're there now,' he sighed, suddenly forgetting to be angry. 'I suppose you'd better stay at the hospital to see it through, and come in and report afterwards.'

It took longer than it should have, owing to the fact that the hospital admin people had apparently never heard that they speak more than one language in China. By that time I'd got used to hanging around in my socked feet with no shoes – not that anyone seemed to notice that, or the roller-blades still hanging round my neck. Well, they finally managed to get someone to question the girl (it was true, she was a girl, only eighteen), in the right language or dialect or whatever they needed. And the story was interesting enough to pacify even the most impatient detective inspector.

No surprise to hear she was an illegal immigrant who'd been brought here with a lorry-load of others from her part of China. From the translated version of her story, the only wonder was that they'd all survived the long journey, land and sea and land again. They'd been put to work in a factory, where they also slept and ate and never saw the light of day. Her pregnancy changed nothing in her drudging routine. But once the birth was due any day, she'd been taken from the factory in some other vehicle (the translator said not a lorry but he didn't know what she meant except that it wasn't a bullock-cart) and dumped in the doorway where I'd found her.

That should start up some interesting investigations, I thought as I trudged into Shady Lane, wearing shoes again at last.

Like, for example, what factory? Where? Who was organising all this? And many other questions.

Chapter 2

Just as Alfie Partridge was rumbling at me 'What d'you think you're up to…' and Derek Michaelson was grumbling at me 'And where do you suggest we look for this man Garcia?' I had one of my brilliant ideas.

But I decided not to reveal it to either of them until I'd made some progress with it. There were problems that needed thinking through first. After all, it had been some time since Juan Garcia had lodged in Hendon, before he went inside. And his landlady at the time, Sleazy Sue Slipworthy, hadn't been too keen on him, then. Also she might not be there herself by now. And for various reasons I felt I couldn't go there nosing about. But I knew a man who could.

Aristotle Anapolis would do anything for me. All I had to do was explain the situation to him. So I had to see him again. Not a hardship, specially as I told my conscience that it was all in the line of duty. I sent him a text message: CALL WN U CAN. YR HLP WNTD, thinking I'd have him on the blower that evening to explain, and maybe we could meet somewhere more convenient for him than schlepping all the way up to Watford again.

As usual, I expected too little of him. When I got home, he'd already let himself in with the key that he'd thoughtfully forgotten to return, and was sitting watching TV and drinking my beer. Normally, I'd have said a thing or two on the lines of people making themselves at home in my place, but since I wanted a favour and he'd come all that way without asking questions, I just gave him a medium-to-warm hallo.

Spelling out what I needed him to do didn't take long, but once he started asking questions about the background to it all, the evening spun itself out until nearly midnight. And I suppose I shouldn't have been surprised when he said he hadn't come by car and didn't think he could get a train back... So there we were again. And what with him being on early turn again, so having to get up at four-thirty to catch the first train, we didn't get much sleep. But it was nice.

'I'll go to that address in Hendon as soon as I'm off duty tomorrow,' Ari said. 'Then maybe you can meet me in Camden Town when you're off in the evening.'

So we fixed to meet at his parents' place in Camden Town, though I was a bit worried about what his mother might say to me. The last time we'd met she'd been ready to kill me because she thought it was all my fault that Ari had been kidnapped and nearly died of dehydration.

As it turned out, it wasn't so bad. She just said, 'Hah! So it's the bad penny turned again!' And Ari kissed her and whisked me off to his uncle's nice Greek restaurant, where he said we could sit and talk for hours without anyone bothering us.

'Well,' Ari said, 'to start with, you didn't tell me this Missis Slipworthy was such a sex-pot.'

I felt a little twinge somewhere in my midriff. But before I could decide if it could possibly – or impossibly – be jealousy, he was going on.

'Twenty years younger and I could have fancied her,' he said, 'but she didn't seem to notice the difference. I could see why your buddy Alfie Partridge couldn't keep away from her, specially the way she dresses, innit. She didn't hardly give me a chance to say what I come for before she had me in her kitchen giving me tea and jam tarts.'

'So she still lives there,' I interrupted this poetic tale of near-seduction. 'Did she say how that came about? I was afraid once her boss was a goner, she'd have done a bunk. Specially when it looked as if she'd been sheltering the murderer. Well, I know Garcia didn't really do it, but it was a bit dodgy for her. And what about her husband? Does he live there too? And is it still a sort of guest-house?'

'All right, lovely girl,' Ari said, laying a pacifying hand on the side of my face and stroking it gently. I liked this, but it wasn't on the agenda for that evening. 'Let me tell you everything my own way, right?'

As I nodded, I could feel a soppy sort of smile coming on to my face. I had to remind myself that this was a meeting, not a date. It was strictly police business, even if unofficial enough to make Detective Sergeant Alfie Partridge's face go the same colour as his ginger beard.

'I reckon she must have been a tart some time,' Ari mused, 'what with that dress and the make-up and that kind of come-on manner with her, and friendly in that common sort of way like they've got in South London an'all, I've noticed since I've been down there. They're different that side of the river, Greta, did you know that? Well, even if she is in Hendon now, that's what she's like. But anyway, I expect you knew all about Sue Slipworthy from your dealings with her before, innit.'

There was a pause while he poured us both some more wine and I tried not to show my impatience. After all, this wasn't really a plod reporting to a detective sergeant, just a kind of informal passing on of information between friends. I decided to keep quiet and let him tell it in his own time.

'There was a board in the front garden saying it was the Homely Guest House, so that give me an easy way in,' Ari said. 'I just asked her if she had any rooms vacant, and she said no but come in anyway, and then there was all that carry-on what I already told you, and we got chatting. Good thing I didn't follow up on all her eyelash batting and that, though, because after a while her husband come in. You never told me about him, maybe you never met him. Great big black bruiser, he is, American and a real tough. Been inside, I could tell. No question there. So the story I give was I'd met this nice little South American feller when I was inside myself, and he said if I was ever looking for a nice place to stay if I happened to be in north-west London, I should look up Mr and Mrs Sam Slipworthy at this address. "Oh," sez Missis Sue, "you're in luck there. Like I said, I haven't got no vacancies to offer you just now, but if you're talking about who I think you're talking about, he's right here on the premises this minute"!'

I gasped. I'd hoped that looking up that address might give us a lead on Juan Garcia, but having Ari claim to be his friend and then coming face to face with him – that could be awkward.

'Well, you can guess,' Ari said simply, 'I nearly shat myself. Got myself in a right pickle there, and this bloody great American looming over me, I could see I was in for some trouble. But it was OK; when she went up to his room she found he was out, after all. So I wrote a quick note to leave him my phone number, and got out fast as I could, innit. And that's all I can tell you, Greta. I know you said it never used to be their own place, but I didn't find out nothing about how they come by the house, nor none of that.'

Well, course I thanked him a million times and made a great fuss of how he'd so bravely put himself in danger for my sake. But I couldn't help thinking that if he hadn't made up that daft cover story, he need not have been in such a pickle, and maybe could have found out more for me. I didn't want to seem ungrateful, though, so I didn't say any of that.

It had been a bit of a long shot. I'd had no reason to believe that Sleazy Sue would still be in that house. And since the last time she'd seen Juan Garcia she'd been giving him a bad time, what with abusing him verbally and tying him up and putting him in a trunk, it was stupid to think he would have gone back to her for shelter. But then I knew that Garcia was a bit cracked, with a tendency to do himself no favours, and if he thought he might be in the frame for murder again, he must have been desperate. Poor silly little bugger. If I could ever have a soft spot for a bungling small-time crook, he'd be the one.

I got straight on my mobile to Shady Lane and gave them his address.

*

As I recalled, when that master-crook Len Gilmore had got himself bashed to death, Sue Slipworthy had been looking after the place in Hendon as a sort of safe house for his 'associates'. Her husband was still in jail, and for a living she had to take in anyone who was sent to her.

At that time, poor little Juan Garcia was caught up in the middle of Gilmore's whole complicated little empire of crime. And as we investigated Gilmore's murder, at one point Garcia was the prime suspect. When she heard that, Sue got pretty angry with him and bashed him one. They'd never got on well together, although they worked for the same firm.

Still, Garcia probably didn't know where else to run except back to his old bolthole. Lucky for him that Sam Slipworthy had a soft spot for foreigners.

It was amazing to me that my boss should think Juan Garcia

capable of murder, whatever the circumstantial evidence looked like. But I knew it was no good pleading for common sense. So the only way for me to help the silly little bugger was to talk to him. And for that he had to be banged up, or at least brought into Shady Lane for a while.

Alfie volunteered to go to Hendon to pick him up, taking a uniformed plod with him. This didn't surprise me, considering the effect that Sleazy Sue had had on Alfie in the past. He was a good man, Alfie, a loving husband and father with a strong belief in the importance of family. But somehow this didn't stop him from being particularly susceptible to a certain kind of woman – the tartier the better, I'd noticed on more than one occasion since we'd been partners. So he probably wanted to renew acquaintance with Sue, but having a plod with him would stop any funny business. I was looking forward to hearing how he got on with her large powerful American husband.

'How did it go yesterday, Alfie,' I asked him next morning, and saw by the way he scratched his ginger beard and mumbled into it a bit that Sue still had that powerful effect on him. I wouldn't have dared tease him a few years ago when he was still showing me the ropes, but these days, now that we're really partners I know I can get away with it.

'Have any trouble with picking Garcia up?' I went on innocently. 'What about the people he was staying with?'

By this time Alfie had twigged what I was up to.

'That's enough of that, young Greta. Your man Garcia came along quiet as a lamb, no problem. And that Missis Slipworthy is as obliging as ever, and I'll have none of your lip about her, either. Mind you, she was telling me about her husband, and what a fine figure of a man he is. My height and build, she says,' he added, puffing out his chest. 'No wonder she missed him so badly when he was inside. Pity he was out when I got there, I would've liked to meet him.'

I wondered if Alfie would really have liked to meet the husband of a woman he'd fancied so strongly, but let that go. Seemed like Ari hadn't exaggerated Sam Slipworthy's size, if Sleazy Sue was telling the truth, and not buttering Alfie up as usual. That Sam must be a big feller. Alfie is six-four if he's an inch, and built like a brick shit-house to match. He towers over me, and not many men do that. Even Ari at six foot is only an inch or two taller than I am.

Derek came in, and I felt my knees dissolving all over again. I find it very infuriating that he has this effect on me, but it's not his fault. As far as I can tell, he doesn't even notice this feebleness of mine. Strange, because Alfie, not the most observant detective on the squad, let me know a long time ago that *he'd* seen how Derek makes me feel. And we both know, without talking about it, that my enthusiasm for Derek isn't at all the same sort of thing as Alfie's weakness for slutty women.

Anyway, Derek was all business.

'About that body in the field, we've made some progress here, I'm glad to say,' he told us both. 'The victim's got a record nearly as long as his life was. One of those incompetents who can't see he's not cut out for crime. Operated mainly down Putney way, although he tried his hand in Richmond and Dulwich sometimes. It doesn't matter how long I'm in this job, I just can't understand these fools who keep trying the same thing and getting caught and yet haven't got the sense to stop. Recidivists have always puzzled me.'

Alfie and I exchanged looks. We'd heard this rant more than once before, and we knew better than to answer. He just had to let off steam for a few minutes, and then he'd get down to business. Alfie cleared his throat. He was very good at that. He could sometimes keep clearing away at this invisible frog for as long as Derek went on about the foolishness of the recidivist.

'Charlie Hampson, otherwise known as Charlie the Chump,' Derek finally revealed. 'And we've even got a report from Putney of some stolen silver which seems to tally with what you saw Garcia offering at the car boot sale, Greta. And the break-in ties up with Charlie's MO, and the prints from the scene are on their way, so if that's a match, we've got the whole thing tied up pretty neatly.'

'You haven't told Greta the other bit, Guv,' Alfie said.

I looked at each of them in turn with my eyebrows up, but neither seemed to want to tell me the rest of this apparently open and shut case. Finally Alfie said, 'It's our old mate Garcia, Greta. He won't talk. We can't get him to say a word. When I brought him in I chatted to him on the way, friendly-like, being old acquaintances, but I couldn't even get a hallo from him. And since then we've asked him everything from does he want a lawyer to does he want a cup of tea, and not a dicky-bird comes out of his little beak.'

Derek gave me his heart-melting smile. God, what a handsome sod, I found myself thinking all over again, and nearly forgetting to listen to what he was saying.

'You managed to get something out of him in the past, Greta. So we thought if you went in and had a little informal chat with him, you know, not an official recorded conversation, he might open up a little. And once you've loosened him up, we can have a proper interview. After all, we've got a pretty good case against him already. He was seen quarrelling with the victim, and his prints are on the murder weapon. But you know we can't just leave it at that.'

'Have we got an open mind, Derek? Or are we starting off convinced that he dunnit?' I asked, taking advantage of being asked an unofficial favour.

As I expected, I got no answer from either of my two dear

male colleagues, so left the room to go and talk to that poor little blighter who I was sure had in some way been framed.

We all knew that anyone could turn out to be a murderer, so it was no good arguing that he wasn't the killer type. But somehow I was absolutely sure that Juan Garcia had not done this particular crime.

I was even more certain when I went into his cell and saw him sitting in a corner, silently weeping.

Silence wasn't his usual style at all.

Chapter 3

This wasn't a time for being the heavy threatening sergeant. Sweet sympathy was what was called for here. It didn't cross my mind at the time that, after some of our past history, Juan might find this even more unnerving. Most likely he vividly remembered how I'd scared him so much at one time that he'd tried to hang himself with his shirt in his cell. Luckily for us all, that ended only in a broken ankle when the shirt tore and he crashed into the lavatory pan instead. But it did mean we got off to a bad start.

So when I said in my most sugary tones, 'Come on now, Juan, things aren't that bad,' he took one look at me and shot off to the corner of his cell and sat there on the floor with his face to the wall, shivering and muttering to himself in Spanish. It took a lot of coaxing to get him away from there and sitting down to listen to me, but finally I calmed him down enough to have a sort of conversation.

Apart from wanting to find out his side of the story, what interested me most was why he was so scared. If he knew he was under suspicion for murder but he hadn't done the crime himself, how did he know it was his mate that was done in? And if he didn't know about the murder, what exactly was terrifying him so much?

I tried to take his hand, but this brought on such a bout of twitching that I decided that I'd better not touch him. I saw then that it was going to be a job to get him to trust me.

Finally I got him to start talking. Then suddenly it was the Juan Garcia from the old days. I couldn't stop him.

'After I see you at the boot sale, my matey come back and he say to me, why I haven't sell yet any of the silver,' he started. 'So I tell him nobody want such stuff, and also about I got a visit from you and I deeden want to stay more there. So we have row and shouting and I walk away and leave him with his boot in the car and the silver. I went to pub and have lunch, and stay long time. Then I theenk is not nice to leave matey there in field when is getting dark, so I go back. Everyone is gone. Is no cars, no people, no boots. I walk roun field, I see my fren on ground with head bashed. Oh no, is like when I see Meester Geelmore all those years before and you say I keel. Then I see what done the job and I take it up, then I drop, then I ron. Then I know I shouden do none of that, so I go to old fren Meesis Sleepworthy for to help me. She has nice husban,' he finished.

It was pathetic.

I gave him a tissue and he dried his eyes, blew his nose and let out a long quivering sigh. I couldn't help feeling sorry for the poor little bugger. Talk about own worst enemy. He didn't have the sense of a flea.

'OK, Juan,' I said briskly, ignoring the way he shied like a startled donkey at my voice. 'First thing is, you need a lawyer, and if you haven't got one already, one can be got for you. Then we need to do a little investigating to see if we can help you. Tell me your friend's name and address, for starters.'

When he willingly gave me his murdered matey's name, Charlie Hampson, and his address in Wandsworth, I knew he'd decided to trust me regardless of our friction in the past, because it all tallied with Derek's information. So I told him again I was on his side and would do all I could to clear him, and left him looking almost cheerful.

Then I went back to the office and told Derek that Garcia was ready to make a formal statement.

'If it's OK with you, Derek,' I said, taking advantage of my success with Garcia, 'I'd like to slope off to the hospital and see that little Chinese girl again. Don't you think we should be trying to get to the bottom of that case?'

'Surely she's a matter for the social services and immigration people,' he grumbled. 'What do you want to stick your oar in for?'

'Well, the factory where she was doing forced labour–' I started.

But he flapped his paw at me and cut me short with a terse, 'Oh, go if you want to, Greta, but don't start getting emotionally involved, just because you were there at the birth.'

I stamped off, grinding my teeth. Emotionally involved! There at the birth! This was one of the times when I couldn't believe I could be so passionate about this little berk. You'd think he'd know me better than that by this time. After all, we'd been working together and good friends (most of the time) for quite a while now. And he still thought I could get emotionally entangled because there was a baby in the case. Even Alfie understood me better than that. Admittedly, I had a soft spot for ferrets. But babies – yuk!

Of course the welfare of the little Chinese girl and her baby were the responsibility of the social services, and the illegal entries were down to the immigration lot. But I couldn't see that the slave labour factory was anyone else's business but ours. And it was up to us to find it and close it down.

What with one thing and another, Derek and I had both forgotten that we had one of our infrequent dates that evening.

He was still now and then on his project of educating me into sharing his passion for opera, and I was still pursuing him just because of my passion for him. I'd put up with long frustrating hours when he'd done nothing but play bits of songs from his favourites and explained the stories to me. Now at last we were actually going to see something called 'Butterfly' at the London Coliseum.

I'd made up my mind that however difficult it might be, I'd stay awake all the way through. He might want to teach me to understand his particular hobby, but I'd made up my mind that he should enjoy something far more physical with me, however much I might suffer on the way to getting him to the point.

On the way to the hospital I sent him a text to remind him what time he was calling for me to go into London. No rebukes about forgetting, no threats of what I'd do if he didn't turn up. Just a cool efficient 'of course you remember'.

By the time I got to the hospital, I was in a muddle of feelings. I was partly looking forward to the evening, but also partly dreading it. I was still annoyed that Derek should accuse me of emotional involvement with the birth of a baby. I was baffled about how to find out more about where the Chinese girl had been working and living.

And I was even more mystified about the murder of Juan Garcia's matey.

None of this was like the cool Greta Pusey I'd always been. After all, if I was going to be the first woman Deputy Commissioner at Scotland Yard, I'd have to keep the brain-box working at top gear all the time. Not get bogged down with problems that a clear head could quickly solve.

This line of thinking wasn't helped by finding, when I got to the hospital, that the Chinese girl had absconded and left the baby behind.

'We're very concerned about her,' the Chief Nursing Officer told me. 'She was in no condition to discharge herself. The effect on her health could be disastrous. And of course there's the babe.'

'How was it possible for her to just walk out? Didn't anyone notice?'

'Well, you know we're seriously understaffed, and there aren't enough nurses to watch over each individual patient…'

'Did she have her clothes with her?'

'No, you see, we took them for laundering–'

'What was she wearing when she left the hospital then?'

'A, er, what we call a nursing gown.' She looked embarrassed.

'You mean she went off out into the street and God knows where after giving birth just wearing a little sort of cotton nightdress that opens all down the front? And no shoes?'

The silly cow drew herself up, trying to look dignified.

'Surely, Detective,' she said coldly, 'that will make it all the easier for you to find her?'

*

I was amazed when Derek told me we were going to the opera by train. What's the good of having a car and being a Detective Inspector if you can't go to the West End occasionally by your own comfortable private transport? But still playing at the sweetness and light strategy, I chatted away to him about Puccini all the way from Watford Junction to Euston, and was grateful that at least we got a cab from there to the Coliseum. I was afraid we'd have to plunge down into the mysteries of the tube, or stand in the rain for a bus.

Actually, I'd been reading up a bit about Puccini – the man himself, not the operas – and I was surprised at how interesting he was as a person. Of course, Derek knew all that already, but he was glad to talk about him and to tell me about a dramatised version of his life he'd seen, starring the late Robert Stephens. (I didn't tell him I thought he was an elderly ham. Why spoil things?)

Well, after all that, we got to the theatre early and Derek was wonderfully generous with the drinks. I'm not all that gone on champagne, actually, but it was exciting to know he thought I was worth it.

I was afraid that all that unaccustomed booze (not to speak of boredom) would send me to sleep, but when it came to it I loved the opera, and even shed a tear or two at one point! This was a first. Calm Detective Sergeant Greta Pusey never cried. Derek said to me afterwards that he was surprised to see me so moved, as I already knew the story off by heart. He didn't know how unusual it was for me to cry at all, ever.

The thing was, seeing it all happen was so different, not like just knowing the story and listening to the music. That poor little tart, taken advantage of by that sod Pinkerton! I didn't tell Derek of the connection in my mind between Butterfly and the little Chinese girl who'd been so badly treated and was now probably wandering round Watford, half-naked, lost and scared. Didn't want him going on again about me being emotionally involved.

On the train back to Watford, I asked Derek to my place for a coffee. (I didn't really mean coffee, and I hoped he'd realise that.)

I got a bit excited for a moment when he said, 'Well, I'd like to come home with you, Greta, but I don't drink coffee so late at night.' But my heart went down like a stone when he added, 'But a cup of chocolate would be nice, if you've got such a thing.'

'Sure,' I said glumly, 'chocolate, cocoa, herbal tea, whatever you'd like.'

But there'd been no need for me to be so cast down,

because the moment we got in the front door he grabbed me and started kissing me in no uncertain manner, and didn't even wait to see if I bent my knees to make it easier for him. In no time at all we were down on the rug, thrashing about nicely, and I thought things were going my way at last. But no such luck. It was a case of stopping short again.

Flushed and panting, I said, 'What is it, Derek? Don't say you don't fancy me, I can tell you do. You can't still be pining for Erica.'

Standing up and zipping up his trousers, which I'd accidentally undone in the heat of the moment, he said, 'I'm really sorry. This isn't fair on you. We mustn't do anything like this again.'

'No,' I agreed. 'Behaving like a couple of inhibited professional virgins is stupid. I'm not asking for commitment, you know. Just normal follow-through.'

I probably spoke more bitterly than I'd meant to, but I was feeling hurt and rejected. And puzzled.

He walked to the front door, and I padded after him, trying to make him see how I felt by my expression. My face must have shown how I felt, even to someone so slow on the uptake. Then I thought I'd try to delay him by saying something – anything.

'So you didn't really want any hot chocolate then?'

'Forget it,' he barked, his hand on the front door knob.

'Well,' I tried. 'Thank you for a lovely evening. The champagne and the opera were smashing. I really enjoyed it, er, them–'

'OK,' he said, and left. I let drop my second tear of the evening.

*

Lots of surprises next morning at work. None of them particularly good, but none as bad as the one of the previous evening. Derek and I were both wearing our professional poker faces, and Alfie occasionally looked from one to the other of us in a considering sort of way. He didn't ask any questions, though. Just as well for him. He'd have got his head bitten off.

Surprise number one was that Juan Garcia had been charged with murder.

The second was that a plod had picked up the little Chinese girl, shivering in her little cotton hospital-issued nursing shift, and she was in a holding cell pending an ambulance coming to take her back to hospital.

The last was the worst. A young, skinny, pretty little blonde.

'This is DC North,' Derek said. 'She's one of the fast-track intake. I want you to take her under your wing, Greta.'

'North,' I said. 'Any relation to a shyster lawyer called Charles North? We met him on the Len Gilmore case, Guv, you remember?'

'Oh yes,' Alfie chimed in, 'a right slimy type, he was.'

All three of us glared at him.

'No,' the blonde said quietly, 'none of my relations are lawyers.'

'Well,' Alfie said heartily, as unsquashable as ever, 'that's just as well. So anyway, you're going to be North of Watford, are you? I expect you know what Londoners always say about North of Watford, don't you? They say there's nothing there. Like, after Watford you fall off the end of the earth.'

*

Of course, by the time I'd finished putting North in the picture – and incidentally in her place when she tried to get friendly –

the Chinese girl had been picked up and taken back to the hospital. So we went there after her.

'So why do we want to see the Chinese girl again, Sarge?' North asked. I'd made sure she understood she'd call me Sarge and I'd call her North. None of this Greta and Vicky stuff, as she'd suggested.

'I've arranged for the translator to be there again, and I want to try to get some idea from her about where this factory might be,' I explained. 'We can't have the whole of the Hertfordshire Force out checking up on every factory in the county to try to find it.'

I looked at the Chinese girl in the bed, still wearing the little cotton hospital-issued nursing shift. Then I looked at the nurse. She was the same hatchet-faced old biddy who'd been on duty when the translator had helped me interview the girl after the baby was born.

'This is the wrong girl,' I said, as calmly as I could.

'Of course it's not,' she snapped. 'Look, she's still wearing the same gown she had on when she skipped off.'

'Oh, I suppose they all look the same to you,' I popped back at her. I had no reason to suppose she was a racist. I just didn't like her. The truth was, I didn't much like anyone that day. 'Well, there's an easy way to see who's right. Give her the baby and tell her to feed it. See what happens, then.'

'What do you think, Mr Wing?' old Hatchet-face asked the translator, who'd been politely standing by, waiting to be asked to do his job.

He was cautious.

'She looks similar to me to the girl I saw first. Her name is Ah Weng So,' he said. 'Shall I ask her something?'

'No, don't worry, I'll get the babe,' the nurse simpered at him. Then we all stood around looking at each other and the girl in the bed in turn, not knowing how to fill the time until the nurse got back with the baby.

I've got to admit, even though I'm not one for kids, it was a cute little thing, like a tiny Chinese doll. The nurse offered it to the girl, who shook her head and stunned us all by saying in near-perfect English, 'OK, I give in. It's not mine, I'm not Ah Weng So. I'm not an illegal immigrant, I'm a British subject. I was born here.'

Just what I needed. Another mystery to solve. And the little rookie I was supposed to be mentoring wasn't going to be much help, either, judging from the way her mouth was hanging open. At least that gave me something to say until I could get a useful thought.

'North,' I barked, 'shut your mouth and open your notebook.'

The interpreter, Mr Wing said, 'It seems you won't be needing my services today, Detective, so I'll leave you now. You know where to find me if you need me in the future.'

Before I'd had a chance to thank him, or gather my wits, the nurse was suddenly shouting at the girl in the bed, 'Well, what are you doing there? Taking up valuable hospital space! Are you going to take this baby, or what? Where's the poor thing's mother? Get up out of it!'

She was working herself up into a regular fit of temper, I could see.

'Have you got any clothes with you, Miss?' I asked the girl in the bed. 'I'll need you to come back to the police station with me to answer some questions.'

'No problem,' she said breezily. 'My brother's out in the waiting area with my things. If one of you would go and fetch him, we can sort it all out in no time.'

That's what you think, miss, I thought grimly, trying to work out what I could charge her with to hold her at Shady Lane.

What offence had she committed? What law had she broken? None that I could see.

It was my only lucky break that day that I didn't need to charge her with anything, real or imaginary. She and her brother both came along willingly enough with us, offering to answer any questions. This seemed very suspicious to me, so when they started by giving their names as Sadie and James Lee, I asked them if they had anything to prove their identities. Of course they did, but I still wished I'd had Alfie with me instead of stupid North, to give me some ideas. She was no help at all, except for scribbling away in her notebook like some prize swot at school.

Now that I had a chance to look at Sadie Lee properly, standing up with her clothes on, I could see there was a world of difference between her and the missing Ah Weng So. She was taller and older, and had a cool, composed air about her that poor little Ah Weng So could probably never achieve even if she was lucky enough to survive another ten years.

Settling herself down, she held a cigarette to her mouth and indicated to James to light it, saying as an afterthought, 'I'm sure you don't mind if I smoke, officer?'

She and her brother, if that's who he was, gave their story as follows.

They'd been strolling about looking around on their first visit to Watford, when they'd come across this little Chinese girl, running along wearing only a little cotton shift, and sobbing pitifully. Even on a warm summer's day, she was underdressed, and what with the crying, it was obvious she was in trouble. Naturally they stopped her and asked, first in English then in Mandarin then in Cantonese, if they could help. She gave them some story about being held prisoner in the maternity ward of a hospital so near to where they were standing that she could point it out to them. Without hesitation James had given her his cotton jacket, then they stood in a bus shelter while Sadie took her hospital shift and put it on.

'Of course James took charge of my own clothes,' she added. Very helpful.

'Good thing we're having some warm weather lately,' I put in, but this went down like the proverbial lead balloon. Sadie just went on with their story.

According to her, Ah Weng So thanked them and ran off as fast as she could, wearing James Lee's light jacket and nothing else. And, just fancy, no sooner was she out of sight than a policeman came along! He promptly hauled Sadie to Shady Lane, from where she was taken to the maternity wing of Watford General Hospital. James just tagged along, ignored by the plod who was taking Sadie in charge.

'And you know the rest, Detective,' Sadie finished. But I recognised that gleam in her eye. I'd seen too many bent customers looking so pleased with themselves when they thought they'd spun a good enough yarn to get them off the hook. What I wanted to say after listening politely to this tale was: *A likely story.*

Instead, I said, 'Excuse me, Miss Lee, but wasn't this a rather impetuous reaction to a perfect stranger telling you what might well have been a pack of lies? I would say your kindness to this *strange girl* was more than generous, it might have been positively foolhardy.'

She shrugged and looked at me enquiringly, as if she was just waiting for the next stupid question. So I gave it to her, although I could see I was wasting my time trying to get any answers.

'And may I ask you, in view of the fact that you speak perfect English, how it was that you didn't point out the mistake to the officer who brought you here or the ambulance driver who took you to the hospital? You just quietly went along, didn't you, without a word. Got into the hospital bed and said nothing to the nurse. Could you please explain that to me? Were you just deliberately prolonging the misunderstanding to give Ah Weng So more time to get away from her responsibility to her baby?'

James butted in. He was another cool customer, like his sister. I had to admit that part of their story – being brother and sister – did seem to be true, because they looked so alike as to be twins. But although I wasn't as dim as old Hatchet-face back at the hospital, for all I knew, Chinese persons of a certain kind always looked like that.

'No, I don't think my sister has to explain anything to you, Sergeant. Your innuendoes are quite ridiculous. All that happened was that we did a kindness to a young girl in great distress. She told us nothing about a baby. We believed her story about being held prisoner. We assumed she was an illegal immigrant awaiting deportation, and of course we felt sorry for her, being of Chinese descent ourselves.'

'And you, Mr Lee,' I barked, trying to be a bad cop now that good cop hadn't worked, 'why should I believe anything you say? Are you and this lady really brother and sister, for example?'

The fact was, I had no idea what to say. Of course it didn't matter a damn if they were related or not. I just wanted to have a go about something. It was all so smelly, but I couldn't put my finger on what to do about it. Anyway, it didn't work. He just got haughty.

'That's enough. We have been sufficiently co-operative, and I think we'll go now. Come along, Sadie.'

Desperately I chucked in one more question.

'And why did you come to Watford? A long way from your usual stamping ground, I'd guess, isn't it?'

'We'd heard it was an interesting little town with a very

good shopping mall,' Sadie Lee said, and shrugged. 'Nobody told us what the police are like here. And anyway it's a pretty dull place.'

North spoke for the first time in this whole muddled incident. In a small timid voice she asked Sadie Lee, 'May I please have your address for my records, Miss Lee? In case we need to ask you to identify Ah Weng So when we do come across her. She has committed a misdemeanour by deserting her child, you see.'

Just to round off the picture of how polite we can be, when Sadie gave her a card, she thanked her so humbly anyone would think she'd got an autographed picture from a pop star. Give her her due, I suppose it was well done.

'Well, North,' I said when Sadie and James had gone, 'what do you make of that precious couple?'

'I think they're in on whatever is going on and they picked up that kid when she ran away from the hospital and she's back now in the factory. All that stuff about Sadie putting on her nightgown and taking her place was just to cover up that she's been taken back to being a slave.'

'OK, so why should they go to all that trouble for one little worker? It couldn't have made all that difference if they'd lost just one…just a minute!' I finished as the truth hit me. 'Of course, Ah Weng So knew something that would lead us to them! They were scared that if we questioned her enough we'd be able to locate the factory! Oh, f– er, dammit, why didn't I think of that before!'

Lucky for her that North stayed quiet for long enough for me to stop swearing at my own stupidity. She'd have got the rough edge of my tongue if she'd dared open her mouth.

Then she said nervously, 'What will happen to the little baby now, Sarge?'

And instead of a kindly enlightenment about the law on

abandoned babies, all she got from me was a grunted, 'How the hell should I know.'

The fact was, I needed a little brainstorming session with Alfie and Derek, but I didn't want to tell them I was stumped so early in the game. Still, there was one thing.

'Give me that card,' I said, and as I'd half expected, it gave an address in Chelsea. I thought it would be either that or Soho.

'Right, North, here's what you do,' I told her. 'Get along to their place and hang around. When one or both of them comes out, follow them.'

'Pardon?'

'Two simple words, North,' I barked. 'Which don't you understand? Follow. Them.'

'But Sarge,' she stammered pallidly, 'how–'

'North, listen. FOLLOW THEM.'

And just to make clear that was her whole instruction with no more details, I smartly marched out of the room and up into the canteen, hoping that at least Alfie would be there to give me some wisdom.

Strange to say, he wasn't but Derek was. Unusual not to find Alfie in the canteen at practically any time of night or day.

'The CPS had the charge reduced to manslaughter,' he greeted me glumly. My mind was so involved with the Chinese puzzle that it took a few seconds to catch on that he was talking about Juan Garcia.

Poor little Juan. I'd really promised myself to help him, but this Chinese business had sidetracked me. It was a pity that Derek and I didn't agree on either of these cases. But that wasn't the only subject where we differed. We seemed to be on opposing sides about everything these days.

Well, it wouldn't be the first time I'd had to strike out on my own.

While I'd been chewing all this over, Derek had been going on.

'Alfie's got some idea about interviewing Garcia's landlady, so he's gone off to Hendon to see her. Can't think why,' he shrugged. 'But I let him go. Couldn't think of anything better for him to do.'

I could easily see why Alfie had gone to Hendon. He'd remembered his pleasant 'tea breaks' in the past with Sleazy Sue Slipworthy, and was using the present case as an excuse to take up their acquaintance again. And he was banking on her husband being out again when he paid this next visit. But his luck couldn't hold forever. Sooner or later he'd meet Sam Slipworthy, and that would be an interesting get-together, specially if Sam suspected something had been going on between Alfie and Sue in his absence. Talk about Clash of the Titans.

I wondered if Alfie would tell me all about it.

Chapter 4

Well, it was turning out to be my summer for getting everything wrong.

When I did next see Alfie, the following morning, he was grinning through his ginger beard like some demented gargoyle.

'Smashing chap, that Sam,' he greeted me.

'Oh good,' I muttered. 'Sam who?'

'You remember, Sam Slipworthy. Little Sue's old man. He might have been a wrong'un in the old days, but now that he's going straight, you couldn't meet a finer–'

'So you didn't pick up where you left off with Sue?' I interrupted.

There went my hopes of an interesting introduction between a jealous black giant and a naughty ginger-bearded copper of the same size. I'd been hoping for at least some entertaining embarrassment for Alfie. Not that I wished him any harm, but he *had* got up to a few carryings-on that he wouldn't want his wife to know about, for instance. And not just with Sleazy Sue, either. He knew I could tell a tale or two about some of his naughty behaviour in the past.

'No, listen, Greta, I'm telling you, this feller Sam is going to help solve the Garsher case. He thinks you're right, that little chap Joo-Anne is too scared of his own shadow to do anyone in. Anyway it turns out he was quite attached to his partner, calling him his matey and all that.'

'You and Derek thought I was barmy, keeping on about

Juan being innocent. You both said it was an open and shut case, with all the evidence, didn't you?'

Alfie went a bit red.

'Yes, well, but–'

'So you're more prepared to take notice of this ex-con, Sam Slipworthy, than of your own partner?' I yelled, suddenly losing my rag.

I was fed up with everyone and everything. I couldn't seem to get started on anything, I didn't know what I was doing or what to do next, and now my partner was getting friendly with the last person in the world I'd expected him to get on with.

Derek came in.

'What have you done with Vicky?' he barked at me, without even a good morning to start with. So it was Vicky, was it, I muttered to myself, grinding my teeth. Not North. He could well ask what I'd done with her. What I wanted to do with her was more like it. Hiding all this as best I could, I told him the instruction I'd given her the previous day.

'For all I know, Guv,' I said, 'the silly little person is still standing outside where those two live, waiting for them to come out so that she can follow them. I don't suppose it would occur to her to call in. Do fast-track people learn to use their initiative, at all?'

Coldly he said, 'Perhaps you've forgotten that I was and still am one of those fast-track people. And is it possible that you've also forgotten that I instructed you to take DC North under your wing? Dumping her outside some place in Chelsea to wait for two people to come out and possibly follow them is not my idea of looking after a rookie. What did you expect her to do if they both came out and went in different directions? Or if neither of them came out at all? And did you think of clearing it with the locals?'

I didn't answer, but avoiding his eye I called her mobile.

She was upstairs in the canteen. Very politely I invited her to join us in the office.

'She seems OK, Guv,' I pointed out.

She seemed more than OK when she came in. If there's one thing I hate, it's a dainty little blonde gazing wide-eyed at Derek while reporting to me. There've always been too many dainty little blondes in the world for my liking.

'I waited there until the end of my shift, Sarge, and nobody came out,' she said, 'so then I went home. That was OK, wasn't it?'

'Very sensible,' Derek smirked at her before I had a chance to say anything. 'I don't see what else you could have been expected to do. In the circumstances,' he added, giving me an unfriendly look. 'Perhaps, Sergeant, you'd like to discuss with us all exactly what you suspect those two people of, and why you wanted them followed.'

Somehow I felt now wasn't the time to give Alfie's favourite answer: 'Buggered if I know'. That just about summed it up. I was floundering. But I knew I'd have to have a go, even if it came out all wrong.

'I know we've got a good ethnic mix in Watford,' I started, 'but we've never had any sizable Chinese community. Surely it's not just coincidence that after I'd found that Chinese girl having a baby in a doorway in the middle of the night, the very next day two more Chinese people turn up? And not just in Watford, but practically on the doorstep of the hospital that she'd just run out of, the day after giving birth. Wasn't it all too handy to be believable that the first two people this Ah Weng So sees outside the hospital are this same Chinese brother and sister, Sadie and James Lee? They live in Chelsea, but they say they came here because they'd been told Watford was interesting! I can't believe I'm the only one who can smell something rotten here.'

After all that, I was panting a bit, so I sat back and waited for reactions. I should have known what I'd get from Alfie.

'Ah Weng So?' he chortled into his beard. 'Is that supposed to be her name? Where did that come from?'

'The interpreter,' I answered coldly, and turned to Derek. 'What do you think, Guv? Something fishy?'

'Yes, maybe,' he said. 'But what? And whatever it might be, I can't see any crime being committed. If the immigration people ask us to help look for Ah Weng So, OK then it's down to us. But as for watching and following Sadie and James Lee, I really can't see–'

'But I really didn't mind, sir,' little Goldilocks butted in, gazing at him brightly. 'It wasn't difficult keeping a watch on their home. I was just sorry that it seemed to be for nothing.'

For nothing. What a sweetheart. With us for less than a week, and getting the knife in already.

I was beginning to feel a bit desperate.

'Look, Guv,' I said, 'Ah Weng So was working in a factory. It must have been fairly nearby. They wouldn't have driven very far to dump her in a doorway to have her baby. That factory must be producing something illegal, otherwise it wouldn't need to have illegal immigrants working there as slave labour. Surely we need to try to find the factory? And if the only people we can get hold of who seem anything to do with the whole thing are Sadie and James Lee, all we can do is see where they might lead us.'

'But why would the factory people first have dumped Ah Weng So in Watford and then gone to all that trouble to get her back?' he argued.

At last I had an answer to something that seemed logical.

'Because they realised that she knew something that might lead us to them! And maybe they only thought of it *after* they'd got rid of her.'

'Sir,' came a small voice from my dear little protégée. 'I

think Sergeant Pusey is right. It all makes sense.'

Oh yes. I needed her support, didn't I. I didn't want to show out what I felt about her, so I glared at Alfie instead.

'What do you think, *Sergeant* Partridge?' I asked in my most sarcastic voice. Wasted on him, of course.

'Yes, Guv,' he spoke to Derek instead of answering me. 'I think the girls have got something there. We ought to chase it up.'

The girls! I could have killed him with my bare hands.

'OK, team,' Derek said. 'I'll go and have a word with the Super, then I'll talk to this other Chinese couple myself. You can come with me to see them, Greta.'

Up piped the little voice again.

'Sir,' she said. 'It's Sadie and James Lee. Here's their card, sir, with their address and phone number and fax number and email address and everything. What shall I be doing, sir?'

I held my breath. If he said she should come with us to Chelsea, I'd probably explode. But before he had a chance, Alfie chimed in.

'You come up to the canteen with me, young North, and I'll put you in the picture about the Joo-Anne Garsher case and his background. We've got a long history with that little feller, I can tell you.'

*

When we all met up again, Alfie was bursting with news. He couldn't wait to get me alone to tell me what a clever-clogs he was.

'The car, see, the car was the clue,' he burbled. 'You know, the estate car what you saw the silver in the boot of when you went to the car boot sale and bumped into Garsher.

He can't drive, the silly little useless bugger, and he never thought of telling you.'

'So?' I prompted, not wanting to let on I couldn't make head or tail of what he was on about.

He didn't notice I was blank about the whole thing. He was too pleased with himself.

'So when somebody bonked that other feller on the head, they must have driven that estate car off somewhere. I got the reg number from Dusty – she's still living at the same place as when she was here with us – and I've put out an alert for it. She got a name with it, as well, but course it wasn't real. She hasn't changed, old Dusty, has she,' he beamed.

What 'old Dusty' was like now or in the past wasn't something I wanted to discuss. So I ignored that bit and concentrated on the important part of Alfie's latest theory.

'I remember that Garcia couldn't drive when he was involved in the Gilmore case, because of how stupid we thought it was that he had to take taxis everywhere that Gilmore sent him,' I said. 'But why are you so sure he hasn't learned in the meantime?'

'Because Sam and Sue told me,' Alfie beamed. 'I told you me and Sam got on alright, didn't I. Now then, Greta,' he added, seeing me scowling, 'we mustn't be prejudiced, you know, we're always being told about institutionalised intolerance, and that doesn't only mean racism. Just because Sam Slipworthy's been a bad'un in the past, we shouldn't think he won't co-operate with us now.'

I couldn't believe this was bigoted old Alfie, lecturing *me* about not being narrow-minded. When I recalled all the times I'd had to stop him using offensive language to certain people...! This wasn't a case of taking a liking to Sleazy Sue's husband. Somebody had been giving Alfie a talking-to.

I'd never heard him using words in the past like 'prejudice' and 'institutionalised' and 'tolerance'.

'Have you been going to evening classes, Alfie?'

'No, why? Oh, you mean…'

He looked coy. It was a strange sight, this great bulky middle-aged cop, with his ginger beard and florid face, suddenly wearing this unusual expression. Then he explained.

'When you were in hospital that time, when you got shot,' he confided, 'we had a chap from the Home Office come here and give us a talk about all that. Then there was that Policing Diversity Course we all had to go on. And my Betty, she said I ought to take it to heart. So I did.'

'Right. So now we're sure that Garcia still can't drive, and whoever bonked Charlie Hampson on the head with a tyre iron drove his estate car away with all the silver in it, so that probably means that Garcia was telling the truth when he said he found his matey Charlie already dead. Have I got all that right?'

He nodded, beaming again.

'So that leaves another question,' I went on. 'Have we now changed our minds about whether that silver was stolen? Because you may remember, Alfie, that when I tried to bring Garcia in for handling stolen goods, Derek chewed my ear off and I had to let him go because Derek said I had no grounds for believing the silver that Garcia was flogging was stolen.'

Alfie shrugged. 'You'll have to ask Derek that for yourself. He hasn't said a word to me about it. Anyway, how did the interview go with those two suspicious Chinese characters in Chelsea?'

'Don't you think you'd have heard all about it if he'd done any good? He tried threatening them with a charge of obstruction of police in the course of their enquiries, and they were dead cool about it. "Go ahead," they said, "but we'll have to consult our solicitor about that." He just couldn't get a useful word out of the pair of them. I've convinced him there's something fishy about them, but we can't think what to do about it.'

'Where is he now then?'

'Having a word with Mr Moon.'

We both knew that Superintendent Moon often had helpful bright ideas when the rest of us were stuck. And although he was still a bit disillusioned with the system which had stopped him getting Derek made up to Detective Chief Inspector at the end of his last brilliantly successful case, that didn't stop him being as keen as ever to solve sticky puzzles.

'And where, may I ask, is little Miss Stick Insect?'

I didn't try to hide from Alfie that I wasn't keen on young DC North, and he didn't pretend he didn't know who I meant.

'Oh, I left young Vicky up in the canteen studying PACE. I gave her a good long talk about the background on that Garsher, so she's up to speed on him. She seems a nice little thing, Greta, I don't know why you don't like her.'

'Must be the name,' I muttered. 'Reminds me of that smarmy lawyer, Charles North, who made things so difficult for us on the Gilmore case.'

'That's not like you, girl. It's a common enough name, and–'

'She's told us she's no relation,' I finished in chorus with him.

I wondered, did I have a gut feeling of distrust of DC North, or was it just my natural hatred of skinny little wide-eyed young blondes?

Chapter 5

I spent a grumpy evening, not even cheered up by a phone call from Ari asking me out on a proper date. 'When we can both get a free day,' he said, 'let's go down to the coast somewhere and have ourselves a really good time.'

'Sure,' I said, 'let me know when you can make it, and I'll see if I can fix the same day.'

But my heart wasn't really in it, and maybe Ari guessed that, because he didn't hang on chatting, but just said he'd call again soon.

Quite late, when I still didn't fancy going to bed, I thought about going out for a mind-clearing turn around Watford on the old roller-blades. But I didn't really feel like it, and anyway, when I remembered what happened last time I'd done that, it put me right off.

Round about two o'clock, I thought I'd better go to bed even if I wasn't going to sleep. This was all very unusual for me. Sleep was generally something I was very good at. My Gran used to say I could win a gold medal if they ever included sleeping in the Olympics.

So I wasn't bothered when my doorbell rang. Normally I'd be fast off and out of it by that time, or if I happened to be awake for some particular reason, I'd be leery of who might be making calls in the middle of the night. This time, more out of curiosity than anything, I looked through the security fish-eye viewer in the front door, and when I saw who it was, I let him in without a flicker.

'Well, stranger,' I said, 'what brings you here in the middle of the night? I thought I'd given you clear marching orders a good long while ago.'

He shoved past me, shut the door behind him and stood with his back to it. He hadn't changed. Bit fatter, maybe, but nothing to be sarky about.

'Look, Greta, this isn't what you think,' he started.

I raised my eyebrows.

'Since when do you know what I think, Jim Robinson?'

He let it go.

'I'm not trying, you know, like, to start things up again between us.'

Jim the Long-distance Lorry Driver had been my kind of regular bunk-up when I'd first got upgraded to CID in Watford. He'd hung around and pestered me about how much he fancied me. He wasn't a real liability like a proper boyfriend would have been, because we had this arrangement that whenever he was passing through Watford on a job, he'd stay overnight with me. It was OK, no great shakes, but convenient for us both, until two things happened.

One was the earth-shaking moment when I'd set eyes on DI Derek Michaelson and fallen madly and dramatically in love with him in an instant. And the other was when Jim's wife attacked me because she'd found out about us and got upset about it. So I'd given Jim the boot. It wasn't easy, because he'd suddenly decided we weren't just having a cosy little arrangement. Oh no. He'd come to the conclusion that he really truly loved me and wanted to leave his wife and kids for me. And he'd got this daft idea that I loved him, too. It was quite a job, shaking him off. But finally, after I'd actually managed to convince him I meant it when I said 'bugger off', that was the last I'd seen of him.

Until now.

Bored, I said, 'Well, Jim, what is it now? Something special, is it, that makes you call on an old friend in the middle of the night?'

He didn't notice the sarcasm. He never had. But this time it wasn't just because he was as thick as ever, but he was all overwrought, as well.

'Listen, Greta, I need your help.'

'I'm not doing B&B any more, Jim, in case you hadn't noticed.'

'No, serious, I'm in trouble and I need protection and I'm scared to go to the police. Officially, I mean. You're the only one I can talk to, because we can keep it quiet between us, so nobody will know what I've done.'

It finally dawned on me that the time for jokes and rough wisecracks had passed. We went in and sat down and I brought him a lager.

'Tell me,' I said, and I wished I hadn't. It all came pouring out in a torrent. On the other hand, the first three words guaranteed my full attention.

'This Chinese bloke spoke to me at the Calais end of the Channel Tunnel, and he asked me if I'd like to earn a lot extra. Course it was obvious it was something illegal, and first I thought drugs. But it wasn't, it was people. You know me, Greta, you know I wouldn't do a thing like that, not for any money. So I told him, nothing doing. Then I found out some of my mates were doing it, smuggling these illegals in under their normal load. Well, least, I'd thought they were my mates till then. That's not the way to make yourself rich, is my opinion.'

I nodded. 'So where's the danger then?'

'One of them I thought was a friend was talking to me about it, and I told him what I thought. And he must have told this Chinky bloke, and then they all got worried because I spoke a bit strong and they must have thought I was going to give them away. So this Chinese, nasty-looking feller he was, he come to me and he said what would happen to me and my family if I told anyone about this racket. Nasty stuff, and he went into a lot of detail, too.'

'Well, that's simple enough; you weren't going to tell anyone anyway, were you? So all you had to do was keep on holding your tongue. You can do that, can't you, Jim?'

I was back to the sarcasm again.

'No,' he said, and I could hear from his voice that he was really desperate. 'You don't understand. The Chinaman said that if I went to the police, anywhere in the country, they'd know and they'd come after me!'

'What! No, that must be bluff. How could they possibly know.'

'I don't know, but that's what's got me all wound up. See, if it's true, they must have some enormous organisation…'

His voice trailed away at the look I gave him.

'Go home to your wife and kids, Jim,' I advised him, 'and forget it. You're getting all hot and bothered over nothing. Don't give another thought to the Chinese or what your mates are up to with smuggling illegals. Don't let anyone kid you they've got this huge set-up spying on the police, or infiltrating, or whatever it is they're on about. And most of all, don't come near me again. I'm not your stopover in Watford and there's no point in us pretending we're old friends, OK?'

And I practically shoved him out of the front door. But I was awake all the rest of that night, thinking over what he'd said. This was unusual, as a rule it takes a lot to keep me from my beauty sleep.

Jim was no hero, never had been, but he was a strong tough feller, and not easily scared. On the other hand, he was never all that great on duty and civic responsibility, and normally he'd turn a blind eye to anything naughty his mates might be doing. So what had got him so bothered now, enough to come bleating to me about it?

At first I'd kidded myself it was just an excuse to start up again with me, but I soon realised that wasn't it. He was really worried, and it must have been because of that Chinese claiming he had an ear in every police HQ in the country.

Yes, I finally decided, that was it. It was just that Jim was too thick to realise that the man was bluffing, and he felt bothered enough about it to come and tell me. Most likely now he felt he'd done the right thing, and it was up to me to take it from there, so he could wash his hands of the whole problem.

By the time I'd come to that conclusion, it was time to get up and I felt really knackered. I'd never been any good at missing sleep, even in a good cause. And Jim and his problem certainly wasn't good or a cause.

I didn't feel any better when Alfie greeted me with, 'What's up with you, girl? Been having a naughty time, have you?'

North offered me an aspirin.

Derek of course noticed nothing.

'Now, Greta,' he said, 'Mr Moon wants you to describe the silver you saw Garcia trying to flog at the car boot sale, in as much detail as possible. Perhaps you'd like to try drawing some of it, if you can. Can you sketch? Then we'll send it out to all the areas where Charlie Hampson operated, to co-ordinate action. Somebody will have a burglary report that matches.'

'Er, excuse me, Guv,' I said, 'but as we haven't recovered the stuff, how will it help to know who it belonged to in the first place?'

He didn't answer, only went on as if I hadn't spoken.

'We've already got the description and registration of the car the goods were in, and that's been circulated. And we got the name and address of the present owner from the PNC. He reported it stolen two weeks ago.'

He beamed round at us all, as if he had the whole thing under control. Alfie scratched his beard, then his head, then coughed, and finally said as heartily as if he really meant it, 'That's good, Guv. What would you like us to do then?'

Before Derek could say any more, North put in her two-pence-worth.

'Sir, may I ask a question?'

He nodded at her in what I could only call a fond manner, if you can nod fondly. He gave it a try, anyway.

'Sir, have the uniformed branch been given a description of Ah Weng So, and told to pick her up on sight?'

'Good point, Vicky,' he said. 'Yes, as it happens that's all in hand.'

'So, er, what's next then, Boss?' I asked. It was obvious he had no more inspiration than the rest of us, so it was up to me, as usual, to rescue him. 'Because,' I went on, 'if you've got time, I'd like a quick private word with you.'

I had no idea what to say to him. I just wanted to get him alone, and also to postpone having to write descriptions of the silver Garcia had been trying to flog. But when Alfie had carted North off to the canteen, I found myself telling Derek about my visit from Jim.

This was funny. I'd convinced myself it was all about nothing, and yet somehow I felt the need to tell it all to Derek. When I'd finished, he thought for a while, and then decided, as I had, that it was all rubbish. So why wasn't I surprised when he said we ought to go and discuss it with Superintendent Moon? I suppose for the same reason that I'd thought it wasn't worth thinking about and then repeated it to him.

'First, though,' he said, 'let's clear up a few points. This was the same Jim Robinson you had a close friendship with before I knew you, was it? The one whose wife beat you up and landed you in hospital?'

'Yes, but what difference does that–'

'Well, there's something I never understood about that. How did it happen that this young woman managed to do so much damage to you, when you've got your Black Belt in karate? And didn't you tell me you'd finished with her husband long before that, as soon you discovered he was married?'

'Yes, but what's all that got to do with–'

'Oh, nothing, really,' he interrupted again. 'Just that I never had an opportunity to ask those questions at the time, and I've been kind of wondering about it all, on and off, ever since.'

I looked at him, hard, and thought even harder. A little idea crept into my head. I'd always known that he was a bit of a tight-arse – in fact, I knew so many things about him that I'd normally dislike, that it was a puzzle to me that I was so barmily in love with him. Of course, he was very handsome and well built in a small compact kind of way, with his big brown eyes and heart-melting smile. But I'd never been one to go just for looks, and anyway, Aristotle Anapolis was every bit as good looking. And taller. No, there was no explaining it, and it was a waste of time trying to solve it. On the other hand, hadn't he just given me a big clue about why he wouldn't give me a tumble?

'Derek,' I said. He looked at me with a kind of neutral expression. I said his name again, trying to put lots of passionate feeling into it. If it worked, it certainly didn't show in his expression. I tried again.

'Derek, do you think any less of me because of my affair with Jim?'

'No, of course not,' he said briskly – but too quickly. 'Come on, let's go and have a word with Mr Moon.'

Funny that he should ask those questions about that business with Jim's wife and then not press for an answer. Not typical at all. Still, I was glad of it. I didn't really want to go into the whole thing again.

So off we went to see the Superintendent.

One of the things I admire about Derek is the way he can express himself. Comes of a university education, I suppose. He explained my story to the Super in a far more tactful way than how I'd told it. Even then I could tell Mr Moon wasn't happy.

'So this long-distance lorry driver fellow confided in you, Sergeant Pusey, because he was afraid to report the matter to us in a formal way? And you believed him, did you?'

'Well, sir,' I muttered, 'I couldn't think of any reason why he'd be spinning a yarn. The trouble is, he's not much in the brains department, and this Chinese feller probably sussed that and saw he could kid to him that he had connections in every police HQ in the country. On the other hand, I thought I should report it…'

I'd known from his expression while Derek was talking that I wasn't the flavour of the month, and when he'd called me Sergeant Pusey that clinched it. There'd been times in the past when Mr Moon had seemed to approve of me, calling me Greta and seeming even to try to make a match between me and Derek. Other times we'd all been scared he'd have a stroke, he'd been so purple-faced with fury at us when we'd made a cock-up of things.

But he was a fair boss and clever with it, and we all respected him even if he did look like an over-Full Moon. Round was the only way to describe our Super, and when he stood next to his tall thin beautiful wife it was a sight to behold. She was at least six inches taller than him. But the fact that they had five children and were obviously devoted to each other gave me hope that the height difference didn't matter between me and Derek.

I'd been thinking all this while Derek and I had been standing in front of Mr Moon, waiting for his conclusions. I was pretty sure he'd send us away feeling foolish. After all, it was pretty stupid. So I was gob-smacked when he said he was going to HQ in Hertford to talk to them about it.

'Might be worth having a word with the Chief Constable, too,' he added. 'But in the meantime, let's keep it between the three of us.'

'You see, Greta, you did the right thing,' Derek said to me as we went back to his office. 'Maybe it wasn't all such nonsense after all. Or perhaps there's something Mr Moon knows that we don't which ties in with your Jim's story.'

I didn't like that last bit. What did he mean, *my* Jim?

Chapter 6

'Here's a bit of practise sleuthing for you to teach young North,' Derek said, fishing something nasty-looking from his in-tray. 'There's been a spate of reports from local vets about food poisoning in cats and dogs. See what you can find out, and give Vicky a lesson on how you go about these things.'

And he handed me the file. I was disgusted. Big deal. Not that I've got anything against cats and dogs, and of course I was sorry to hear that the poor little buggers were being poisoned. But hardly a job for a Detective Sergeant, was it, specially with a trainee in tow. I don't mean that I think our work should always be exciting and violent, catching master-criminals and so on. On the other hand, surely the uniforms could handle this one.

Still, far from me to argue with the beloved boss, so off I went to the canteen to rescue DC North from endless lectures by Alfie. I did wonder if I could get him to join us, but thought that would be stretching it a bit. Two detectives looking for someone with a down on pets was bad enough. Three would be ridiculous, specially with two of them being sergeants.

'So how do we set about this then, Sarge?' North asked, gazing at me seriously with those baby-blue eyes.

I didn't really have any idea, but I wasn't going to tell her that, was I.

'First we get a list of the vets who've been reporting this apparent crime, then we go and talk to a few of them and find out what they can tell us.'

It was boring work, and North's difficult questions didn't

help, such as: 'Why do you think this came to CID and not the uniformed branch?' and others that I'd have liked to be given the answer to myself.

Finally, though, we did have a chat with a really handsome vet who seemed quite gone on North's youthful charm, and ended up asking her for a date. When she accepted, it was good news for me. I'd been afraid she was after Derek.

Also, he was the fourth one we'd seen and he confirmed what the previous three had said, so that was a help, too. Turned out all the vets had been in touch with each other. And they'd narrowed the poisoning down to pet food shops that sold loose food, that is, not in tins or other pre-packs. Seemed that some owners of cats and dogs thought this muck was healthier than the factory stuff, and there was quite a number of shops selling it.

So off we tooled to the nearest one, happily named 'Moggies and Woofers', which sold all kinds of gear for pets, and also toys for the little darlings, and live fish in tanks and birds in cages. I hate that. I'd had to give away Felix, my lovely little ferret, because I couldn't bear to keep him in a cage to stop him eating the furniture. Prisons for criminals are bad enough even if they are necessary. But why put animals in prisons?

There was only one person in the shop, so I showed him my warrant card and asked to speak to the manager.

'I am the proprietor of this establishment,' he said, fluffing up his bouffant hairdo. I'd expected some sort of hardware-selling type person, probably wearing one of those useful brown coat overalls like Ronnie Barker in that TV series. But this chap looked ready to go to a dance, wearing a maroon velvet jacket, and a silky-looking purple shirt with a maroon cravat tucked into the neckline. The cravat had little animals dancing all over it, in different colours. What with one thing and another, he was quite a sight. If you met him anywhere else, you'd take him for a hairdresser.

'How may I be of assistance, officer? My name is Rodney Price, and as you see, I have a lovely selection of birdies and fishies available, all in the best possible condition.'

Struggling to keep a straight face, I said, 'We've been asked to look into a number of cases of food poisoning amongst pets in Watford, Mr Price. And it seems possible that some of the contaminated food came from this shop.'

He went red, his rosy lips trembled and his long curly eyelashes fluttered. I thought he was going to cry. He waved a shaking hand in a sweeping gesture to take in all his premises.

'I can assure you, officer, everything here is beautifully clean and hygienic. I wouldn't dream of putting any of our fellow creatures in danger of ill-health.' He swallowed hard, several times, almost dislodging his cravat. 'May I ask exactly what it is that I'm accused of?'

Then there was a confused scene. Mr Price was protesting his innocence of anything at all so hysterically that he couldn't hear what we were saying. So North and I had trouble reassuring him that we were just making routine enquiries. Anyway, once we'd convinced dear Rodney that we hadn't come to nick him, he calmed down a bit and gave us the name of his animal feed wholesaler.

'I don't get everything from him, you understand,' he said, still sniffling a bit, 'just the fresh food for the moggies and woofers. The other stuff, the dried food and seeds and so on, I get from–'

'No, thank you, Mr Price, that's really all we need to know,' and I shoved North in front of me and out of the place as fast as we could go. I've got to admit, some of my dislike of her went for a burton when I saw she felt the same as I did about

Mr Price and his moggies and woofers. We sat in the car and laughed till we cried.

'Birdies and fishies,' she said, and I answered, 'moggies and woofers.'

'Oh, Sarge,' she finally said, drying her eyes, 'to think I was afraid this was going to be a boring case. We ought to be paying entertainment tax for people like Rodney Price.'

'Yes, and you've got a date with that good-looking vet, too,' I reminded her. 'There's a lot to be said for routine cases. Danger's exciting, but this can be fun.'

Fun! I thought. Since when did I talk this girlie-stuff? What happened to tough Detective Sergeant Pusey, ambitious one of the lads? I pulled myself together.

'Right, now North, you can do the next bit on your own,' I snapped in a sudden change of tone. 'Just go round to all the rest of the shops selling this so-called fresh pet food and check that they've all got the same supplier. I'll drop you off at the next one, and then you can make your own way. See you back at the nick this afternoon.'

That made me feel a lot better and more like myself. Also with luck it would give me a chance to write up my description of that silver stuff Garcia had been trying to flog at the car boot sale. Then maybe I might be able to have a little chat with Alfie about this and that.

I sat at the keyboard with my eyes shut, trying to picture exactly what I'd seen in the back of Garcia's estate car when I'd come across him at the car boot sale. The trouble was, my mind kept drifting off to my original reason for going there, and Derek and his love of opera and our puzzling state of affairs. Affairs! If only.

He liked me, I knew that, and surely all that snogging must mean he fancied me, too. So what was the problem? It couldn't be just that he knew I'd had it away a few times with

Jim. Not even the most narrow-minded prig (was Derek a narrow-minded prig? No, he couldn't be – I couldn't love anyone like that) would expect a woman of the world such as myself to be a virgin.

I shook myself. I had to pull myself together and concentrate on the damn silver. What had I actually seen? A teapot, a milk jug, a sugar bowl, two candle-sticks, a vase, a big bowl, a big sort of serving dish, some cutlery…there was more but I simply couldn't picture it. I described it all as best I could, printed out a few copies, dropped them in Derek's in-tray, and went to look for Alfie.

Not in the canteen – what a surprise. I roamed about, asking passing plods if they'd seen him, and finally ran him down in the CAD (Computer Aided Dispatch) room, making a nuisance of himself to the catchers. When I finally got him alone, he was so full of it he didn't give me a chance for a word.

'We think we've found who that silver was burgled from! I got this idea, well, Derek and I got it together, and we went through lists of B and E's where silver was reported stolen. We found this one that matched with that little toe-rag Charlie Hampson's usual patch and method, and we've asked the locals to fax us copies to see if it matches up with what you saw at the car boot sale.'

'Well, what was so marvellous?' I sneered. 'Derek said he'd got an almost match from Putney days ago. I was supposed to fax them my description of what I remembered seeing Juan Garcia trying to flog, to see if it tallied.'

Alfie wasn't put down by this.

'Wait!' he went on. 'You don't know the best bit. The name of the person what reported that particular theft to the local nick in Putney. It's his name what's the interesting thing. The bloke's name is Chang!'

Beaming, he waited for my reaction. He must have been

well pleased with what he saw on my face, because he burst out laughing.

'See,' he said, rubbing it in, 'it's the Chinese Mafia again. Everything you do lately takes you to the Chinese, doesn't it. Go on then, tell me about Derek interviewing those other two down in Chelsea.'

'We couldn't do any good,' I had to admit. 'Derek really pressed them, asking if they didn't know where Ah Weng So ran off to, and trying to get James Lee to admit he went somewhere with her while his so-called sister wandered about in her hospital gown waiting to be picked up in mistake for her. They just stone-walled. Derek asked James where he was when his sister was apprehended by that PC, and he said he was just loitering nearby. He asked Sadie why she didn't say anything in English when she was picked up, brought here and then to the hospital, and she just said she didn't feel like speaking. Can you believe it, the barefaced cheek of it.'

'Well, why didn't he charge them with obstruction or something?'

'I asked him that afterwards, and he said he didn't think it was worth the paperwork. We could always get them another time if we decided it was worth bothering, he said. He's with Mr Moon now, talking it over.'

I had another thought.

'Did he know about this latest Chinese connection before he went to see Mr Moon, do you know?'

Alfie shrugged. 'Don't think so. Do you want to go up and tell them both?'

I did.

'And this little Chinese girl who had the baby, what was her name?' Superintendent Moon asked.

'Ah Weng So.'

'Yes, I remember,' he nodded, 'well, has anyone seen

anything of her since her latest disappearance? And what's happening to the baby, does anyone know that? What will become of the poor little mite?'

Derek cleared his throat.

'Erm, I don't think that comes within our purview, sir. I believe the social services will be taking care of that problem. Our immediate concern is the involvement of this couple claiming to be brother and sister, James and Sadie Lee. And now we have a further coincidence of the silver having been stolen from yet another Chinese person, this Mister Chang. What do you advise should be our next course of action?'

As usual, I was full of admiration. I thought I'd been pretty good coming out with the expression 'Chinese connection' to impress Alfie, but Derek always used words I never would have thought of. Purview, I thought. I don't think it comes within our purview. I must remember that one. Maybe I could have used it about the stupid mystery of the poisoned pet food. I nearly lost the trend of the conversation, I was so taken up with my lovely Guv.

Mr Moon was saying he thought we should liaise with the local Chelsea cop-shop to bring James and Sadie in on a charge of obstruction, and see if that would help. We didn't tell him Derek had already decided against that idea.

'Meanwhile,' he said, 'while Greta's dealing with that, I suggest you call on this mysterious Mister Chang and see how he strikes you. Take a list of what Greta remembers seeing at the car boot sale as your excuse for going to see him, and just see what you can suss out. I agree it's all too far-fetched to be a coincidence. I've heard of the Yellow Peril,' he said, suddenly giving a big chortle, 'but this is ridiculous!'

You had to like a man like that; he's so human.

Derek and I hurried out, grinning like Cheshire cats.

While I was on the blower to the Putney nick about picking

up James and Sadie Lee, young North came bouncing in, full of herself. I waved at her to sit down and shut up, but she was so over-excited she couldn't, and kept pacing up and down all the time I was talking. Very distracting. Mind you, I found everything she did irritating, including breathing. Nothing new there, then.

Finally I put the phone down and snapped at her, 'Well?'

'They're such a load of plonkers,' she burst out.

That was a bit of an eye-opener. Up till then she'd spoken so refayned and proper, I wouldn't have expected her to know any slang, let alone use it to a superior officer. Still, I didn't let on.

I just said, 'Go on. Try starting at the beginning.'

'Six of them, Sarge, six! And not one knew anything about their supplier except his name and mobile number. Address? No, they all said, they didn't need it. Delivery van, make, colour, registration? None of them had noticed. And this geezer's been delivering to them all for months! So then I tried to get a description of the man himself, Dan. Dan who? Who cares, they all said. Then you'd think the descriptions would match up a bit, wouldn't you? No, not even slightly! He was tall, short, fat, thin, brown curly hair, bald, middle-aged–'

'Alright, alright, I get the picture. That's part of the job you'll have to learn, North. There's always a lot of frustration when you're dealing with the public. You should have learned that by now. Five witnesses, five different accounts. But did you at least get his mobile number? I suppose they just phoned him when they wanted something and he came and delivered it?'

'Yes, so I expect now we'll call the number and ask him to come in to Shady Lane and answer–'

'No, of course not. Give me the number and we'll get his name and address and go and call on him.'

She went all round-eyed.

'I didn't know we could do that with a mobile number, Sarge.'

Pushing a grin off my face, I said sourly, 'Well maybe there's a lot you can still learn, Detective Constable North. Even fast-trackers don't know everything from their first day. Training can't cover everything.'

While we were waiting for the information to come through, she popped up to the canteen and brought us back a cup of tea each. We were sipping at it in peace when she suddenly went pink and starting clearing her throat and humphing.

'Come on then, North,' I snapped. 'Out with it. What now?'

'Well, er, Sarge, er – do you mind if I ask you something personal?'

Here we go, I thought. She's going to start asking about Derek. I knew she was after him all along. Oh well.

'Go on then,' I said, putting on my most unfriendly face.

I could see it was difficult for her, but I wasn't going to help. I just sat and waited, looking as much like an Easter Island statue as I could.

'Where do you get your hair done?' she blurted.

What. This was the last thing I would have expected. Still, not difficult.

'I don't. It's naturally curly, and I shampoo it myself under the shower, and when it needs cutting, I cut it. Why?'

The pink deepened to almost scarlet. But give her this – once she'd got her teeth into something, she didn't let go. I could tell I'd knocked the stuffing out of her quite well by now, but she wasn't going to give up. She had to speak very fast, though, so as not to lose her nerve. So it all came out nearly as just one word.

'Well, Sarge, I don't know if anyone's ever told you, but you're very pretty, and if you wore some make-up and had your hair done professionally and dressed a bit smar–'

'Thank you, North, for your kind advice. I'm sure you mean well. Now let's just get on with the job.'

It was lucky for her that the message came through at that moment with the name and address of Dan, the pets' meat supplier that we'd been waiting for. Otherwise she would have gone a few more colours, not just pink or scarlet, by the time I'd done giving her a piece of my mind. The cheek of the kid. I was fuming.

We went off to see Dan Bush in hostile silence. I could see she was already regretting what she'd said. I was trying to think up ways to make her curse herself for opening her cheeky mouth. Very pretty, indeed. As if I needed someone like her to tell me I'm a cracker, when I've got Aristotle Anapolis panting after me. Not to speak of Jim Robinson and a few others I could call to mind. I reminded myself how many men had told me that with my height and figure and face I could have been a model.

So I was in a right frame of mind to give Mister Daniel Bush a hard time by the time we got to his address. It was in one of the worst parts of Watford, where the old workmen's cottages hadn't been knocked together and gentrified and made all posh by all the high-earning incomers emigrating from Swiss Cottage. His house was at the end of the terrace, and he'd stuck a kind of lean-to shack at the side of it, and outside it was a rundown van that had once been white. His windows were uncurtained and dirty and it must have been a good century since a lick of paint had been near the place. Just to make it all more inviting, when we got out of the car and walked towards the place, a terrible stink hit us. We were both coughing and choking, and I nearly turned round and walked away. What kind of man was this Dan Bush, I wondered.

After a bit of banging on the front door and the side of the van, he came out of the wooden shack on a wave of pong. I deduced in my best detective way that this was where he stored the pet food. He was a short round greasy-looking person, bald and shiny, and his general allure wasn't added to by several warts where his hair should have been. No surprise that this didn't tally with any of the descriptions North had got from his customers.

'What can I do for you ladies?' he asked with a charm-free smile, not helped by several teeth being missing. The rest were different colours – some brown, some black and one green. Definitely not an attractive article, but I did somehow manage to smile back at him.

We showed him our warrant cards and I explained how we'd arrived at his doorstep. He was very impressed that we found his address from his mobile number, but didn't have much else to say.

'There's nothing to tell, see,' he explained. 'I buy this stuff from this geezer, and these pet shops phone me when they want some, and I deliver it.'

Wearily I said, 'I know, don't tell me, you don't know his name or address, and you just phone him when you need more supplies, right?'

'No,' he said, all surprised. 'He comes round to me regular every Wednesday, and if I want some, I buy it, cash, and if not, I tell him to come again the following Wednesday. I never phoned him, why should I?'

'Great,' I said. 'So you don't know how to get in touch with him then? What will you do if he doesn't turn up one Wednesday?'

Then, seeing the words starting to come out of his blubbery

lips, I quickly added, 'I mean, if he suddenly stops calling at all, any Wednesday? Where will you get your supplies then?'

'No bother, I'll just get on with my other lines of business. See, I buy and sell all sorts of things; second-hand furniture, clothes–'

'OK, Mr Bush, I get it. Well, as it's Wednesday tomorrow, we'll be back to see if we can have a word with this supplier of yours.'

On the way back, North asked, 'Where are we going with all this, Sarge? I mean, when we see this other supplier, what then?'

I'd been wondering the same myself. The whole thing had seemed a waste of time to me from the first. But as she spoke, I had a flash of inspiration. So of course I answered her as if I'd had a plan all along, hinting it should have been obvious to her as well if she'd had half a brain.

'We'll go there in two cars tomorrow, and you'll sit round the corner in yours while I talk to this supplier and ask him questions about where he gets his stinking pet food. Then when he leaves, you'll follow him. When I leave, I'll call you and you can tell me where you are and where you're heading.'

'Of course!' she cried with what seemed like admiration. 'That way we can find out the source of the stuff and…and… and what, Sarge?'

'See what it's all about, naturally,' I answered with a confidence I was far from feeling. Buggered if I was going to tell her I didn't know what I was doing.

More to change the subject than because I was interested, I asked her casually, 'Why did you ask me where I got my hair done?'

She got embarrassed all over again. But give her credit, she had guts. She went right on with it.

'Well, I just wondered if you, er, you know, if you'd like to try mine, because she's just starting up and she could do with a few recommendations. I'm sorry about the rest of what I said, I didn't mean to offend–'

'Alright, never mind. Give me her name and number, and maybe I'll drop in some time if she needs customers. You should have said you were trying to help someone. How old are you, anyway, North?'

'Twenty-one.'

'And how long have you been in the Job?'

In an even smaller voice she said, 'Three months.'

'And that's fast-track, is it. When I was your age I'd been in for three years in uniform, and it had taken me that long to get into CID. You've got a long way to go, haven't you.'

'Yes, Sarge,' she said humbly, and there was no more conversation all the way back to Shady Lane.

But I thought a lot about what she'd said about make-up and clothes. Maybe that was what I needed to get Derek more interested.

Course, I had no intention of following up the advice of young DC North. Getting myself all prettied up wasn't my thing at all. What did I need with all that? Still, I thought I'd just go and have a peep at this hairdresser friend of hers. So finding myself in that direction on my way home that evening – well, not much of a detour, anyway – I stopped outside Marilyn's Miracles to see what it was like.

What it was like was what my Gran used to call Casey's Court. Whenever there were people all rushing about and shouting and babies crying and toddlers eating and being sick and nobody seemed to know what they were doing, her name for it was Casey's Court. And that was what Marilyn's Miracles should have been called.

That decided me. Only someone who needed treatment

for the inside of her head would go in there to have the outside of it improved.

Before I could change my mind, I went straight in to make an appointment. I spoke to Marilyn herself and asked her what she could do for me.

'Well, it depends what you were wanting,' she said. She was a tiny blonde with a strong Irish accent. 'Was it a complete makeover, or just a tidy-up?'

So I made an appointment for the whole works on my next day off, and went home regretting it.

It was lucky that Ari was there unexpectedly to cheer me up, so the evening wasn't a complete loss. And he told me my new exercise plan was paying off because I was getting back to my proper shape. I didn't tell him about the scheme for the new me. He was more than satisfied with the present one, anyway. Unlike some.

I told him about this stupid job we were on, about poisoned pets.

'There's been a lot on the news about that sort of thing,' he said. 'Farmers selling condemned meat illegally for pet food. You keep tracking, and you'll end up with a big case there, innit.'

He beamed at me in his usual fond way.

'You've always been clever, lovely girl, even when you got on the wrong track sometimes.'

It wasn't fair. He knew I always melted when he called me lovely girl.

So much for Miss Fast-Track North and her beauty advice.

Chapter 7

Before going off with North to intercept the latest pet food delivery, I had an early breakfast in the canteen with Derek and Alfie. I was glad to see North hadn't turned up yet.

'Course, if Mr Moon says bring them in on obstruction, that's what you've got to do,' Alfie observed, talking through a mouthful of fry-up as usual. 'Mind you, I couldn't see why you didn't want to in the first place.'

Derek ignored him, and said to me, 'CPS is dropping the case against Garcia. We'll have to let him go.'

'What! But it's only a few days since they said they were reducing the charge to manslaughter.'

There was no getting away from it, Derek was well choked.

'Now we've got an unsolved murder,' he muttered, 'as if we haven't got enough mystery with this Chinese puzzle. Did you believe what your friend the long-distance lorry driver told you about the Chinese chap trying to get him to take illegal immigrants, Greta?'

'He's not my friend, but I did believe him. He hasn't got the imagination to make up something like that. And I could tell he was really worried.'

'OK then,' and Derek gave a big sigh and gazed off into the distance.

'Here,' said Alfie, spraying crumbs, 'Greta, did you know that a lot of the top brass at Scotland Yard are women?'

'Yes, course I did. What's your point?'

'Well,' he chortled, 'I can remember when you first joined

CID and I was your partner, you told me and my Betty that you wanted to be the first woman Deputy Assistant Commissioner at Scotland Yard. My Betty couldn't hardly believe you was serious. Ambitious, you said you was, and not interested in men nor marriage nor none of those normal things for young girls.'

'Yes,' I said coldly, 'and I still feel the same. I want to get to the top in the Job, even if I won't be the first woman to make it. People don't stop climbing Everest just because somebody else got there first.'

I cast an eye at Derek to see his reaction. He wasn't even listening. He was far away in some intellectual thought-world of his own. And anyway, why should he care about my ambitions.

North came bouncing in, all fresh-faced and full of energy.

'Thought I'd find you here, Sarge,' she announced. 'Ready?'

I was. We left. On the trail of the mystery pet food poisoner. Was this what I'd joined the police for?

We hung around Dan Bush's stinky establishment for an hour or so, waiting for his anonymous supplier. I decided not to tell North I'd made an appointment with her friend Marilyn the hairdresser. Every now and again she'd ask me a question about the background on Juan Garcia. Turned out that gradually, more to pass the time than anything, I told her the whole complicated case that he was involved in. She claimed to be full of admiration for how we'd handled it. That was a load of baloney. She was just practising her buttering-up skills. I noticed she was most interested when Charles North the oily lawyer came into the story, but that was probably only natural because of the coincidence of their names.

Finally this geezer turned up in a nice clean newish blue Vauxhall van. He was as different from Dan Bush as a greyhound from a donkey. If I'd met him casually, I couldn't have guessed his trade in a million years. There was something about him that called for politeness on my part. He looked more like a City gent than a horse meat trader. I walked up to him as he was talking to Bush.

'Excuse me, sir,' I said, showing him my warrant card. 'May I have a few words?'

Say this for him, he had princely manners.

'Certainly, Sergeant, what can I do for you?'

North had nipped off round the corner back to the other car when he'd arrived, as we'd arranged. So I had to take my own notes as he told me his name, address, phone number, fax number, email address. I already had the make and reg number of his van. Probably if I'd asked for more detail he'd have gone on with his date of birth, marital status and where he went to school. He seemed positively eager to co-operate. Bush stood there looking gob-smacked.

'You never told me all that,' he accused.

'My dear man,' Edward Franklin replied in his gentlemanly way. 'You had but to ask. I have no secrets.'

'I'm glad to hear that, Mr Franklin,' I butted in. 'What we really need to know is where you get the supplies of pet food you sell on to Mr Bush.'

'Why of course, with pleasure. It's a little processing plant near a farm up towards Tring, just past Berkhamsted. You know Northchurch? No, well, never mind, it's not difficult to find. I'll just write down the exact address for you. The name of the chap in charge is Bentley. 'Fraid I don't know his first name. May I ask if there's a problem?'

Naturally I wasn't giving him any information. I was there to collect it, not give it out. I'd thought of getting a sample of his supplies to take in for analysis, but I was glad I hadn't done that when I saw how troubled he was at the thought that there might be something wrong. What we needed was for him to lead us to the source of the stuff, not be alerted beforehand.

And I left. Then he left. Then North got on the blower to me to tell me he was driving, not north-west towards Tring, but east towards Radlett. On we went, the three of us, him seeming not to know he was leading a convoy, but North keeping me in the picture all the way.

The direction he was going wasn't towards the processing plant nor his business or home address he'd given me. By the time we'd gone through Hemel Hempstead, St Albans, Hatfield and Hertford, I was beginning to think maybe he did know we were tailing him and was purposely leading us a dance.

Still, we stuck to him, up the A10 by-passing Stevenage, until North said, all excited, 'Wait, Sarge, he's slowing down, I think he's going to turn off, I'm just getting to the signpost, he's gone off to the left, it says…' her voice wobbled, and I thought we were going to lose contact, but then it came back strongly – 'It's nasty, Sarge!'

'Never mind that, North, we mustn't care about that, just tell me the name on the signpost.'

Now I could tell why her voice had sounded so rocky. She was laughing.

'That's the name on the signpost, Sarge. It says "Nasty, one mile". I think we've arrived.'

Then she couldn't hold back any longer. She just whooped. And I couldn't blame her. I thought I knew the whole of the county of Hertfordshire, but I'd certainly never heard of a place called Nasty.

When she could speak, she said, 'I'll wait for you at the turn-off, Sarge. We'd better go in together, in case there's anything–'

And she was off again. I've got to admit, I saw the funny

side myself, of going to a place called Nasty in case there was anything nasty there, and I did laugh a bit. But I didn't go off half-cocked the way she did. She was like a little kid, hooting and gurgling away. I had to speak to her sharply when I pulled up alongside her. I left my car on the verge and got into hers.

'Come along, North,' I snapped. 'Calm down and get going. Let's see where our friend Mister Franklin has led us. It certainly isn't the address he gave for his supplier in Northchurch, nor his home in Bovingdon.'

We could tell we were on the track before the place came in sight. The stink was horrible, and the noise was nearly as bad. No doubt of it, we were coming to some sort of factory doing something really smelly.

'I think it's round this next bend, Sarge,' North said.

Then my mobile rang. It was Derek.

'Where are you?' he asked, unreasonably in my opinion. Probably he'd forgotten he'd sent us on this wild goose chase himself. Then, before I had a chance to draw breath to answer, he followed up with, 'What are you doing? Is North with you?'

'Stop the car,' I told North. Then I explained quietly to Derek where we were and why. It took a lot of willpower not to snarl at him, much as I love him.

'Come back,' was all he said at the end of my account.

'But Guv, we're just getting somewhere on this case. Couldn't we just suss out this place to see what–'

I remembered too well our conversation when I'd tried to arrest Juan Garcia at the car boot sale and he'd put a stop to that. And look where that had taken us. It was as if he deliberately wanted to muck up everything I tried to do, right or wrong.

Normally at this stage he'd have got all boss-like, called

me Pusey or even Sergeant, and ordered me to do as I was told. But this time he sounded as if he was pleading with me.

'It's like this, Greta. We've got to let Garcia go, now that the CPS has decided there's no case against him. And he says he wants to talk to you. If we let him go now without talking to you, we'll have the devil's own job finding him again. The thing is, we don't know what he wants to say, but it might be important. So leave your cat food case and come back to Shady Lane now.'

'Sarge, I can do it,' North interrupted. 'Please tell the Boss we've got two cars here, and you can go back and I can go on and find out what's happening here.'

I told Derek what she'd said.

'But she's only a rookie,' I added, 'and I don't know about leaving her on her own here.'

'No, it's OK, Greta,' Derek said. 'It's not as if it's anything dangerous. It'll be good experience for her. Just tell her to take it slowly and not do anything rash. No arrests or anything like that, just careful investigation.'

It was against my better judgment, but of course I had to do what he said. North drove me back along the road to my car and then turned round to go back to Nasty. I went as fast as I could to Shady Lane. Juan Garcia was waiting for me in an interview room, all beams.

'See, Sergeant darling, I tole you I was innocent,' he greeted me. 'You and Missis Sleepworthy and her husban', you are all the frens I got in the worl', now that my poor matey Charlie he got bashed.'

'Good. Now what?'

'No need being shy, Sergeant. I know was you got me free here. Now I do for you somethееn. I tell you somethееn about Charlie.'

I expected one of Garcia's rambling cock-and-bull stories,

but I thought I'd better listen, just in case it gave us a clue in the re-opened Charlie Hampson murder enquiry. So I gave Juan one of my best friendly smiles, and waited.

'See, Charlie he knew he wasen very clever with the burgling. So he got what he call a connection, and got himself a boss. When you got a boss in his business, you do better, see. But he make a mistake. The first job the boss give him, he go to wrong address. The boss tell him, give back the silver. But he theenk, OK if he give me to sell in car boot. Maybe the boss so angry, he have him keel. What you theenk?'

'Yes, Juan, that's a possibility. Not a very good one, but who knows. So can you tell me who this boss is who took on Charlie the Chump?'

'No, well, my matey Charlie not such a chump like you theenk, Sergeant. He don't tell even to me, his fren, the name of the boss. But he tell me important theeng about him. He is a Chino. You see? Is important I tell you thees, right?'

I couldn't believe it. A Chino could only mean Chinese in Garcia's fractured English. But just for this little scrap of information I'd left North on her own following a hot lead on another case. Surely Derek or Alfie could have got that much from Garcia, without hauling me back from the far north of the county?

Then it hit me. Another Chinese strand? Were we going to find a Chinese at the bottom of everything we did these days? Were they taking over the country? Or was there some impossible connection between the late Charlie Hampson, his new boss, Ah Weng So and her new baby, Sadie and James Lee, and the mysterious Chinese who'd threatened Jim Robinson, the Long-distance Lorry Driver, with unknown intimidation if he didn't smuggle illegal immigrants into the country?

I checked with Juan Garcia that I could find him again at

the Slipworthy's house in Hendon (so much for not being able to find him again), gave him a quick thanks, and rushed to tell Derek this hot news. I'd feel better if I dumped it on him, I was sure, even if all he could think of was to dump it on Mr Moon in turn at the end of the line.

When I got to Derek, he was furious. I couldn't get a word in about Garcia. He was pacing up and down, doing a good enough imitation of Mr Moon in his most purple-faced rage. I'd only ever seen Mr Moon once in that state, and never wanted to repeat the experience. Couldn't blame him at the time, mind you. He'd thought Garcia had committed suicide in a holding cell, and when he'd discovered he'd only broken his ankle falling into the lav and then escaped from the hospital on crutches, the poor man nearly exploded.

But this wasn't Derek's usual style, and I couldn't make out at first what it was all about. I'd never have dreamed that Derek had such a temper. I should have guessed what the reason was, of course. It was his precious North again.

Finally I managed to piece together what he was foaming about. She'd called in to say she'd gone into the factory in Nasty and asked to see the manager, then enquired what they did there. Apparently they processed animal parts not suitable for human consumption, which they got from the abattoir next door, packed the stuff in cans and sold it under the label of 'Luvapet'. That was all she learned.

So she started off back to Watford and found she had four flat tyres.

'Four!' Derek ground out through gritted teeth. '*You* know what that must mean, even if she doesn't. Somebody wanted to give her a warning. What right had you to leave a young rookie all alone in that hazardous situation? Why didn't you bring her back with you when I called you in? What's the matter with you, Pusey? Can't I trust you to do anything right these days?'

'But you gave the OK yourself,' I finally managed to squeak, loud enough for him to hear while he went on pacing up and down. 'I asked you–'

'Don't you dare try to put it on me, Pusey. If you'd put me fully in the picture I'd have realised the danger. Anyway,' he added, quietening down a bit, 'we've sent the tow-truck out and Alfie's gone with it to make sure she's alright. I told her not to try to do anything until he got there. And you'll be pleased to know that he's offered to take her under his wing from now on, so you need not feel responsible for her any longer.'

I was fuming a bit myself by this time, but I could see it was no good arguing. I had no idea what Derek thought had happened to his poor innocent young maiden, but it couldn't be anything like as bad as I wished.

Now I could see why I stood no chance with him. It was because I wasn't a young blue-eyed skinny little blonde. Simple as that. And whatever Marilyn, the mad Irish hairdresser, could do for me, it wouldn't make me over into his type.

Hopeless, I trudged out of his office.

I still hadn't told him what Garcia had said, and I didn't even care.

I was going home to brood.

Alone.

*

I stood in front of the full-length mirror in my bathroom and tried to give myself a cool assessment of what I saw. In detail. Naked. Every bit. OK, so I wasn't a skinny little blonde, and I wouldn't see twenty again – or twenty-five, come to that. But I still had my model's figure, good legs, fine tits (a nice handful, Ari always said. NO, I wasn't going to think about Ari. This was about Derek).

Nothing wrong with being tall, either, if you're graceful with it. Even nearly six foot in heels. Didn't get my Black Belt in karate just for chopping blocks of wood and bricks and stuff with my bare hands, you have to know how to move properly, too.

Not a bad face, even if I say it myself. Ordinary nose, funny-coloured eyes (Ari was always asking if they were green or blue. NO, never mind about Ari. Had Derek ever noticed my eyes? Probably not). What's known (kindly) as a generous mouth, maybe ready to smile too much. Better than sulking, I suppose.

The hair. Yes, that was the trouble, the hair. Always untidy, mousy-brown, too curly, looked as if it had been cut with a knife and fork.

Now that I'd decided that after all Marilyn's Miracles were the answer to my problems, I put my clothes on and thought about work. Better than thinking about Derek, and wondering why he was such a bastard to me. If only I could hate him, how much better off I'd be. I could settle down to a happy comfortable sex life with Ari, who thought the world of me and was tall dark and handsome in the bargain. Fun, too, sometimes. Except I didn't love him, I loved Derek.

Oh, bugger that. Think about the job, I told myself. Nothing happened. My head stayed buzzy and muddled and full of my own vital statistics and maddening mental pictures of Derek with his arms round dear little North.

Maybe I needed to go out for a mind-clearing speed around Watford on the trusty old roller-blades. No, didn't fancy that either. What about the bike? Hadn't really used that since I'd acquired a car and started putting on weight. Not much weight, though. Not enough to put a man off.

Just a minute. What about if I took the bike and did a recce of my own around that smelly factory in Nasty? Kill three birds with one stone: get exercise, fill in time instead of brooding, find out something that could be useful by nosing around where Miss Smarty-Pants North had got all the answers!

Let's see. In our cars, it had taken us less than an hour to get to Nasty. It must have been between thirty and forty miles. I could cycle at about ten miles an hour, erm, say it would take me four hours to get there, an hour to poke around, another four to get home (knackered), that would just about give me time to shower and change and get back to Shady Lane. Was I any good at the job after zero hours sleep? No. Should I do it anyway?

I decided to go. Anything was better than moping around trying not to think about Derek.

Thinking about what routes to take to avoid the motorways took my mind off the way my legs started aching almost from the start. And by the time I was back into the rhythm of cycling, I started to enjoy myself. But when I got half-way there, I decided it didn't matter if I went as far as Nasty or not. I felt better already. And what could I find out there anyway?

So I turned around, cycled home, fell into bed and got a good night's sleep instead. Probably a better idea.

Next morning, even though I had aching legs and a sore bum, I felt great and ready to take on the world. Or even Derek. I went storming into his office ready to demand an apology for how unreasonably he'd behaved to me the previous day.

Didn't get a chance, did I. While I was still opening the door and drawing breath to start, he was already at it.

'...Don't know what's the matter with you these days, Greta. Used to be able to rely on you. Even when you made mistakes, you were still a good copper. But to go flouncing out like that just because you had a telling-off–'

That was too much, really over the top. I stopped wondering how he'd known who was coming in the door before he'd even seen it was me, and waded in myself.

'Flouncing! What do you mean? I've never flounced in my life! And while we're at it, I might ask what's the matter with you these days. Not like you to let a skinny blonde turn your head–'

'Skinny blonde! What are you talking about? I'm talking about the standard of your work. What's skinny blondes got to do with it?'

We both stopped for a moment, panting for breath. He was bright red and I could feel heat in my face, too. We'd never had even the smallest argument before, and here we were having a first-class row. What was I thinking of? We'd always acted like colleagues and friends, but he was still an Inspector and I was only a Sergeant, even if we were sometimes on smooching terms.

In a much quieter voice he asked me, 'Maybe you'd like a transfer? How about Drugs? They're always short of manpower, and they could use a bright Sergeant like you.'

That was below the belt, and he knew it. He certainly hadn't forgotten that I had a hang-up about drugs because my teenage mother had died in public of an overdose when I was two years old. I felt the heat draining out of my face as I saw he was already regretting what he'd said.

'What's wrong with you, man?' I asked, more calmly, thinking we were both getting more rational now and maybe could have a sensible conversation.

Wrong again. It was as if I'd lit his fuse again.

'Man!' he flared. 'Where do you get off talking to me like that?'

Right away I was back at full fury.

'Why the hell shouldn't I call you man? Alfie calls me girl all the time and I'm not supposed to mind. Or maybe there's some reason you don't want to be referred to by your sex?'

Oh hell. My turn to have gone too far. I'd really overstepped the mark this time, I could see by his face.

'I'd better go,' I mumbled, and made for the door.

'Greta, wait. Why are we quarrelling like a couple of kids? Come and sit down and let's talk properly. You're right, I did give the OK for you to leave North on her own at Nasty, and it was my mistake, not yours.'

Another switch. I was beginning to wonder if my dear boss was suffering from some sort of hormonal imbalance, behaving like a man on a roller coaster. I sat in silence and we looked at each other in a measuring sort of way, like boxers before the round two bell rang.

Derek put his elbows on his desk and his face in his hands for a moment. Then he gave a great sigh, ran his fingers through his hair (wouldn't I just love to do that myself) and looked at me, straight in the eye, seriously.

'The fact is, I may as well tell you, I've got this feeling that I'm fucking up everything I try to do.'

This was a turn-up. First of all, for Derek to actually admit he wasn't on top of the job, but even more, for him to use that sort of language. He was usually such a posh gent. What with one thing and another, I didn't know what to say. There was no need. He was going on.

'Tell me about your conversation with Juan Garcia.'

I did, and when I'd finished we sat looking at each other more like dummies this time, not like opponents any more.

Finally I said, 'I know you think I've got a bee in my bonnet,

Derek, but you've got to admit it's too much, the way the Chinese keep cropping up. And we both know that in our business there's no such thing as a coincidence.'

Of course, naturally Alfie would choose that very moment to come bursting in with the biggest coincidence of all.

'Guv, Greta, listen!' he yelled, waving a bit of paper. 'It's our case. A body, a young Chinese girl, and what do you bet it's that one, you know, whatever her name is, the one you helped with the baby in the doorway, Greta!'

'Ah Weng So,' I said automatically as I got up and made for the door. 'Where was she found?'

'Fill in the details on our way,' Derek said, coming to life at last. 'Where is it? Who found her; when; do they know how she died? Who's on the scene now? Come on, Alfie, calm down.'

'You know that multi-storey car park they're building opposite the hospital?'

Of course we did, and even if we hadn't, by this time Alfie was driving us towards it at top speed with lights and sirens going. This didn't stop him from shouting all he knew of the case at us as we raced to the scene.

'Turns out the foreman is one of the old school, cares about the work, you know. So before they installed the lift he told his gang to get rid of some of the rubble and other rubbish they'd been chucking down the bottom of the lift shaft.'

'Unusual,' Derek remarked.

'Yes, well, some of it was old food, see, and also the Portaloo had been taken off the site, so they'd been using–'

'So that's where they found the body, when they cleared out some of that muck?'

'Right. The foreman phoned it in and there's a couple of uniforms at the scene now, waiting for us.'

I knew what was coming. Derek confirmed it.

'They'll need you, Greta, and maybe a nurse from the hospital too, to identify if it really is your Ah Weng So. But we'll have to do all the usual at the scene first, anyway.'

'Spect it is your girl, Greta,' Alfie interrupted. 'Be a bit of a turn-up for the book if it's still another one, won't it. We'll be up to the eyebrows in them. They say,' he went on chattily, 'that every third person that's born in the world is a Chinese, and I reckon–'

'Yes, OK, Alfie, we get it. When you get over to the hospital to pick up that nurse then, Greta, Mr Moon has been wanting to know what's happening to the baby, so you might as well find that out too, while you're there. Sorry about before,' he muttered quietly.

As usual, Alfie's hearing was most acute when you didn't want it to be.

'Sorry?' he boomed. 'What's been happening then?'

He never got an answer. We'd arrived at the multi-storey car park, and a uniform waved us down and directed us to the lowest floor. It was only later, when I wasn't so focused on the crime, that I remembered that Alfie had spoken to him by name.

'Thanks, Taz,' he'd said. It was the unusual name that stuck in my mind.

I looked at the mucky little body that they'd hauled up from the bottom of the lift shaft. It was Ah Weng So, alright. What a sad end for the poor kid, after not much of a life at all.

I had a strong feeling I knew who'd done this to her, but there was no point in telling Derek. He had no time for instinct or prejudice, and this was both. How I'd ever get any evidence to prove my case was beyond me. Just now, though, we had to go through the usual formalities, with Derek starting the ball rolling by bawling out the foreman for moving the body.

Of course, he said she might have been alive, but a child could have seen she couldn't possibly have been...

The medic arrived and pronounced her officially dead. Then we all got on with our routine, with all the photographers and forensic guys doing their thing while we talked to the foreman and his work gang. He was quite a bright guy, and he'd even sent one of them to fetch the security man who'd been on duty the previous night. But nobody could tell us anything useful. We just heard a lot of grumbles about the Portaloo having been taken off site prematurely.

So after a pretty useless morning, I went over to pick up the nurse from the hospital and we followed the sad little body to the morgue.

On the way back after we'd both identified Ah Weng So, I remembered Mr Moon's interest in the baby, and asked the nurse how it was.

'It,' she said. '*It*, Sergeant, is a little girl, and just like a doll. Seeing nobody's got any idea of finding a next of kin, the Social will take her over and try to find a home for her. Mind you, now that my own three are all at school, I've an idea to put in to adopt her myself. The pity of it, a poor newborn infant with nobody caring for her.'

'What about the pity of the poor young mother being murdered?' I argued.

She shrugged. 'Oh, murder, was it? I thought she'd just fallen down a lift shaft running away from her responsibilities.'

What strange priorities of pity some people have. We parted coldly.

Back at Shady Lane I found young North reading and munching an apple.

'Busy?' I asked. And before she could answer, I went on, 'Where's everyone?' hoping she'd understand by this that I meant to tell her that she was no-one.

If I thought having this little go could dent her self-confidence, I was living in a dream world. She just answered calmly, 'The Inspector's with Mr Moon and Alfie's in the–'

'Yes, I know, in the canteen,' I finished for her, noticing that she was reading PACE again, the little swot.

I was just asking her sweetly if she was studying for promotion, when Derek came back, looking as if his Portaloo had been removed too soon, too. But I could see he wasn't in the mood for that sort of crack. Not even what I would have said at similar times in the past: 'What's up, Doc?'

I just waited for him to say something. He did.

'Mr Moon doesn't think this team is pulling its weight,' he growled. 'Apparently we have the lightest case-load in the whole of Hertfordshire CID, and we still can't come up with any results.'

Before he could say another word, North put her book down and walked out of the room. I still waited, I didn't know for what. I wasn't going to tempt fate by saying anything about North's behaviour. Just as well. She quickly came back with Alfie. The little pest had just gone to fetch him from the canteen.

Then Derek read us all the riot act, telling us to get our fingers out, etc. I could see this wasn't the time to argue with him about the stupid poisoned pet food case, which I still couldn't see could be a CID matter.

Still, the day was nearly over, and the next day was a free one for me, so I stayed shtum and started looking forward to my hair makeover at Marilyn's Miracles.

'I've detailed DCs Fred Archer and Kevin Burton to go over to the multi-storey car park and sift through all the muck that was in the bottom of the lift shaft,' Derek said.

Alfie was never one to shirk speaking up if he thought it was called for.

'Why them, Guv?' he said. 'They always got all the dirty

jobs when they first joined us from uniforms, but we've got ourselves a newer recruit now.'

And he looked pointedly at DC North.

Derek sighed.

'Yes, OK Alfie, you're right. Vicky, you'll have to go with Fred and Kevin to learn how it's done. It's a mucky job, but we all had to do it at some time or other.'

I was fuming again. How sympathetic he sounded to his dear little Vicky.

I couldn't remember him ever apologising to any of the rest of us when he gave us dirty work to do.

And it was 'Vicky' again, after only knowing her for five minutes!

Grrr.

Chapter 8

I was really nervous. I had to remind myself that I was a tough Detective Sergeant, scared of nothing.

'What are you going to do?' I mumbled at Marilyn, who was fingering thoughtfully through my hair.

'Leave it to me,' she said. That was the start of hours of being marched backwards and forwards from mirror to basin and basin to mirror, having tight things rolled in my hair, being anointed with all sorts of smelly puddingy stuff, having a sort of cap put on my head and then painfully having some hair pulled through it with a crochet hook, and finally having a drier waved at my poor aching nut while Marilyn carefully tugged at my hair again with a strange-looking brush.

Didn't look all that clean, either, after all that.

During all this time, people came and went, some eating and some drinking, some with little kids bawling or running around under everyone's feet, and everyone talking at the tops of their voices. Seemed as if Marilyn understood all that was going on and shouted commands at them all like a desperate captain on a sinking ship. Anyway, everyone seemed to survive, so maybe we were manning the lifeboats. By then I didn't care anything about anything except getting out of there in one piece and getting rid of my skull-splitting headache.

I'd kept honestly to Marilyn's instruction not to look in the mirror until she said I could. Finally she gave the word.

'Now then,' she said, beaming and holding a mirror behind

me so that I could see back and front at the same time.

I couldn't believe my eyes. I looked a proper tart. My hair was short and straight (how had she stopped it being curly?) and stood up in sort of tufts, each one a different colour. I didn't know whether to scream, cry or bash Marilyn round the head. Clearly she didn't suss my reaction at all.

'Isn't that great,' she said, 'how we've changed your image completely. Hasn't it brightened you up? You look like a new person, and if I may say so, you look a lot younger, too.'

Hm, younger, eh? I hadn't thought of that. Maybe I'd get used to it, after all.

See what Ari said. I had a date with him that evening, and he'd said he had a surprise for me. Well, whatever it was, it wouldn't be as amazing as the one I had for him on the top of my bonce.

Just as I was getting over the shock of the new me, I got another one when Marilyn told me how much I owed her.

'Don't worry,' she said, 'we take cheques or credit cards.'

And while my knees were still weak, she went on, 'Would you like to make your next appointment now, or will you phone?'

It took a lot of will power not to give her the answer I first thought of and to leave there still smiling bravely.

On the way home, I suddenly realised that Derek hadn't told any of us what happened when he went to see Mr Chang, the victim of the late Charlie Hampson's last silver burglary. I was tempted to pop in to Shady Lane just to ask about it, but then I realised I was just making an excuse to myself to see him even on my off-day. And anyway, if I happened to see North as well, I'd have to start questioning her about what really happened in Nasty. She still hadn't given me any details of that episode. Definitely not worth breaking up my free time.

So I decided to buy some clothes instead, something I hardly ever do because I feel most comfortable in jeans. Still, since I had this expensive new hairdo, I thought I might as well tart myself up to get the max out of it.

Ari got the max out of it alright that evening. I thought he was going to have a heart attack. He'd never seen me before all done up in a short tight skirt, heels and full make-up. And the new hair was just the cherry on top of the sundae. His mouth dropped open, he went all colours, and he made a funny noise, like 'Aarghgh'. Then he sat down. Then he stood up and walked over to me.

'Why?' he said.

I gave him a drink and he settled down a bit, but I could see he was shaken, though I wasn't sure in what way, plus or minus.

Finally, he said in a croaky kind of voice, as if he'd just got a sore throat, 'We were invited to my home to have dinner with my mother and father this evening. Shall I phone and say you're not well?'

I'd met his mother once and she'd made clear she didn't think much of me. I didn't want to see her again, ever. Still, Ari might have asked me first. And I didn't like his reason for calling it off now.

'Any particular reason in mind, why we should have dinner with your parents?' I asked, trying to sound off-hand.

'Yes, my mother wanted to explain to you how keen she is for me to get married. She doesn't think you're suitable, she wants me to marry a nice Greek girl, but now she knows you're the one I love, she says she'll help me persuade you.'

'Well, why can't you just tell her I don't want to get married. It's not you, tell her. I can see she must think her darling son is a great catch, but if you tell her it's not personal–'

'You know that's not true. If your wonder-boss the Inspector asked you, I bet you'd say yes like a shot.'

Ari sounded bitter. I couldn't blame him really. You might

say if you were one of those women who like reading those Mills and Boon romantic books that I'd been toying with his affections. My own view was that we were just having a great sex life and enjoying each other's company. I couldn't see why marriage had to come into it at all. And he was wrong about Derek.

'No, you're wrong,' I told him, trying to sound as believable as I could. 'Honestly, Ari, I just don't want to get married at all, ever. Not to you, not to Derek, not to the Prince of Wales, not even to George Clooney. So maybe it would be a good idea if you phone your ma and say I'm not well.'

'OK,' he said, taking out his mobile. 'She's been saying all along that all English girls look like tarts, and if she saw you tonight–'

Luckily for him, he got through to his mother just then, otherwise he'd have got a good old mouthful from me. All English girls look like tarts! What a cheek! Anyway, I could tell he didn't just say what we'd agreed. The conversation went on and on, in Greek of course, so I wandered into the bathroom to take another look at the new me. Hate to say this, but he was right. I looked like a tart, maybe an expensive one, but still nothing like a loving mother would want her son to marry.

Anyway, after we'd got over squabbling about whether all English girls looked like tarts or it was only me in my new look, I washed my hair a few times and kind of smoothed it down a bit so it didn't look so bad. Then we had a smashing evening together and ended up as usual, the best of friends.

The result was, next morning I breezed into Shady Lane feeling on top of the world, even though my hair had kind of sprung back to the way Marilyn had done it. The good feeling didn't last.

Wouldn't you know, the first person I saw was my pet hate, Knockout North.

'Oh Sarge,' she said in her smarmy way, 'I've written a

full report of what happened in Nasty after you'd left. Shall I give it to you or the Inspector?'

'I thought you were helping Fred and Kevin sifting through the muck in the lift shaft for forensics yesterday?'

'Yes, they're nice chaps, aren't they? And that was very useful experience for me. But we don't know if we found anything interesting. We just bagged it all up and Fred passed it on to forensics.'

Trust her to think of that disgusting job as useful. I'd have to think up something even worse for her some time to see how she liked that.

'But then,' she was going on, 'I did the report last night after I'd got home and showered the smell off. At least, I hope I did get rid of it. You can't smell anything, can you, Sarge?'

I had to admit she smelled as sweet as violets and took the report from her.

'I'll hand it on to DI Michaelson when I've read it. Just as well to make sure you've covered everything in it.'

'Thank you, Sarge. Love your hair!'

And she fairly skipped out of the room. I'd give her something to skip about. I scanned through that report like a bad-tempered school teacher reading the homework of her least favourite pupil. Not one mistake could I find. But I was happy to spot quite a few omissions. An excuse to have a go at the little darling.

'North!' I barked when I found her in the canteen with Alfie, as usual having his second breakfast. 'This report. You haven't mentioned if you saw any of the actual factory, any of the workers in it, if so what nationality they appeared to be, the name and nationality of the manager you interviewed–'

'Hold on, Greta,' Alfie interrupted, spraying crumbs as he always did. 'Give the kid a chance. And anyway, I thought

Derek had passed her over to me. I should be vetting her reports before they go to him, not you.'

'Please yourself,' I snarled, flinging it on the table in front of him. 'I've got better things to do with my time, anyway.'

As I marched out, from the corner of my eye I could see Alfie scratching his head, looking puzzled. I have to admit it's pretty unusual for me to speak to him that way. He's miles my senior, even if we are both sergeants. He took me under his wing when I was a rookie, he and his wife Betty have been very kind and hospitable to me, and I really respect him for his knowledge and experience in the Job. And I'm kind of fond of him. He must have wondered what had happened to his pal Greta that day. So did I.

'That *was* Mr Chang's stolen silver, as far as we can make out,' Derek greeted me when I got to his office. 'But all I got from talking to him was a demand to know when we'd recover it for him. And we've charged Sadie and James Lee with obstruction, but of course we couldn't detain them.'

'So where are we now, Guv?'

'Up against a blank wall as far as I can see, and Mr Moon is well and truly on my tail. Any ideas?'

He sounded really glum. I thought I couldn't make matters worse.

'Look, Derek, I really think we've got to chase up everything we can think of. Any news about the cause of Ah Weng So's death? I know you don't like hunches, but I'm almost sure James Lee killed her while his sister took her place. OK, it was our error in letting uniforms take her back to the hospital in mistake for Ah Weng So, but that must have been her intention. And why should she have done that, if not to give her brother time to get rid of Ah Weng So? Wait…' I held up my hand as he was about to argue. 'You're going to say "what motive", right? Well, what if they're part of the outfit that was getting forced labour out of Ah Weng So and who knows how many other illegals? And they were worried in case she led us to the factory where she was working. So they tracked her down to dispose of her before she could tell us anything?'

'Yes, very good,' Derek said grudgingly. 'But that's all theory. What have we really got in fact?'

'OK, let me try an even more far-fetched theory on you. How about a connection between Charlie Hampson's Chinese boss, plus Mr Chang the burglary victim, and the Chinese who tried to get Jim Robinson to smuggle illegals, together with Ah Weng So and James and Sadie Lee, and the smelly factory at Nasty?'

Derek burst out laughing. Well, I'd managed one thing. I'd got a smile out of him. Not quite what I'd been trying for.

Then he looked at me, fully and properly, for the first time since I'd come into the room.

'What happened to your hair?' he asked, not in a putting-down kind of way, but really puzzled. 'What have you done with all your lovely curls?'

Not a winner there, then. He'd actually liked it better before I'd spent all that time and money on trying to look more twenty-first century. And younger. Anyway, I got the feeling he didn't really want an answer, and I was right. He was still laughing at my theory.

When he calmed down he said, 'Sorry, Greta, listening to your theory was very entertaining, but you're a better copper than that. You know that's not real life. And anyway, we've got nothing to go on except your imagination. Let's try to be rational now, shall we?'

'OK, have you got any reasonable theories?'

He sighed.

'Come on, never mind theories, it's facts we need, or at

least some information. Get on to Charlie Hampson's record and see if you can get some more background on him. Or better still, what about getting on to his fence, the one he told Garcia was no good any more? We might get something out of him. Forget the theories, Greta, at least for a while. Let's do some real police work.'

*

'Well done, Vicky,' Derek beamed, while I tried to stop scowling. 'That was a very well written report, clear and concise but with all the details, and I can't fault your spelling or punctuation, either.'

Alfie cleared his throat and looked at me, a bit hurt. I didn't say anything, but I knew he took it personally. Spelling, punctuation, grammar and all that stuff not being his strongest points.

'Guv,' he said, 'what do you think about me and Greta going back to that place and trying to find out a bit more. Like,' he hurried on, seeing Derek frowning and starting to shake his head, 'sussing out what happened to that other feller, you know, the one that Vicky and Greta were following that took them to Nasty.'

'Franklin,' I supplied. 'That's right, he seemed to disappear, and there's nothing about him in your report, *Vicky*.'

I hadn't used her first name before, but the way I said it this time wasn't meant to tell her we were going to be friends. She took the hint and studied her feet, going a bit pink.

'OK then,' Derek said, 'you two go back, if you think it's worth the bother, and Vicky and I will go and see what we can find out in Putney and Chelsea.'

This wasn't in my game plan at all. The last thing in the world I wanted was for Derek to be alone with North. Anyway,

Alfie was supposed to be her mentor, so she should have gone with him to Nasty, and I should have been with Derek. I glared at Alfie, who smiled back innocently.

'It'll be like old times, girl,' he said, 'you and me working together again, wunnit.'

So I swallowed it and we all went off, North gazing adoringly at Derek as usual, me looking like thunder, and Alfie and Derek not noticing a thing.

The first thing I observed when we got to Nasty was that the smell had gone. North's report had explained that inside the factory it didn't smell at all, because they had powerful extractor fans that gave all the locals the benefit instead. The manager, Mr Blenkins, had told her they had very few employees because the place was fully automated, so there was no point in showing her around. And her report said she'd seen no need to call on the abattoir, which he pointed out to her almost next door. I couldn't blame her for that. Who'd want to visit a place like that, if they didn't have to.

'Mr Blenkins admitted,' her report said, 'that the Luvapet factory and its employees were extremely unpopular with the local inhabitants for obvious reasons, and suffered a certain amount of harassment which they had never reported to the police. He denied all knowledge of supplying a wholesaler named Edward Franklin, although I told him we had arrived at his premises by following Mr Franklin. When I found my tyres had been let down, I assumed it was part of the local harassment to which Mr Blenkins had referred.' And so on.

The village of Nasty was tiny. It had no church, shop or post office. Nor did it seem to have anything like a factory or an abattoir. I couldn't believe it.

'I can't believe this,' Alfie said. 'If it's not here, what did you smell?'

What Nasty did have was a pub. The Dragon was the

kind of pub that must have existed in rural areas at the beginning of the twentieth century. It was closed, of course. We tried to look in, but the windows were too filthy. Alfie banged on the door for a long time. Finally a gravelly voice shouted from inside, 'Not open yet!' and Alfie shouted back who we were. Grudgingly the door creaked open, we showed our warrant cards, and the mucky unshaved publican let us in.

It was about the sort of place you'd expect in a grungy village like Nasty. Dark, dull, badly furnished, a padded bench under the windows with dirty stained cushions and a smell of stale cigarette smoke. But nothing like the smell North and I had been knocked out by on our first visit to the area.

Alfie had got his name from over the door.

'We hope you can help us with our enquiries, Mr Jonas,' he said briskly.

'Wodjer want?' Jonas growled.

'About the Luvapet factory,' I said.

'Nevererdofit.'

After a moment, Alfie unscrambled this.

'What do you mean, you've never heard of it? It's the factory that was making all the smell and making all your locals complain. It was getting its supplies from your abattoir here–'

Mr Jonas came to life.

'You've come to the wrong place,' he said. 'This 'ere is The Dragon pub, in the village of Nasty, population one 'undred and four. The four's my kids,' he added with a leer. 'We've never ad no factories ere. Years ago, in my grandfather's time, there was a abatt– a slaughter-ouse for the local farmers, but that's been closed near on a 'undred years.'

'But–' I started, but once wound up, Mr Jonas wasn't going to stop so easily.

'I've lived 'ere all my life and my father before me and 'is father before 'im and I can tell you we've never 'ad no factories nor any industrials stuff 'ere, never. So you come to the wrong place, see. Perlice!' he added bitterly. 'If I run over my license hours, they'd be on me like a ton of shit. Get on with solving some crime, why doncher, 'stead of chasing wild geese.'

And he more or less shoved us out of the door. Not that it wasn't a relief to get out into the air, what with the smell of the pub and its owner, who seemed not to have bathed or shaved since the previous Christmas. But *THE* smell was missing. I was fed up. I was absolutely ready to believe that North had made up every word of her report, but the trouble was that I'd smelled the smell of Nasty myself, and I knew that much at least was true.

'More mysteries, Alfie,' I said gloomily. 'You can't imagine a smell. So what was it, and where did it go? And where did Edward Franklin go? And if North didn't invent it, where did the factory go? And her Mr Blenkins? Let's knock on a few doors.'

We looked up and down what seemed to be Nasty's only street, at the sad dilapidated little dwellings. Alfie marched up to the first door after the pub and banged on it.

It was opened by an old dear in a grubby cardigan and wrinkly stockings (I suppose they were her stockings and not her legs), who seemed to have the same ideas of personal hygiene as the publican. Alfie stepped back a smart pace or two and started bawling questions at her; but sad to say, she was friendlier than Mr Jonas and invited us in for a cup of tea. Phoo! The windows seemed to have been sealed up and the place ponged something awful. Awkward really, to talk about a smell that had disappeared to someone who clearly wouldn't have noticed such a thing.

Still, I tried. I explained the whole thing, from beginning to end, including North's report, her Mr Blenkins, the factory, the abattoir, her tyres being let down, the lot. I mentioned our following Edward Franklin and getting hit by the smell, and left nothing out. Then Alfie told her about Jonas the publican and what he'd said. Mrs Puckridge listened carefully while we all had a cup of tea, which seemed to have been made with rancid milk. Sometimes she nodded, occasionally she gave a dry chuckle. None of it seemed funny to me, but maybe she was just doing that to show she was paying attention.

'Well, young lady,' she said to me when we'd finally finished, 'I must say it's lovely to have visitors. We hardly ever see any new faces in our little village, you know. It was all very interesting, what you told me. Now, what can I do for you?'

I managed not to groan, but I looked hard at Alfie, who hadn't said much so far. Give him his due, he took it up right away.

'Was there ever a pet food factory in Nasty, Mrs Puckridge?' he started.

Then he took her through the whole thing, and drew an even blanker blank than we'd got from Jonas the publican. He tried another line, bless him, suggesting that maybe there was another village nearby that North had gone on to, and found the factory, not realising that she wasn't still in Nasty. No, Mrs Puckridge swore that she knew all the surrounding area and there was no such place anywhere near or far.

'Something wrong with that tea,' Alfie grumbled, burping as we got back into the car, waving back at Mrs Puckridge standing on her doorstep. She seemed sad to see us go.

'Bugger the tea,' I said. 'There's something wrong with everything. Let's just drive out of sight of your friend

Mrs Puckridge and then go over the possibilities before we go back to Watford.'

We did, and between us we came up with a whole lot of ideas, all stupid. But there were plenty of questions.

If North had invented her report, why did she do that, what happened to the smell, and who let her tyres down?

If North's report was all true, what happened to the factory, Mr Blenkins, Edward Franklin, the abattoir, and why were the villagers lying?

If North's report was true but she'd somehow gone on to some other nearby village, how had she made that mistake and why didn't Mrs Puckridge know what other village had the smelly factory?

But the biggest problem of all was this: I knew I'd smelled that terrible smell on the road to Nasty, and it had to have come from somewhere and something. Now it had gone. How?

When we got to this part, Alfie started giving me a funny look.

'Listen, Greta,' he said, 'now don't take this wrong and go all huffy on me, but are you sure about smelling this smell in the first place?'

I didn't bother to answer. Alfie often said I'd got too much imagination, but I couldn't imagine a smell, specially if North smelled it, too. I got on my mobile, got the number of the local Environmental Health Department, and spoke to the head of the Department herself. I gave her an outline of the problem, not too much detail. When she called me back to confirm there was no pet food factory anywhere within a ten-mile radius of Nasty, that at least cleared up one question, even if it raised another.

'Look, Alfie,' I said, 'I've made no secret of the fact that I don't like young North, so it's just as well we're together on this job, otherwise you and Derek might think I was trying to do her down. But you've seen and heard all that I have, and we can't get away from the fact that her whole report must be an invention from beginning to end. Now, the question is, why?'

'No, girl, there's another two questions. Where did the smell go? And if her report is a pack of lies, what are we going to do about it?'

We drove all the way back to Watford without speaking another word. Not that there was any bad feeling between us. Just that neither of us could think of anything to say. No need to spell out to each other that this was serious. It didn't matter that the whole pet food enquiry was a minor job. That wasn't the point any more. Falsified reports were major, on any subject.

I don't know what we expected, or even if Alfie's thoughts were the same as mine. Maybe I thought that if we confronted her with the facts, DC North would break into floods of tears and beg for another chance. Or perhaps I pictured her white-faced accepting instant dismissal from Superintendent Moon. I suppose that was what I really hoped. What happened was the last thing I could have guessed.

We'd reported to Derek with North present. Alfie did most of the talking. Derek listened to the end and then turned to North.

'Well, what have you got to say for yourself?'

'I don't know what to say, sir,' she said. Her head was up and she didn't look the least bit worried or bothered. 'All I can tell you is that every word of my report is absolutely correct, and I'm sorry I didn't get a signed affidavit from Mr Blenkins, but it didn't seem necessary at the time. When I left the village of Nasty, the smell was as virulent as it had been when DS Pusey and I first got there.'

We all went quiet, then suddenly she burst out, 'Sir, I have it! DS Partridge came to Nasty with the tow-truck when I called in about my four flat tyres.' She turned to Alfie. 'You must have smelled it then, Alfie. And so must the truck driver...'

Alfie looked blank.

'You didn't say anything,' he muttered. 'I can't say as I remember any particular smell. Sorry, girl. Can't help you out there.'

North at last started to look desperate.

'What's happening? Why are you all ganging up on me? What's going on?'

This was great. Now she was the victim suddenly instead of the culprit.

'Just a moment,' Derek said. 'Let's deal with one thing at a time. The smell. North, when you came out of the factory, was it as powerful as when you arrived? Was it dispersing at all? Perhaps by the time the tow-truck arrived it had completely gone. That would account for Alfie not noticing anything when he got there.'

I was dead chuffed he'd started calling her North again, but I didn't like the way things were going. It sounded as if he was trying to help her out, when he should have been down on her like a ton of bricks. No, just a minute. If he was saying there really *was* a smell, that meant that he believed *me*, nothing to do with accepting her report.

Whatever he was up to, she wasn't playing along.

'No sir,' she said stubbornly, 'it was just as bad all the time I was there.'

Stalemate. Deadlock. Where did we go from here. We all looked at Derek.

'I'm afraid you'll have to be put on suspension, North,' he said. I could see he didn't want to be saying this, but he couldn't see a way out. 'Come with me now to see Mr Moon.'

When he came back on his own, all he said to me and Alfie was, 'Come on, you two. It's not a minor case any more. We're all going back to this smelly village of yours. Nasty, eh?'

Chapter 9

Going back to Nasty with Derek and Alfie wasn't a complete waste of time, because on the journey Derek filled us in on his trip to Putney and Chelsea. According to him, the local CID was very helpful and didn't just show him reports, but had a long off-the-record jaw with him.

'Was DC North in on that?' I asked. I knew this might be treading on a tender spot with him, specially in her present situation, but it seemed to me that if she wasn't to be trusted, the less she knew the better. Of course I wasn't going to say that out loud, but I could see he picked up the message.

'No, as it happens, she wasn't there. This was an informal chat between officers of equal rank,' he said at his most pompous.

Alfie cleared his throat so lengthily and meaningfully that we both looked at him, expecting some comment. All he said was, 'Keep your eyes on the road, Greta.'

Pick the bones out of that, Greta, I thought.

I got the feeling Derek didn't quite trust us with absolutely everything he'd learned, either. Just that the fence Charlie Hampson used before he decided car boot sales were more profitable WAS ALSO CHINESE!

'Oh, is that all,' I said, trying not to sound sarcastic. 'Seems as if they're everywhere, doesn't it. I don't suppose North said this Mr Blenkins, the so-called manager of the so-called pet food factory, was Chinese too, by any chance?'

Well, of course, when we got back to Nasty, there it was

as we'd left it. No smell, no factory, no abattoir, same miserable little pub.

'Here's where young Vicky was with her four flat tyres when we come with the pick-up for her,' Alfie pointed out. 'She said she left it here and walked the rest because the road was widest here.'

'I don't suppose you asked exactly where she walked, by any chance? And when you and Greta interviewed the publican and the old lady here, did you ask them about a smell?' Derek asked, speaking directly to Alfie by way of showing me that he was a bit off me at the moment.

Alfie admitted that we'd asked about a pet food factory and an abattoir, but only mentioned in passing that the locals were supposed to have complained about the smell.

'Course I never asked where the factory was. Why should I?' he added, reasonably enough. 'They said there wasn't one.'

'Right,' Derek said grimly. 'Let's try again. There's not many houses along this – I suppose this *is* the main street – so we'll just go door-to-door, three each, and ask those simple questions. Do they know of a pet food factory anywhere around here, and has there ever been a bad smell here that people have complained about? Come on, let's get on with it.'

So there we were, back to being PC Plods, doing stuff that was a pain in the neck and useless, and probably all because Derek was still trying to clear his little darling's name. And as Alfie and I could have told him, it was all a waste of our time, because we met with nine blanks.

'What next?' Alfie sighed when we got back into the car.

'Surrounding countryside,' Derek said.

'Oh, come on, for Pete's sake!' I burst out. 'This is crazy and you know it.'

'I know what you think, Greta,' he said, 'but this isn't just about North. You've said yourself there's a mystery here and it's probably not just about pet food any more. I'm a senior officer, and do you really think I'd be wasting my own time as well as my two best sergeants' if I were only concerned about a probationary detective putting in a fictional report? Just remember, if you yourself hadn't referred to this terrible smell, there'd be less of a puzzle. So let's leave personalities out of it, shall we, and get on with the job?'

Of course he was right, but even he couldn't have guessed how right he was.

We started by driving to the next village, Puckeridge (that must have been where old Mrs Puckridge came from), which was a whole lot of an improvement on Nasty. Nothing of interest there, so I drove on, not caring about signposts or wondering where we were going. With hindsight I realised I should have taken more notice of my route, so that we could find our way back to civilisation easily.

So it happened that when we all started smelling THE SMELL again, I didn't really know where we were. I hadn't even thought to check the odometer to see how far we'd travelled from Puckeridge. I stopped the car and we all got out. Nobody needed to take the lead. We all followed our noses in the same direction. Through a field, through a little stand of trees, too small to call a wood, and out into some rough sort of heathland.

And there it was. A mouldering heap of bodies. The stench was unbelievable. A hundred times worse than what I'd smelled on the road to Nasty, but the same sort of horrible stink.

My first reaction was to turn round and run back to the car, but Alfie and Derek bravely walked on towards the shocking sight. So of course I had to follow them. As we got closer, we could see that the bodies were all kinds: animals, chickens, people. Some even looked like children.

Derek took command. He sent Alfie back to the trees to

break off some branches, as thick as he could. He sent me back to the car to phone for back-up and medical help and ambulances and the forensic team, while he got on to Mr Moon on his own mobile, to report what we'd found.

He shouted after me as I ran back to the road, 'And bring that bottle of water back with you.'

I couldn't imagine what that was for, but I did as he said. I didn't think of it at the time, but afterwards when I came to turn over the day's events in my mind, I remembered this was what I most admired about Derek. He might have been a bit of a prat in some ways, but when it came down to it, he was a real man and a leader of men.

Still, as I say, at the time there was no room in my mind for anything except our awful discovery. In a way, what followed was even worse, though in another way I suppose it was better.

When we re-grouped, Derek took out his handkerchief and soaked it in the water from the bottle I always kept in the car, tied it round over his nose and mouth and told us to do the same. Then, each of us holding one of the strong branches gathered by Alfie, we slowly went towards the disgusting heap.

Derek got there first and cautiously prodded at the nearest body. He swore, tore off his wet hanky, flung down his stick and swore again. Alfie and I were a few paces behind him so he had time to do all this before we caught up and saw what had caused this reaction.

The body he'd touched so carefully with his branch was a shop-window dummy.

'All those fucking precautions,' he shouted. 'And where does this bloody stink come from? Somebody's having us for fools. I'll have them for this.'

And he went on like this for some time. But while he was standing there swearing and fuming, Alfie went round to the other side of the mound and I, like a fool, followed him. What we saw there was no hoax. They were real body parts alright, and some of them looked pretty old, too. Not the man I thought I was, I went over to the nearest ditch and quietly threw up, leaving Alfie to break the latest news to Derek.

The rest of the day was like a continuous nightmare, which I'm glad to say I can't much remember. What I can recall is Alfie coming home with me and making me drink three big gulps of brandy, a drink I hate. But it did the trick, knocked me out and kept me sleeping until the alarm went off next morning.

And that brought its own weird news. Preliminary report from forensics was that they'd gone through the whole foul pile and discovered that there were some dummies (what they called manikins, although some were women and some children), some dead chickens and other birds, and some human parts, which they said were probably what they politely referred to as 'hospital waste'.

'What does that mean, Guv?' Alfie asked, looking a bit green.

Derek held his head.

'I can't believe this,' he said. 'If what they suggest is true, what they seem to be saying is these are amputated diseased limbs stolen from hospitals instead of being incinerated. It's not just repellent, it's hard to believe. Hospitals have a strict protocol, which is always rigidly supervised. And anyway, who would want to steal body parts? What for? It can't be. I expect,' he added, brightening up a bit, 'when we get the final report from forensics they'll admit their first assumption was fallacious.'

This sounded more like the real Derek, not the hopping, swearing, furious one we'd seen yesterday. 'Their first assumption was fallacious', eh! I couldn't have put it better myself. Although whether it was fallacious or not, I couldn't see for the life of me where we could go next. The whole thing was a farce.

'Well, in the meantime, I have to tell you two,' Derek went

on, 'that North has made a direct appeal to Mr Moon, and he has agreed that she might come with a couple of us to the area and point out exactly where she claims she went to this Luvapet factory and interviewed the manager.'

'What!' Alfie said, which was lucky because I was dumbstruck. 'You mean she's still saying her report is true, after we all went round everywhere looking for her factory and couldn't find a thing? And let me remind you, Guv, that you and me and Greta all spoke to people what *live* there, and they've never seen nor heard of such a place neither.'

By this time I'd got my breath and added, not as noisily as Alfie, 'And nor has the Environmental Health Department.'

'Nevertheless,' Derek sighed, 'Mr Moon wants us to give her the chance to actually go to the very spot and either point to the factory or admit that she's lying and tell us why.'

'Why?' Alfie and I said in chorus.

'Well, if she lied she must have had a motive, and Mr Moon would like to know what it might be.'

It ended up with all four of us driving off in the direction of Nasty again. Derek had to go because he was the senior officer, I went because I'd been with North when we'd first followed the disappearing Edward Franklin to Nasty, and Alfie's excuse was that he was supposed to be North's mentor.

'And that's another thing,' I pointed out to Derek as I drove once again past Hatfield and Hertford along the A10, 'what happened to Edward Franklin? This whole mess all started, remember, because we were following him on the trail of the supposed poisoned pet food.'

We did the rest of the journey without another word from any of us. We hadn't heard a peep from North since she'd joined us in the station car park. But when we took the turn-off to Nasty, she sat forward in her seat and started looking round carefully, so I obligingly slowed down to five miles an hour.

I'd been along this road several times recently, but I'd never noticed a giant hoarding that suddenly appeared round a bend in the road.

'There!' North shouted, pointing at it. 'It was there, where that big poster is now.'

I was more than a bit fed up with all this by now. With a sigh I stopped the car and we all got out and climbed over the fence. All four of us walked round the hoarding a few times. That's all it was. A hoarding, with a big poster on it advertising some sort of pig food, judging by the picture, although the wording – 'BEST FOR YOUR WEANERS' – didn't tell me much.

North had tears in her eyes, and even I could see she was trying not to break down completely.

'I can't help it if it's not there now,' she said in a shaking voice. 'I can't help it if you don't believe me. I tell you there was a factory there, and it smelled terrible outside but didn't smell at all inside. I went into an office and spoke to the manager, Mr Blenkins. Would you like me to describe him to you? Should I describe him to the computer artists so that you can have a picture of him?'

We all looked at her and at each other. I didn't like her, never had and never would. But she sounded so truthful and desperate, I didn't know what to make of it all.

In fact, I just didn't know what I thought about anything any more. There'd been too many mysteries lately in this neck of the woods.

And some of them were much more sickening than anything North could invent.

*

Back in Shady Lane, Derek told us, 'I've had another chat with Mr Moon, and he's been in touch with the Chief Constable in Hertford. We've got clearance to continue our investigations around Nasty, although it's well out of our area. But the best news is that HQ in Hertford is willing to lend us some extra bodies if we need them.'

'What would we need them for?' Alfie asked. 'Forensics have gone over and over that field where we found what was causing the smell. And once they found out how the heap of dummies and body parts got there, by them tractor tracks and all that, what do we need more plods for? What else is there to do?'

'We're not going on looking for North's missing factory, are we?' I put in, trying not to sound how I felt. Fed up and sarcastic.

Derek kindly took no notice of how sour our questions sounded, and explained himself.

'No, we need uniforms and forensics to check up on that field behind the hoarding.'

'What, you mean where young North thought she saw a factory!' Alfie didn't trouble to hide his feelings. 'Will you tell us what we're doing with all this, Derek?'

He didn't always use Derek's first name. Mostly he called him 'Guv' or 'Boss', but sometimes he seemed to feel like saying 'Derek' was the only way to talk to him. If Alfie had known the word, he would have said he felt patronising. And I thought, too, that Derek was going a bit over the top with all this stuff about what happened or didn't happen in and around Nasty.

'After all,' I said, doing my best to sound reasonable, 'we've got much more serious cases to work on, like a couple of murders for example.'

Oh yes, in the meantime the autopsy had confirmed that Ah Weng So had been murdered. Some kind soul had broken her neck before shoving her into her last resting place, and it was clear that the drop down the lift shaft wasn't the cause of death. So now we had two separate murders: Juan Garcia's former 'matey' – the useless burglar Charlie Hampson – and that poor little Chinese girl.

'I think those body parts in a field could be considered a serious matter,' Derek said, 'even if they were found in an area outside ours. What do you think about that disgusting find, Greta?'

'Looks to me as if somebody's trying to wind us up,' I said. 'Somebody with a perverted mind thinks they're having a laugh.'

'That's hardly an explanation,' Derek said. 'It's no help at all.'

There was no answer to that, and I didn't want to try to think of one. He was right to squash me. What I'd said didn't mean a thing.

My mind drifted for a moment, and I remembered something I'd been meaning to ask Alfie about. Anything was better than this daft obsession Derek seemed to be chasing, of proving that North wasn't a wholesale liar.

'Alfie, do you remember when we went to the building site where they found Ah Weng So's body, and you spoke to the uniform there?'

'Oh yes,' Alfie was happy to join in this change of subject. 'You mean young Taz. He's a dead keen young bobby, wants a transfer to us, and I'm, you know, encouraging him, because we haven't got many brown faces, have we?'

'Bobby', I thought. Did anyone but Alfie use that word any more?

Derek gave a sort of irritable grunt.

'Taz,' he said. 'Short for Tasmania, is it?'

Seeing this was heading for one of those stupid wars of words about nothing in particular that Alfie and Derek sometimes had, I thought we'd better get back to Derek's hobby-horse.

'OK then, Derek, what do you want us to do? Go on looking for this so-called missing factory, or what?'

'Oh yes, and by the way,' Alfie added, not to be shut up, 'is young North still on suspension? Because I think you ought to consider young Taz to take her place–'

And then it happened. Derek just held his hand up, palm towards Alfie. And Alfie shut up. If I hadn't seen it for myself, I wouldn't have believed it. Nobody could stop Alfie in full flow, not even Mr Moon himself. That's what I love so much about Derek. One of the things, anyway. He might not be very tall, but he's got power. Not just the power of being our superior officer. I mean a sort of *inner* power. Even Alfie feels it sometimes. And who wants tall dark and handsome if they can have a powerful man. I do. If only…

'Off you go then,' Derek said, 'and you'll meet Sergeant Best, your liaison from Hertford HQ. I told him to speak to you, Greta.'

I'd loved to have asked him what he'd be doing while we were mucking about out in the country, but I thought better of it. He didn't look as if he wanted to chat.

So Alfie and I went trooping off to this empty field behind the billboard advertising pig food to start an inch-by-inch examination. Wearing gloves, of course. Why? Did we expect to find more bodies, or what?

There was a small group of uniforms standing around when we got there, and one of them came up to us, looked us both up and down, and said to me, 'Detective Sergeant Pusey?' Only he pronounced it like something full of pus, like you might say, 'Yuk, it was all pus-y.'

'*Pusey*,' I corrected him, but he just smiled and held his hand out.

'Sergeant Best,' he said with a stupid grin, 'but you can

call me Tom. I suppose I can call you Greeta?'

'It's Greta,' I said, taking no notice of his hand.

'Greta?' he said, all amazed. 'Then why isn't it spelled with two Ts?'

I let it go, and just explained to him what we were all doing there. Greeta, indeed! It didn't help that Alfie was having a good old snigger to himself.

I don't think Derek himself had any clue what sort of thing we might be looking for, or even if he thought we might find something. When we finally told him what it was, I expect he was as surprised as we were at what we did find, although he was his usual silver-tongued self, hiding how he felt.

It wasn't obvious at first, because of not knowing what we were doing. But bit-by-bit we discovered a large rectangular indentation in the grass and weeds growing there. And in it were smaller ones, different sizes. When I made a suggestion to my new 'friend' Tom, one of his men got hold of some white paint and painted all the impressions, some deeper than others, some just flattening the grass and others biting right into the earth. Then we all stood and looked at the result.

One of the plods said to Tom, 'It's like the sort of marks you get when there's been a Portaloo in a field, isn't it, Sarge.'

'Yes, maybe, but much more than you'd get from that,' he said. 'Or perhaps it was a sort of mocked-up construction made to look like a real building. If it's only temporary, it wouldn't make any marks you'd notice unless you were doing an inch-by-inch inspection.'

He turned to me.

'Is this the sort of thing we were looking for, Greeta?'

'Maybe,' I said, but then Alfie interrupted with the whole story.

'Well, Tom, it's like this,' he said. 'One of our officers thought she'd seen a factory here but we couldn't find it. So it could be that there'd been some sort of temporary building here that got packed up and taken away after she'd gone.'

He seemed quite excited, and I expect he was pleased that North might not have been telling us a pack of porkies. So we thanked all our helpers, even Tom Best, who still insisted on calling me Greeta, and they put up POLICE NO ENTRY tapes round the field and we all went our different ways.

Alfie and I went straight home and didn't report to Derek till next morning. It had been a strenuous day. Inch by inching is very tiring.

Derek seemed as pleased about it as Alfie. I tried not to show that I wasn't exactly thrilled at the thought that North might be reinstated.

'If this fellow Franklin who you were following had gone on straight past this field and through Nasty,' Derek asked me, 'was there anywhere he could have gone, or did the road just stop after Nasty?'

'No, there were two roads, you remember we took one that led to the smelly heap we finally found, and the other one goes to several more bigger villages–'

'So what would you say, Greta? Do you reckon we're on the way to solving some of our Nasty pet food factory mystery?'

'No, Guv.'

I knew he'd be annoyed at me for being stubborn, but I couldn't help that.

'I think we've got even more of a mystery now. Why should anyone go to all this much trouble to confuse us just because they're doing something fishy about pet food that might be poisoning a few cats or dogs? It's not exactly the crime of the century, is it. There must be much more to it to make it worth going to all this bother.'

I was relieved to see he was nodding. So no arguments this time, then.

'You're right. Clearly there's something much bigger going

on, with more important business involved. Still,' he brightened, 'at least we've made a few discoveries.'

And much good that did us, I thought, but had the sense not to say.

'Anyway, Greta,' he went on, 'you'll be glad to know that we've brought James and Sadie Lee in on a charge of attempting to pervert the course of justice. Mr Moon was impressed with your hunch that James Lee murdered Ah Weng So, and he even thought your theory of his motive was worth considering.'

'Perverting!' Alfie marvelled. 'Not obstructing enquiries then?'

'No, Mr Moon thought we could get away with the stronger charge, and that might scare them into making a more believable statement than the rubbish they've offered so far.'

'Has Mr Moon seen them himself?' I asked. 'You saw what a tough couple they are. Don't you think it's a bit OTT to expect them to crumble now?'

Derek was tight-lipped.

'We'll see,' was all he'd say.

It was one of those times when I wondered what I saw in him.

'What was that theory of yours, then, Greta?' Alfie asked, and Derek gave a weary sigh and looked at the ceiling for patience.

But I was glad to go over it again, if only to be able to reconsider whether I was being an idiot. So I started at the beginning.

'I found Ah Weng So having a baby in a doorway. She said she'd been brought from China as an illegal immigrant and made to do slave labour in a factory until the birth was due, when she'd been brought here to Watford and left. And I think whoever dumped her realised later that they'd made a mistake and that they should have put her right out of the way so that she couldn't give away anything that might damage them–'

'But you said she couldn't tell you much anyway,' Alfie interrupted.

'But how could they know how much we might get out of her?' I argued. 'Anyway, I think they sent those two, Sadie and James Lee, if those are really their names, to make sure that she didn't do any talking at all. And did you know, Alfie,' I went on, getting my second wind by now, 'that Charlie Hampson's boss was Chinese, and so was the victim of his last robbery, and so was the man who tried to get Jim the Long-distance Lorry Driver to bring in illegal immigrants? Do you believe that's all coincidence?'

'Ho no,' Alfie grinned, 'course I see it all now. It's a world Chinese conspiracy, right? They're taking over everything, starting with Watford, that's it, isn't it?'

He started laughing, and slowly (and I hope reluctantly), Derek joined in. I quietly slipped out of the room and left them to it. Full marks to me for not slamming the door. But in my head I slammed more than that, starting with Alfie's outsized middle.

Of course, by the time they both joined me in the canteen we'd all got over it, and started talking seriously again.

Derek said, 'I've just had a phone call and a fax from your friend Tom Best in Hertford, Greta. He said he'd just finished giving hell to one of his men because he'd found something at the entrance to the field which he didn't think he needed to report because he thought we were only interested in the field itself. I wouldn't have expected even a new recruit to be that daft! It was only a piece of paper with a design on it, but Tom thought it might be useful, so he faxed it over.'

He showed us the paper and Alfie and I gawked at it,

mystified. The only thing on it was a sort of rectangle with a diagonal line drawn across it. It looked like a doodle or a bit of a child's geometry homework. Certainly nothing worth making a fuss about. We were no further forward.

Mr Moon gave us all permission to use Shady Lane's latest and proudest new acquisition: a one-way glass to observe an interview. I thought we might have been the first cop shop in the UK to get such a thing, although judging by films, they were quite common in America. Mr Moon himself was conducting the interview with James and Sadie Lee, with Derek partnering him, a uniform on the door, and obviously the Lees' solicitor there too.

'Listen and learn, Greta,' Derek hissed in my ear before he went into the interview room. 'Mr Moon can give us all lessons on how to do it.'

I could have made a few cracks there about the size of Mr Moon's family, but I could see it wasn't a good idea. So there we stood on the other side of the glass, me and Alfie, him with his big meaty hand on the shoulder of happily reinstated North, both of them looking pleased with themselves.

Mr Moon started by pointing out that the charge against the Lees was a serious one, but there could still be an even graver one in the offing. Their solicitor, Mr Woo, asked for an explanation.

'A young Chinese girl has been murdered,' Mr Moon said. 'And we are continuing our enquiries into the circumstances of her death.'

At the word murder, all three Chinese hissed in an identical manner and looked at each other with no facial expressions but pretty tense body language. After a pause, Mr Moon went on.

'Our investigations are pointing in a certain direction.

Would Mr Lee or Miss Lee wish to make any statement in the matter at this time?'

Woo shook his head.

'They know nothing of this death,' he stated. 'You already have their statements, that they came across a Chinese girl running along wearing only a little hospital shift, and in an obvious state of terror. As humanitarians they did what they could to help her.'

'Particularly because they were all of the same ethnic origin?' Derek put in.

Mr Woo shrugged. 'Probably.'

'Did the Chinese girl you met,' Derek asked Sadie Lee, 'by any chance tell you her name?'

'Yes, she said it was Ah Weng So,' Sadie said, looking the picture of innocence.

'Ah Weng So was under investigation as a self-confessed illegal immigrant,' Derek went on. 'When you, Miss Lee, took her place and wilfully impersonated her, you must have known you were obstructing the police in the course of their duty.'

'No,' Sadie said. 'How could I have known that? I was just helping someone in distress.'

Then her expression changed. It looked as if she was trying to seem upset, but it wasn't all that convincing.

'Are you telling us,' she asked, 'that this Chinese girl who was murdered was Ah Weng So? But that must mean that she was correct to be so afraid, and we were right to try to help her.'

'But you deliberately let us and the hospital authorities believe that, like Ah Weng So, you spoke no English,' Derek said. 'This was a deception, however you might choose to describe it.'

Woo spoke up again, this time allowing an expression to

creep onto his face. A sneer. Chinese sneers look a lot worse than English ones, I noticed. 'You might have a hard time proving that to a court, Inspector. I don't believe you can make this charge stick, and nor do you. I think you are simply trying to intimidate my clients into making a false admission.'

Next to me, Alfie gave a grunt and dropped his hand from North's shoulder.

'He's got a point there,' he muttered.

But Mr Moon was calm.

'No court would accept that Miss Lee and Mr Lee just *happened* to be present in Watford, on exactly the same spot as Ah Weng So when she ran from the hospital,' he said. 'Especially since on their own admission they'd never been to Watford before that day, and had no particular reason for being there just then. And then we are asked to believe that Miss Lee changed places with this complete stranger who she *happened* to encounter, just because she was in distress and they were of the same ethnic origin.'

'Some people do have sudden impulses of kindness, Superintendent,' James Lee joined in. 'It's not unknown, even in this heartless day and age.'

'Yes, Mr Lee, I do agree,' Mr Moon said, looking him up and down with an expression I'd never seen on his chubby face before. It could have been hatred. 'And your *sister's,*' (he put a sarcastic note into the word sister), 'impulse of kindness extended to allowing herself to be mistaken for Ah Weng So. By your own account, you were the last person to see Ah Weng So alive.'

Woo quickly butted in with, 'What are you implying, Superintendent?'

Blandly, Mr Moon said, 'It is quite believable that the reason for Miss Lee's ploy of wasting the time of the police and the hospital staff was in order for Mr Lee to take Ah Weng So to a nearby building site and there take her life and dispose of her body.'

Like puppets joined by one string, all three Chinese simultaneously sprang to their feet. Mr Woo was frowning, but Sadie looked as if she was going to spit at Mr Moon, and her brother's face was positively black with fury.

They all spoke at once, so of course we couldn't tell what any one of them was saying.

Still very calm, Mr Moon said, 'Please sit down and speak one at a time.'

The three of them sat down and started a fast conversation in Chinese. Sadie and James Lee seemed to be disagreeing with each other, but they were both clearly telling their solicitor what to say. Finally, he had the last word, shaking his head at them as if to say 'leave it to me'.

'Is that your case, Superintendent?' he finally asked. 'Do you have any actual questions you wish to ask my clients? So far we've heard only suggestions and innuendo from you. You cannot possibly have any evidence against them, particularly in the matter of murder. False accusations, as you must know, are useless.'

So much for learning from Mr Moon, I thought. I wasn't at all impressed with his interviewing technique. But that was an opinion I had sense enough to keep to myself.

'Well,' he tried again, though it seemed to me the solicitor was winning on points, 'perhaps you yourself could tell me if there is any reason why I shouldn't, here and now, charge Mr Lee with murder and Miss Lee with being his accomplice?'

There was a silence you could cut with a knife. The three of us watching through our posh new viewing glass held our breath.

'As I have already said, Superintendent, how about lack

of evidence?' the solicitor said smoothly, smiling like the cat that swallowed the goldfish.

'Well, I think we'll hold them both on the lesser charge for now, of attempting to pervert the course of justice,' Mr Moon said.

On cue, Derek read out the charge to them both, with the usual warning, and took them off, I suppose straight to the custody suite. Mr Moon switched off the tape recorder, stood up and had a little stretch.

At the very moment that he clicked that switch, an even louder click sounded inside my head, like one of those light bulbs going on in a cartoon. I suddenly thought, for no reason that I could explain to myself at that moment, of that nice little interpreter who'd helped us talk to Ah Weng So while we still had her in hospital. I'd have to look up my notes and get his name and address.

Maybe by then I'd have worked out why I wanted to talk to him.

Chapter 10

I found little Mr Wing's name and address in my notes alright, but I couldn't for the life of me work out why I wanted to see him. There was no way he could know any more about poor little Ah Weng So than we did, and I couldn't think of anything to ask him. But something was nagging at the back of my mind, and I just couldn't get hold of it. Maybe if I'd talked it over with Derek or Alfie they might have been able to jog my memory, but I'd had enough of them taking the piss out of my theories, and I didn't want to give them another chance to have a go at me and my imagination.

In the end I decided to go and visit Mr Wing anyway, and just have a sort of informal chat with him, see if anything came to me. I phoned first, and he said he'd be pleased to welcome me at his humble office.

But when I broke the news to him about Ah Weng So being murdered, I could tell he was sorry he'd said he'd see me. Not all Chinese are inscrutable, and he certainly wasn't. I thought he was going to cry, he was so upset.

'Ah, that poor little girl,' he said when he was able to speak. 'She had suffered so much in her short life, why could we not do more for her? And – the baby? What will happen to her helpless child?'

I felt really guilty. Of course I was sorry about Ah Weng So being murdered and her baby being left an orphan practically from birth, but I hadn't really taken any of it to heart as Mr Wing was doing. After all, I knew the girl and her baby better than he did, considering that I'd been, as you might say, in at the birth. And Mr Moon had been concerned about the baby, too, I remembered. Did this mean I was hard-hearted?

'I'm sorry…' I started, but Mr Wing just put his hand over his face and sat there. I thought he was sort of mourning or something, but it turned out he was thinking.

'I will consult Mrs Wing,' he said at last, 'but I'm sure she will agree with me. We must go to the hospital and ask for the procedure for adopting the poor motherless baby. Thank you very much for informing me of the sad event, Sergeant Pusey. It was kind of you to take the trouble.'

I didn't like to tell him that wasn't the reason for my call, specially as I still didn't know what my purpose was anyway.

'Do you want to talk to your wife straight away?' I asked. 'Or could we have a little chat first?'

'Yes, let us talk now. Can I help you in any way? I would be pleased if I could be of assistance in bringing those evil people to justice.'

'Those people? Do you think more than one person was involved in the murder of Ah Weng So?'

'No, perhaps not directly. But I recall every word of her sad history, and there are a number of wicked and corrupt people implicated in that.'

I was impressed with his knowledge of English. I'd admired his perfect pronunciation when we'd met before, but his vocabulary was almost as good as Derek's.

'Well, of course I have all my notes on the case, Mr Wing, but since you remember your conversation with Ah Weng So in detail, perhaps we can go over it all again.'

'Yes, but there's something else troubling me. How are we going to locate her husband and the rest of her family to inform them of this tragedy? She didn't actually tell me the name of her village, or even which province she came from.'

I started feeling guilty again. I hadn't given a thought to any of that.

'Husband?' I said, more to cover up than anything. 'You didn't tell me she was married.'

'But it's obvious. Surely you realised that such a virtuous girl must have been married to have a baby.'

I hadn't thought whether she was particularly virtuous, either. It seemed I was about to learn a lot more about this victim after her death than I had while we were interviewing her in the hospital. Then again, that was if I accepted that anything Mr Wing told me now was accurate, and not suppositions he'd added out of sentiment. He did seem an amazingly emotional little chap, not like my previous impression of someone all businesslike and detached.

'I will tell you my complete recollection, Sergeant Pusey. Probably your own notes will have much the same information, but of course I didn't translate every single word to you.'

'What! But that was what you were there for–'

'Yes, but you only wanted to know pertinent facts. Now I will tell you every word that I remember. Ah Weng So was elected by her village to take the hazardous trip to England, to work and raise enough money for her family to join her. They in turn would do the same for the rest of the village. I believe part of the reason she was chosen was because she was young, strong and intelligent. The transport man was paid and she then became one of many making a nightmare journey. During that time she discovered that she was pregnant, but told no one. Do you want the details of how they all suffered while being transported?'

Speechless, I shook my head. He went on.

'Perhaps that is best. One man died, and his body was just left by the roadside. To continue. All of the travellers had been led to believe that on arrival they would be given accommodation and work. This was more or less true. What the entire lorry-load was not told was that they would work and sleep on the same factory premises, never be allowed out, and receive no money. Nor were they permitted any communication with the outside world. They were actually slave prisoners.'

This time my head shaking was in sympathy. So I wasn't completely cold-hearted, then. It was a relief to know that.

'Then they found out she was pregnant and dumped her, I suppose?'

'Yes, she thought she wasn't taken away in the same lorry she'd arrived in, but that was all she could tell me about being taken to Watford. However, she did have a clear idea of how long the journey took, and perhaps that small piece of information might help you to find this terrible factory. She was counting, you see, because of the birth pangs beginning. And she thought it took about twenty minutes from when they put her in the lorry until they left her in the shop doorway where I believe you found her.'

I didn't like to tell him that wouldn't help. He seemed so pleased that he was giving me a real clue. About twenty minutes at what speed? How could we search the countryside on the basis of such vague information?

'Was she able to give you an idea what sort of work they were doing in that factory? Were they making clothes, for example?'

'Oh no, nothing so clean and safe to handle. All she could tell me was that the smell was disgusting and they seemed to be preparing dead animals for some purpose.'

'Dead animals? You mean, like chickens or horse meat, something like that?'

'Yes, but not only that. From the way she spoke, I thought she meant all kinds of parts of animals, such that she didn't always know what they had been in life. And always a terrible smell.'

I couldn't believe it. Coincidences didn't happen, specially in police work. But I had to admit that the smell in Nasty and North's so-called missing factory did seem to add up to Ah Weng So's illegal immigrant slave factory. It wasn't only the smell that was the link. There was that disgusting heap of *things* we'd found in the field not far from Nasty. But then again, if we were going to believe North, the factory she went to had no smell…

No, anyway, there was another piece that didn't fit. At any speed it wasn't possible to get from anywhere around Nasty to Watford in twenty minutes. Unless, of course, a frightened young girl about to give birth alone in a foreign country might make a mistake about the passing of time? I held my head and gave a small groan. What could I say to Derek and Alfie now?

'I am sorry,' Mr Wing said, 'I have upset you. You are more sensitive than I first thought. You seemed so unsympathetic when I was helping you to interview that poor young girl, a typical police officer only concerned with facts and legalities. But I see now I was wrong. I apologise.'

Unsympathetic! I'd held the little blighter's hand, hadn't I? I'd stood up to Derek when he'd ordered me back to Shady Lane, and told him I couldn't desert the poor kid! What more could anyone want from me, I wanted to ask Mr Wing. But I didn't, mainly because my mind had shot off somewhere else.

Supposing there really was a connection between the illegal immigrants' slave factory and what we'd found in the countryside around Nasty? That could mean that anything at all that was found in the vicinity could have some meaning. I decided to try a long shot. What did I have to lose at this stage?

I took a crumpled bit of paper from my pocket, smoothed it out and handed it to Mr Wing. It was the fax of the diagram they'd found on a bit of paper just outside the field behind the pig food hoarding. Probably it would mean as little to him as it did to us, but what the hell…

'Does that mean anything to you?'

He only needed one glance.

'Yes, of course,' he said. 'Zhong Guo. China. The Chinese name for China translates as central nation or kingdom. And this pictogram, of what *you* would call a rectangle with a diagonal line across it, represents in all languages of China the word Zhong, or central. You see, China has always believed itself, as I believe many much younger nations do, to be the centre of the world. Zhong Guo. China,' he repeated, probably taking my amazement for disbelief.

I was numb. 'Zhong Guo,' I tried to echo, and kindly Mr Wing corrected my pronunciation several times until he said I had it just right.

'Does this help you to find those terrible people and their loathsome trade?' he asked, and I was tempted to give Alfie's standard answer: 'Buggered if I know'.

But instead I mumbled some standard police formula about furthering our enquiries, thanked him really sincerely for all his help, and staggered off. My poor brain was buzzing in all directions. Even my busy imagination couldn't cope with all this unbelievable stuff. All the way back to Shady Lane I was muttering to myself, 'Zhong Guo, Zhong Guo, Zhong Guo. Derek and Alfie will never believe this.'

And then, getting my head together a bit, I thought, maybe that'll stop them making fun of my Chinese conspiracy theory. They're everywhere, wherever we look we find Chinese. I hope Mr Moon can make sense of this, because I certainly can't…

What did I mean, I couldn't make sense of it – of course I could. A bit of it, anyway. Was I a detective, or what? One of Ah Weng So's fellow slave prisoners, working in the factory with her, had managed to get a piece of paper and a pencil, and had scribbled this tiny message: Zhong Guo. And why would he do that? To let someone know that there was a Chinese person being held captive in the depths of the English countryside, that's why! It was the best he could think of to make a cry for help. Maybe he couldn't get a bigger bit of paper to write a longer message, or if he could, he couldn't think what to say, or he was afraid that a bigger piece would be found by the wrong person. So he was hoping for a sleuth to find it, right?

For at least five minutes I was thrilled with myself at working this out. Then reality hit. We'd pretty well decided that there'd been a temporary structure where we'd found the traces of a building in the field behind the pig food hoarding. A temporary building couldn't be a factory. It wouldn't be strong enough. So that couldn't have been where the slaves were working on what Mr Wing had described as 'preparing dead animals for some purpose'.

No, wait, I had another inspiration. This one was better. Preparing dead animals for some purpose had to mean PET FOOD! We'd found the illegal pet food factory. No, we hadn't actually found it, as such. We'd probably discovered a link between unsound pet food accidentally poisoning animals, and the slave factory where Ah Weng So and her friends had been imprisoned. So now at least we knew what they were doing and why, so all we needed to find out was WHERE.

Hot to reveal all this brilliance, I rushed into Derek's office, flushed with discovery and pleased with myself. He and Alfie sat quietly listening without a flicker of expression as I poured it all out. When I'd finished, Derek still didn't say anything, although I thought he was beginning to look a bit grim.

But of course Alfie had something to say, as always.

'What's the point, girl?' he boomed. 'Where does all that get us? Theories are all very well, but the question is, what do we do next, eh?'

'OK, Alfie,' Derek said, 'let's leave that. There's something more serious we've got to investigate now, Greta. I'd just finished telling Alfie when you came in. It seems that some twisted person in a local hospital has been disposing of amputated body parts in an unorthodox fashion.'

Feeling sick and shaking a bit, I started, 'What–' but Derek shook his head and went on, 'I know it's hard to believe, but instead of these, these items going into the hospital incinerator, they've been, it's now suspected, selling them for pet food.'

Patting my shoulder kindly, Alfie said, 'Don't worry, girl, I don't believe it either.'

'So this is a priority investigation now,' Derek said, talking as if he'd just had a local injection in his mouth by an inexpert dentist. And I couldn't blame him. Even thinking about it was disgusting, and talking about it must have been worse. I wanted to ask him for orders, but I couldn't seem to find my voice.

*

After a few interviews at local hospitals, I didn't feel like ever eating or drinking anything at all again, ever. Just the same, I went straight to the canteen because I knew that's where Alfie's always to be found if you don't actually trip over him lurking in a corridor, jawing at anyone who'd listen.

There he was, rabbiting away as usual, this time to an

audience of one. It was the young PC he'd called Taz, who was dead keen to join us in CID. The way I felt at that moment, he was welcome to my job. Alfie waved his arms at me and shouted, 'Over here, Greta,' as if I wouldn't have spotted him without this much guidance.

'This is young Taz, what I was telling you about,' Alfie said, through a mouthful, as usual.

Close up I could see this feller wasn't such a kid as I'd thought. I gave him a small nod with my mouth shut. I was surprised when he stood up and gave a sort of small bow at me.

'I'm so pleased to meet you at last, Sergeant Pusey,' he said. 'My name is actually Tariq Tazhim, so you can see why I'm called Taz.'

'Tashim?'

'No, not exactly, but it doesn't matter if you pronounce it correctly or not, Taz will do. You see, it's not an easy name for people who don't have an alphabet which corresponds to the one in which it was first written.'

'See how educated he is,' Alfie said admiringly. 'Knows more than one alphabet. I told you, Greta, he's a bright boy. We could do with one like him, couldn't we? What about you putting in a word for him with Derek, eh?'

'I really don't think we should be thinking about recruiting just now, Alfie,' I said. 'We've got more important things to think about. A lot of problems to deal with,' I added to Tariq Tazhim.

I didn't want to discourage the lad, if he was keen. After all, he was only trying to follow the route I'd taken to get to where I was. Although maybe he wouldn't be so anxious to join us if he knew what we'd been going through recently. As if he'd been reading my mind, Alfie then launched into an account of our current cases. I wasn't at all sure this was a good idea, but there's never any stopping Alfie once he'd got rolling, so I leaned back and let him get on with it.

When he'd finally ground to a halt, I said to Taz, 'What we don't know is if we're dealing with several different cases or if they're all connected in some way.'

And while he was digesting this, I said to Alfie, 'And you don't know where I've been since you last saw me, either. You're lucky to have missed it. The incineration plant in a hospital is not a good place to visit.'

I felt myself going a bit green just remembering it, but I managed not to throw up again, as I had in the hospital grounds. Derek hadn't held my head, either. Nothing like that. Not tender and concerned, as I might have hoped. He'd been so furious and embarrassed I expected him to walk off and leave me there, heaving. He hadn't done that, but he hadn't spoken a word to me on the way back to Shady Lane nor since. As if I'd done it on purpose. Anyway, I left that part out of my description to Alfie, just told him how it all worked.

'So it was no help then, going there?' he asked. 'Nobody knew anything about bits not being incinerated that should have been, I suppose.'

It was quiet while we all thought about this blind alley.

Then Taz said to Alfie, 'I heard you got some uniforms from HQ to do an inch-by-inch in that field where the factory was supposed to have been near that village called Nasty. Why couldn't you have used us? We can do that as well as any of them. How can I get the experience I need to apply for a transfer to your branch, if you use plods from somewhere else when you could have us?'

Alfie was saved from having to answer this sudden challenge by Derek suddenly appearing in the doorway of the canteen.

'Partridge! Pusey!' he barked. 'My office, now!'

That didn't sound good. Unfriendly, to say the least. And didn't make us look great in the eyes of our young wannabe colleague, either. Or maybe it would just put him off enough to stop him pestering Alfie for help in getting a transfer. Who'd want to work for a bad-tempered sod like that, he might ask himself.

Turned out that all Derek wanted was to pass on a rollicking he'd just got from Mr Moon. It must have put his nose out of joint, not being the Super's blue-eyed boy any more.

'Wandering around the countryside chasing up meaningless leads,' he told us, 'while the case-load of Shady Lane CID is growing like a mountain. It won't do, it's not good enough, we've got to take our share. Just stop fumbling about on this case that doesn't seem to be going anywhere.'

'Right, Guv,' Alfie said, at his smartest, 'what would you like us to do now?'

Derek clutched his head.

'Just give me time to go through this lot,' he said, pointing to his in-tray, 'and I'll assign something worthwhile to both of you.'

Alfie and I turned to leave, and Derek called after me, 'Alright now, Greta? Got over it, have you?'

His voice was so unfriendly and sarcastic, I didn't bother to answer, just followed Alfie back up to the canteen without a word.

Taz was still waiting for us.

'I've been thinking,' he greeted Alfie, 'about hospital incinerators.'

Well, what a fascinating subject.

'You know that case up in Scotland where they found the body parts in the caravans–'

'What case? What body parts?' I interrupted.

'Sorry, I thought you must have read about it,' he said. 'It was in the papers. Well, there were some caravans out of season in a caravan park, and somebody noticed blood dripping out of the bottom of a couple of them. So they called the police who broke in and found these body parts that turned out to be what's officially called hospital waste.'

I could feel my lips going all tight and dry. I didn't really want to know any more about hospital waste than I'd already learned that day, but at the same time, it could be something useful. Alfie must have thought the same, because he urged Taz to go on with the story.

'Well, you probably know that not all hospitals have their own incineration plant, and that means they have to contract that work out to specialist companies. So the police in Scotland finally tracked down this rogue company that had been taken on by several hospitals to dispose of their waste matter. Turned out they'd just been storing the stuff in these old derelict caravans that they towed to out-of-the-way caravan sites and just left there!'

'What, with all that horrible human stuff rotting inside!' Alfie exclaimed in disgust. 'Good thing we didn't come across one of those, eh girl,' he said to me. 'What we did find was bad enough. How long did they reckon it had all been left there, then?' he asked Taz, who was looking as gob-smacked as we felt.

'But, but surely you read about it?' he stammered. 'If you didn't see it in the newspapers, it was in the *Police Gazette.*'

Alfie and I looked at each other. I could feel my face going red. We both knew what an important connection this could be to our own baffling case, and yet neither of us knew a thing about it. We must look a right couple of kippers to this keen young plod, I was thinking, and by the expression on his face, Alfie was on the same lines.

Taz saved the moment by jumping up and saying, 'I think

I've got something about it in my locker. Hang on and I'll go and see.'

'Alfie,' I said urgently, 'we've got a problem here. If we tell Derek about this, he'll think we're trying to hang on to a dead-end case instead of taking on one of the new ones he's on about. But if we don't tell him…'

'Never mind telling Derek, we've got to get the proper story first,' Alfie said. 'There's too many holes in this. It might just be somebody getting hold of the wrong end of the stick, and it's not what it seems. You know what journalists are like.'

Dear old Alfie. So thick and insensitive sometimes, so surprisingly sharp when you least expect it. Of course he was right. The more I thought about this tale as told by young Taz, the less likely it seemed. When he came back a few minutes later clutching a whole wad of papers, before he even sat down Alfie was on to him like a bull terrier.

'Listen, lad,' he said, 'none of what you told us made sense. How could this outside firm get a disposal contract from hospitals without being looked into first? They'd have to show their factory or plant or whatever it's called to some pen-pusher in the health authority, wouldn't they? And I expect they'd have to show they were a proper outfit, with references and bank accounts and company accounts and all that. No, I'm sorry,' he said, firmly waving away the heap of papers Taz was shoving at him, 'I don't care what it says there, it's all rubbish.'

I looked at him fondly. I couldn't have put it clearer myself. Taz meanwhile was looking more and more sorry for himself. He was just starting to protest, 'But, Sarge–' when Derek came storming back.

'I thought I'd find you two back here,' he said, and you

could almost see the steam coming out of his ears, 'come on, I've got work for both of you.'

And he marched out, with us two trailing after him like two naughty school kids, without even a glance back at poor Taz sitting there with his pile of useless newspaper cuttings.

Back in Derek's office, he handed Alfie a report.

'Here you are, Alfie,' he said, without cracking a smile, 'here's a nice juicy stalking case for you. Off you go.'

And he turned to me, still serious and unfriendly.

'A friend of yours has been attacked,' he said, handing me a file. 'You'd better go and see what you can find out about it. It's your little friend the translator, Mr Wing.'

As I opened my mouth to, well, I wasn't sure what: to say what a surprise, or he wasn't really my friend, or just to gasp, or even to say that wasn't really a CID matter, Derek held up his hand.

'I know, I know,' he said. 'It should be one for uniforms. But Mr Moon and I thought, in view of Mr Wing's connection with our ongoing case, you should take this on. And don't bother to argue that you thought that wasn't an ongoing case, just for this once, Greta, do me a favour and just do it, right?'

Did he mean just do it right for once, or just do it, right?

I took the report and left without a word, but with lots of them churning round in my head. Surely it must be a coincidence? Why on earth should anyone want to attack little Mr Wing just because he was the translator for poor Ah Weng So's statements to us? No, I decided, it couldn't be connected to the Ah Weng So case; people get attacked all the time for all sorts of reasons or sometimes for no reason at all. But probably Derek was right, and I'd better go and talk to him to make sure he thought it was coincidence, too.

I almost went to the wrong place. I'd already started off for his home when, stuck for ages at the traffic lights at Watford

Junction Station, I idly flipped through the folder on Mr Wing's case, and saw that he was being kept in hospital. Not just treated in A&E. He must have been more seriously injured than I'd realised. When I parked in the hospital grounds, in exactly the same spot I'd had earlier that day when I'd disgraced myself by being sick in public, I took the time to read the case report thoroughly. Sloppy police work, I told myself, is time wasting. I should have read it before I left Shady Lane. Just as well I read it now, though, because it partly prepared me for the sad sight of poor Mr Wing. This was no random attack. Someone had meant to do him some serious damage.

The nurse I got hold of told me that his back and shoulder had been severely bruised, obviously with a very heavy weapon – maybe even an iron bar – his leg had been broken in two places ('Looked as if someone had jumped on it,' she said), and due to having his nose broken as well, he had two black eyes like over-ripe plums. He being so small and frail anyway, and of that yellowish colour naturally that all Chinese people are, the total sight was one of the most horrible I'd seen in my time in the police. And I'd seen a few, too.

I sat by the bed and took his uninjured hand.

'Mr Wing,' I whispered, 'can you hear me? It's Greta Pusey.'

From our previous conversations I already knew what a sweet gentle man he was, but even then his response startled me.

In a cracked voice he said, 'Oh, Detective Pusey, how kind of you to come. I'm so sorry I can't see you just now, my eyes don't seem to want to open. Please excuse my condition.'

I'm usually pretty tough, I like to think. But this was so touching, I could have cried. Also, I got that little creeping feeling of guilt again I seemed to keep getting when I was with Mr Wing. Somehow I got the idea that I'd brought him into something that was too big for him to deal with. This was stupid of course, because I wasn't the one who'd got him to come to the hospital to be Ah Weng So's translator. But I just couldn't shake off the feeling of responsibility.

'Do you know who did this to you?' I asked him, still holding his hand. 'Or why?'

'No, I don't know those people, I'm glad to say. There were three large men. They came into my office and didn't say a word, just set about me. I have no idea why. But my wife believes it was something to do with our trying to adopt that poor little orphaned baby.'

Oh yes, I'd forgotten. He'd told me that he and his wife wanted to try to adopt Ah Weng So's baby. And one of the nurses at the hospital had told me that she wanted the same thing.

There wasn't much more Mr Wing and I could say to each other, so after muttering the usual meaningless good wishes for his recovery, I left him alone. Alone? That was strange.

On my way out, I asked the nurse why Mrs Wing wasn't there, and she said she didn't know. In the car, I got on my mobile to Derek and asked him to arrange for a plod to check on Mrs Wing to make sure she wasn't getting a dose of the same as her husband. Then I rummaged through my notes to find the name of the nurse who'd said she wanted to adopt Ah Weng So's baby.

Chapter 11

I found the reference in my notes to the nurse who wanted to adopt Ah Weng So's baby. It made no difference what her name was, I didn't get to the hospital. For once, uniforms had responded quickly and reported back on Mrs Wing. She was OK, but she wanted to see me, urgently. So I turned back and went to see her instead of the nurse. As it turned out, just as well.

She was a neat little doll of a woman, just right for Mr Wing. Her pretty Chinese doll of a face was all creased up with worry, which wasn't surprising, considering the state of her husband. But it turned out that wasn't all of the problem.

'My husband, you know, is a very truthful honest man,' she started.

'Of course I know that –'

'But this time he didn't tell you everything. He didn't lie, you understand,' she insisted, 'he just didn't tell you everything. But I told him, now that both our lives are in danger, it would be best if we left nothing out in future when we talk to you.'

'Both your lives! Is that why you're here and not with him at the hospital? Do you want police protection?'

'No, no, Sergeant, wait, you are too impatient, let me explain in my own way, please. But I'm forgetting my manners. Can I offer you some tea?'

I couldn't believe it. Here was this couple apparently in a serious fix, and she was offering me tea. No wonder people reckoned the Chinese were inscrutable. So as not to offend her, I said I'd love a cup, then had to wait, fidgeting with impatience, until she brought it in. It was horrible, too. I'd never tasted green tea before, and never wanted to again. Then at last we could get on with it.

'We went to the hospital to find out about the baby,' she started. 'There was a nurse there who wanted also to adopt her. So we all have to see the social services people and go through the adoption procedures. Perhaps they will see that it is more suitable for a little Chinese girl to be with a Chinese family than an English one, particularly as we already have two little children of our own.'

I marvelled at her perfect English, which was just as good as her husband's. And for someone who thought her life was in danger, she was amazingly cool, too. She seemed to read my mind, because she smiled, and gave me a little more explanation.

'I call myself Chinese, but perhaps you will have guessed that I was born and educated here in England, and in fact I think of myself as English. But I understand that to most people I will always appear Chinese. This will also be the case for the child of the unfortunate Ah Weng So, which is a good reason for her to join our family.'

'I do understand how you feel, Mrs Wing, but you know it doesn't matter what I think about the future of Ah Weng So's baby. My concern is what happened to your husband, and why, and whether you are in danger yourself.'

I could hear myself coming across all pompous and formal like Derek at his most irritating, and really all I wanted was to shout at her, 'Get on with it! Get to the point! Shove your bloody green tea out of the way and cough up some information!'

It was no good. She was going to keep on at her own pace, and there was nothing I could do about it except fidget a bit and pretend to sip politely at this disgusting tea.

'When we left the hospital after enquiring about the baby,' she went on, 'I told my husband that I thought we were being followed. But of course he just laughed and teased me about watching too much television. We *were* being followed, and when we stopped outside here, the car behind us stopped also, and three large men followed us into the office and two of them set about beating my husband. You saw how thoroughly they did that. The third one just held me out of the way until they had finished. Then they left and I phoned for an ambulance.'

'Did you give a description of the men? Can you tell *me* anything about them?'

'Yes, they were all of Chinese appearance. Whether immigrants or born here I couldn't tell, because they spoke no words.'

'And you thought this was all to do with your wanting to adopt the orphaned baby?'

'No, this is what I have to tell you, Sergeant. I have had some short opportunities to talk to my husband since the attack. While we were waiting for the ambulance, and then afterwards in the hospital, we exchanged a few words. This was all we needed, because we have had many long talks about Ah Weng So ever since my husband first spoke to her. You see, translating isn't always an exact science. So it wasn't that my husband withheld anything from you that Ah Weng So told him, it was more a question of translation.'

By this time I was near exploding with impatience.

'I'm sorry, Mrs Wing,' I said, trying not to bark at her in my most bad-tempered voice, 'I just don't understand what you're trying to tell me. Could you please explain a little more clearly, do you think?'

After all, I couldn't yell at her the way I'd carry on at, say,

Juan Garcia, could I? But I felt like it. Anyway, finally she got to the point. Talk about long-winded. Sweet little Oriental doll and friendly witness she might have been, but a pain in the butt she certainly was.

'The trouble was, you see, Sergeant, the word "factory". This is not a precise word in any of the Chinese languages. For such a word we will use phrases such as "the place where things are made from other things" or "working with machines" or "a large place where many work together". And so on. Whereas in English there is just this one word, factory. And when poor Ah Weng So told my husband about the place where these illegal immigrants were forced to work and sleep, it seemed to him that the best way he could convey to you what she was saying, was to tell you she worked in a–'

'FACTORY!' we both finished in chorus.

'Yes, you see,' she said, 'then you understood a large manufacturing building. But it need not have been what you mean by a factory. It could have been a large shed, or a barn, or even – although perhaps this is an extreme example – a marquee.'

I clutched my head as all the implications burst on me.

'Oh my God,' I groaned, 'this changes the whole case. Do you realise, Mrs Wing–'

Remembering all that she couldn't know, I shut up. But the little wheels were still going round.

'What has this got to do with your husband being assaulted, then? I don't see the connection.'

'Just simply, I believe,' she said, 'that they think we know a lot more than we've told you. They, whoever they are, are warning us that whatever Ah Weng So told my husband in the hospital that he hasn't already told you, he must keep to himself. And in case he has confided in me, I too must not reveal any more information to the authorities. But–'

'But you won't be intimidated,' I finished for her.

She nodded. 'Can I get you some more green tea, Sergeant?' she asked calmly. 'It has many healthful properties.'

I certainly didn't want any more of that muck, but I needed time to think. So as graciously as I could, I thanked her and said I'd love some more green tea.

My head was buzzing with thoughts and ideas, but luckily in the time Mrs Wing took to come back with some more redundant tea, one clear item had floated to the top. Everything that had happened recently had seemed like too many coincidences. And now we had another one. Wasn't it strange that just about the time when our investigations seemed to show that DC North's 'factory' had been a temporary structure, Mrs Wing should decide to explain about the many possible meanings of that word in Chinese?

On the other hand, neither Mr nor Mrs Wing could possibly know what had been discovered in that field near the village of Nasty. So it must have been just luck that now we had one of our mysteries explained by a vagueness in translation. Luck? No way. Even less likely than coincidence. So whichever way I looked at it, I had to be suspicious of Mrs Wing. I scowled at her. She dimpled politely back at me. It was tough, but I had to do it.

'What made you decide to tell me about this just today, Mrs Wing?'

'To tell you about...?'

'To tell me about this difficulty in translation. After all, Mr Wing could have explained it to me at any time since he first spoke to Ah Weng So on our behalf. So why have you chosen just today, when your husband was attacked and you yourself might be in similar danger, to bring this possible problem to my attention?'

There I went, sounding all la-di-dah again. But I couldn't

find the words to ask this question in a friendlier way, and I certainly didn't want to come the tough stuff with her. And the more I thought about it, the more important it seemed to get an answer. It didn't look as if I was going to get one, though. She just sat there, looking polite and puzzled. Everything I'd ever heard or read about the inscrutability of the Chinese, and the Yellow Peril, and all those other prejudiced racist remarks, started going round in my head.

'Did you tell me all the truth about the men who attacked your husband? Is it true that they didn't say anything? Maybe give you a warning about anything?'

She just shook her head. Not a word. I saw then that I'd have to give it a long shot.

'Do you know a Detective Constable called Victoria North?'

She flinched. She pursed her lips. She shook her head.

I could see I was on to something. But what?

She must have been lying. Dear little Vicky was somehow in the thick of all this, and had prompted the Wings to give this story to cover her version of the factory at Nasty. But how did the assault on Mr Wing fit into this? Surely DC North couldn't have arranged for Mr Wing to be attacked so that he and his wife would spin this tale about translation complications? Oh hell, none of it made sense.

How could Vicky North be in the middle of this baffling case? However much I disliked her, I couldn't see her as some great mastermind handling all this stuff about illegal immigrants, factories processing disgusting human waste from hospitals, slave labour…

I suddenly saw yet another impossible connection.

Surely nobody could be going to all this trouble just to manufacture and sell dodgy pet food?

I must be losing my conkers, I thought.

I was trying to tie up several separate cases into one enormous convoluted master-plot.

I needed to go home and put a cold wet towel on my head.

I smiled politely at Mrs Wing.

'Thank you for the information and the delicious tea, Mrs Wing,' I said insincerely. 'You've been very helpful. Please let us know if you feel the need of protection. I do hope Mr Wing will soon begin to recover.'

And after this pretty little speech, I left with false smiles and a splitting headache.

I didn't know what to do next.

It didn't seem as if there was any point any more in going to see the nurse who wanted to adopt Ah Weng So's child.

My thoughts were too jumbled and senseless to try to discuss it all with Derek or even Alfie. I was completely out of ideas, a strange thing for me – I usually had too many, so that my most common problem was which to choose to follow up.

And having a headache was even more peculiar. Apart from times when I'd been bonked on the nut by some weirdo, I'd never had such a thing in my life. Well, first things first. I stopped at the first chemist I came to.

After an idiotic conversation, with the pharmacist keeping on asking me what I usually took and whether I'd had an accident and if I could see OK, I finally managed to buy some pills. I got back in the car, washed a couple down with a swig of the water I always keep there, and sat and waited for an effect. I felt a bit swimmy, but the headache was still there...

Loud banging on the window woke me. The familiar uniform topped by an almost familiar face unblurred.

'Sergeant Greta!' Taz said. 'Are you alright? Please open the window.'

Not my best day, all in all.

On the other hand…I needed to sound out some of my thoughts. I didn't want to go over it all with Derek or Alfie. I didn't really want any opinions. I just wanted to hear myself telling the whole story, and I didn't fancy talking out loud to myself. What could be better than just a pair of ears attached to no one in particular, like young Taz.

'Get in,' I said, opening the passenger door.

He was keen. He practically hurled himself in.

'What is it, Sergeant Greta? Do you need help? Is anything wrong?'

Bad start.

'I'm fine. Are you on duty?'

'No, I know I should have changed out of my uniform before I left the station, but–'

I wasn't interested. He was wrong anyway. PCs are only instructed to change from uniform after their shift in designated dangerous areas, where people who didn't get on very well with the police might follow them to their homes to do them or their families a mischief. I couldn't be bothered to explain all this. Taz should have known it anyway.

'I need to talk about the case I'm on,' I interrupted him. 'Understand, I'm not asking your opinion about anything. And I don't want any of this to go any further. I just need you to listen, OK?'

He looked a bit baffled, but nodded obediently, and off I started.

'I don't believe in coincidences, but recently my life has been full of them. An illegal immigrant Chinese girl had a baby, was temporarily impersonated by another Chinese girl, then the first one got murdered. An inquiry about pet dogs being poisoned leads to an animal feed factory, which disappears. Then it looks as if the murdered Chinese girl had been a slave prisoner in that same factory. The Chinese interpreter who first worked with the murdered girl gets beaten up, then his wife goes to a lot of trouble to explain to me that in Chinese they have the same word for a temporary building where people make things as for a factory. Like as if she was trying to tell me how the animal feed factory could have disappeared. But how could she have known anything about a disappearing factory? That's the puzzle, you see, the puzzle and the link.'

I stopped for breath and looked at Taz for the first time. Up till then I'd just been looking ahead through the windscreen, almost thinking I was talking to myself. But then I remembered he was there. He was mopping his face with a large impressively white handkerchief. Hardly anyone carries those these days, either they use tissues or they cuff it. For the moment I was distracted from my problems by imagining some devoted Asian mum in a sari, carefully ironing his hankies, underwear, socks...

'Well, come on, Taz,' I barked at him. 'Don't just sit there sweating. Say something.'

'But you told me to keep quiet,' he pleaded, looking at me with big brown eyes like a kicked spaniel. 'Do you really want an opinion, Sergeant Greta?'

My headache had gone, but I was feeling really irritable.

'Why do you keep calling me that? You don't call Alfie Sergeant Alfie.'

'No, I just call him Sarge, but I thought it would be more respectful to call you–'

'Oh, pack it up. When we're off duty you can call me Greta, and at the station you can call me Sergeant Pusey. How's that? Will that do you?'

I didn't know why I was picking on him like that, except for the need to kick someone because I was so fed up. My outline of my problems hadn't helped at all, and I could see he wasn't going to make any contribution.

'OK Greta,' he said, suddenly very brisk. 'Here's what I think. You've got a straight choice. Either you believe in coincidences or you don't. Since you say you don't, then you have to choose to believe that everything you've just said has a connecting link. And as that's the very same word you already used yourself, that's what you've chosen. But what you haven't pinpointed is what makes the link. You've got to look for a common factor that runs right through, joining everything up. Maybe it's because of the recurrence of all the Chinese–'

'Oh yes, there's more of them that I didn't even mention. Like the little burglar who tried to sell some silver at a car boot sale and then got murdered. Not only did he steal the silver from a Chinese gentleman, but he was working for another Chinese at the time! And it turns out that he burgled the wrong house anyway. Is that a separate case, or does that fit into the puzzle, too?'

Taz did some deep breathing. Either it was because I'd foxed him with my latest lot of Chinese, or he'd lost his train of thought. Anyway, after a while he picked up and went on.

'But have you thought that maybe there's something else linking all these different events? Not just the Chinese element, but one single basic racket that all the rest just feeds into?'

I took a long swig of water and cracked open the window a bit. This kid was bright, no getting away from it. I thought about Jim, the Long-distance Lorry Driver and his story about being approached *by a Chinese man* to smuggle illegals. Maybe this was what it was all about. Smuggling Chinese illegals into the country to work as prison labour in illegal factories. And then was all the rest just incidental, little off-shoots of the main criminal activity?

Taz suddenly grabbed my hand and I let out a little yip of surprise.

'What…?'

'Greta,' he said urgently. 'There's something I've got to tell you. You are the most beautiful wonderful brilliant woman I've ever set eyes on. You are my inspiration. You are the main reason I want to be transferred to CID. Greta, I admire you more than anyone I've ever met. In fact, I may as well be completely honest with you' – he was practically panting by this time – 'I love you, Greta Pusey.'

And he sat there, gripping my hand between his two sweaty ones, looking at me with those doggy eyes, and I was thinking, oh shit, why does this always happen to me? Haven't I got enough trouble?

I managed to get my hand back, and patted him on the knee, partly to dry off some of the sweat.

'Come along, young Taz, don't be silly,' I said in what I hoped was a motherly way (or at least auntly). 'This is just a crush. We all go through this sort of hero-worship stage. I mean, look how much older I am than you. And anyway – I, er…'

I didn't know what anyway was, so I just dried up. He was still looking at me with this soulful look, this time as if I'd kicked the spaniel, but I'd had a hard day and just couldn't deal with any more problems. What I really wanted was to tell him to bog off, but I could see I couldn't talk to him the way I'd talk to Jim, say, or even Ari. He was so young, it was pathetic.

After a while he said, 'I didn't want anything from you. I know you couldn't feel anything for me. Please don't think I was trying to make advances to you. I just wanted – I just *had* to tell you how I feel. Please forget it.'

And he got out of the car, closing the door very carefully and gently, and walked away. Bit of a let down, really. As an afterthought, I wouldn't have minded a short grapple in a steamy car. No strings, of course. Just a bit of physical contact.

I decided to go to karate instead.

*

So after all the heavy thinking and the headache pills and the snooze in the car and then a good hearty karate session, you'd think I'd be knocked out. Specially since I'm a champion sleeper as a rule, and I've been told I could sleep for England if it was part of the Olympics. But that night, could I sleep? Could I hell.

It all kept going round in my head. The link, the link. I knew I was missing something that should have been obvious, but I just couldn't get hold of it. Finally I decided I must be hungry, so I made myself a nice thick bacon sarnie and a cup of tea.

And it was while I had a mouthful of this specially early breakfast that it came to me: where had all this wild goose chasing started? What had led us to Nasty and the factory that disappeared and the repulsive heap of bodies and not-bodies? Of course, it was that mysterious smoothy, Mr Edward Franklin, who had been so forthcoming about the supplies of pet food he sold on to the unsavoury Dan Bush. And what a pack of lies he'd told us about the processing plant where he got the stuff.

Forgetting my bacon sarnie in my excitement, I started pacing about the place, waving my arms and talking to myself.

'Think, woman, think!' I shouted, regardless of the neighbours.

Deaths of pets, visits to vets, tracing the origin of the pet food that was the probable cause of the deaths. Following Edward Franklin, who'd told us his supplier was in Northchurch, just past Berkhamstead, and who'd led us to Nasty instead! What was the link between the heap of body parts we'd found near Nasty, the factory processing lethal pet food, and the Chinese illegal immigrant slave labourers? The pet food itself, of course. And Edward Franklin, probably, if that was his name, if we could ever find him.

In a rare state of excitement, I phoned Derek.

It wasn't until he snarled at me that I realised it was a bit early.

'Greta! Are you mad? Do you realise what the time is?'

I glanced at my watch. Hmm. Maybe it was slightly unreasonable to call him at twenty to four. Still, a breakthrough was important enough, surely? He didn't seem to think so.

'Go back to bed,' he growled, 'and take all this up with me in the morning.'

No good pointing out that it was morning already. I went back to my cold bacon sarnie and scummy tea.

Even with all the bad temper, Derek must have been a bit impressed with the bit I'd managed to blurt out before he hung up on me. Because I got to Shady Lane at six-thirty (keen, eh?) and he was already there.

'Come on then, Greta, let's have it all,' he said before I could open my mouth. 'I can see you've worked out one of your marvellous theories and you're just busting to get it off your chest.'

I suppose I should have been encouraged that he'd even noticed that I had a chest, but the way he said it, it was so unromantic, I don't think it had anything to do with sex.

After all, it was a good thing he hadn't listened to me when I'd phoned, because in the meantime I'd had a chance to put my thoughts in order. It was a wonder to me, because I'd always thought I'd be like a wet rag if I didn't get my full quota of sleep, but here I was as bright as the glitter on a tart's eyelids, and ready to set it all out to him.

Then, just as I opened my mouth, he said, 'On second thoughts, hold it. Hang on until Alfie and Vicky get in, so we can have a proper brainstorming session about whatever it is you've come up with.'

That bloody Vicky again! Alfie, OK. But Vicky! Who needed her?

Chapter 12

As it turned out, I did. Need Vicky, I mean. It chokes me to admit it, but she was the only one who saw the sense of what I was saying, and gave me her wholehearted support. Derek and Alfie weren't exactly arguing, more sort of so what-ish. And Alfie pointed out some of the times I'd gone charging up blind alleys and chasing red herrings, as he put it.

Which of course Vicky North couldn't have known about without Alfie kindly passing on this vital information.

'Maybe so,' I said. 'Nobody's always right. We all have to learn from our own mistakes. But all our cases have worked out fine so far, haven't they? I wouldn't be a sergeant by now otherwise, would I?'

Then I thought maybe it wasn't such a good idea to remind Alfie of my commendation for bravery, because he and Derek had both said at the time that there was a big difference between being foolhardy and being brave. But the brass didn't see it that way. Anyway, that's water under the bridge. Now was now.

'So what are you actually suggesting then, Greta?' Derek asked in his most snooty voice. 'What actual action do your theories lead to?'

I really had a strong desire to kick him at that moment, but instead I gave him a really smarmy Vicky-type smile, and said, 'If we could get hold of some of that pet food and get it analysed and get the DNA, and then compare it with the same from that horrible heap of stuff we found in that field outside of Nasty–'

'DNA! Do you know what you're saying?' he said. 'That work costs the earth. And to what end, may I ask? If it was shown that there was a link, an actual provable physical link, between those two sources, what would that tell us? How much further forward would that take us?'

Vicky saved me. I could have killed her. Or at least blacked her eye.

'See, Guv, if we could get some DNA from Ah Weng So,' she put in eagerly, 'and *that* gave us a match too, then we've got a definite link between the slave factory where she was held, the missing factory, the poisonous pet food, and the stuff you found in that field.'

'Right you are, Vicky,' he said, all thoughtful consideration. 'And that would probably tie up with the chap who approached Greta's lorry-driver friend to bring in Chinese illegals. Maybe it would be worth making a hole in our budget, after all.'

I rolled my eyes at Alfie, who like a true friend came to my rescue. Thick he may be sometimes, but even he understood that I'd rather have my theories blown out of the water than taken up because Vicky pushed them.

'But Guv, like you said, even if we prove all that links up, it doesn't take us any further in actually solving anything, does it? I mean–'

'OK Alfie,' Derek said rather wearily, 'I'll have to have a think about all this. Maybe run it past Mr Moon. Anyway, in the meantime, I want you all to see what you can do to track down this mysterious Edward Franklin.'

'Which of course isn't his name,' I offered gloomily. 'Every word he told us was a lie, so that must be false as well.'

'Something to get your detective teeth into then, isn't it?' Derek was cold and unsympathetic.

And the three of us trooped out to leave him alone to ponder.

'Let's go back,' Vicky proposed in her loathsome eager way, 'to where we first met Edward Franklin, and see if we can pick up his trail from there.'

Pick up his trail! What did she think we were, Boy Scouts?

'OK,' I said, 'we can give it a try. Let's go and visit the smelly Dan Bush again, and see if he's had any more calls from his supplier, whatever his name is. Certainly won't be Edward Franklin,' I grumbled as we set off.

Another surprise. Ain't life full of them, though.

Dan Bush told us the so-called Franklin had gone on calling and delivering just the same as he had before our visit. I felt a bit of a fool about that. I'd been so sure that every word he'd told us was a lie, I hadn't even thought of trying his phone or email. So I made out that we had to see him personally, and all we had to do was hang around all over again and wait for him to turn up. Except of course, I suggested this time we should stay well hidden in case he saw us and took off.

Well, I always knew that there'd be a certain amount of repetition and boredom in detective work, although I hadn't reckoned with being stuck with a Victoria North (aka pain in the bum). She tried to chat, but all she got from me was grunts.

'Good hairdresser, isn't she?' she tried.

And, 'Aren't we lucky to have a boss like Derek?'

And, 'What a good sort that Alfie is, isn't he?'

And even, 'That little uniform who hangs around Alfie, Taz is it? I think he's sweet on you…'

But it was all useless. She couldn't get a word out of me. That didn't mean that a lot wasn't happening inside my head. I just didn't want to let on to her that anything she might have to say to me might ring a bell. And I certainly didn't want to let on that I could see that all that stuff we'd been burbling about DNA was probably ridiculous rubbish.

Finally, at six o'clock, Dan Bush came and found us.

'Didn't think he'd turn up today, girls. I did tell you he came on Wednesdays,' he said helpfully. 'You might as well go home and put your feet up.'

Thanks a bunch, I thought but didn't say. Just nodded and drove off.

Bright and early next morning we were at it again, me feeling even more of a Charley because I'd forgotten about Franklin always calling on Bush on Wednesdays. Waiting. This time Vicky seemed to have given up on the friendly conversation. Suited me.

I wondered what Derek and Alfie were up to while we were hanging around like two lemons. We silently swigged water, munched crisps and peed behind bushes.

Finally of course it all paid off. Mr Edward Franklin turned up.

'Block his exit,' I told North as I got out of the car.

Strolling up to Franklin, I said in as friendly a voice as I could manage (considering I was well fed up by this time), 'So sorry to bother you again, Mr Franklin, but I'd just like to ask you a few more questions, if you can spare the time.'

I sounded sarcastic to me, but he answered politely enough, 'Of course – er, Sergeant Pusey, isn't it? How can I help you?'

That was pretty cool, all things considered, and nearly threw me off. But at least this time I remembered to consult my notes.

'You gave us the address of your supplier, Mr Franklin, in, er, Northchurch, near Tring, just past Berkhamsted. But then, when you left here that day, you drove in quite a different direction, up the A10, and to a little village called Nasty. None of the addresses you gave me are thereabouts. Can you explain that to me, please?'

I was being extra polite to him because as soon as I started talking to him, I'd realised what a huge clanger I'd dropped about this whole thing. After we'd lost him at Nasty, I hadn't bothered to check up on the information he'd given me – what a berk! I couldn't blame Derek for not picking it up, either, because he had a lot more on his mind. So I couldn't even accuse Franklin of giving false information.

Smiling with difficulty, I waited for his answer. And when it came, I felt even more of an idiot. And in front of Vicky North, too! What would Derek say when I told him? Ouch. As I expected by then, he had a believable answer.

'But Sergeant, I didn't say I was going directly back to my supplier. What a pity you didn't ask me where I was going next,' he said, smooth as silk. 'I could have saved you the trouble of following me. In fact, I was going to visit my sister, who lives in Wood End. Do you know it? It's another village, just past Nasty, and quite a bit bigger. Now, is there some other way I can be of assistance to you?'

I muttered thanks and backed off, outwardly calm and inwardly cursing. Not Franklin or Dan Bush or even Vicky North. Just myself.

Silently daring North to say a word of sympathy or ask a question, I said, 'Right. Let's go and call on Franklin's supplier in Northchurch.'

And we drove off in an atmosphere you could cut with a blunt fork.

We'd been quiet for so long that when North did speak I gave a great jump. I'd mercifully forgotten she was there. Wishful thinking.

'I'm sorry, Sarge,' she said, and she sounded it, too. But why?

'Why, what did you do?'

'Well, I know you've got a lot on your mind, what with Ah Weng So and her baby and all that, so when you forgot to follow up on Franklin and the story he told us, I should have reminded you...'

She'd wrong-footed me again, the little pain in the neck.

'Not your fault,' I said, trying to sound gracious and sounding more as if I'd got something caught between my teeth.

But when we got to Northchurch we both felt as if we'd been reprieved. It wasn't really a village, more a sort of nearby suburb of Berkhamsted. It was a bit bigger than Nasty, but not much. In any case, it was easy to cover its area quite quickly and to be sure that it had nothing like a factory, farm or abattoir. And the actual address Franklin had given us didn't exist.

This time we wanted to make sure, so we went back to the little cottagey police station in Berkhamsted to check. They were very welcoming, offering us cups of tea and opinions and advice. But the main thing was, they definitely confirmed that there was no such place in or around Northchurch or Berkhamsted. Nor, as far as they knew, anywhere in the area. They gave us a map with all the local farms marked clearly, and we drove round them all. No factory or anything like one. What a relief. So we were off the hook about that one.

'But that doesn't have to mean that Franklin lied to us about himself,' I said, determined not to miss anything this time. 'We've still got to check up on his personal information.'

'OK Sarge, I'll see what I can find out by phoning him.'

'No, don't do that, I don't want to alert him. Let's drive straight to the address he gave us. We can check up the phone number and fax and email later.'

I glanced at the time.

'You're not in a hurry to go off duty, are you?'

This was only a formality. I had no intention of letting her go at this stage of the game. Funny how I found I needed her just now.

'No, Sarge, let's chase him up. It's in this direction anyway. If you give me your notebook I'll get on to the Police National Computer and get them to check up on his van while we're on our way. This is fascinating, isn't it. Talk about the plot thickening, eh Sarge?' she chattered away.

You don't like her, I kept reminding myself. But suddenly I felt a strangely sort of warmish feeling. A bit like I'd felt towards Alfie when I first knew him. It must have been to do with 'we're all in this together' or something, because I'm glad to say that by the next morning I'd completely got over it. And disliked her as much as ever, specially when she was 'helping' me report to Derek.

Telling Derek about the dead end we'd come up against wasn't so hard. It sort of got me off the hook for forgetting to follow up the info that Franklin had given me in the first place.

Of course the name, address, telephone and fax numbers, email address and registration number of his van were all false. And the street he claimed to live in didn't exist.

'Where does that leave us?' Derek asked in his gloomiest voice, and true to form, Alfie answered, 'Buggered if I know.'

Finally I decided that I'd have to tell Derek about Mr and Mrs Wing. What I had to tell him was pretty vague, but I still had a bad feeling about them. It was a shame that I should be suspicious of them, specially as from the start I'd taken such a shine to Mr Wing. When I'd first met him in the hospital, interpreting for poor little Ah Weng So, he'd seemed quite a sweetie. But now I was beginning to think perhaps I'd made a bad judgement there. And of course Alfie would be quick to point out it wouldn't be the first time I'd got somebody wrong. So what? Nobody's perfect, are they.

Anyway, I got my thoughts together and blurted out, 'I think there might be something fishy about Mr and Mrs Wing.'

'What, the interpreter? What do you mean, you can't think the fact that he was attacked has anything to do with our case,' Derek said, lifting his eyebrows in a particularly scornful way.

This was too good an opening to miss. I abandoned the Wings for the moment to ask the big question that had been bugging me all along.

As politely and respectfully as I could, I asked Derek, 'Which case is that, Guv? Can you please explain how many cases we're running just now? The missing factory, the poisoned pet food, the body parts in the field, the murdered burglar, the murdered Chinese girl, the mysterious Mr Franklin – are they all one case, or half a dozen different ones? Or are some of them connected, but not all? Honestly, I'm confused.'

I stopped for breath and looked at Alfie and North. What a relief! They were both nodding. So I wasn't on my own and being thick. It really was all as baffling as I thought. And that meant if I had to add Mr and Mrs Wing to Sadie and James Lee and all the other Chinese elements, it wasn't going to be too far-fetched.

Derek was looking as if he'd been hit over the head with a wet sandbag. This was the man I'd looked up to (in a way, though of course in a different way he had to look up to me – when we were both standing up, that is), and who I'd thought so much cleverer than anyone I'd ever met. I could see he couldn't think of a thing to say. Alfie came to his rescue.

'Go on then, girl,' he urged me. 'Tell us what you were going to say about the Wings.'

'Mrs Wing went into a long explanation about how difficult

it is to give an exact translation of some words. And she gave me this example of how they don't have one word for factory, and it can mean lots of slightly different things…and anyway, in the end, she was telling me that where I'd found that bit of paper that said 'China' in Chinese, there could have been a sort of temporary moveable place where they were making things. Well, not even necessarily making things, maybe just putting things together or packing them, or something like that.'

'So?' said Derek, stony-faced.

'So when Mr Wing said that Ah Weng So said she worked in a factory, it need not have been a factory as we understand the word.'

'And this means?'

'Well, it seemed to me that this meant someone had told them that we'd found evidence of a temporary structure in what's now an empty field, where previously we'd thought there was a proper factory.'

Derek gave up his interrogation and just looked at me. I felt I had to go on, because I could see he wasn't impressed so far.

'If someone told them that, and I think they were both lying about who attacked Mr Wing and why, then surely that implicates them in some way?'

'Sounds likely to me,' Alfie put in his two penn'orth. 'How about inviting them to come and have a chat with us here, Guv?'

'Mr Wing's still in hospital,' I reminded him.

'Come on Alfie.' Derek suddenly stood up, all brisk and full of life.

'Where we going, Guv?' Alfie asked, lumbering to the door.

'To the hospital to see Mr Wing, of course,' Derek snapped and hopped it before I had a chance to point out that he hadn't even tried to answer my question.

So I still didn't know if he thought all these cases were

connected or not. And worse still, I didn't know what to do with myself and bloody North while he and Alfie went to talk to Mr Wing.

'What do you think we should do next, Sarge?' North asked.

'One of the things we'll have to do is wait till next Wednesday and nab that so-called Edward Franklin and charge him with obstruction.'

'How's that?'

'Well, he knew we were pursuing enquiries, and he deliberately gave us misinformation on two separate occasions.'

'Is that enough?'

'It'll have to be.'

I'd made up my mind somebody had to suffer for how out of it I felt, and I couldn't think of anyone else just then. But in the meantime, until next Wednesday, what?

'I'll tell you what you can do, young North,' I barked. 'I want you to sit down and write a complete record of everything that's happened to you personally since you joined this team. Don't leave anything out, even if you think it's unimportant. Put in every name, description and other details you can think of. Of course you'll have notes to refer to, but if you think hard you might remember stuff you didn't bother to write down.'

'Do you mean absolutely *everything*, Sarge? I mean, even things like I thought this chap's false teeth didn't fit too well, silly things like that?'

'Yes,' I said firmly, 'leave nothing out. Nothing at all.'

That'll keep her quiet for a few hours, I thought with glum satisfaction, marching up to the canteen with longing thoughts of a bacon sarnie.

But it wasn't to be.

My mobile vibrated. Not many people had that number.

It was Ari. He had no business calling me while I was on duty. Specially if he was on duty himself.

'What!' I barked. I was in a barking mood that day.

'Listen, Greta,' he said, and I knew it must be something serious because he hardly ever used my proper name – 'lovely girl' was what he usually called me – 'this is important. I've just had to arrest your little chum Juan Garcia for drunk and disorderly. In the middle of the day and in the middle of the road. And guess what he said when I took him in? He thanked me.'

'So?' I said. 'What do you expect a drunk to say?'

'No, you don't understand. He *wanted* to be taken in. For safety.'

Then I caught it. Garcia thought he was in danger. Clever Ari had twigged it and thought it was urgent to let me know.

'If I come there right now, can I see him?'

'Yes, course, come now, quick.'

Well, even if I'd gone on the siren I could hardly get from Watford to Brixton in half an hour. But by the time I did finally arrive, sweating and swearing at the traffic, Juan Garcia seemed to have sobered up. Always supposing he'd been drunk in the first place. That was the first question I asked the custody sergeant.

'Was he really drunk? Or just so disorderly that PC Anapolis assumed he must be?'

Put my foot in it again, didn't I? The sergeant looked me up and down in a really down-your-nose way.

'I don't know how you proceed with these matters out there in Hertfordshire–' he started, in a really snooty voice, so I interrupted before things got too unfriendly.

'Sorry, Sarge, didn't mean to question anyone's judgement. Just that I know this little feller from a long way back, and he's good at acting a part when he's scared. And I've got reason to suspect he's right to be nervous. I think he's got into something too big for him to understand, never mind be part of it. That's his form, you know,' I moved smoothly into the chatty approach, 'whenever we've come across him, he's always up to his neck in something outside his range.'

'Go on,' said the custody sarge, and I could see I'd got him interested regardless of the bad start I'd made. So I gave him a brief history of our dealings in the past with Juan Garcia, and soon had him roaring with laughter about the time the little bungler had tried to top himself and ended up breaking his ankle instead. After that it was a piece of cake to get in to see Juan on my own.

No surprise to see him crouched in the corner of the holding cell, sobbing quietly to himself. I had to resist the temptation to say: 'Here's another fine mess you've got yourself in, Stanley', (like Hardy always said to Laurel), because I knew it would start us off on the wrong foot. I didn't want to start having to explain to him about Laurel and Hardy. Ordinary conversation was hard enough.

'Come on, Juan,' I said briskly instead, 'pull yourself together.'

When he saw it was me he jumped to his feet with his arms out, and for one gruesome moment I thought he was going to hug me. No, it was OK. He was just going to wave them about a bit in his usual way.

'Oh, Sergeant darling, I should have know you would come to save me, like always,' he blubbed, and I got ready to dodge in case he got too close in his excitement. He stopped and thought for a moment, and I could see the wheels going round. 'What you say when you come in about to pull myself?'

I didn't want to waste time on one of those silly explanations about English expressions that we used to get so tied up with when I first knew him. I just told him to sit down, and stood over him (not too close).

'Now then, Juan Garcia,' I said in my sternest sergeant's voice, 'tell me what you've been doing to get yourself so scared that you had to be arrested to feel safe. And don't try telling me any silly stories. I want the whole truth this time, or I won't be able to help you again.'

'Am being followed, Sergeant, peoples following me all the time.'

He looked at me appealingly, but I stayed shtum and waited.

'Is those Chinese peoples,' he explained. 'I don' know who they are, just all the time I go, Chinese peoples follow. So I come all down to these part where I don' know where I am, and still they follow. Is not nice. So I come in here for to be safe.'

'Why didn't you come to me in Watford? Or phone me? You know I'll always help you if you're in trouble.'

'Yais, but Meeses Sleepworthy, she say not to trouble you more. She never liked me before, but now is being very kind, and husban' also. Teaching me speaking more better English, and telling me advices.'

'Well,' I said with marvellous patience, though I say it myself, 'I don't think much of their latest advice. If you'd come to me in the first place, I need not have come all the way down here to see you. Lucky for you I've got a friend here who called me to say you were here. Anyway, do you recognise any of these Chinese people who you think are following you?'

Juan got excited. 'Am not just theenk, Sergeant. Is real. Following all the time, and what for? What they want from me? I don' know no things about why they keel my matey–'

He clapped his hand over his mouth. Too late. He'd really let the cat out of the bag this time. So he knew all along who'd done that murder he'd been accused of. But he'd been too scared to say. Now how was I going to get the rest of it out of him? I'd have to think of a trick or two, but not the ones that worked on him before, in case he still remembered how I'd fooled him in the past.

I had a hell of a job getting the custody sarge to let me haul Juan back to Watford. Even after I'd got so chummy with him and made him laugh and given him a bit of the old body language to make him think I fancied him! Some men are hard to get round. He kept pointing out the rules and the paperwork and stuff till I nearly gave up.

But finally after I'd suggested getting our Super to talk to his Super he agreed to waive the charge against Juan and 'give him into my custody' as he put it. I couldn't make out if he thought he was blinding me with science or something, but it turned out all he wanted was a date. So I fixed one with him. Didn't have to turn up, did I? Might even send DC Victoria North in my place. That would give them both a bit of a turn, wouldn't it. This seemed such a good idea to me that I couldn't stop grinning to myself all the way back to Watford.

'What for you smiling like thees, Sergeant?' Juan asked me nervously. 'You not going to give me the degree again like before?'

Recalling the time when Alfie and I had scared him so much he'd tried to top himself, and how we'd both nearly ended up on a charge ourselves, I promised him sincerely there'd be nothing like the third degree when we arrived at Shady Lane.

'I'm going to look after you, Juan,' I told him. 'Haven't I always been the one you could rely on when you were in trouble?'

'Yais, mm,' he agreed. But I could see he still had his doubts.

So did I. I hadn't got the smallest idea what to do with him when we eventually got to Shady Lane, but I was trusting to luck that something would occur.

Meantime I'd made a mental note to thank Ari in a suitable manner for his help. If he hadn't realised who he had on his hands and how useful it could be to let me know, we might not have got the breakthrough I hoped we now had. If we did.

And by the way, I thought I'd have a less than friendly word some time with Juan's landlady, Mrs Sue Slipworthy, and suggest that she stop giving her lodger useless advice. Telling him not to trouble us might have well wiped out our latest lead. Unless, of course, that was her intention. We'd see about that.

Meanwhile, I popped Juan into an interview room and rushed to tell Derek the latest. This time he'd have to be pleased with me. Probably he would have been delighted, but he was out. What now, I asked myself. I didn't want to wait till Derek was available, because Juan might go off the boil and deny spilling the beans about the murder of his little friend, the incompetent burglar Charlie 'the Chump' Hampson. No, I'd have to take a chance and go it alone.

I wasn't exactly shocked to find Juan having another snivel to himself when I went back to talk to him. In fact, I was a bit surprised to find him still there at all. It would have been typical of him to have done a bunk at this stage of the proceedings, being fed up with himself opening his mouth when he should have kept it shut.

'Come on now Juan,' I said in my kindest voice, 'there's nothing to be afraid of. Tell me what's worrying you.'

After another sniffle or two, and a swipe of the nose on the cuff, he mumbled something. Holding myself back with a struggle from barking at him, 'Speak up, man!', I went on with the sweetness and light.

'Who was that you said?' I cooed. I had no idea if he'd mentioned a name, but I thought I'd gamble on it.

'Chang was the name. My matey Charlie, he robbed from Mr Chang the silvery things what you saw me selling from the boot,' Juan explained.

This was no good at all. We already knew the name of the victim of Charlie's latest robbery. But I kept my patience.

'Yes, Juan dear,' I said with even more of an effort, 'but why does that worry you so much?'

'Poor Charlie, he make mistake and go to wrong house. Mr Chang what he robbed from, he was best friend of Charlie's new boss. Charlie's new boss tell him where to do job, Charlie get orders wrong. New boss angry, promise Mr Chang Charlie be punish. You see what they do to my poor matey, then make it look like poor Juan Garcia do it!'

And he burst into loud sobs again. This was getting us nowhere. It was raising more questions than it answered. The first problem was how could Juan have got hold of all this stuff? And why should this be a reason for him to be followed and frightened by Chinese men? Even if it was true, he certainly couldn't prove that Charlie Hampson's boss had been so angry with him that he'd had him killed, just to make his friend Mr Chang feel better about being burgled by mistake.

Anyway, who was this mysterious boss of Charlie's? Did Juan also claim to know this? OK, next question. First, with the least possible physical contact, I patted Juan slightly on the shoulder and gave him a tissue to dry his face.

'Come along now Juan, stop snivelling,' I advised him.

Mistake.

'I don' know what is snivelling,' he muttered miserably. 'I don' know what to do about everytheen. Maybe I should go back to Colombia. Is no Chinese there.'

'No, no, Juan, you can stay here and help us, and we'll look after you. Don't be afraid. Now tell me,' I went on as he seemed to calm down a bit, 'did your matey Charlie ever tell you the name of his new boss, by any chance?'

'Sure,' he said, 'is what I am worry for. If I know hees name, he knows mine, what will happen to poor Juan? Going same way as poor Charlie?'

'Poor Juan will be fine,' I assured him hypocritically. 'Come on, just tell me the name, please?'

I've got to admit that the one syllable he came out with was a big surprise to me. Maybe I should have guessed or even suspected. But I didn't.

'Lee,' Juan said.

*

After I'd got Juan nicely and safely tucked up in a cosy cell, I finally found Derek. And I couldn't wait to pass on my bombshell. Except that as far as Derek was concerned, it was a dud.

'Lee?' he said, not quite sneering, but more or less. 'I suppose you couldn't have come up with a really common name like, say, Wong? Lee for Chinese people is like Smith or Jones for us. You want me to think it's that so-called brother and sister act, James and Sadie Lee, don't you? Well, I'm sorry, but we both know that Juan Garcia is an unreliable witness at the best of times. And to start accusing those two of murder on just his say-so, well, how ridiculous do you want us to look, Greta? I'm surprised at you, I really am.'

I was squashed flatter than a bed bug in Brick Lane.

'Well, what do you think we should do with Juan, then?' I asked. 'I more or less promised him safety from these Chinese he says are following him…'

'Oh, alright,' he said irritably, 'I'll go and have a word with him.'

'Derek,' I said in my smallest voice, 'before you go, could I have a word on a private matter?'

'Go on then,' he said, looking at his watch meaningfully.

'You remember when you took me to the opera and how much I liked it,' I started, and was glad to see his expression lighten up right away. 'Well,' I went on, 'I know we're too snowed under for anything like that now.'

He just nodded, but he was looking much friendlier by the second, so I felt brave enough to keep at it.

'So I was wondering,' I finished all in a rush, 'if I could come round to your place some time and you'd play me some records of other operas and tell me about them, because I'm really into that stuff now.'

I knew that would remind him of how I shed a tear at my first opera and how surprised we both were at toughie Greta turning out to be such a softy. It worked.

'Of course,' he said quietly, 'that would be very pleasant. I'd like that. Soon.'

Then, suddenly changing back to being the DI, he added, 'Meantime, what are you doing about apprehending this Edward Franklin? For all we know he might be the key to the whole thing.'

I explained again, 'He goes regularly to deliver every Wednesday, and North and I will be waiting for him there. But before that, we've got no idea where to find him or even what his name is. What do you mean, he might be the key...?'

'Oh, I don't know, what makes you think I understand any of this any more than you do, Greta? We're all just stumbling through a maze. Even Mr Moon's run out of suggestions.'

North came trotting in, looking pleased with herself. She plonked a thick wodge of papers in front of me.

'I've done what you said, Sarge. Written down absolutely everything, typed it up, printed it out, there it is!'

I had to admit that was pretty quick. But I wasn't going to

give her any praise for sorting out all her notes and unwritten recollections, specially in front of Derek.

'You're a fast typist,' I said, all sarky. 'Did you take typing lessons before you enrolled at Hendon?'

She was unsquashed. Took it as a compliment, in fact. Like a rubber ball, that girl, always bouncing back. Pain in the neck. And everywhere else, too. Worst of all, Derek picked up the top few sheets and started reading. Reading and nodding and smiling.

'Very good, Vicky,' he said. 'Well written, coherent but not verbose.'

I had to distract him from all this.

'What happened when you spoke to Mr and Mrs Wing, Guv?'

Still leafing through Vicky's 'coherent but not verbose' report, he answered absent-mindedly, 'No, not much, I didn't get much further than you. We'll have to think about those two, though.'

'Is there anything we should be doing now, Guv?' North asked, at her smarmiest. 'We seem to have run out of steam, don't we?'

'Yes, Vicky,' he said, looking at her the way he should have been looking at me, 'we'll just have to hope for another lead. I suppose if you two have all your paperwork up to date, you might as well go home.'

'See you later, then, Guv,' I said in what I hoped was a meaningful voice as I left, making sure that I shoved North out before me. I wasn't taking the chance of leaving her in his office with him.

At home I couldn't settle. TV was boring, the latest crime novel somehow wasn't gripping me the way it had at the start, I couldn't be bothered to do any laundry or other domestic stuff. Finally I gave in to myself and did what I'd wanted to do from the moment I got back.

I phoned Derek.

What a relief – he sounded pleased to hear from me.

'Yes, Greta,' he said, 'pop round now and I'll order a pizza and we can listen to some music. I think we both need a distraction this evening from the mess we've got ourselves into at Shady Lane.'

Well, it wasn't ecstatic, but it would do for now. Perhaps after a few glasses of his favourite Merlot and telling me about his beloved operas, we'd get a bit cosy.

Chapter 13

Trudging home after another frustrating evening, looking for something to kick – a pebble, a tin can, anything to let off steam – I gave myself a stern lecture. Why had I rushed around frantically deciding what to wear for what I'd hoped would be a romantic evening, thinking whether to drive, walk, cycle or roller-blade, how much make-up to put on, or whether I should use some of the exotic pong Jim, the Long-distance Lorry Driver had brought me from foreign parts years ago? Why did I keep getting my hopes up every time Derek just got a bit friendlier? Did I really think I could seduce him if he didn't want to be seduced?

Well, probably from his point of view it had been a satisfactory, quiet, pleasant evening. He played records and explained about them. We ate pizza and drank Merlot. (Had I decided not to drive because of drinking, or because I'd hoped to be staying the night and going to Shady Lane together next morning in his car?) We chatted about music and other things, anything except work. But that was it. Not even a friendly kiss passed between us. Nada, as Juan Garcia would probably say. Nix. Nothing. Face it, I'd misread everything that'd happened between us in the past, and he just didn't fancy me.

'Fool, Greta!' I suddenly shouted out loud, causing a passing cat to let out an alarmed yowl.

Seeing that prowling animal reminded me of Jim's well-meant kindness in presenting me with a ferret when he thought

I was lonely. I've never been lonely in my life. I like being on my own, and anyway in recent years I'd had a lot of company, what with Jim and Ari. But now I didn't want to be alone, or with Jim or Ari. All I wanted was Derek, who'd ruined all my plans for concentrating on my career and not bothering about love and all that soppy stuff.

My Gran always used to say that a woman on her own was sending a wrong message if she had a cat. Like she was saying, this is all the companionship I can get. Did that apply to ferrets, I wondered, or was that a different message?

Just as I was thinking that, a little dog trotted by. Dogs shouldn't be out on their own, night or day. I called to him and he came over to me, wagging his tail and looking pleased to see me. He had no collar. Thinking I'd take him home with me and call the dog warden in the morning, I went to pick him up, but he dodged me and I just couldn't catch him. I could see by the look in his eye that his head was full of plans for the night, and I wished him luck and hoped his night worked out better than mine had. He didn't seem to care about my good wishes as he trotted off.

I got home feeling sorry for myself. Even a stray dog had better plans than spending the night with me. I looked in the mirror and decided too much make-up was the problem. Next time I'd try the natural look. What did I mean, next time? Was I crazy? Why didn't I know when to give up? Was I really too conceited to believe there was a man who didn't want me?

Strangely, after all that frustration, I slept like a log, and got up bright and early all fresh to start a new day.

No sooner had I got in than there was a call from the front desk.

'There's a woman here, I think she's asking for you, Greta,' the station officer said. 'Only she's saying she wants to speak to Gerda, and you're the nearest I can think of.'

'Well, what's it about? What's her name?'

'She won't say. You'd better come down.'

I took one look and remembered everything about her. Marion Sestina, who'd helped us with a case in the past and then got the hots for Ari. In fact, come to think of it, when I'd dumped him, he went out with her for a while. Another little dainty blonde who made me feel like a clumping Amazon. Not that I disliked her personally, only that I was against dainty little blondes on principle.

'Gerda?' she greeted me timidly. That's another thing I don't like. Women who speak in that mousy way. Specially ones that get my name wrong.

'Greta,' I snapped back at her. 'What can I do for you?'

In sort of a trembly voice she said, 'I'm really sorry to bother you, but I wondered if you could possibly tell me how to get in touch with Aristotle Anapolis.'

'No, I'm sorry. I certainly wouldn't give such information about a fellow officer. I'm sure if he wants to see you, he'll contact you himself. I assume you're still at the same address?'

'Oh, but–' she started, and I suddenly felt sorry for her. A fellow sufferer in love, she seemed like.

'OK, just give me a message or a note or something and I'll pass it on. That's the best I can do,' I offered.

Her eyes filled with tears. I was disgusted. I didn't remember her as one of those weepy ones. Seemed to recall she was a bit of a toughie. See, that's what love does to you. Mucks you up. I'd never be as much of a wuss as that, but I did sort of know how she felt.

'If you'd just ask him to phone me, I know he's got my number,' she said.

Then what I'd said before suddenly clicked, and in a

different tone of voice she went, ‘What do you mean, fellow officer? He’s not in the police, is he?’

‘Yes, he re-joined the Met. Decided not to be a private detective any more. He was no good at it, anyway. Next time I see him I’ll tell him to phone you,’ I said over my shoulder as I walked away from her.

But she wasn’t having that.

She called after me, ‘Just a minute, I want to ask you something else. Come back, please.’

Oh well, as least she didn’t call me Gerda again.

‘What?’

‘What did you mean, next time you see him? Do you see him often? Does he work at this station? Are you, is he, I mean–’

‘If you mean, are we an item, mind your own damn business,’ I snarled, and this time I really walked out on her. Not that I knew the answer to that question myself, even if I’d thought she was entitled to ask. What exactly was my relationship with Ari?

I had no chance to turn this over in my mind, because no sooner had I got back upstairs than Derek pounced on me (not in the way I’d like) and barked, ‘What day is this, Greta?’

Puzzled, I said, ‘Wednesday, of course…’ and my voice trailed off as I realised I shouldn’t even be there. Wednesday was the day North and I were supposed to be lying in wait for the elusive Edward Franklin.

‘Yes, right, Vicky has just called in to say she’s there at Dan Bush’s place waiting for you. Maybe you remember that you arranged to meet there rather than go together from here?’

With a final scowl he marched off, not even giving me a chance to apologise.

So off I scooted to the rendezvous with Darling Vicky,

praying that Franklin didn't turn up before I did. I broke all the speed limits getting there so as not to give her a chance to cop him on her own, but I need not have done, because then we had hours of waiting. And just as I was beginning to think we were wasting our time for a change, there he was, driving up again in his spotless van, smooth as you like.

We jumped out of our cars and got to him at the same time.

'Edward Franklin,' I said, 'I am arresting you on a charge of obstructing the police in the course of their enquiries...' and all the rest of the rigmarole.

I was all braced to tackle him if necessary, but he made no attempt to bolt, in fact he just stood there not moving a muscle until I'd finished waffling away, then quietly got into my car with me without a word. Silence all the way back to Shady Lane. Only when we were at the custody desk did he say, in his usual courteous way, 'Is this the time for me to ask to phone my solicitor?'

Naturally, when I got back to Derek's office, North had beaten me to it and told him of 'our success', and he was congratulating *her* on a job well done! Still, he did say I could come with him to interrogate Franklin, and didn't try to include her in that. On the way down, I asked him what had happened about Juan Garcia.

'I've arranged for him to be held in protective custody,' he said. 'Bit of a job convincing Mr Moon to approve it, but he's willing to take your word for it that there is some danger there. Personally, I don't believe a word that Garcia says, but he does appear to be genuinely scared, so we'll keep him for a while. Don't know how long for, though. As for this idea of yours that Sadie and James Lee are somehow tied up in everything that's going down recently, I just can't swallow that. I didn't even suggest it to Mr Moon. Don't want to get laughed at,' he finished moodily as we went into the interview room together.

The so-called Edward Franklin and his solicitor were already there.

Surprise, surprise! His solicitor was a face well known to me and Derek: Charles North, who we'd had some very dodgy dealings with in the past. What! Charles North, of Abel, Levi and North, those extremely expensive Mayfair solicitors, now working for a supplier of pet food? That same Charles North who'd had a very dubious involvement in a high-profile case that had finally earned Derek and me so much approval from High Up?

And of course, didn't we absolutely believe PC Victoria North when she'd told us that she was no relation of his, in fact had never heard of him. So the two of them on our premises was just a coincidence (not). Talk about fishy!

On second thoughts, pity she hadn't come with us to the interrogation. It would have been interesting to see their two faces when they saw each other. Even if they'd been blank, we might have read something into that.

However, question one had to be, who was Edward Franklin anyway?

What kind of catch had we accidentally got while fishing for tiddlers?

Smooth as ever, Charles North said, 'Inspector Michaelson! And Sergeant Pusey! What a pleasure to see you both again, after all this time.'

I switched on the tape recorder and said all the usual things into it, and Derek said stonily to Charles North, 'We have reason to believe your client is involved in the sale of contaminated meat which has caused the death of a number of animals. He has also given us a false name, address and other details of himself and the factory from which he claims to obtain this food. The number plate on the van that he drives is also false. Is your client prepared to give a statement on these matters?'

In his old oily way, North said, 'This is all very official, Inspector. I wonder if it would be possible to switch off the tape for a few minutes while we have a little informal chat?'

'Edward Franklin' was also smiling ingratiatingly. I felt like banging their heads together, but Derek didn't see things my way, as usual. Without a word he signalled to me to switch off – without even saying into the machine that I was doing it! Not like Derek to consider anything so improper.

'Well?' he said.

'If my client was willing to give you all the details of the whole network, Inspector, which I can assure you is far bigger than you can imagine, how would you then regard him and his fairly minor misdemeanours?'

I could see Derek was tempted by Charles North's offer. Clear up all the messy mysteries, and bag a big case too! But whatever Derek might or might not be, one thing was certain: he was straight and did everything by the book (except that little matter of switching off the tape).

'Sorry, Mr North,' he said. 'Either officially on tape, or no deal.'

And he signalled to me to switch on the machine again.

'Right,' he said, 'if your client is not prepared to make a statement or even give his real name, we will proceed with the charges as I have already outlined.'

Suddenly, there was a complete transformation in 'Edward Franklin'. From being the suave English gent, out of the blue he broke down completely. He clutched his head, ruffling that smoothly combed hair, his face went all crumpled and most scarily, his eyes filled with tears.

'No, no,' he said frantically, turning to North, 'you can't let me go to jail. Do something, that's what you're here for. You can get me out of this, you know you can.'

The most amazing thing about this change of character was that his accent was different, too. From being the typical English public school type, he had become some sort of foreigner who spoke very good English. I was still gaping at him, when Derek cut across anything Charles North might have been going to say, by asking the simple question of Franklin, 'What is your nationality?'

And I don't know who was most surprised when he answered, 'I suppose you could say I'm a German national, but I haven't lived in Germany since I was a small boy. And to anticipate your next questions, most of my life has been in Shanghai, and my name is Edvard Franz.'

He slapped something down on the table between us. Derek picked it up, and turning the pages, said into the machine, 'For the record, Mr Franz has just handed over a passport. It is out of date and was a document issued by the German Democratic Republic before it was merged with the Federal Republic of Germany. So you come from East Germany, Mr Franz?'

Charles North said urgently, 'I must advise my client to say no more until we have had a private consultation.'

'Too bad, Mr North, too late,' and Derek went on to charge Edvard Franz with the sale of contaminated meat and giving false information to the police.

Of course we all knew there was much more behind it than that, but it was enough to hold him on for the time being. During this, Charles North was looking less and less smooth and smug, and more like a man with big troubles. You could almost see the bags developing under his eyes. He didn't wait for his client to be handed over to the custody sergeant, but just left without another word to any of us.

All this time the word 'Shanghai' was going round in my head.

'What do you think was biting our old friend, the oily solicitor?' I asked Derek.

But before he could answer, I was suddenly doubled up with a terrible pain. I'd been suffering from some sort of indigestion recently, which was a nuisance and an interference in my normal life. I'd always had perfect health, never having had even the usual childish ailments when I was little, and even on those rare times when I'd caught a cold I managed to shake it off quicker than most people. And as for all this PMS business that some women complain of, I just didn't know what they were on about. So this indigestion-type thing was a big puzzle, not to speak of a bit of an embarrassment, as I didn't know how to deal with it, and didn't want to ask anyone either. And now, just when we might have some sort of breakthrough in this case, and I was about to point out yet another Chinese connection to Derek, this!

I think the pain must have made me go deaf for a minute, because the next thing I knew, Derek was holding me by the arm and saying something, but I couldn't tell what. It was awful, I was actually gasping for breath.

'...sit down, Greta,' I heard, but I couldn't sit or stand, I just fell down.

When I opened my eyes, Derek was bending over me, looking all concerned. Any other time I'd have been delighted that he cared that much, but just then all I wanted was to die. It was that bad.

'What is it?' he was saying. 'What's wrong? Speak to me, woman...'

And then his voice sort of faded out. And so did I. What a girlie way to behave. When I looked back on it later I was thoroughly ashamed of myself. But at the time it was all too confusing to think of anything. The next thing I knew, I was being wheeled along on a gurney, with an ambulance woman on one side and a paramedic on the other, with Derek trailing along behind looking like a spare wotsit at a wedding. Or maybe funeral. I tried to ask what was going on, but my voice didn't work. I had a passing thought that maybe I'd been attacked, but mostly I couldn't think of anything but the agony in the very middle of my body.

A lot more happened after that, but it was all too muddled to really remember it properly. The upshot was, I finally woke up in hospital to be told I'd had peritonitis because I'd neglected doing anything about the symptoms of appendicitis.

'You could have saved yourself a lot of grief if you'd gone to your doctor,' some officious little tart of a medical student scolded me. 'An appendix removal is a much simpler procedure than surgery for peritonitis. It could have been fatal.'

And when I said I'd thought it was indigestion, she had the cheek to say a grown woman should know more about her body than that. I was really pissed off about the whole thing. Still, I started to perk up when Derek arrived with a bunch of flowers and an anxious look. That look was worth a lot to me. But before we could have a proper conversation, Alfie and his Betty came clomping in with bunches of grapes and a box of chocolates.

The big surprise was how much time I'd lost.

'Three days!' I said. 'What do you mean – I can't have been unconscious for three days.'

'No, dear,' Betty said, 'not exactly unconscious, but when we came to see you after the operation, you didn't seem to know any of us, you were that feverish, and nothing you said made any sense. So we just kept coming till today, and now you're more like yourself, and very glad of it we are, aren't we, Alfie?'

And they both stood there nodding and smiling like a pair of giant teddies. Great waves of gratitude swept over me that I had these people who really cared about me. I knew that Aristotle Anapolis loved me and wanted to marry me, but that was different. It was only because he wanted me for himself. But Alfie and Betty gave me that warm feeling of being loved that I hadn't had since my Gran died. And when I looked at Derek, I could see the same sort of concern. I felt all choked, as if I was going to cry. Talk about being girlie! It must have been the anaesthetic that affected me... I'd heard it made you feel weak for a few days. *Come on, toughen up,* I told myself.

'Well,' I said in what was meant to be a brisk businesslike voice (but it wobbled a bit, I had to admit), 'so what have I missed? What's been going on in the real world?'

Betty and Derek spoke together. She was saying something about my not minding about work until I was better, but what he said was much more interesting.

'Edvard Franz was refused bail on our recommendation. Investigations are going on, but he won't say another word. But the really interesting thing is, Charles North has disappeared!'

'What do you mean, disappeared?'

Derek forgot where we were for the minute, and his voice took on its usual note of irritable impatience.

'What do you think I mean? I mean nobody knows where he is. His wife, his office, his clients have all reported him missing. He was last seen driving himself off, he said to see a client, although there was nothing in his appointment book, his secretary knew nothing about it, and he didn't specify the name of the client. His car has been found dumped on

Hampstead Heath, nowhere near his home or his office or the addresses of any of his known clients. Forensics found nothing suspicious in the car.'

I closed my eyes to digest all this and have a little think. Maybe I was still a bit woozy, maybe I shouldn't have blurted out the first thing that came to mind, but on the other hand, maybe Derek shouldn't have reacted the way he did.

I said, 'And what does dear little Vicky North say about this? Still claims she's no relation to Charles, I suppose?'

All Derek said was, 'Oh really, Greta, you haven't improved at all!' and he stamped out.

'Why should having an operation improve me?' I asked Alfie, but he just sort of tutted a bit and shook his head at me in a sad kind of way.

'Bit of a red herring, that, if you ask me, girl,' he said, breaking off a branch of grapes and munching them. 'What difference does it make if young Vicky is related to that slime-bag lawyer or not? What's that got to do with the case?'

'Well, what about the case? Any progress?'

Alfie sat down and prepared himself for a long chat. But Betty had other ideas. She could be really forceful sometimes, too.

'Come on, Alfie, leave Greta alone,' she said. 'She's tired herself out. Look at her, she can hardly keep her eyes open. We'll come and see you again tomorrow, dear,' she told me. 'First just tell me if there's anything you'd like us to bring you. Do you want to give me your keys and I'll fetch you some things from home?'

Where would we be without the practical Betties in life? She was right, I must have been really tired, I was not only getting sentimental, I was turning philosophical as well.

When I woke up I had two more visitors. A big surprise. Ari stood there gazing at me with a soppy look on his face, but instead of making me feel better, I felt worse when I saw who was standing beside him: Marion Sestina. I ignored Ari and glared at her.

'What do *you* want?' I muttered. It was meant to be a shout, but it didn't come out right.

'Marion heard about you collapsing and she phoned me to tell me,' Ari said.

Oh yes? I thought. Marion heard? How? Thought she didn't have his number? And how come Ari didn't hear for himself? As if I didn't have enough to think about, now this. It was all too tiring.

'Go away,' I said to them both. 'I'm tired, I don't want any visitors, I want to sleep. I've had an operation.'

I don't know why I said that, they must have known, but anyway it worked. They went without another word.

When I woke up later I found I big bunch of roses and a lovely card from Ari. Only Ari, I was glad to see. Not Ari and *her*.

Bit of a puzzle, that. If I didn't want him, why should I mind if he teamed up with her? It was clear that she was keen enough for both of them.

The ward was a bit busy by this time. It looked as if one shift of nurses was handing over to the next one, some orderlies were coming round with trolleys of food, and there was one who seemed to be trying to polish the floor under my bed. Into all this came marching the most immense bunch of flowers I've ever seen. Everyone stopped what they were doing to look at this sight. It was so big you couldn't see who was carrying it – just this sort of walking flowerbed and a pair of legs.

My luck. It stopped by my bed. And of all the people who weren't on my mind at that moment, who should it be carrying this barmy offering but my latest admirer, Taz.

He stood there like a joke bride left at the altar, and looked at me with doggy eyes. I could see he wasn't at all sure of his welcome, and he was right about that. Maybe I should have been a bit more kind and tolerant, but I'd had a difficult day already, and this was too much.

I was too tired to think of a tactful way to say it, so I just said, 'Go away, Taz. And take that stupid joke with you.'

I shut my eyes, and when I opened them again he'd gone, together with his complete florist's display. But of course he'd left a note. It said, 'Wishing you a speedy recovery, with all my love and all my heart. From your hopeless admirer.'

No name. It didn't need one. Only Taz could do that. I'd have to find a way to shake him off.

My life was difficult enough without being stalked by a puppy.

Chapter 14

No surprise that when I woke up next day I was feeling completely different and not a bit sorry for myself. In fact, the only thing I felt bad about was having been so rotten to everyone. Well, not everyone, because Ari actually deserved a bit of stick, turning up like that with Marion Sestina. But I could have been a bit nicer to poor little Taz. I'd make it up to him, I decided, as soon as I got a chance.

Trish, one of the nurses, came to take my temperature and stuff.

'You're doing alright with the men, aren't you, my girl,' she said, rolling her eyes. 'I've never seen a patient with so many worthy specimens coming in one after the other. Which is *the* one, then? Not the one with the biggest, er, bunch of, er, flowers, eh?'

And she burst into such a fit of giggles that she had to sit on the bed with me to recover. My Gran used to work in a hospital and from what she'd always told me, things had got a lot less formal these days. This showed up even more when a young doctor came strolling in and sat on the bedside next to Trish, the two of them nearly knocking me off the other side. He didn't want to know how I was getting on; all he asked was if he could share the joke.

'Can I go home now?' I asked in my best and loudest Sergeant's voice. 'I feel OK and I'm not used to three in a bed.'

Instead of this putting a stop to their mucking about, it just sent them off into more silly sniggering.

Louder still and getting a bit irritable, I said, 'Well, I'm glad to be so entertaining to you all, but I've got a job to do. How about giving me my exit permit?'

Turned out I need not have made such a production of it. That's what they were going to do anyway. But not for work. Just home and rest for a week, they said.

Not likely, I thought, hailing a cab outside the hospital entrance.

'Shady Lane Police Station,' I told the driver.

Wouldn't you know it, the first person I saw there was young Taz. In uniform of course. Have to say he looked quite handsome. So it was fairly easy to make a gracious apology to him and explain I hadn't been feeling quite myself.

'Of course I understand, Sarge,' he said. 'It was a bit of a cheek on my part to come marching in like that. But surely you shouldn't be here yet? Have you been signed off?'

'No, well, course I can't come back to full duty yet, this is more an unofficial semi-social call,' I explained. I didn't really need to tell him anything – none of his damn business – but I was trying out what it sounded like so as to be ready for whatever Derek or Alfie were going to say when they saw me.

'Just want to let everyone know I'm out of hospital, and to thank you all for your good wishes, and so on…'

It sounded a bit lame. Wouldn't do.

So when I got to Derek's office, I breezed in all casual-like and said, before they had a chance to raise their eyebrows, 'Hi fellers, I just popped in on my way home to let you know I'm out of pokey!'

Then I saw their expressions. They certainly wouldn't be looking like that just because I was out of hospital. Alfie and Derek were looking really grim.

'What, what…' I started to stammer, but before I could put the question Alfie interrupted.

'You know Charles North is missing,' he said. 'And now

young Vicky hasn't come in. Doesn't answer her phone. We haven't heard a word from her.'

'So you're short staffed,' I said stupidly, not getting the point. 'If it would help, I could stay–'

'No, Greta, you're not fit,' Derek said. 'Go home. We were just thinking of asking Mr Moon if we could temporarily co-opt young PC Tariq Tazhim. He's very keen for a transfer to CID. Don't worry about it.'

I could tell I wasn't quite OK, because my brain couldn't seem to get into top gear.

'PC who? Oh, you mean Alfie's friend Taz. Oh yes, why not,' I said miserably slumping down in the nearest chair. 'He's a bright lad, I'm sure you'll manage fine without me.'

Derek answered in his sternest voice.

'Don't start acting up, Greta,' he said. 'Nobody's suggesting this young lad can take your place. And we're glad you're out of hospital, aren't we, Alfie? But we've got some serious business happening here, and we can't afford to waste time considering if you've got feelings of being left out. Just go home and rest, and when you've fully recuperated and the doctor says you can come back, you know we'll be more than pleased to have you back on the team.'

Alfie took pity on me. He could see I still wasn't getting the full story.

'Looks as if there really is some connection between Charles North and young Vicky, after all,' he said. 'If they've both gone missing in the same few days, it must mean something. Can't be coincidence, like she claimed it was with the name. I believed her,' he went on, 'because she seemed such a straightforward little person, and anyway, it's a common enough name, North. But now we don't know.'

Derek glared at him and cleared his throat meaningfully.

'Yes, course, Derek's right, Greta,' he added, all in a hurry.

'You must go home now. We'll manage with young Taz. Like Derek said, he's keen.'

My head was thumping so much that it was a wonder I found my way home after all that. Why should Charles and Vicky North have disappeared? Even if they were related or just connected in some way, what could have caused them both to buzz off like that? And together? No, at the same time didn't need to mean together.

I was disgusted when the phone woke me up. As soon as I got home, I'd just sat down to have a good think about this latest news, and blow me if I hadn't fallen asleep then and there without even taking my shoes off. Maybe they were all right, and I wasn't quite fit enough yet to go back on active duty. But that didn't mean that my brain needed sick leave. There was no reason why I couldn't sit at home and try to work something out. And not waste half a day sleeping.

It was Aristotle Anapolis on the blower. At full volume. I could tell he was upset because his English was worse than ever. You'd never think he was born here.

'Why didden you tell me you was going home. I phoned the hospital to ask about you, and when they said you wasn't there no more I nearly had a fit, diddeneye. Thought you was worse or something.'

I knew I'd have to cut in, otherwise he'd have gone on like that for half an hour. Anyway, I didn't see why he was so put out. I didn't have to report to him about my health or anything else.

In my most sarcastic voice I said, shouting him down, 'Well, Ari, it was very nice of you to come to see me and bring Marion Sestina with you, but how did you know I was so keen to see the two of you?'

After quite a long while (for him), he answered in a different tone of voice, more sort of hopeful and cheerful, 'What, did you mind her tagging along? It's jealousy, innit? You care, donchya, Greta?'

'Not a bit,' I said. 'It's just that you might have checked first to see if I was well enough for visitors, that's all. But you can come and see me here if you like. Only let me know beforehand how many of you there'll be, so I can put the glasses out ready.'

I knew I was being sarky and rotten to him, but I was so pissed off I had to take it out on someone, and Ari was available. I didn't give a toss if he wanted to take up with Marion Sestina or not. Nothing to do with me. After all, he was a free agent and he knew I was in love with somebody else, so he could do what he liked. I had no claims on him, and didn't want any, either.

So I told myself, anyway.

But I did wonder how she came back on the scene the way she did.

We'd first met her when she'd contacted Ari anonymously, calling herself *flyonthewall.com*. After he'd had a lot of publicity about having been kidnapped, he was sort of a local hero for a while, and got a lot of fan mail. But her email was different. She'd said she could help us with a case of corruption in the Town Hall because she worked there. It turned out to be true, and she'd been instrumental in the case being cracked. But even though after a while she'd tried to become very friendly with me, I never really took to her, partly because she was one of those dainty little blondes who get on my nerves, and also, I've got to admit, because she was very keen on Ari.

So I hadn't seen or heard anything from her, and I thought Ari hadn't either, until that day when she'd come into Shady Lane asking me to help her get in touch with him again. Then the next thing I knew, *she'd* told *him* I was in hospital and got him to bring her along when he came to see me! It didn't add up, but it didn't matter anyway. Just the same, if he was supposed to be so madly in love with me, how come he was taking up with *her*? Not that I cared.

Anyway, Ari said could he come round on his own that evening, and of course I said yes, mainly because I wanted someone to talk to, and Derek and Alfie seemed too busy. But I did phone Shady Lane later that evening, before Ari came, to ask if there was any news of Vicky North. She hadn't turned up, didn't answer her landline or her mobile, and didn't seem to be at home at all. And for some reason it wasn't considered necessary to break into her home to see if she'd come to some harm.

'What about her next of kin?' I asked, but the night shift was too busy for that. After all, she was only a little trainee DC skiving off and letting herself in for a disciplinary when she did turn up for work with some excuse or other.

I didn't see it like that, but seemingly nobody cared what I thought while I was officially off sick. Except Ari, of course. When he turned up with his usual giant pizza and beaming smile, we had a long talk about the Norths, Charles and Vicky, and he agreed with me that she was somehow involved in the whole complicated mess. That made me feel better, and so did the very careful little cuddle he gave me before he left.

'Nothing more than that for us for a while, lovely girl,' he said, 'but you know it's not just for the sex that I love you.'

I really wished I could truthfully say the same to him. He deserved it more than Derek. But who ever said life was fair?

*

When I woke up next morning, I was disgusted to see how late it was. So this was convalescing, was it, sleeping till the middle of the day? I didn't like this at all; I was turning into a slug. Slugs didn't get to be Assistant Deputy Commissioner at Scotland Yard, did they? Even if I wasn't physically a hundred percent, that didn't mean I couldn't exercise the brain-box a bit. I crawled out of bed, wondering what happened to all my energy, and while I was eating my cornflakes I pondered what I could do.

Once I'd showered and dressed I felt more like it, so I drove over to Shady Lane (see, conserving energy by not walking) and wheedled Vicky North's home address out of the station officer. Then I went there.

Course, she didn't live in common old Watford, like the rest of us. No, she had to live in expensive Radlett, and by the looks of it, in a pricey flat, too. No answer to ringing the bell and banging on the door, so after a little trot round to sum up the place, I found a back door and broke in. I don't mean I knocked the door down, just sort of eased it open using a trick I'd learned from Alfie. He need never know I broke my promise not to use it, I told myself.

Well! It was obvious from the word go that this little cop wasn't living on what she got from being a DC. The furniture, carpets, rugs, ornaments, pictures and so on must have cost a small fortune. Not so small, either, I saw when I nosed a bit into a drawer or two and saw some expensive clothes. But what was even more clear from looking around was that the little bird had flown. There were gaps in the wardrobe and empty drawers and no suitcases anywhere around. That would have told you, even if you weren't a detective, that she'd done a flit, but either in a hurry or somewhere she couldn't take a lot of luggage. Otherwise she wouldn't have left such good stuff behind.

Now the question was, why and where to? Two questions. I searched more carefully. No passport. No safe. No photographs. No address book. No mobile phone. I picked up the landline phone and pressed the redial button.

'Good afternoon, Abel, Levi and North, can I help you,' a posh voice answered. I hung up. That was some connection and a half. My head buzzed. Again. This head-buzzing was a new development, and seriously interfered with thinking. I sat down and gazed into space for a while. Then I must have dozed off again, because I suddenly woke with a start, hearing voices. I tiptoed into the kitchen and found myself face to face with young Taz.

'Greta! What are you doing here?' he said. 'Did you find the back door open too? I thought you were off duty this week.'

There were too many questions there, so I answered with one of my own.

'Who's this?' I asked, pointing at the young plod with him. He looked slightly familiar, but I didn't know all the uniforms at Shady Lane by name these days. Turned out he'd been sent with Taz to see if they could rouse DC North, acting on the theory that as nobody had heard from her, she must be ill.

'She's scarpered,' I told them. 'No suitcases or passport here, and some clothes obviously missing.'

I decided not to tell them about the last phone call she'd made. None of their business. I'd wait till I could tell Derek and Alfie.

'What about the phone?' Taz asked. 'Has she left a mobile here? Have you tried the redial button on her landline? Could be interesting to know the last call she made.'

'Prob'ly to a airline,' the plod offered, 'making travel arrangements, like.'

Before I could start saying what a bright idea, Taz had picked up the phone, pressed the redial button, listened and hung up.

'Who are they?' he asked me. 'Do you know this firm of

Someone, Someone and North? Must be to do with Vicky. Same name.'

'Yes,' I had to admit. 'It's a firm of solicitors called Abel, Levi and North. Charles North is acting for that feller calls himself Edward Franklin.'

'What, the cats' meat man?' Taz said, all surprised. 'What can that have to do with Vicky?'

I had to fall back on Alfie's favourite.

'Buggered if I know,' I said.

Taz called in to Shady Lane what he'd found at DC North's flat, and got the message to come straight back.

'What will you do, Greta?' he asked, and I just shrugged and said I supposed I'd have to do as I was told and go home to continue recuperating.

Naturally, I was lying, and being a better driver, I actually got back to the nick before he did. First person I saw was Alfie.

Before he had a chance to start going off at me that I wasn't supposed to be there, I asked him straight out, 'What's occurring, Alfie? Something's new, isn't it? Come on, you may as well tell me.'

'Got no time to stand and chat,' he said, unusually serious for Alfie. 'If you want to know, you'll have to come in the car with me and I'll tell you on the way.'

Normally I'd do anything to avoid being driven by Alfie, who's in line for a prize for being the world's worst driver, but I could smell that there'd been an important break. So I'd even put up with that test of nerves rather than miss what was going on.

Off we went then, Alfie as usual asking me the way before even telling me where we were going. Turned out it was Chelsea. I should have known it! Who lived there? Sadie and James Lee, of course.

'Prob'ly fuss about nothing,' Alfie grumbled, crashing his

gears in a frightening way. 'But Sadie and James Lee were out on bail, you know, and Chelsea nick called Derek today to say they hadn't reported in. So they sent one of their CID to call on them, and he says he can tell there's someone in but they won't answer the door or the phone. Derek's oppo in Chelsea asked what he wanted them to do, and Derek reckons we'll go there ourselves and have a decko.'

I felt a bit let down.

'Is that all?'

'Dunno what else you want,' Alfie grumbled, swerving dangerously round a parked van. 'You've put me off now, I've forgotten where you said we come off the A40. Tell you what,' he added, brightening up as he drove at full speed into Tesco's Hoover Building car park, slammed on the brakes and nearly dislocated our necks, 'bet you're fit enough to drive now, why don't you go the rest of the way?'

That was a relief, but of course before we could set off again Alfie had to pop in to Tesco's to get a bit of nosh.

'Had early breakfast this morning, and might not be able to get much by way of refreshment in Chelsea,' he explained, scattering Kit-Kat crumbs as usual.

I wiped the steering wheel and we were on our way again. Although when Alfie casually mentioned the name of Derek's oppo at Chelsea, I nearly did a bit of Alfie-type driving myself.

'Carruthers?' I went, getting control of myself and the car. 'Nobody's called Carruthers; it's not a real name except in old black and white adventure films. You know, Carruthers is the Englishman who always dresses for dinner in the jungle and ends up being eaten by lions. Decent sort, Carruthers, and all that,' and that was when I discovered that I hadn't quite recovered from my operation, because it still hurt to laugh.

'Can't see what's funny about that, girl,' Alfie mumbled. 'What difference does it make what the feller's name is. Far as we're concerned, he's DI Rex Carruthers, and that's all there is to it.'

Derek was already there when we got to Chelsea nick, and when he saw me I thought he was going to tear me off a strip, but he just scowled and muttered he'd talk to me later. I never did find out why he and Alfie hadn't gone there together, but knowing those two, it was probably something as stupid as Alfie being in the bog and Derek too impatient to wait for him.

Anyway, then we got to meet this famous Carruthers. He was as different from Derek as if Central Casting had looked for an opposite. He was as ugly as Derek was handsome, as tall as Derek was short, and as skinny as Derek was well built. I must say, the contrast made Derek look even more sexy and desirable than ever. But I've got to admit, when it came to brains, it didn't seem there was much to choose between them. And he did have a nice smile, which came out when he was introduced to me.

'Call me Rex,' he beamed at me, and I nearly bust a gut trying not to laugh again. Carruthers was a barmy enough name, without it being teamed with a dog's name. What could his parents have been thinking of? It was lucky he didn't realise I was smothering a bad attack of sniggers. He must have just thought I was returning his big smile and warm handshake with interest.

'Well, Rex was just saying before you two arrived,' Derek said, 'that he thought we should treat this as a siege situation. Two of his men have been observing and neither Sadie nor James Lee has come out, but they believe they've seen someone moving about inside, not too near the windows, of course.'

'Siege? Why siege, Guv?' Alfie asked. 'Why can't we just break in and fish the pair of them out?'

'We don't know what weapons they might have in there,'

DI Carruthers said grimly, 'and surrounding the place with armed SO19 people and challenging them might just bring them out unarmed and safer for all concerned.'

So it was agreed and set up. Meanwhile, apart from some polite intro words to Rex, I hadn't murmured a word. It was weighing on me a bit heavy that I shouldn't really have been there at all. Tell the truth, I was feeling a bit the worse for wear. But I'd rather have dropped in my tracks than admit that to Derek or Alfie. As usual, though, I'd underestimated Derek.

First opportunity he got, he said to me quietly, 'I think you should just slope off home now, Greta, and we'll come and see you later and tell you all about it.'

And for once I wasn't sorry to do as I was told. I told Alfie I'd take his car and leave him to come back to Watford in Derek's, and I'd see them later.

You'd think I'd be upset to miss all the action, but the truth was, it was all I could do to keep my eyes open driving back home, and I couldn't wait to flop down and go fast off as soon as I got in. There was something in this recuperation business, after all, and it wasn't just the medics being officious. Anyway, by the time I woke up it was quite dark and I was so out of it I couldn't remember what time of day it ought to be.

What was that ringing? Was it the alarm to get me up and on the job? No, silly arse, I was on the couch and it was the phone.

Yippee, it was Derek and he wasn't even cross with me for turning up again when he'd specially told me to go home and rest.

'Are you alright, Greta?' he asked, so anxiously that I could feel my face splitting into a big grin of joy. He cares, he cares, I thought, getting all hot with excitement. 'You looked really groggy when you left Chelsea, and we were all worried about you.'

Oh, not so good. Who were the 'all' who were worried about me? Why wasn't Derek right there on my doorstep waiting to hold my hand and stroke my forehead, and any other bits he fancied stroking? How much did he really care? (My usual question, as usual left unanswered.)

Anyway, then the switchback took another swoop upwards as he said, 'Are you well enough for me to come and see you? You might like to know what happened after you left.'

And in a weird echo of Ari, he added, 'Shall I bring you something to eat?'

Still, there the resemblance ended. He arrived with a carrier full of Chinese take-away and a bottle of his favourite Merlot. And while we settled down to stuff ourselves and swig the booze, he filled me in on the Chelsea/Chinese scenario.

Turned out that Rex's fears were justified, and the Lee brother and sister (if that's what they were, which hadn't yet been verified) really had been armed, and had tried to resist. But after a lot of megaphoning and a fairly small exchange of shots, as usual SO19 had done their bit, and the two of them were now in custody.

'Was it a big buzz?' I asked, not trying to hide how sad I was at missing all the excitement. 'I've never been in on a siege situation. Did you feel as if you were in a film or something?'

'No, actually, I know you thought you were missing something special, but in fact it was rather dull. It was mainly hanging about waiting for something to happen. You should know by now, Greta, that police work is like that. Every shift is seven and a half hours' boredom and half an hour more action than you could really do with.'

I thought sadly that that was what my love life was like,

specially where Derek was concerned. But I didn't really feel fit enough to start leaping on him again, although I fancied him as much as ever. I changed the subject.

'Didn't you want to laugh when you found out their DI's name was Rex Carruthers? I mean, Carruthers is bad enough, but Rex! Bet he got teased a lot at school, poor bugger.'

'Well, actually, after it was all over, we had a cup of tea together and a bit of a chat, and it turns out that he's a rather high-class chap, went to public school and all that, and a name like Rex Carruthers wouldn't cause as much hilarity in those circles. Apparently it's an aristocratic name, and it's even spelled in an unusual way – you might like to make a note of it, in case you ever have to write to him or refer to him in writing,' (and can you believe, he actually spelt it out for me) 'it's C-A-R-O-T-H-E-R-S.'

'Oh, I see,' I said, not trying to stop laughing this time, 'you mean CARROT OTHERS.'

I thought Derek would go all snooty on me, but he joined in laughing, and somehow one thing led to another and we ended up in each other's arms. So when we stopped laughing, he kissed me. And it was as perfect as ever, but I really didn't feel strong enough to urge him on. So we just had a bit of a snog, and in case I've never said it before, I want to place on record here and now, that this man was and is the best kisser I've ever had the pleasure with. Not to speak of being the love of my life.

*

What with going to bed in a state of bliss after a lovely long snog with Derek, and this strange need I had recently for lots and lots of sleep, it wasn't till late the next morning that my brain started to get into gear. And even then it took a long shower and a hearty breakfast to wake me up properly. It was round about then that I worked out what had been in the back of my mind all along. There was something they weren't telling me.

Sadie and James Lee had been charged with attempting to pervert the course of justice. I remembered distinctly that there'd been discussion at the time whether it shouldn't have been obstructing the police in their enquiries. They'd been bailed and instructed to report to their local nick every week till their case came up. So far it all made sense.

What didn't add up was, when they failed to report, what was so crucial that a siege situation was called for? SO19 were only called in when there was a really serious crime involved, like a kidnap or hostage situation or some loony popping off a gun at passers-by, or if a known wanted criminal was holed up with an arsenal of weaponry. Something like that, anyway. But when two people on a relatively minor charge just failed to report, all this carry-on didn't make sense. And no responsible officers like Derek and his new pal Rex would call for that sort of action in these circumstances.

So what did everybody else know that I didn't? And why hadn't Derek or Alfie told me the full story?

Chapter 15

Even though I was longing to get back to Shady Lane and find out why SO19 had been called in to winkle Sadie and James Lee out, and anyway I was missing the Job seriously, I decided for once to be sensible and not go in. I could see I could be a serious nuisance hanging around not quite well enough to be of use. And after getting on such good terms with Derek the previous night, I didn't want to spoil things.

So I decided to do a little private sleuthing on my own. I went out to Radlett to Vicky North's flat, and gave a friendly 'Hi' in a 'you-know-me' kind of way to the young cop on duty there before letting myself in the back door again. Of course he'd seen me when he'd arrived there with Taz and I was already there, so he took it for granted that it was OK for me to be there again. Well, he should have asked to see my identification even if he thought he knew me, but I was lucky he was so inexperienced. I nosed about the place again, more thoroughly than I'd had a chance to do when I was there before, but I couldn't find anything helpful.

I decided to do a little door-to-door in the neighbourhood, starting with the other ground floor flat and then going on to the upstairs flats in the little block. There wasn't much chance of finding anything out, but it was worth a try before Alfie got here himself or sent Taz to snoop around a bit more.

What I hadn't expected was to hit lucky at the first go. The front door opposite North's was opened by one of those women who was fighting age and flab without any signs of success. Her four-inch spiky heels and pointy toes must have been killing her, but maybe not as much as the small sparkly top and tight leather mini stopping a long way above her chubby knees. And I could see she'd ladled her make-up on with a spoon. The whole thing was topped off with an up-to-the-minute white blonde hairdo, which might have looked great on a twenty-year-old.

'Can I help you?' she grated without changing expression, and even someone as out of touch with current fashions as I am could see right away that Botox had been much in use there. Maybe she actually wanted to smile, but that's something I'd never know.

I showed her my warrant card and asked myself in. Her flat was done as expensively as North's, but in that minimalist style where there were hardly any chairs and when you found one you wished you hadn't. Still, I sat in the one she offered me, and told her I was after any information she could give me about her neighbour.

'Well!' she said. 'I'm surprised you have to ask. She's one of you lot, after all, isn't she? So you ought to know all there is to know about her.'

Her face didn't change – it probably couldn't – but her body language said clearly, 'Are you going to give me some dirt?'

She leaned towards me so far I was afraid she'd topple right over, what with being a bit top-heavy anyway. And some of her upper body looked as if it was trying to escape from the rest. Couldn't blame it for that. Not a pretty sight, even if she might have thought it was, herself.

'We're very worried about Detective Constable North,' I said, trying to sound all formal and official. 'She's a most conscientious officer, and has always been very punctual and reliable. But now she seems to have disappeared without a word to her superiors. Naturally, we're afraid she may have been the victim of foul play. Can you give me any information which may help in our investigation?'

I felt very pleased with myself about that. I'd tried to sound as much as possible like Derek being his most pompous. Didn't do much good, though. Not at first. Got plenty of words, but not helpful ones.

'Well, I can tell you that while she's been living here she hasn't lived like a young girl should, in my opinion. Nothing like what I was like at her age, I can tell you. I never heard any loud music from her place for one thing, and I never saw any other young people calling on her, not male nor female, and she looked to me like she never did anything but going to work and coming home.'

Well, that was that. I started to thank her, but just when I was trying to ease myself out of this apology for a chair and be polite about her useless information, the flood of words started up again.

Before I could finish my goodbyes, she interrupted, 'But that's not to say she didn't have *any* visitors. One of them was an older man, and I can only hope he was her father, because he was certainly old enough, and I could tell it wasn't anything, you know, of a sexual nature, because he never stayed overnight or even long enough for, you know, a bit of that. But the other man, he was older too, as far as I could tell, but you can't always be sure with them, because he was some sort of Oriental. I *think* he was Chinese, but you never know with them, do you?'

Well, this Mrs Atkins might have been a bad judge when it came to her own appearance, but she was a first-class observer of other people. I got a description of the 'older man' from her, and it was exactly Charles North. Just as good, she was able to tell me how often he came, and how often the Chinese man came, and what the average was of the times they arrived together or separately. She couldn't have had much of a life herself, poor thing, taking so much detailed notice of her neighbour's visitors. I wondered if she kept the same tabs on everyone else in the block. Didn't ask her, of course. She was such a useful witness I even accepted a cup of her disgusting herbal tea. Camomile, I think she said it was.

Shrewdly she said to me while I was sipping it and trying to pretend I enjoyed it, 'It's very good for people who haven't been well. Have you had the flu recently, Sergeant?'

I managed not to blurt out about my operation. I can't stand people who go on about things like that. But after the original shock of what she looked like, I came to the conclusion that Mrs Atkins was quite a nice sympathetic person after all. And I did feel the need to talk to an understanding person sometimes. It was tempting to stay and have a little personal chat, but I resisted. I thanked her and warned her we might ask her to come to Shady Lane to make an official statement, and trudged on upstairs. My luck didn't hold up there. No answers from any of those flats. Still, I hadn't done too badly at first try.

Now the question was, should I go to Shady Lane and tell Derek what I'd discovered. That would mean confessing I'd been poking my nose in again when I was supposed to be lolling around at home, reading magazines and eating grapes and stuff.

But what else could I do? Couldn't go to Charles North's office and ask questions there. Either Derek or Alfie or both of them together would have covered that. And I certainly couldn't keep this new stuff to myself.

Sadly I drove back to Shady Lane, going over how I was

going to answer the latest telling-off I was sure to get from Derek.

Wrong again. He was so delighted with what I told him, he actually forgot I wasn't supposed to be there. And he wasn't half-hearted with his praise, either. I wouldn't call it a generous apology, but probably as near as I was going to get from His Lordship.

'You said all along you didn't trust young Vicky, and you were right. And didn't you even hint at one time that she might be something to do with Charles North, too? I've got to hand it to you, Greta, your instinct was spot-on this time. But the trouble is, we've got all these disconnected pieces of information, and nothing seems to make a whole picture. Or anything like it. You were right about the Chinese link running through everything, but so what? How can we tie up the little murdered Ah Weng So and the disappearing factory where she worked with the Chinese visitor Vicky North had before she did the vanishing trick herself?'

'*And* the Chinese boss Juan Garcia said his murdered friend worked for,' said Alfie, not to be left out, 'and James and Sadie Lee, and the Chinese victim of burglary. And how does that Franklin, or whatever his name is now, fit in? Why should Charles North come and be his brief? How do they even *know* each other?'

Just beating Alfie to it, Derek said, 'Buggered if I know.'

But we didn't laugh, because he looked so serious and fed up. And I felt the same way myself. I could see Alfie wasn't his happiest, either. The worst of it was, none of us could think of any action to take next. Just sitting around Derek's office and talking round and round the whole thing certainly wasn't going to solve anything. We needed some sort of breakthrough.

I went home and had a nap.

The phone woke me up again, and this time it was Ari, calling to ask how I was getting on. I felt like snapping his head off, but that wouldn't have been fair. It wasn't his fault if we'd got bogged down in a complicated case.

'Yes, I'm much better,' I said. 'You can come round with a pizza if you like.'

If he liked! Never any need to ask Ari that. It seemed as if there was nothing in the world he liked better than my company, with or without sex. And I still felt nothing like the with. So it would be pizza and chat only.

Good old reliable Ari, he arrived faster than I would have thought even he could, with the usual supplies of goodies. He put the carrier bag down and gave me a very careful gentle hug and kiss.

'What's up, lovely girl?' he asked. 'Got the convalescent blues?'

So I poured it all out. Not about loving Derek and him not loving me, of course, but all the rest. About how stuck we were with these bits of a puzzle that didn't fit together, and how I kept sneaking about trying to help and getting more information that made it all even more baffling. And how fed up the three of us were about it all.

And how I kept sleeping all the time. Hearing myself telling it all, I ended up feeling even more sorry for myself than I had at the start.

Munching his pizza and slurping his lager, Ari listened all through without saying a word. Even when I'd finished talking, he still didn't make any suggestions. That wasn't like Ari at all. I could see he was turning it all over, but he didn't say anything till we'd finished eating and he'd gone into the kitchen and made us a mug of coffee each.

He plonked my mug in front of me and said, 'Well, lovely girl, let's start off with that Charles North. You've had to deal with him in the past, haven't you? And a right slippy customer he was, too, by what you've told me.'

'I don't think he's just slippery,' I said, 'I think he's a bit barmy, too.'

'What, you mean, mad, bad and dangerous to know?' Ari said. 'Like that Lord Brian?'

This took my mind off the main problem for a moment.

'Lord Brian? Who's he?'

'You know,' Ari said, 'he had a lot to do with Greece, that's how I know about him. Lord Brian, you must have heard of him, lame feller he was, had a friend called Shirley. Funny name for a feller, innit, but he was a poet, and you can never tell with them, can you.'

I didn't have to dig back far into my school days to twig he was talking, for some reason, about Lord Byron and Percy Bysshe Shelley. But when I mentioned to him that he had the names slightly wrong, he just shrugged and said it made no difference, it was just something he'd heard. He was right there. It was absolutely off the subject.

'OK then,' he said, 'let's leave Charles North for a sec. I've got another idea. I'll make up a story to fit all the facts as we know them. Doesn't matter if it's far-fetched, innit. Then you pick holes in it, right? Then we'll try again together. By the way, you left out a strand, dincha. You forgot your old mucker, Jim, the Long-distance Lorry Driver. He come and told you a tale about a Chinese too, didden'e? OK then. Listen up.'

I was so taken up by this new approach I even forgot to tell him about Jim doing so well he had a little fleet of lorries of his own these days. Well, I'd tell him some other time. Because even before Ari started on his theory, I was feeling better. Just the thought of somebody – anybody – trying to make something of this mess, had to be good. And apart from being soppy about me, Ari was no fool.

'No,' he said. 'Wait,' he said. 'Jussa minute,' he said. And then, while I sat quietly fuming at this sudden turn, he paced up and down, muttering to himself. Finally I couldn't stand it.

'What!' I snapped. 'Come on Ari, spit it out, whatever it is. Stop playing hard to get.'

This brought him out of his trance, alright. Even if he didn't know what irony was, he'd have said this was it. For *me* to say that to *him*, after the years of run-around I'd been giving him, was a joke too far. He sat down, looking serious, and I thought he was going to tear me off a strip.

Instead, he said, 'What you never told me was, what did this Charles North's family say? What did his secretary and other people in his office say? Who reported him missing, and when? How did they know he was missing? Was there a note? How do they know he never just done a bunk?'

It wasn't often that Ari made me feel a fool, but this was one of the times. I had to admit that I didn't know the answers to any of his questions.

'Well, why don't you just ring Alfie and ask him?'

Ari seemed to think it was that simple. All it did was make me feel even more stupid. So I took a deep breath, forgetting all about how it hurt my operation, and told him the truth.

'See, Ari, the thing is, none of our lot did any of that interviewing. Turns out that this feller he was acting for, this Franklin or whatever he says his name is now, he rang North to have a word about his case, and his office told him he was missing. So he said, had they told the police, and they said, yes, the local station was on the case. Got to hand it to him, he was sharp enough to ask what station it was. Then he told Derek, who got on to, Bow Street I think it was, and they faxed over a report to him. Course, Derek couldn't tell them we've got suspicions about North being tied up with all this other stuff, all he could say was, he's representing a prisoner we're holding. So they just sent over the bare bones.'

'There you are then!' Ari said, full of himself again. 'That's your answer, innit. What you've got to do is get all them people properly interviewed, like, probing, you know, to find out more of what you need to know about how much North is in all this muddle you're trying to sort out. Like, I'm not all that gone on your boss, but he knows his job, and I bet he'll winkle out more stuff than those Bow Street cops what think they're just clocking up a MISPER.'

And he sat back, well pleased with himself. But I wasn't going to let him off trying to solve the case so easily.

'But you said you were going to make up a story to fit all the facts as we know them. Doesn't matter if it's far-fetched, you said, it'll make a starter, then we can pick holes in it together and try again. That's what you said,' I said, all tetchy and irritable, 'and where's all your theory now?'

'Alright then, don't get so moody,' he said nervously. 'I'll have a go.'

He took a deep breath, leaned forward, took my hand and gazed into my eyes. Oh no, I thought, he's going to start all that romantic business again to try to take my mind off work. But I was wrong. He was really going to try to help.

'What about this,' he started. 'This Charles North, he's like a junior partner in a racket being run by the Chinese. And he signed up his niece, this Vicky North, to join the gang. And what the Chinese do is, they smuggle Chinese into this country to work as slaves in a dodgy food factory. The illegals, they can't do nothing but stay where they're put, because they can't speak the lingo here and they're told if they're caught they'll spend the rest of their lives in jail eating foreign food and never seeing the light of day. Or something like that. So these factories, they're like lightweight temp'ry buildings, because they don't need no machinery, because with slaves you can do it all by hand. No automation, see. So they buy up rotten condemned animals what should have been burnt, and bits chopped off from people from hospitals, and all horrible stuff like that, innit, and flog it off cheap to these animal food people.'

He had to stop. I could see why. He'd made himself feel sick making up this story. His face had gone a funny colour, and his eyes starting watering. I patted his hand and gave him a little kiss. I could see he needed a bit of encouragement.

'I know it all sounds too horrible to be true,' I said. 'But it does fit the facts so far. And I suppose you're going to say that Ah Weng So got murdered because they were afraid she might put us on their track? And James and Sadie Lee are part of the gang?'

'Right,' Ari said, making a quick recovery, 'and I tell you what else. This head Chinese, whoever he is, doesn't only do the business with the illegals, innit. He's got a burglary business going too, see. That's where Juan Garcia's friend come in, poor little bugger. Then, there's your friend Jim and what he told you. They didn't just try to get him in the racket, did they? No,' he said, full of it by now, 'I'll tell you what else. They said they've got police connections all over the place, didenthey? They planted that Vicky North to take the fast-track at Hendon to keep them in the picture if the cops know anything about them and what they're up to, and I bet you they've got little Vicky Norths all over the country in cop-shops, spying on us!'

And he beamed at me, thrilled with himself. Last thing in the world I'd want him to know was that what he took for me giving him back a loving smile was really me trying not to pee myself with choking back a big laugh. Well, he *had* said his story would be far-fetched. But he hadn't said how ridiculously far his exotic Greek imagination would take him. Still, I had to hand it to him, he'd really had a go. My only problem now was how to knock holes in his daft theory without hurting his feelings too much.

Keeping a tight hold on my voice, I asked him, 'So what do you suppose has happened to Charles and Vicky North now, then?'

'Obvious,' he said, now in full swing and believing his own mad guesses, 'they looked like being sussed out, so they done away with them, in case they give the whole game away, innit.'

'If you're right,' I said, still trying to go along with it, 'that means we'll never find the bodies. But how are we going to put all this to the test?'

Ari shrugged.

'Not my problem, lovely girl,' he said, 'I done my bit, innit. Well, got to go. Early turn tomorrow.'

He gave me a lovely loving kiss, and was gone. That left me with a lot to think about. But I found that instead of bending the great Pusey brain to the big problem, I was wondering why it was so comforting when Ari called me 'lovely girl' but still so annoying when Alfie called me 'girl'. None of it kept me awake, though.

But it must have been in my head, in some compartment or other, because I had the most terrible dreams. I hardly ever dream, or if I do I don't remember anything when I wake up. This was so disgusting, though, that even after I'd got up and showered and dressed and everything, I still felt too sick to have any breakfast. It was so detailed and the colours were so real that I kept seeing it all, going round in my head.

Even now I can't bear to think of it in detail, but what it

was about was Charles and Vicky North being processed in the dog food factory. I blamed Ari for his theory about their Chinese boss doing away with them, but it was really down to my own imagination working out what he'd have done so that the bodies couldn't be found.

I had to do something to wipe it out. I didn't feel fit enough for karate or cycling or roller-blading, and I've never been much of a one for swimming. So physical activity was out. The only thing then was to go to Shady Lane and take a chance on getting an earful from Derek about waiting for the Med Officer to give me the OK to go back to work.

Then having psyched myself up for that, I was disappointed when neither Derek nor Alfie was in the office. Taz was, though.

'They've gone up to Bow Street,' he said. 'But I thought you were on the sick-list, Greta.'

'Don't you start, young Taz,' I snapped. 'I get enough of that from those two. I suppose they've gone to find out more about the missing Charles North. Any news of Vicky?'

'No, only that her neighbour has confirmed that it was Charles North who was her most regular visitor. They showed her photographs of some Chinese men, but she couldn't help there. She said they all looked the same to her. So that wasn't much help.'

He sighed and went quiet, but instead of going back to his computer screen, he just sat and looked at me all doggy-eyed and sort of devoted looking. Well, it had taken me long enough to stop Ari doing those soppy looks, and I didn't see why I had to put up with it from young Taz, so I sloped off to the canteen.

The pictures in my head were beginning to fade a bit, so I managed a decent breakfast after all. And I spun it out right till Alfie came in. I knew he'd make straight for the canteen when they got back from Bow Street or wherever else they'd been, and I'd rather catch him on his own than face Derek, who'd probably be in his worst mood. So I got him some grub and while he was stuffing his face, I asked him what progress.

'No progress,' he said, talking with his usual mouthful, 'just verifying and cross-checking.' He washed his food down with a good gulp of tea, and went on a bit more clearly, 'Charles North has disappeared alright. They found his car half-way between his office and his home. No sign of foul play. All neatly locked up, legally parked in a quiet side street, clean and tidy. No clues, no fingerprints, no forensics of any kind. He's just gone.'

'And what about Vicky?'

'Ah, now, that's different. Looks as if she packed and done a bunk. What we don't know is, if she had another passport and she's gone abroad somewhere, or she's still in this country. That's in hand, but it's my view we'll no more find a trace of her than we will of her uncle. Might just as well have been kidnapped by aliens, the two of them. I'll have another of them rock cakes, Greta, if you're treating. Not as good as my Betty's, but they fill a space.'

'Space,' I said. 'Is that where you think Vicky and Charles North are now?'

'No,' he said, stuffing a whole rock cake in his mouth and talking round it, 'more likely in that mystery portable factory we're chasing.'

I felt myself go pale. Not just me and Ari, but Alfie too! Maybe there really was something in this mad theory, not just my nightmare.

Of course, wouldn't you know it, Derek chose just this moment to walk in.

'You're looking very pale, Greta,' were his first words. 'I hope this is just a social call, and you're not thinking of coming back on duty yet.'

Normally I'd be thrilled he even noticed if I was pale or

flushed, but this time it didn't seem to matter. I'd started to feel sick again.

I'd never liked Charles North, in fact we'd all agreed that he was the slimiest brief of all the scumbags we'd met in our line of work. And I'd made no secret of the fact that I had no time for Vicky North, either. I'd done my best to make her life difficult, and the more Derek had seemed to try to help her, the more I'd tried to give her a bad time.

But what some of us seemed to be thinking might have happened to the pair of them, that was a fate we wouldn't have wished on the worst villain we had to deal with, dead or alive. The worst of it was, it made sense in a gruesome kind of way.

'If, *if*, Vicky had something to do with all this stuff that's going down,' I managed to stammer out, 'do we think she was planted in the police to pass information back to her uncle – if Charles North *was* her uncle, that is.'

'Yes,' Derek said, grim-faced. 'It looks as if that was the case. Although it doesn't make a lot of sense when you come to think about it.'

'Well then,' I said. 'Do you remember what Jim Robinson reported that Chinese feller said to him when he refused to take any illegals through the Tunnel? He said they get information from inside the police all over England.'

At least that got the first laugh of the day.

'What!' Alfie said, laughing so hard that some of the food fell out of his mouth. 'What d'you mean? That little Vicky Norths have been planted in every cop-shop in the country? Come on, girl, sounds like you need a bit longer convalescence before you come back to work.'

And even Derek was laughing a bit, though not as unappealingly as Alfie, naturally, because at least he didn't have a mouthful of food.

Chapter 16

Wasn't I just glad to see young Taz rushing into the canteen to put an end to all this fun at my expense. Specially when we heard his message.

'Mr Moon thought you ought to know about this, sir,' he said to Derek. 'Looked like it was nothing to do with us, but Mr Moon, he put two and two together, and he thinks it's all to do with us. Very much so,' he added, looking round at me and Alfie to make sure we were paying proper attention to his important news.

'Come on then, lad, spit it out,' Alfie encouraged.

'Five homeless taken to Watford General with some sort of poisoning, and one died in the ambulance,' Taz went dramatically, milking it for all he was worth. So far he could see none of us was very impressed, so he rushed on, falling over his words in his hurry to amaze us. 'But one of them, sir,' he was now speaking only to Derek, 'one of them was still conscious. And *he* told the ambulance men, before he passed out too, that they'd all been eating dog food. Not in tins. Got it loose from the pet food shop; the owner said it was fresh in that day but he'd give it to them as an act of charity, like. Course, they'd made out to him they had a couple of dogs to feed and they couldn't afford to buy them anything.'

He stopped for breath, and Derek prompted him, 'And the Super thought it might link up with one of our cases, did he?'

Taz had run out of words. He just nodded dumbly while the three of us looked at each other, all thinking hard.

‘Come on then, Alfie,’ Derek said, ‘we’d better get over to the hospital and see if we can find a link between these vagrants and what we’ve already got on our plates.’

Nobody except me seemed to notice he’d accidentally made a very bad joke, so I swallowed it and said, ‘What about me? Can’t I come too?’

‘I have to remind you, Sergeant,’ Derek said in his most bossy formal voice, ‘that you are still on sick leave and should not even be here on these premises. Go home, Greta, and get out of our hair. Come on Alfie, let’s go.’

Taz and I looked at each other.

‘Are you going?’ he asked.

‘No,’ I said, ‘I’m coming back into the office with you, even if I have to just sit and watch you catching up with your paperwork. It’s the only way I can keep in touch with everything that’s going on.’

‘No need to watch me, I’ve got a good book you might like a look at. Do you like crime novels?’

‘You bet,’ I said, ‘unless they’re about those pain-in-the-arse women detectives who go for five-mile runs every morning before having an hour in the gym and a brisk cold shower before they’ve even thought about breakfast.’

‘Why, you mean to say you don’t do all that, Greta?’ Taz had the good sense to laugh while asking this daft question, otherwise he would have got a dusty answer.

Or even a thick ear.

Then he got serious, and said, ‘Do you think there’s any connection between our case and that business in Morecambe that time with the Chinese cockle pickers? It seemed to me as if the same people might have been involved.’

I didn’t want to stick my neck out any more, after Derek and Alfie laughing at me for suggesting nationwide infiltration of all our police forces, so I just shrugged and said, all off-hand, 'Your guess is as good as mine, Taz. So where's this good book you offered me to look at while I'm sitting around here?'

Well, he gave me this big fat book of nearly seven hundred pages to see if I fancied reading it, and I started leafing through it. For some reason, it fell open at a page where I read this:

He had recognised early on that educational achievement and liberal humanism were not exactly episematic qualities in the still very traditional police force. A common soldier may have a field marshal's baton hidden in his knapsack, but he was never going to get the chance to wield it if he didn't learn the language of the barrack room.

Naturally Derek had a dictionary in his office, so I used it to find out what I'd just read. I got the general message (one that Derek had to learn the hard way on his climb up the ladder) but came to the conclusion that it wasn't exactly my sort of reading matter. I've never fancied books that make you keep going to the dictionary to find out what they're on about, and then you see they're just taking a poncy way of saying something that everybody already knows. No wonder it was such a long book. The writer was too keen on showing off for my liking.

I handed it back to Taz with a mutter of 'Thanks but no thanks' and wandered back up to the canteen for another cup of tea and a heavy think. Although it didn't need a great brain to figure out that the poisoned people Derek and Alfie had gone to see at Watford General must tie up with our poisoned pet food and Chinese slave labour factory cases. The real question was, where did we go from there?

At last I got an idea. This made me feel as if maybe I really was coming to the end of this boring convalescence. Maybe I'd better make an appointment with the Station Med Officer to get the OK to come back to work officially, instead of sneaking in and getting chucked out all the time. Still, that was by the way.

The idea that struck me was, why not go back through all my notebooks right from the beginning of all this and see if there was anything we'd overlooked? This was what I'd got Vicky North to do at one point, and it seemed like a good idea to follow my own advice now. Except I wasn't going to put it all on computer like she'd done. Just reading it all through would do.

Now then, what exactly was the beginning? Was it when I found Ah Weng So in labour in that doorway in the middle of the night, or when I saw Juan Garcia selling dodgy silver in the car boot sale? Anyway, I got out my whole pile of notebooks, shoved them in a big evidence bag, and sloped off home with the lot.

Turned out this was more gripping stuff than any of those big heavy novels like Taz offered me, and either it was as exciting as I thought or I was really recovering, because I didn't fall asleep through all the hours it took to read. The first thing that struck me was how easy it was for things to fall into place when you looked back at them.

For instance, the time when Vicky suddenly got four flat tyres and had to be rescued. Of course, that was a delaying tactic which she'd fixed up with the factory people in Nasty! They'd had to have time to pack up and move on, bribe the villagers, clear the air of the smell, all before we got back to investigate further. Still, that was by the way.

Two real leads I'd lost sight of: talking to Juan Garcia again, and having a really tough interview with Mr and Mrs Wing. I remembered now how suspicious I'd become of the Wings after he'd been bashed up and she'd suddenly decided to explain the difficulties of accurate translation to me. Before that, I'd been really taken with them, specially Mr Wing, who seemed a dear little person to me at the time. But other things, more pressing, had arisen, and I'd almost forgotten all about them.

I was getting a bit more cautious, though, about taking things up all by myself. I phoned Taz at the station.

'Want to come on a little visit with me?' I asked, thinking, well, he's keen on me, he'll say yes to anything I want. Wrong. He was no Ari, who'd do whatever I asked him without a word of argument. Taz wanted to know who, what, where, why, had it been cleared with the Inspector, and all that. So I said, never mind, I'd go by myself, and then he must have got the wind up, because he suddenly changed his tune and said he'd come and pick me up right away and I could fill him in on the way to wherever we were going.

Before he got there, it occurred to me what a long explanation I'd have to give him to put him in the picture, and what a short drive it would be from my place to the Wings, so by the time he arrived I had a pot of coffee brewing. I sat him down with a mug of full strength and a biscuit and gave him a complete background about where the Wings fitted into things and why I'd started to worry about them and then forgot. By the time he'd finished his coffee and I'd finished talking, he was as keen to have a word with them as I was. So off we went.

Mr Wing's office was really a shop, only of course he had nothing to make a display of, so he just had blinds and his name and occupation painted on the window. It all looked well and truly shut. It had that sort of dusty neglected look that places have when there's been nobody there for a long time. Just the same, we rang the bell and banged on the door for a bit, then we found the way round to the back and had a go at that.

When I'd been there previously, I'd gone through the shop

and up the stairs, but of course there was an outside stairway at the back, which was to get up to their flat without going through the shop. Taz and I tooled up those stairs, and I had to admit to myself that I wasn't as fit as I thought I was, and got a bit puffed by the time we got to the top. Anyway, we rang and banged and tried to look through windows, but no luck.

If I'd been on my own I'd have gained entry the way I did to Vicky North's flat, but I couldn't very well do a breaking and entering with a young cop with me. So I suggested we try the neighbours. We went down and round to the front, and took a next-door shop each.

I was lucky with mine – a nice friendly plump lady who sold what used to be called haberdashery, but now it's just handiworks or something like that. Embroidery stuff and knitting wools and patterns and sewing things and all that. Mrs Patel, her name was, and she was keen for a chat. I could see why. There was no great rush of customers lining up to buy what she was offering. It was a wonder she could make a living. Still, none of my business.

'It was so unusual,' she said. 'Whenever they've been going away in the past, they've told me beforehand, given me their keys, asked me to pop in to see everything's all right, water the plants, you know, like neighbours always do. They did the same for me. But this time, I never even saw them go. I hadn't seen them for a day or so, but you know how it is, sometimes you just miss each other, but then the milkman came and asked me if they were away. So we went together to see if we could get an answer, then I came back and rang them, and they didn't even have their answering machine on. I couldn't understand it. And it's the middle of school term, and as a rule they wouldn't dream of taking the children away when it's not holiday time.'

She paused for breath, and I asked, 'When was this that

you realised they'd gone? Can you tell me an exact date?'

'Oh no, not exact,' she said, 'but it would be about two weeks ago now. I think that's how long. It must have been soon after Mr Wing came out of hospital. Did you know about his accident? He was in a bad state. And that's another thing, I don't think he was fit to drive.'

'Where do they usually keep their car? Do you know if it's gone?'

'Oh yes, if the car was still there I'd have been on to you lot right away. I mean, a whole family missing and their car still there, I'd have suspected foul play, wouldn't you? As it is, I've been wondering whether to tell the police. But what could I tell them? It's not against the law to go away without telling your neighbour, is it?'

I'd been making notes like mad, and now I looked up from my notebook and saw that this poor lady was very upset. It had been a bit thick of me not to realise that it really was a worry to her, and she was glad that she'd found someone responsible to pour it all out to.

'Don't worry, Mrs Patel,' I told her, 'now that you've explained it all, we'll take it up. You don't think they've come to any harm, do you?'

She was quiet for a while, and I could see she was making up her mind whether to tell me something else. So I kept my mouth shut and waited. Wouldn't you know it, though, just as she started to speak, Taz came marching in, saying, 'My lot couldn't tell me a thing, said they kept themselves to themselves.'

I gave him a hard look and he shut up, but it had been enough to put Mrs Patel off her stroke. Then I realised there was something else I'd nearly overlooked. I couldn't believe that I could get so out of practice of spotting things in such a short time.

'You mentioned the children, Mrs Patel. I only knew Mr

Wing as our official interpreter, so I didn't know they had any children. Can you tell me about them?'

She brightened up.

'Oh yes, they had two girls and two boys, and they were real little smashers. Not just good looking, I don't mean, but lovely manners and so friendly. Always popping in here to ask if I needed any errands, or just for a chat. It never gets very busy in here, you see, and they knew I got lonely sometimes…'

Her voice sort of tailed away as she must have realised in the same moment that I did, that she was talking about them in the past. As if they were dead, or at least gone for good. Her chubby brown face went pale, and her eyes filled.

'What do you think could have happened to them, Sergeant?' she asked in a shaky voice.

'I'm sure there's nothing to worry about,' I said in my most efficient police voice. 'If anything had happened to them, a road accident or that sort of thing, we'd know and we'd have come to you before this, looking for relatives and the like. People do go off suddenly sometimes, you know, even if it's unusual for them. Maybe they've gone to visit relatives in another part of the country, or the world even, or just decided that Mr Wing needed a long convalescence after his "accident", and thought they'd better take the children with them.'

Looked as if I'd at least half convinced her, because she started to pull herself together a bit. But she still didn't tell me the other thing she'd thought of. That about wound it up: she knew Mrs Wing had relatives in Chinatown in London, and Mr Wing's family were all still in China, but she couldn't give us any more information than that, so we thanked her and sloped off.

When we got in the car, Taz said, 'Well, you did a lot better than I did. My lot was positively hostile. Didn't speak to the Wings, didn't like Chinese people, didn't like the fact that next door on the other side there's an Asian lady, took no notice of offending me in the meantime, just couldn't get rid of me fast enough. Man called out "Good riddance" as I left and I couldn't tell if he meant me or the Wings. It was a greengrocers, and I hope all his apples go rotten.'

This was strong stuff from usually mild and quiet Taz, and I could tell his feelings were hurt. Not just by the racist greengrocer, but by the fact that I'd done better than he had. Poor Taz just wanted to make a good impression on me, and it never came off.

When we got to my place I asked him in, but I expect he could tell it was just politeness, so he said he hoped we could talk it all over tomorrow, and drove off. I wasn't sorry, because I wanted to think over what I'd heard. I remembered that the Wings had been talking of trying to adopt poor little Ah Weng So's baby, but I'd had no idea that they already had four children of their own. This made me re-think my suspicions of them, but I still wondered about their possible connection with the main Chinese gang. What should I call them? Triad?

I wrote up my notes and went to bed early, still turning it all over in my head.

But next morning something happened that nearly made me forget all the questions about the missing Wings.

In with the usual junk mail, the postman brought me a personal letter. Hand-written. I never get personal letters. I don't know anyone to write to, so nobody writes to me. And this was an airmail one, and I certainly don't know anyone abroad. I turned it round and round in my hands, peering at it, before I got a knife from the kitchen and carefully slit it open.

I looked at the end first, to see if it was from anyone I'd ever heard of. It certainly was and I certainly had.

It was from Vicky North.

Chapter 17

'Dear Greta
I know you never wanted me to call you that, but there's nothing you can do about it now, is there? See, I'm in Antofagasta, which is a very nice town on the coast of Chile. And in case you've never heard of it, that's fine, because I don't want to be anywhere you know anything about. Like Colombia, for example. Surprised? I bet you didn't realise I knew so much about your past cases, and about Juan Garcia and where he came from.'

I didn't know at this stage whether I wanted to go on reading or rush to the atlas to find out the exact whereabouts of Chile and even Antofagasta, if such a place existed and wasn't just something Vicky had made up to confuse me. I went on reading.

'Don't start looking Antofagasta up with the idea that you'll come out here to find me, Greta. I've got a different name and a whole new identity, and anyway by the time you got here I'd be looking so different my own mother wouldn't know me. Or my dear Uncle Charles, who's probably been fed to the fishes by now.

'I know how you hate not knowing what's going on, so this is the only reason for this letter. Believe it or not, I really liked you and wanted you to like me. I never really understood why you didn't. You seemed to take against me long before you could have had any suspicions about me, that I'd been planted. See, we've got similar backgrounds, and I always wanted to tell you that, but

you never gave me a chance. The difference was that my mother gave me to her brother Charles and his wife as soon as I was born, so when she knocked herself off with an overdose (just like yours, right?) I didn't find out till years later. Of course nobody had any idea who my dad was (choice of many whose names she didn't bother to ask, probably) and I'd always been told Uncle Charles and Aunt Sophie had adopted me, but the details came much later.'

By this time I was just hopping mad. How could she have found out all those facts about my mother and my birth and my Gran bringing me up and all that? I'd always been so careful who I told, and nobody who knew could have said anything to Vicky North or Charles North. So where could she have got all this stuff?

'You're probably wondering how I got all this information about you. Well, you see, the organisation that Uncle Charles worked for is very thorough, and even though they didn't always tell us foot-soldiers everything that was going down, they made sure we knew all about the people we were going to be "working" with. I mean, for example, were you aware that your beloved boss, the lovely little Derek Michaelson, was married and only got divorced when he left his wife for that gorgeous city whiz-kid, Erica? Who soon got fed up with him and chucked him out? Still, that's all by the bye.

'The main thing is, you want to know about me and what I was doing with you lot in Shady Lane. Well, when I got involved with Charles North's employer, no one could tell in advance that I'd be posted to Shady Lane. I was just sent to get police training at Hendon, put into the fast track and told that wherever I ended up being posted, I was to keep Charles informed of everything that the cops knew and didn't know, and to find out all that I could

about every ongoing case, and use my initiative to impede any investigations that I could without arousing suspicion. I certainly didn't realise at the time that I was one of many, and there were little Victoria and Victor Norths being posted all over the country. And in some cases, more than one of us in a police station, not necessarily being informed about each other.

'So you'll want to find out what it was all about? Well, naturally, your guess was right. You're generally a good guesser, although we did have records of some of your real bloopers in the past. We were (and I suppose the Organisation still is) about lots of things: people smuggling, illegal factories, burglary, you name it. Every sort of organised crime, and all flowing from Charles North's boss. I can't tell you his name. And I wouldn't even if I could. But I can tell you for a fact that he's a Chinese gentleman who speaks perfect English because he had a top-notch private education in England. I've got no idea what Charles did to upset him, but as soon as I heard that my poor uncle was for the chop (and I'm not going to tell you how I found that out), I used the plans I'd had ready for a long time, and got out fast.

'Now you're nearly as much in the picture as I am, so it's good-bye and I'm really truly sorry we were never friends. When I made that suggestion about changing your appearance and going to my hairdresser, I was really trying to help you to get the handsome Derek to see how attractive you can look if you try. I honestly do admire you, Greta, and I hope you get your man ***and*** *the promotion you want.*

'The woman previously known as Detective Constable Victoria North.

'PS Just a thought: why don't you take a good hard look at Taz.'

I sat down with a thump, and only realised then that I'd been reading all this walking up and down. I was so angry I couldn't think what to do with myself. I tried a bit of screaming and throwing things, but it didn't help. Finally I went into the kitchen and broke a couple of plates and jumped on them. That made no difference, either. Trouble was, I couldn't tell exactly what it was that I was so furious about. That she had so much info about me, and more about Derek than I'd been able to find out in all this time we'd been working together? That she'd fooled us all? That she'd got away? That she'd had the cheek to write that letter? That she pretended she'd liked me all along and wanted to be my friend?

Finally I calmed down and started to think a bit straighter, and I realised that what was really upsetting me was that I could see I'd have to show her letter to Derek and Alfie and probably Mr Moon as well, and I really didn't want any of them to read the bit about how I felt about Derek. I did mind that she'd sussed it, but I cared much more about it being told to everyone. But it would have to be done. Probably.

Even then I didn't go rushing off to Shady Lane waving this letter under Derek's nose. I made myself another mug of coffee and sat down to have a good hard think. Because another angle had occurred to me. It was obvious, really.

As soon as Mr Moon read this confession from Vicky North, he would simply have to pass the whole thing over to Scotland Yard. Even taking into account that we didn't have to believe every single word of it, the possibility that there actually was a nationwide conspiracy of infiltration of every police service in the country *including the Met* had to be taken seriously. So this would no longer be a Watford case, or even a Hertfordshire case, but a national case. And we'd have no more to do with it. This wonderful, mysterious, baffling, exciting case would be taken away from us. The best and worst case

I'd ever been on. All they'd want from us would be reports, reports and more reports. But no action.

The more I thought about it, the less reason I could see for showing Vicky's letter to anyone at all. After all, it was a private letter from her to me. It wasn't evidence. Maybe it wasn't even a confession. It could be just a whole work of fiction, all made up to have a go at me. I had to admit I'd been a bit hard on her, so why shouldn't she give me a smack in the eye back. I looked at the envelope again. True, it did seem to have been posted in Chile, but what did that prove?

I cleared up the broken plates and made myself another mug of coffee. I wished I had someone to talk this over with, but there was no one. The only person I'd ever been able to talk to about my problems and troubles since my Gran died was Ari. And I certainly couldn't show him the letter or even tell him about it. It had too much stuff in it that I wouldn't want him to know. So I had to argue it out with myself. And anyway, being a straight-up sort of guy, he'd naturally say I must do the right thing and pass it on to my superiors. Also, having an excellent memory, he'd remind me that Jim, the Long-distance Lorry Driver had given us a hint of the national extent of this case when he'd told us about being approached to smuggle illegals through the Channel Tunnel.

Finally I came to a sort of conclusion. There was no hurry to decide what to do about the letter. Even if I did hand it over to Derek and Mr Moon, they'd have no way of knowing when I'd got it. So I could take my time. Think about it for a day or two. Or, say, a week.

In the meantime I got on the blower and made an appointment with the Station Medical Officer for my final check-up and OK to get back to work officially, instead of sneaking in and being chucked out all the time.

That would give me a breathing space to argue it all out

with my conscience. Why conscience? Well, it could be seen as a duty to hand the letter over. Or I could just chuck it away. Of course, there was also that mysterious PS to think about. What could Vicky have meant about taking a good hard look at Taz? Was she suggesting that he was one of their plants at Shady Lane? She did say in her letter that sometimes there was more than one of them in one Station, and they didn't know each other. But why should she suspect him of being one of her lot? Or was she just having a bit of a stir to get us looking in the wrong direction? I thought back to all the contact I'd had with Taz since I first met him, and couldn't think of a single reason to be suspicious of him. Not like the way I'd felt about Vicky from the start. I'd always known there was something fishy about her. Little skinny rat.

*

There's no such thing as coincidence. So when Ari phoned to ask if he could see me that night for a serious talk, I knew it couldn't be about my problem. But it was a bit of a worry, because Ari didn't usually go in for serious stuff. Except when he was talking about marriage, of course. Oh hell, I hoped it wasn't that again. I had enough to worry about without fending off more proposals from Ari.

Well, in a way it was. But not exactly like it had been so far.

'See, lovely girl,' Ari said, munching on our usual giant pizza, 'you know I love you and I always will. But my ma is right when she says it's time I settled down, innit. And if you've really made up your mind it's not worth me waiting for you, I've got to do something else.'

Something else? I thought. What else was there, if you

wanted to get married and you couldn't get a yes? I soon found out.

'It's Marion,' Ari said.

'What? That Marion Sestina again?' I burst out. As if I didn't have enough to worry about, without that little creep coming into our lives again.

'Yes, well, see, she keeps phoning me and that,' Ari said. I could tell he wasn't feeling exactly comfortable.

'What do you mean, "and that"?' I snarled. 'You haven't been having it away with both of us, have you, you dirty dog?'

'No, course not,' Ari was quite put out that I should think such a thing. 'But you know how she first got in touch with us, over that case at the Town Hall. She still works there, by the way.'

'I don't give a toss where she bloody well works,' I interrupted.

'No, but, you remember, she was sending emails through my cousin George and his Internet computer what he's such a whiz at, innit. Well, she's been sending me emails and George showed some to my ma, see, and she said, "Who's this girl what's so keen on you that she doesn't care who reads about it." '

'So you think if you can't have me, you might as well have someone who wants you,' I said bitterly. 'Even if she's not a nice Greek girl like your ma has always wanted for a daughter-in-law.'

I wouldn't have taken on so much about it in the usual run of things, but I'd had a difficult enough day, what with that little rat Vicky giving me problems. And now it looked as if I was going to lose Ari. Not that I loved him or anything, but we did have a very nice kind of, well, I suppose it was a relationship.

I'd been so busy being offended, I hadn't noticed how Ari

was feeling. But at this moment I looked at him, really looked properly, and I was shocked to see his eyes were full of tears. Ari didn't cry. True, he was emotional, which was only proper since he was a Greek, but crying was a bit over the top. Still, I suppose I was flattered in a way.

'Why can't we just go on the way we always have?' I asked him, in a much nicer voice. 'What's all this about getting married all the time? Is it just because your ma wants grandchildren, is that it?'

'No, lovely girl,' he said miserably, 'it's because I love you and I want to marry you, but you never will, so I've got to get over you, innit. And Marion's dead keen…'

His voice trailed off and he looked at me like a puppy waiting to be kicked. What could I do? I did the obvious. And it took all night. I was dead pleased to notice that I'd recovered enough from the hacking-about I'd got at the hospital to be able to perform as well as previously. I wondered if I should mention this to the Med Officer when I went for my check-up and sign-off, then I decided best not.

And when Ari got up first thing next morning because he was on early shift, there wasn't another word about marrying or getting over me or Marion Sestina, or his mother wanting grandchildren. He brought me a cup of coffee and gave me a lovely smooch, and said, 'Want to go out for a special dinner tonight at my uncle's place in Camden Town, lovely girl?'

I was so pleased I couldn't say a word, just nodded and smiled and gave him a big hug. So that was all right. One problem settled, and one more to go.

But the one still to be solved, that was really serious. Even if I laughed off anything Vicky North said about how I felt about Derek, the big question was about what it would mean to all of us if I handed her letter over to Mr Moon. First of all, it was obvious it was my duty. And I've always prided myself on being as straight as my grandfather, Sergeant Pusey, who I'd never met, had been. Old-timers at Shady Lane still spoke of him with respect as well as liking, and I wanted to be in the same league. But what would it do to our self-respect if we lost that whole big case, with all its ins and outs, that we'd been tracking through all its difficulties and complications? And there was no question about it, Mr Moon would have no choice but to call in Scotland Yard once he read what Vicky said about the infiltration of police services all over the country. Whether he believed it or not.

There again, Derek and Alfie had laughed at me when I'd suggested that moles had been planted amongst the police all over England, but it turned out that I'd been right after all, and they'd have to laugh on the other side of their faces when they found that out. One in the eye for them? Why should I care about that? There were more important things to think about.

Just a minute, that was the other angle. Why should I – or Mr Moon or anyone – believe a single word that Vicky had written? Come to that, how did we know that letter really was from her at all?

I groaned and made myself another mug of coffee. I could see where I was going with this. I was going to have to come clean to Derek and Mr Moon and let them decide what action should follow.

Maybe after all Mr Moon might say, well, perhaps it's just a wind-up and we should take no notice but carry on as before.

Maybe. Or maybe not. But finally I'd decided what to do.

As soon as I'd seen the Med Officer and got the OK to get back to work, I'd ask Derek to come with me to see Mr Moon.

Right. That was definite.

Chapter 18

It didn't help that I had a bit of a barney with the Med Officer.

'Light duties only,' he said.

'Come on, Doc,' I said, 'you know I'm fit for full duties. Look at me. Picture of health, aren't I?'

'We're not talking about pictures here, Sergeant,' he said, all tight-lipped. 'You're lucky I'm not putting you down for desk duties only. You must know as well as I do that you're not fit enough to start chasing villains up and down, or having to wrestle with them to take them into custody. No, it's two weeks at least of light duties, then I'll have another look at you and decide if you're fit.'

'Well, I'll make bl– I mean, I'll make quite sure of it, *sir*,' I snarled. 'I'll get right back to my karate and roller-blading and cycling. Then you'll see how fit I am!'

I tried to make that sound like a threat without being too insolent to a superior officer, and bounced out. I didn't really feel all that spring-heeled, but blowed if I was going to let him see that.

So I was able to breeze into Derek's office waving the MO's bit of paper but with Vicky North's letter still safely in my pocket, and say to him and Alfie, 'Well, aren't you both lucky! You've got me back again!'

All businesslike, Derek proceeded to put me in the picture. They'd got the addresses of his customers from Edward Franklin, and got them all closed down by joint action with the RSPCA, who'd notified vets. One of the homeless who'd eaten the muck being passed off as pet food had died, and the others seemed to be recovering. Sadie and James Lee were in custody, remanded without bail. They'd had to kick Juan Garcia out, although he'd kept asking for protective custody, because as Alfie said, we didn't run a hostel for unsuccessful crooks. He'd gone back to Mr and Mrs Slipworthy's place, and Alfie had promised to keep an eye on him.

'I get on well with them two Slipworthys,' he said with an innocent smile.

I wondered if Mr Slipworthy guessed how friendly Alfie had been with Sleazy Sue Slipworthy while he'd still been inside. But Alfie could take care of himself.

There were more important things.

'No trace of Charles North or Vicky so far,' Derek said gloomily, 'although we've got their descriptions out nationally. And we haven't been able to get a word from Franklin about his suppliers – or I suppose I should say his employers.'

'And did Taz tell you the Wings have disappeared?' I asked.

'Wings?' Alfie looked baffled. 'What wings? Wings off what? What are we talking about here? Birds? Or what?'

Derek was being unusually patient today.

'Mr Wing was our official interpreter for Chinese people,' he reminded Alfie, 'and he was attacked, we don't know why, and he said he didn't know either, and Greta interviewed his wife and got some more information about translations from the Chinese word for factory. Remember it now?'

'Oh yes, those Wings,' Alfie nodded. 'No, Taz never said nothing about them. What about them?'

'Well, unofficially, while I wasn't really working,' I explained, avoiding Derek's disapproving eye, 'I thought I'd just pay a friendly visit to Mrs Wing to ask how Mr Wing was recovering. They seemed a nice couple, and I wanted to know if he was OK. But according to a friendly neighbour, they and their four children had just upped sticks and gone, and it's unusual, she said, because up to now they've always told her where they're going and asked her to look after their place. Also, it's school term-time, and they've never taken their kids out of school before to go away. I told Taz and I thought he might have told you.'

'No he probably rightly thought it wasn't important,' Derek said, and I thought again about the PS to Vicky's letter.

Vicky's letter! It was burning a hole in my pocket, and my conscience wasn't all that cool, either. I'd have to do something about it, and soon. Well, the little devil in my head whispered, why soon? How would they know when you got it? It's got no date to even say when she sent it. Leave it for a while.

'Well, Guv,' I said, 'so where are we now in all our investigations? Have we decided it all links up? And what do we do next?'

My respect for him went down a notch when all I got from him was Alfie's traditional reply, 'Buggered if I know.' And there we sat and looked at each other blankly.

Time to produce my bombshell.

So I thought. But before I had a chance to put my hand in my pocket, Alfie gave forth.

'Course you know, Guv,' he said heartily, combing his beard with one hand and waving the other one in the air. (This was always a sign of deep bother on Alfie's part, but I hardly had time to wonder why before he went burbling on.) 'What we've got to do is, we've, er, we've, erm, we've got to find out from Hertford HQ about another Chinese interpreter, and we've got to get on to my old mate Barney Blue in Soho and get him ferreting away in Chinatown to find out if them Wings have got any family there. And that's only for starters,' he added, mopping his forehead.

I twigged. This was Alfie being loyal and not letting Derek

think we were up against a blank wall. Well, good for him. But it wasn't going to save me from what I had to do.

'Alfie's right, Derek,' I said, 'of course there's always more to be done. And I think I might have something a bit useful.'

I fished the crumpled paper from my pocket.

'I've got a letter that seems to be from DC North,' I started, 'at least she says that's who she is, but it need not be, of course.'

This was no good. I was just talking rubbish. I shut my gob and handed the letter to Derek, and he sat down without a word, with Alfie leaning over his shoulder and breathing heavily down his neck as they both read it. When they both got to the end I waited for some reaction, but all that happened was that without a word from either of them they both went straight back to the beginning and read it all over again. Couldn't blame them for that. I remembered how I felt when I got it.

Although it was obvious they didn't have so much reason to be angry as I did. Wrong again.

When they looked up at me, Alfie's face was nearly purple with fury and Derek had gone all white round the mouth.

Alfie was the first to get his breath back.

'She's having us on!' he shouted. 'Little minx! Done a bolt alright, then thought she'd get us going with this fairy-story. Thought she'd get us running round chasing Chinese warlords, didn't she! She's no more in South America than I am–'

'But it could all be true,' Derek said quietly. 'Or part of it could be…'

I noticed he was avoiding looking straight at me, and I knew why. I'd have to get over the personal bit and concentrate on the criminal part.

'Do you think we should show it to Mr Moon?' I asked.

They answered together.

'Certainly,' Derek said.

'Course not,' Alfie said.

We both glared at Alfie.

'Stands to reason,' he said, at his most reasonable. 'What if she's winding us up, like I said. And Mr Moon takes it all serious and goes off to the Yard and they all put their mighty brains to rooting out all the moles in the police in the whole country. And she's off somewhere laughing her head off at getting us all running around chasing our tails, right? Or if Mr Moon doesn't take it serious, but he worries in case it is, then what? What's the good of it all? No, what I think is, we should go on with our normal investigations, nice and quiet, but keeping this letter in mind. And if we turn up anything that makes it seem as if some of what it says is true – not all, mind you, just some of it – well then, we can take that letter to Mr Moon and let him decide what to do with it.'

Then Alfie won me over with my own thought.

He added, 'There's no way of telling when this letter was posted, nor when you got it, Greta. So no bother about withholding, or anything like that.'

Alfie and I turned to Derek to see if he was going along with this. Looked as if he was when a small smile crept across his handsome phizog.

'OK,' he said, 'tell you what we'll do. You follow up your own suggestions, Alfie, of finding about another interpreter to replace Mr Wing, and contacting your friend Barney in Soho to see if he can help us. Meanwhile Greta and I will go and have another look at the Wings' flat to see if there's anything further we can find out there.'

And I was stunned to see that he then gave me a big wink on the side that Alfie couldn't see. I could hardly wait till we got in the car to find out what that meant. I didn't have to ask, though. He told me.

'Did you think I didn't know how you got into Vicky's flat, Greta?' he said. 'I didn't want to embarrass you by asking any questions, especially as I knew the answers already. So I'm going to be looking in the front of Mr Wing's shop while you are at the back entrance, miraculously finding the door unlocked so that we can go inside without any bother.'

I could have hugged him, and not just for my usual reasons, either.

Mind you, when we did what he said, in a way I wished we hadn't, because the sight we saw when we did get into their home was a real smack in the eye. I'd expected to see some untidiness, a look of hasty departure, that sort of thing. Maybe even an unwashed cup or two in the kitchen sink. Generally, I thought it wouldn't be quite as spotless and beautiful as it was when I'd last seen it.

Maybe in the back of my mind I had a little dread that we might also see signs of violence, but if so, I didn't really expect to see anything really shocking. I didn't really believe that Mr Wing's assailants had come back to have a go at the whole family. And I was right there.

What we did see was a previously perfect home undisturbed except for huge daubs of Chinese writing all over the walls, on the carpets, on the pictures, in fact anywhere where this black and red paint would stick. And it was in every room. Whatever it said, it must have been some sort of warning, because it had been enough to make the Wing family bolt. And even without knowing what the message was, I felt I couldn't blame them. Those huge letters looked threatening enough before I even found out what they meant.

'Let's hope Alfie's managed to find us another interpreter,'

Derek said. 'Although we can presume it's all some sort of threat. It's my guess that they think Ah Weng So told Mr Wing enough for him to be a danger to them, and they want him thoroughly intimidated.'

'What, even after they'd beaten him up?' I said. 'You think that wasn't enough to keep his mouth shut?'

'We're dealing with people who are very thorough,' Derek said, sounding very gloomy. 'If they think there's a slightest risk, they'll just get rid of people. I link this with the disappearance of Charles North. But I wonder who could have known he'd offered to give us information in return for Edward Franklin's release? And why should Franklin have been so important to him that he'd take such a risk for him? We've still got a lot to find out on this case, Greta, and I'll tell you honestly I'm not very optimistic about it.'

Before I could think up something encouraging to say, he went on, 'But what we've got to do now is try to copy down these Chinese characters. I've certainly no intention of letting another interpreter, or anyone else for that matter, into this place to see what we've got here.'

Well, at least there was something I'd got that would cheer him up.

'I've got the camera in the car,' I said. 'I'll just pop down and get it.'

But by the time I got back he'd already filled page after page with careful copies of what was written all over the Wings' deserted home.

How could I not love such a clever man? And he'd been so tactful about Vicky's hints about my feelings for him, too. Not just clever, but kind and thoughtful, as well. I just wished he wasn't so secretive about his personal life. Apart from what Vicky had told me about his past, there must be something else hidden in it that made him swerve off from me every time we seemed to be getting somewhere.

But he was right. We were nowhere with this case. And I couldn't see Vicky's letter helping much, either.

*

See, that's the difference between people who are parents and the rest of us. As soon as we told Alfie what we'd found at the Wings' home, his first reaction was, 'What about their kiddies! How must they have felt? First their dad gets knocked about bad enough to go into hospital, then some buggers come and scrawl threats all over their walls, and they have to scarper. Poor little things. How old are they, Greta?'

And when I mumbled that I hadn't bothered to ask their friendly neighbour what were the ages of the children, or their names, or any such details, he gave me a strange look. I'd have expected him to be a bit annoyed, and even to give me a little lecture about how he'd always taught me to get every detail whether I thought it was important or not. He didn't, though.

He just gave me this look that seemed like pity. As if he was sorry for me for some reason. But he'd always known I wasn't interested in children, or marriage, or any of that stuff. I'd told him from the first that all I wanted was to go far in my career, rise up to be an Assistant Commissioner at the Yard, even.

'Anyway,' he said, sighing a bit, 'I've got the info about an interpreter and he should be with us in about an hour. Difficult name, though, not an easy one like Wing. Here, I've written it down: C-H-E-U-N-G. Don't know how you say it. Choong, would it be?'

'Never mind, Alfie, he'll tell us himself,' Derek said. 'But did you speak to your friend in Soho?'

'Yer,' Alfie said, 'but he reckons it'll be like looking for

Smith in a London directory. Or I s'pose Patel would be just as hard, these days. He'll have a go, anyway, and let me know if he's getting anywhere. Take a time, though.'

Alfie being one of the old school used to have a tendency to say names like Patel in a certain way, but since we'd all been on the Diversity Course, he seemed to be a lot better. I just hoped that the prejudices he'd got rid of extended to Chinese people too. You could never be sure with Alfie.

Well, when Mr Cheung did turn up I think we were all a bit taken aback. For no sensible reason I for one had been expecting someone on the same lines as little Mr Wing. Mr Cheung couldn't have been more different. It wasn't just that he was large – well, to be honest, fat. He had such fat cheeks that the bottoms of his rimless glasses dug into them, and when he took them off to clean them with a spotless silk handkerchief, you could see the ridges where they'd been. Also he seemed to be wearing an Armani suit, though it was a surprise to know you could get them in that size. All in all, he was a model of what the fat rich fashionable businessman was wearing this year, with his shirt, tie, socks and breast-pocket hanky all in smart matching maroon. And I wouldn't have been surprised if his shoes were hand-made, too. He put down his leather laptop carry case and beamed round at all of us.

'Inspector Michaelson?' he said, singling Derek out straight away. 'I believe we share a Christian name. I am Derek Cheung,' he went on in perfect BBC newsreader English. 'I understand you require my services.'

Naturally, Derek recovered quicker than Alfie and I did, and shook hands and introduced us both without batting an eyelid. He showed Mr Cheung his copies and the photographs of what was on the walls of the Wings' flat.

'Ah yes, very interesting,' Mr Cheung murmured, sitting

down and spreading it all out on Derek's desk. He started muttering stuff to himself, which must have been what the messages said. Some of it sounded like this: 'Syau ning, yi wan, suanle,' though of course it might not have been that at all.

'Yes, I see,' he finally said. 'Do you want to tell me any of the location or other circumstances where you found these words, or do you simply require a translation of the messages? I mean to say, my dear Inspector, I can probably extrapolate a great deal more if you tell me the background of this incident. On the other hand, if it's sensitive information…' and he spread his big fat hands as if no more need be said.

'Let's just start with the translation, if you please,' Derek was at his most crisp and officious, 'and perhaps we can have a wider discussion after that.'

'Very well,' Mr Cheung said. 'Here it is. The messages are addressed to someone being called "little person". This can be a reference to his physical stature or his lack of importance in the scheme of things. They say that whatever has happened to him so far can be done ten thousand times more. The actual term used can mean either ten thousand or just a very large number. But the admonition repeated most often is an instruction to forget. "Forget this", it says, or sometimes just "forget". Do you find this helpful at all?'

Before Derek could say a word, I stuck my oar in.

'Is it always so difficult to give an exact translation from Chinese to English?' I asked. 'The interpreter who helped us before seemed to find it very hard to tell us in English a word that he first said meant factory in Chinese, but then we were offered a whole collection of possible meanings for the same word.'

Mr Cheung settled himself more comfortably and started in on what sounded like the start of a long lecture on the subtleties of Chinese linguistics. Lucky for us Derek cut him short, otherwise we'd have been there all night.

'I think perhaps it would be useful if we took you into our confidence,' he said, and Mr Cheung gave such a big beam that his glasses must have cut even deeper into his fat cheeks. So Derek gave him an outline of how we first came to use Mr Wing's services and what happened to him after that. Fat Mr Cheung couldn't have been as much of a villain as he looked, because when Derek was telling him about Ah Weng So and what happened to her eventually, he had to take off his glasses and mop his eyes. I really began to like him then.

'So,' he said finally, 'are we to assume that Mr Wing actually knew something that the criminals were afraid he would tell you, or that they wrongly assumed that he was in possession of such information? I would guess that they were uncertain which was the case. From what you tell me of them, if they had been sure that he was in a position to harm them, he and his family would all be dead by this time.'

Alfie spoke for the first time since he'd been introduced to Mr Cheung.

'How do you come to that?' he asked. 'Have you got any experience of gangs like this? Triads, are they? Do they just do so many murders for, like, insurance?'

Mr Cheung spread his fat hands out again. 'It's what they did to that poor girl, Ah Weng So, isn't it? And I have to say that no, I have no direct experience of such criminals, I'm happy to say, but one hears things, you know.'

And we all sat quiet for a while, thinking it all over.

After a bit, Mr Cheung asked, 'And may I enquire what happened to the newborn baby? I believe you said that Ah Weng So gave birth to a little girl, Inspector?'

Derek looked as embarrassed as I felt. I could see he'd forgotten all about that kid, just like I had. Well, a lot had happened since then, I was excusing myself to my conscience, when Alfie spoke up.

'Yes, I've been keeping track,' he said. I tried to stop my mouth falling open with surprise. 'There's a nurse at Watford General Hospital, where the baby was born, who's keen to adopt her. There's a whole lot of formalities to go through, with social services and everything, but they've let her take the child home on a fostering basis in the meantime. That nurse – Sheila Mackenzie's her name – is younger than we are, my wife and me, so we've let her get on with it. But otherwise we were thinking of putting in for the child ourselves.'

Now I really was gob-smacked. I knew better than to take it up with Alfie in front of a stranger, but I was certainly going to have some questions to ask him when we were alone again. Like, why didn't he tell me any of this? If he'd been going to the hospital, he could have said. And if he and Betty were thinking of adopting a baby, it would have been matey to have told me and Derek about it. Also, I was feeling bad because I'd forgotten all about that poor little babe who I'd sort of helped into the world, and Alfie had been as caring as I should have been.

Anyway, all that happened at that moment was that Mr Cheung said how glad he was that the child hadn't been abandoned, and then he went back to our main subject.

'I've never had the pleasure of meeting Peter Wing in person,' he started, and again I gave a sort of jump of surprise, this time at Mr Wing's first name. He didn't seem like a Peter to me, more like a Fong Wo or that sort of thing.

'Of course,' Mr Cheung was going on, 'his name was known to me, since we are both more or less in the same occupation. Although there are differences. Mr Wing was solely a professional translator and interpreter, and he worked for many business people, publishers and so on, as well as being an official police interpreter. Whereas I myself am a business person, and merely offer my services as an interpreter to the police when Mr Wing is not available. As for example in the present circumstances.'

Knowing Derek so well, I could tell just by looking at him that his little wheels were going round at a hundred miles an hour. He wasn't just taking all this in, he was working on some deductions that might come out of it.

'How interesting,' he said in a positively smarmy voice (not like Derek at all, I thought) 'and may I ask what type of business you are in, Mr Cheung? Might it, for example, be anything which could be of use to us in our enquiries?'

Ho, I thought, he's thinking of movable factories and pet food. If I was right about that, he was disappointed in the next minute.

'Certainly,' Mr Cheung was all graciousness, taking out a posh little case of what looked like ivory (illegal! the buzzer went in my head), and giving Derek a business card from it. 'As you see, I'm in the import-export business. And before you ask, I deal mainly in works of art and artefacts, such as Oriental pictures, vases, ornamental screens, and sometimes small items of furniture. I import these from China, Japan, Vietnam, and so on, and sometimes sell them in this country, or to interested parties in America, Canada, South America, et cetera.'

I've got to admit, I was impressed with Mr Cheung. He had a marvellous vocabulary, but it wasn't just that. Mr and Mrs Wing both seemed to know more English than I did, and I just thought it was because they had the benefit of more education than me. Mr Cheung had this great way of talking, as if everything he said was important, like a politician making an election speech. It was partly to do with his size, but it was something else. As soon as he'd gone, being taken down to the reception area by Alfie, I asked Derek about it.

'Yes,' he said, 'I noticed it too. It's called presence. Must be useful to him in both his lines of business.'

I could see Derek wanted to brood a bit, so I shut up and waited. Of course, Alfie wasn't so tactful, and as soon as he came back he burst out with, 'I reckon there's something fishy about that man, Guv.'

And before Derek could rouse himself to answer, he went on, 'Wouldn't surprise me if he was the Big Boss they're all so afraid of. Seems like just the kind who'd be the head of a big crime organisation.'

I'd had enough shocks and surprises for my first day back on duty. And anyway there were so many arguments that could come out of Alfie's latest, it made me tired just to think about it all.

'I'm off home,' I said, and left the two of them to battle it out without me.

Chapter 19

Next morning, another shock. Another letter. After a lifetime of getting nothing but bills, circulars and official notices, now suddenly I get two letters in one week. And both hand-written, too. I could see right away that this one wasn't from hateful Vicky North. It had a UK stamp and was post-marked Brixton. The writing wasn't of the best. I turned it round and round, looking for clues, before giving up and opening it. Of course I looked at the end first to see who it was from, and got even more of a surprise to see it was from Ari.

What was he doing, writing to me? What was wrong with phone, email, text? I read it. The first few words told me something was wrong. No 'lovely girl' stuff here.

'Dear Greta,' (it started)

'I can see I don't mean anything to you. We had a date and you didn't turn up. I phoned and you were out. Somewhere with your precious Derek, I suppose. Well, I'm fed up with being your plaything' (What! Plaything? Where did he get these words from? This didn't sound like Ari at all) *'and this is the end. You won't hear from me any more. I might not care about Marion Sestina, but at least she cares about me. You don't.*

'Your heartbroken discarded lover,
Ari'

I couldn't believe my eyes. Ari couldn't have written this. I couldn't tell if he did, actually, because I'd never seen his handwriting. But the words! Ari wouldn't know words like *plaything* and *discarded.*

Mind you, he'd have been entitled to be a bit off me. It was only now that I remembered we'd agreed to have dinner in his uncle's restaurant in Camden Town – when was it? – two or three days ago? And what with one thing and another, it had gone clean out of my head. I looked at the clock. I didn't have time to phone him now, but I'd try to get him that evening. I had a sneaky idea he'd told that Sestina woman about me standing him up, and she was the one who'd written this stupid letter. She certainly had the vocabulary for it. Ari wouldn't just drop me. He loved me too much.

I rushed off to Shady Lane, nearly late, and only on my second day back on duty, too. Derek and Alfie were waiting for me.

'We've got a meeting with Mr Moon,' Derek told me, 'and another five minutes and we'd have been late. We've got a lot to tell him, and we're badly in need of his advice, so come on, Greta, let's go.'

I thought we'd be with Mr Moon maybe an hour or so, but our meeting went on so long that he sent out for sandwiches for lunch. We told him all the details, even stuff that didn't seem important, and he asked hundreds of questions and made us go over and over the same ground. I was waiting all the time for Derek to show him the letter from Vicky North, but that was the one thing he never mentioned.

We couldn't shut Alfie up, though, and he went on for what seemed like hours (but maybe was only a few minutes) about his belief that our new interpreter was the Big Boss. Mr Moon was his usual kind thoughtful self, and after listening carefully to Alfie, asked him if he had any definite reason for his opinion.

'After all,' he said to Derek and me, 'Alfie Partridge has

been in the police longer than any of us, and we should take notice of his knowledge and experience.'

Alfie got all red and embarrassed.

'Well sir,' he admitted, 'nothing actually what you might call concrete. No real evidence, not really. But it's a feeling you get when you know you're looking at a real villain. It's like what you might call a sixth sense.'

'I respect this gut feeling of yours, Sergeant,' the Superintendent said seriously, 'but unfortunately you're going to have to find something to back it up before we can do anything about it.'

What a gent our Mr Moon is! He as good as told Alfie he was talking rubbish, but without hurting his feelings, and we could see that it had done the trick.

'So to recapitulate,' Mr Moon went on, 'we have a few small fry in custody, the so-called brother and sister Sadie and James Lee and the man we knew formerly as Edward Franklin. Of course they're being held without bail pending trial, and in the meantime efforts are being made to find out more about their backgrounds. But Charles North and DC Victoria North continue to be missing, and we don't know what has happened to Mr Wing and his family.'

'That's it in a nutshell, sir,' Derek said gloomily, 'and the fact is, we don't know what to do next. What further action is there that we could take?'

This was Mr Moon's chance to give the standard reply of 'Buggered if I know' and it wouldn't have surprised me, either. He was so human and like us, it was sometimes hard to remember that he was our superior officer. But of course he didn't say what he could have said. Too much of a gent, probably.

He just said, 'Let me think it over. You are sure, Derek, you've told me all you know?'

And he gave Derek such a keen look, it was as if he knew

all the time about Vicky's letter burning a hole in Derek's pocket and was just waiting for Derek to come clean about it.

But Derek just said, 'Yes sir,' and the three of us sloped off. Three blank faces sat in Derek's office and looked at each other.

'Paperwork all up to date?' Derek asked us, and when we both nodded, he said, 'Well, you may as well both bugger off home, then.'

As soon as I got in my car I started trying to get Ari on my mobile. Got his message service, left a message, sent him a text and an email, all humble, apologising and asking him to forgive me for not turning up for our date and not letting him know I couldn't come. But I didn't say a word about that letter. That could wait till I could look him in the eye. If he was still speaking to me by then. But the more I thought about it, the more certain I was that he hadn't written such rubbish.

Sure enough, when he called me back, he was the same old loving Ari, asking when he could come and see me again.

I don't know why I told Ari I couldn't see him that night, but it must have been that I do things right sometimes – maybe I have a gut feeling that works when I least expect it. Anyway, it turned out OK because then he said that he'd be on late duty, so we fixed a date for the weekend, and to make sure that I didn't forget or get it wrong, he said he'd come and pick me up from home.

But the instinct that was working in my favour on this occasion was a bit of a breakthrough with Derek. He asked if I'd like to go out to dinner with him that evening! Would I?! It was going to be our first real actual date. I didn't count the times when we'd been at my place or his, or when I'd sort of wangled things so that he took me to see an opera. This was progress.

Of course, I got into a panic about what to wear and if

he'd feel worse about me being so much taller than him if I wore heels. Finally I decided that dressing up and looking as great as I could was more important than our height difference – after all, even in my usual flatties he was a bit shorter than me.

So I did myself up to the nines and he came and called for me and off we went to a nice quiet pub restaurant out in Chipperfield. Very posh and select and I was glad I'd got myself dressed up. We ordered and he picked a very expensive-looking bottle of wine, and I was getting quite thrilled. He was treating me like a woman, a date, a proper person, not just a sergeant whose boss he was.

Then he said, 'Now, Greta, I want to make one thing clear. We are definitely not going to talk any shop tonight. I don't want to give a thought to crime or criminals, real or possible. This evening is personal, just about us.'

By this time I was nearly passing out with excitement. I could feel bits clenching and unclenching, and parts that weren't doing that were sort of quivering with anticipation. This was IT! At last, all the waiting and hoping had worked out worthwhile. I was thanking my lucky stars I'd put clean sheets on my bed that morning.

All serious, Derek said, 'You must know by now that I don't like to talk about my personal life. But since Vicky has partly spilled the beans, I thought it would be only fair to tell you the rest. After all, we are friends as well as colleagues, and we should trust each other.'

I didn't like the sound of this. It wasn't smoochy leading-up-to-sexy-times talk at all. But I smiled and nodded and made agreeing noises, wondering how I could get this to lead to the subject that interested me most.

'The fact is,' he went on after a good slurp of wine, 'I'm very bad at personal relationships, especially with women.

You know how often I unintentionally offend you or Alfie, and you knew something of my association with Erica, and how badly that ended.'

I hated Erica, who was some smart-ass something in the City, little, dark, slim, clever, vivacious, and all the rest of those marvellous things that I'm not. On the other hand, it was because of her, while he was living with her in Highgate, that Derek got himself transferred from Durham to Watford. So I owed her that, at least. But she did chuck him out in a most heartless thick-skinned way while she was having a party, leaving him not only heartbroken but homeless too. Anyway, while I was grinding my teeth about Erica, Derek was talking on.

'But what you don't know is that before I met Erica, I was married,' he said.

Not a word about how Vicky North came to know all this.

I noticed that neither of us was eating the delicious-looking food that had been sitting in front of us for the last half-hour.

'I thought I was the luckiest, happiest man in the world,' Derek said.

I could have hit him. What about my feelings? He didn't seem to notice the effect he was having on me.

'I was getting on in the Job,' he went on, 'I had a decent home and a lovely sweet-natured wife, and we were beginning to talk about starting a family. Juliet, that was my wife's name, went out to work, but she wasn't very happy there, so she was thinking of giving it up so as to be a proper housewife and mother. And then it happened. The heavens fell.'

'What? What happened?' I asked.

Now I was really concerned. I thought, oh God, he's going to tell me she died tragically or something, and he's never got over it.

'She left me,' he said simply.

We sat there in silence for a while, me not knowing what to say and him sort of brooding over his smoked salmon. Finally, maybe because it seemed like a way of breaking the tension, or it could just have been that we were hungry by then, we both picked up our knives and forks at the same time, and set to. Good thing too. I was starving.

Well, I had to take the conversation on a bit, so I asked him why she left. It seemed as if he was waiting for that.

'Old story,' he said, quite bitterly. 'The reason she wasn't very happy at work was because she was having an affair with her boss and she wanted him to leave his wife so that they could go off together. But of course he kept making excuses. So she was using our so-called plans to start a family to threaten him that he'd lose her altogether. Naturally he gave in, and I couldn't blame him for that. Nobody in their right mind would want to lose Juliet.'

We'd finished our first course and his hand was on the table, so I took the opportunity to put mine over it. I stroked it a bit in what I hoped was a sexy way. He didn't take his away, so that was a good sign, maybe. What was the best thing to say now, I wondered.

'How lousy for you,' I said, 'was she a blonde, your Juliet?'

'How did you guess that?'

'Well, it was obvious, Erica being so dark, you just went for the opposite. And I suppose Juliet was a perfect home-maker, because Erica was a good-time girl – if you don't mind my saying so,' I added.

I didn't want to put his back up, just when we were getting on so well. He was saved from answering by the arrival of three waiters – *three*, mind you – to serve our next lot of grub. I was glad to see the helpings were generous. The first course had been delicious but a bit small. I suppose these posh restaurants go in for this dainty stuff, not like Ari's uncle's

Greek place in Camden Town, where they got upset if you didn't leave staggering with all the food and drink they'd shoved at you. All so delicious you couldn't leave any of it, too.

What! Why was I thinking about Ari when I was with Derek? Usually it was the other way round.

We tucked in, and I was glad to see that talking about his miserable past hadn't put Derek off his grub. I always think there's a connection between a man's appetite for food and drink and his other physical appetites, so that was a good sign. Ari was a champion eater – NO! STOP THINKING ABOUT ARI!

After both of us doing a lot of silent munching and slurping, being on our second bottle of wine by this time, Derek started up his story again.

Tell the truth, I was getting a bit fed up with all this sad stuff. I wanted us to get on to talking about us, him and me, not him and all those other women. I wanted to say to him, *I'm not like them, if you take me on I'll never desert you,* but at least I had more sense than that. I knew enough to realise that something like that would put him right off.

'My mother left my father, too,' he suddenly said. 'And me and my brother, of course. He was seven and I was five. We never heard from her again. It makes a difference to how you look at life, you know.'

I could have told him he was lucky to have a mother and father, but I didn't. We weren't doing Greta's sad history today, we were doing Derek's.

'So you see, Greta,' he went on, 'that I've always been unlucky with women. Even my own mother didn't care enough about me to stay with my father to look after me and my brother. And I wanted you to know that if I've sometimes seemed a bit stand-offish with you when we've been in a, er, a, erm, an intimate situation, it's no reflection on you, or how attractive you are or how I feel about you.'

That's more like it, I thought.

'I think you're an extremely attractive woman,' he said, out of the blue, grabbing my hand with the fork still in it, 'and in other circumstances we might have made a go of it. But I just feel I can't take any more chances, and there'll be no more heartbreak for me, because I won't let myself in for it. I hope I'm not misreading the signs,' he said, 'and speaking out of turn. But I did get the clear impression that you were, that is, you are, that is to say, you had some interest in me apart from work and friendship. Oh hell, I'm making a mess of this.'

He put down my hand and his knife and fork and blew his nose, and I saw that there were actual tears in his eyes. As for me, mine were already rolling down my cheeks and probably leaving big mascara tracks on my careful make-up.

I wanted to ask him, is this final? *Won't you give me a chance to try to change your mind?*

But I could see it was hopeless. He'd made it clear enough.

I was never going to get anywhere with Detective Inspector Derek Michaelson. And it was nothing to do with our differences in height, education or rank. It was because he'd given up on women.

Time for one last throw of the dice.

I mopped my cheeks and said in what I hoped was a sexy voice, 'Well, that was all very sad. But I don't know what makes you think it's your heart I'm after, Derek. I just thought we might have a little fling, seeing we fancy each other something rotten. You can't deny that, can you?'

He looked stunned. But after a while he started to laugh. So did I. He poured us some more wine.

Chapter 20

It was a funny thing about letters. In my whole life I'd never got any, then I got two. First the one from Vicky North, and then that other stupid forgery. I never mentioned the second one to Ari. There was no point. There was no need for him to know I'd had a letter written as if it was from him, when I knew very well it wasn't. It must have come from Marion Sestina, and I could sympathise with her. I knew what it was like to be keen on someone who didn't feel the same way.

Anyway, it was a third letter that finally cracked the case. Or led to us finally cracking it, I suppose I should say.

Derek got a letter from China!

It said so much, it was more like a little package than a letter. And it had taken weeks to arrive, partly because it was just addressed to 'Detective Inspector, Watford Police', and it had done the rounds before it landed on Derek's desk. And probably another reason it took so long was because the postal system in China wasn't all that efficient. I didn't even know they had post offices and stamps and stuff out there.

It was from Mr and Mrs Wing.

It started off explaining why and how they'd gone back to China. I say 'gone back', though that wasn't the case for Mrs Wing, who'd been born in London and thought of China as a foreign country. I thought it must have been really difficult for her and the children to adjust to living in such a strange place. But according to the letter, it was the only way they felt they'd be safe from who they described as 'the gangsters' who'd become such a threat to their lives.

'Before I was called to the hospital to act as translator for Ah Weng So,' the letter said, *'we had been living quietly and happily on what I could earn as an official police interpreter and as a translator of text-books for a well-known publisher.*

'But my downfall was my curiosity. After hearing what Ah Weng So told me, I started doing my own investigations. The trouble was, she had told me a lot more than I passed on to the police. I had been able to work out how far she had been brought from where she had been found giving birth in a shop doorway. Then, making the rounds of all the possible places, I accidentally hit on the temporary factory in Nasty on the one day in its existence when the Big Boss was paying it a visit. That was long before the police got there.'

He went on to explain that even then, he could have saved himself and his family a lot of grief if he hadn't managed to work out that the man he'd met there that day actually *was* the boss of the whole set-up. After all, until then he'd just known him as a rich businessman who did a bit of interpreting work for the police as a sort of hobby when the regular translator wasn't available. But what partly gave the game away was the way the manager of the factory bowed and scraped to him, and was distinctly really scared of him. And of course what clinched it was the beating-up and threats to his family that Mr Wing suffered afterwards.

'But at the time when we met at the factory,' Mr Wing wrote, *'Mr Cheung was so affable, I thought I must be mistaken. He displayed great surprise at seeing me there, and asked my business. When I told him about Ah Weng So, he just seemed interested and sympathetic, asking about her baby and so on. However, when he suggested I should not pass*

on my knowledge to the police, I became a little suspicious. Being a very polite person, I did not express this to him, nor was I so ill mannered as to ask him his business in such a disgusting place. On discussing the matter with my wife, we decided I should take no action. But then my beating took place, and you know what followed.'

So Alfie's instinct was right. Fat rich businessman Mr Cheung, who helped the police out by filling in as a part-time interpreter, was the Big Boss. So what? Mr Wing's letter, although clear and helpful, wasn't proof, and certainly wasn't evidence, any more than Alfie's intuition. We were no further forward.

Again, like so many times in the past, the three of us were sitting looking blankly at each other, waiting for one of us to say 'What next?' so that another one could give the same old answer: 'Buggered if I know'.

It didn't happen, though. What happened next was a huge surprise. Derek lost his temper. He suddenly went red in the face and let go with a string of words I'd never imagined he'd know, never mind say out loud. He swore without stopping for a few minutes, while we both looked at him as if we'd never seen him before. Well, in a way we hadn't. Not this side of him anyway.

Then he said, 'That bastard's not going to beat us! All those other people like Ah Weng So, they're all still suffering somewhere. And he's going on with it, too, taking their savings and bringing them over here to be slaves until they're a nuisance, then dumping them or killing them. And he's laughing at us. He got Mr Wing beaten up and those warnings sprayed on his walls, then he had the cheek to come and tell us what they said! As if he didn't know beforehand!'

Trust Alfie to take the drama out of a situation.

He said, 'All those cats and dogs getting poisoned too, with that muck they're making in his mobile factories.'

He must have thought he was just adding to Derek's list of terrible things our villain had done, but it was so much less criminal than the rest, that I nearly burst out laughing. Good thing I didn't, though, because Derek was still seriously furious. As he slowly started to calm down, though, I could see his mind beginning to work. I thought we'd wait to see what would come out, but Alfie beat him to it.

'We've got a few people we can lean on a bit, Guv,' he said. 'If we give them a hard squeeze, we can get a lot more out of them. We've got those two, Sadie and James, who claim to be brother and sister, which I for one never believed. Then there's that Edward Franklin or whatever his real name is. And that other feller, wotsisname, you know, the one in the hospital we nicked for selling amputated limbs – we could find out who he was selling them to, for a start. And p'raps Greta could get a bit more off of her little pal Juan.'

'But doesn't it make you fed up, Alfie,' I said, 'that all the best leads we've got so far are from letters from abroad where we can't follow them up?'

'Course it does, girl,' he allowed, 'but we've got to get on with it and make the best we can of what we've got, haven't we? About time we showed those letters to Mr Moon, too, isn't it, Guv?'

By this time Derek seemed to have got over the worst of his fit of the furies, and was back in charge of himself. Right away he agreed with all Alfie's suggestions, and said he'd go and show Mr Moon the two letters immediately.

'And, Greta, we don't have to tell him when you got that one from Vicky North,' he said, 'it could have come any time. Meanwhile, Alfie, before we start following up your ideas and re-interviewing all these people, maybe you'd like to have a tactful word with your young friend Taz.'

'What! You can't think he's got anything to do with all this!' it was Alfie's turn to explode. 'Just because that Vicky North hinted he might be one of them–'

'No, that's not the only reason. And Greta,' he turned back to me, 'will you get in touch with your friend the long-distance lorry driver and ask him if he'll come in and have a chat with us? I think we could use his help, too.'

And before I could ask him what help that thickie Jim could be, he'd gone. He was suddenly in a great hurry to see Mr Moon, I thought, running after him and yelling that he hadn't taken the other letter off me. He'd forgotten he'd given it back to me. Even then I didn't get a chance to ask him anything. He just took the letter from Vicky North out of my hand, gave me a mumble of thanks, and was off again.

Well, whatever was going on in his great brain, and however things were between us off duty, in this situation he was still my boss, so I set about trying to locate Jim, probably the second-last person in the world I wanted to see. I didn't really fancy phoning him at home in case he wasn't there and his wife answered, as we weren't really the greatest of friends. Not surprising, considering I'd spent a lot of time in bed with her husband before she'd attacked me and put me in hospital. She was the one who was the very last person I ever wanted to see or speak to again. Maybe she owed me one for not pressing charges after she'd knocked me out in my own home, but it was kind of fifty-fifty that she bore me no grudge for having it away with her old man. Still, even if all that was water under the bridge, I didn't want to start leaving messages for Jim with her. All things considered.

I tried his mobile, hoping that if he wasn't actually driving, he'd have it switched on and would answer it. No such luck. Too much to hope he'd have a hands-free. So I left him a message saying that Detective Inspector Derek Michaelson would like a word with him at Shady Lane Police Station, Watford. Jim being so thick, if I'd said he should call *me* back, he'd have thought I wanted to start up with him all over again, and that was something I didn't fancy at all. And anyway, I didn't really know what Derek wanted him for. But I guessed it was something to do with the Chinese feller who'd tried to get him to use his lorry to bring illegal Chinese immigrants into the country.

Well, finally Jim got the message and came into the station, and he and Derek and Alfie and I sat down together for Derek to reveal his master-plan.

Talk about far-fetched!

Apart from the fact that trying to trap a Big Boss like Cheung with a flimsy trick like that was obviously daft, using somebody as dopey as Jim Robinson was just asking for trouble. He'd be bound to cock it up somewhere along the line, and then we'd be no further forward and Cheung would be even more on his guard.

'And we know that Cheung doesn't care who he kills for the sake of convenience, never mind to save his own skin,' I argued. 'Look at the way he had Juan Garcia's little chum knocked off, just because he'd made a stupid mistake and burgled the wrong house. And Ah Weng So, and Charles North, and who knows how many more. So what about the danger to Jim? If he susses out what Jim's up to, Jim's life won't be worth a light.'

Jim came as near as a big fat slob can come to shrivelling and shrinking into his chair. He didn't just look terrified, he looked ill.

'I'm sorry,' he mumbled, 'I'm not sure what you're all talking about. What danger? Why should anyone want to kill *me*?'

I shot a meaningful look at Derek. I tried to make it send him the message, 'See? This is the dope you want to use in your clever plan to trap a master-criminal?'

It didn't work, though. Maybe Derek did understand it, and maybe he could be as ruthless as Cheung when it came right down to it. But surely he couldn't get an OK from Mr Moon to use an innocent member of the public like that?

Derek said, 'Tell you what. Greta, why don't you take Jim out for a nice quiet dinner somewhere, and tell him the whole case from the beginning. Explain it all to him. I'm sure that once he understands all that's involved, he'll be glad to be of service to the police.'

Jim's face lit up. This was a part of Derek's idea that he understood.

'Don't let's go out,' he offered, 'let's go back to yours, Greta, and order in a pizza and some beer, like the old days, and make a night of it.'

I gave Derek my most hate-filled glare. He looked back at me like a Detective Inspector looking at a Detective Sergeant. Nothing more than that. Jim saying 'make a night of it' meant nothing to him.

'OK,' I said. 'Come on, Jim, let's go.'

Naturally, Jim being Jim, I was having to give him a karate demo before the pizza had even arrived. No sooner had we got into my place than he was all over me like a bad case of dermatitis.

'You missed me, didn't you,' he went, grabbing at the nearest part of my anatomy. 'You tried to keep away so as not to upset my stupid wife, but you couldn't, could you.'

It was no good telling him he was wrong and he should let go of me, I knew from experience it was a waste of time. So I had to throw him down and give him a good bit of what-for to convince him that he'd got it all wrong. Again. Then he sat there looking like a moonstruck calf. Why did I have to go through all this every time? It was all Derek's fault.

I kept his mouth full of pizza and beer while I told him our whole case from beginning to end, as per Derek's instructions. From time to time he nodded, mumbled and looked enquiring, but most of the time he just looked completely mystified. I could see why. Even if he understood everything I'd told him, which was hard enough for someone of his low IQ, we were both baffled as to any reason for him to be given all this info in the first place. All I knew was that I was following my boss's orders, but poor old Jim knew even less than that. So I couldn't blame him when at the end of my long tale, he just sat there, burping away as usual and looking like a bump on a log.

Then he surprised me, which was a shock enough in itself. Jim was usually the most predictable unsurprising person in the whole universe.

He said with amazing shrewdness, 'So I suppose your boss wants me to find that Chinky feller and say I've changed my mind and I want to bring in some illegals on my next load after all?'

'Yes, that's what he said,' I admitted, 'but what I can't see is how that's going to help us to prove anything against Big Boss Cheung. Even if we're right and he really is the Big Boss. Could be that we're following the wrong track altogether…'

'Well, anyway,' Jim said, 'why should I? Don't give me stuff about being a good citizen and doing my duty. You said yourself I might be putting myself in danger with this Chink, and p'raps I might end up on the wrong side of the law an'all, and what for, I'd like to know? You won't even make it worth my while with a bit of the other for old times' sake.'

And he made another grab at me. This time I let him. But

even thick Jim could tell my heart wasn't in it, and after slurping at me for a minute or two, he gave up and sat down and just looked at me.

'You don't love me!' he accused.

That was really swift of old Jim. I'd been telling him that ever since I'd first known him, years ago, and it had taken this long for it to sink in. Full marks, Jim.

'I never said I did,' I pointed out.

'Yes, but that was because you didn't like to say,' he argued. 'You did at first, and all that time when we was having such fun together, right up until my old woman came and give you a walloping. But it's not like you to be put off by a little thing like that. What happened? I still love you.'

I was getting tired.

'Oh, Jim, leave it out. Just let's forget the personal stuff and concentrate on what I've been telling you. My boss thinks you can be of great help to us, and the only reason I've been telling you the whole story is to convince you to do what he suggested. This is a really horrible man and we've got to bring him down somehow, to stop all these terrible things he's doing.'

'No,' Jim said. 'You and your lovely little boss can talk till the cows come home, I'm not doing it, and I haven't got to. Say whatever you like about my duty as a citizen or a subject or whatever it is I'm s'posed to be these days. I won't do it. And I can tell you now, even if you'd given us a tumble for old times' sake, I'd still say no at the end of it. I'm not doing it, and that's flat.'

I started to speak, but he hadn't finished. I'd never known Jim to make such a long speech, all in one go.

'And I'll tell you something else for nothing,' he went on, fully wound up by now, 'and that's this: it's a rotten idea. Even if I'd said OK, I'll give it a try, it wouldn't work. How do you think me taking on a load of illegal Chinkies would put me in touch with your Big Crook Boss? What do you think, he comes down to the dock to meet every driver who takes on one of his loads? I know you've never thought I was all that bright, but if you ask me, you and your dear little boss are downright thick.'

He stopped for breath and while I was trying to think what next, two other things happened. In the way that life is, the doorbell and the phone both rang at the same time.

'I'll go,' Jim said, lumbering to the front door.

It didn't seem like a good idea, but as he'd started, I let him go and I answered the phone. Boringly, it was Derek to ask about my progress with Jim. I told him it was no go and hung up.

Jim came back from the front door with Ari.

'Look who's here,' he said. 'Come here often, do you, son?'

Ari was no better.

'What's *he* doing here?' he asked me.

The air was thick with testosterone. There was only one thing to do. Politely but firmly and without any explanations, I asked them both to go.

*

I got in to the cop-shop early next morning, after an unusually bad night. The three men kept going round in my mind like a revolving door.

Jim had had his uses in the past, considering what a useless person he was in most ways.

Ari was great company, but he wanted to marry me and although I was very fond of him, I didn't love him. And anyway I didn't want to get married at all, to anyone. I just wanted to concentrate on getting on with my career.

Derek had been my great passion, but now that I'd found out why all the women in his life had dropped him, I wasn't sure how I felt about him.

And much as I'd tried to concentrate on the mysteries of our Chinese master-criminal and how to catch him, my mind kept straying back to those three men in my life. So I got up at five and listened to the radio to shut off the ramblings of my half-numbed wits.

For reasons that I never found out, Derek and Alfie were even earlier, and were in the middle of a conversation when I got in.

I had no chance to say or ask anything.

'Right,' Derek said, 'now that you're here at last, Mr Moon wants all three of us in his office asap. Come on, Greta, we've been waiting for you.'

I didn't point out that it wasn't quite seven yet. I just followed them both up the stairs.

Mr Moon looked like I felt. He was usually a beaming little fellow, Derek's height but twice his width. I'd seen him angry once (and hoped never to again) but mostly he was full of good nature, and you couldn't ask for a better Super.

But now he looked as if he'd had all the troubles of the world heaped on him, and he hadn't slept for a month. Not ill, just terrible.

Without a word of greeting or telling us to sit down or anything, he started off right away with, 'What makes you all so sure this Mr Cheung is our man? And don't tell me it's just because this other fellow, Wing, says so.'

There was a quiet bit while Alfie and I looked at Derek to see if he was going to say anything, and when it was clear that he wasn't, Alfie said, 'He's a wrong'un alright, Guv. You know as well as I do, when you've been in the Job as long as

I have, you can smell 'em. And we all thought he was laughing at us when he gave us the translation of what it said on the walls of Wing's flat.'

'OK Alfie,' Mr Moon said. 'I'll give you that. He probably is some kind of crook. And if it's to do with his import-export business, that's up to the Customs and Excise people. But what have we got to tell us he's this big cheese we've been looking for?'

Another silence.

Then Mr Moon went on, 'I've been studying all your notes and reports on this case, re-reading those two letters you gave me, Derek, and turning it all over in my mind. One of the things that struck me is that if this fellow is as big and powerful as you think, what else is he doing with his scores of illegal Chinese immigrants? You've discovered this moveable cats' meat factory where he's got slave labour, but how many of those can he have? It seems that he's got some sort of burglary firm going, but he wouldn't use illegals for that. So where are the rest of them, and what are they doing? If it's a steady business, there must be hundreds of them by now. The only suggestion I can make is that they must be in those farm-working gangs, or something like those unfortunate cockle pickers who were in the news a while ago. That's one of the things you should find out,' he said, fixing Derek with a downright unfriendly look.

'Then there's forensics,' he went on, after waiting in his usual polite way for a reply and getting none. 'I see it was possible to establish that the only fingerprints in the Wings' flat were those of Mr and Mrs Wing and the four children. OK, I accept that the intruders wore gloves. No DNA on Ah Weng So's body except her own. Her murderer wore gloves too, did he? I seem to recall that was a warm summer's day, and that was how the two Chinese girls were able to run about the streets in turn in the same little hospital gown. Have you been able to obtain Mr Cheung's fingerprints by any chance?'

By this time, I could see that all three of us were getting a bit hot under the collar. But Mr Moon hadn't finished.

'We have access to excellent forensic investigation,' he lectured us, as if we didn't know that, 'so are we availing ourselves of this? What I would like to see is some analysis of the paper, ink, envelopes, stamps and saliva of those two letters on which you seem to be basing some of your conclusions, Derek.'

Now he had me. I was completely baffled. What was he going on about?

'Right,' he said to me and Alfie, 'you two go and set about more interviewing. Derek, you stay here. I've got a few more things to take up with you privately.'

*

It was useless. We'd been over it all a million times and come up against a brick wall. We couldn't even prove the existence of the illegal Chinese immigrants or the slave factory.

This case was like my personal life: at a standstill.

But anyway, Alfie and I started to talk over a fresh approach to re-interviewing James and Sadie Lee, Edward Franklin and Tom Eagles, the hospital worker who'd sold amputated bits of bodies instead of incinerating them.

'Let's tell them we've already got their boss in custody,' Alfie said, 'and see if that gives them a start. They might see everything all different if they're not trying to keep him a secret.'

'No, that's no good,' I argued, 'how would they know who

he is? And anyway we'd have to say his name, and suppose it's not Cheung at all? They'd all just laugh at us, wouldn't they?'

'Course it's Cheung, I'm telling you I know it as clear as if he'd confessed to us in writing.'

Derek came in looking like death, just in time to stop us losing our tempers with each other.

We both waited for him to speak, not having the nerve to ask him what was the matter. He sat down, slumped, not like his usual upright way, gave a groan and put his head in his hands. This was getting worse. Bad enough he'd gone that sort of greenish colour, but now it was not just like bad news, more like the end of the world. Of course Alfie's patience ran out first.

'What is it, Guv?' he asked, oozing sympathy.

Derek looked up, all haggard, like a man who hadn't slept for a week.

'Mr Moon is of the opinion,' he started, 'and I'm afraid he may be right, that I've mishandled this case from beginning to end. Well, when I say end, of course, I mean up to date. Because we're nowhere near the end. Due to my incompetence,' he added bitterly. 'He didn't say so in so many words, but I got the clear impression that my job is on the line over this case.'

Apart from Alfie's sharp intake of breath, there was a shocked silence. After what seemed like an hour, Derek sort of pulled himself together and started talking a bit more normally. Well, normally for him in his usual posh sort of way.

'Greta, I want you to brief PCs Archer and Burton about the situation in the village of Nasty. Give them enough background so that they are well enough informed to re-interview each one of the villagers to see if any or all of them will revise their story of knowing nothing of a factory or smells of factory activity. Tell them to pay particular attention to the landlord of the pub. And find out if anyone there had any pets.'

'I didn't know that Fred and Kevin were back on our team,' I started, but Derek interrupted with a sharp, 'OK, Greta?' so I muttered that it was OK and scarpered out of the room, only too glad to get away from Derek and his face of doom. But I did kind of linger within listening distance for long enough to hear Derek tell Alfie that the two of them were next going to interview PC Tariq Tazhim.

So that meant that the Superintendent had paid enough attention to Vicky North's hint about Taz to think that he might be a second mole in Shady Lane!

I scooted downstairs to find Fred and Kev, anxious to get them going quickly so as not to miss what might happen next. Now that Mr Moon seemed to have taken charge, I was sure we'd get all sorts of surprises.

That was a safe bet. When the three of us met back in Derek's office, he told me that Taz had been suspended.

'Why? Did he admit–'

'As good as,' Alfie said, by now nearly as glum as Derek. He was fed up because he'd sort of taken young Taz under his wing and got him onto our team. 'Derek tripped him up good and proper by telling him that we'd looked at his bank account and found he was getting money regular from a source we'd traced. And he went all talkative about having an uncle who gives him an allowance. So then I says to him, was this uncle by any chance a Chinese gentleman, and he just sort of folded up and said we'd got him fair and square.'

'Yes,' Derek said, 'I think we'll leave him to think for a while, and by the time we question him again we'll get the full story.'

'Well!' I said. 'That's a good start.'

Then I thought a bit, and had to admit, 'So that Vicky North wasn't so bad after all, was she. She didn't need to have told me about Taz. Come to think, she didn't need to write to me at all. I thought at first she was just having a bit of a laugh at me, but–'

'Yes, maybe she had a conscience after all,' Derek finished for me. 'Now, you two, I need to talk to forensics, so you can get on and re-interview James and Sadie Lee. Separately, mind!'

As if we needed telling that. Looked as if the bollocking he'd got from Mr Moon had made him extra cautious.

Anyway, on the way down to see James Lee, Alfie said to me, 'Greta, you remember years ago when you put the frighteners on that Juan Garcia? You used a shoe from another case to kid to him that we'd got proof he'd trod in the victim's blood, then we had to lose the tape of the interview…'

'Yes, of course I remember. You nearly shat yourself at me taking such a liberty with the truth. But it worked, didn't it.'

I could tell Alfie was hot about something, because he didn't even complain about my language, which was what he usually did.

'Well,' he went on, 'how about doing a bluff like that with this James Lee? Only don't tell me beforehand what you're going to pull, so I can look shocked an' all.'

I didn't bother to tell him I was already working out something like that.

'Well, Mr Lee,' I greeted the prisoner, 'I've got some important news for you. We've been able to obtain some further forensic evidence on the murder of Ah Weng So, and in addition to that, a witness has come forward. So our next step is to take you back to the custody desk and charge you formally with this crime.'

True to form, Alfie was looking all amazed, but he rallied round enough to ask James Lee, 'Is there anything further you want to tell us before we go ahead?'

James Lee was not looking as superior and cool as he had up till now whenever I'd seen him. In fact, he looked rattled and a bit scared. Too scared to challenge us about the witness I'd just invented. Bit of luck for me there, at last.

'But I've told you over and over again that I had nothing to do with her death,' he bleated. 'I wasn't even there when she was pushed down the lift shaft–' He stopped, but it was too late.

'Oh really, Mr Lee,' Alfie joined in, by now enjoying the whole thing. 'And may I ask how you know exactly when it was that she was pushed, if you had nothing to do with it?'

Lee tried to side step.

'What makes you think there was time for anyone to tell me to kill her, anyway?' he said. 'Surely you don't think I would have done such a thing on my own initiative? And if you think I killed her on instructions, when do you think I might have got such an order?'

'Just a moment, Mr Lee,' I said. 'We're the ones asking the questions here. Just try answering my colleague's question. How do you know exactly when this event happened, if you were not involved?'

I gave Alfie the eye that he knew meant he shouldn't say any more. So the three of us sat there shtum while we waited for Lee to work something out. It came off.

After what seemed like an hour, he suddenly burst out, 'It was Wing! He heard what she said when he was supposed to be interpreting for you lot, and he told her to run. He even told her where to go and hide. Then we all met in that multi-storey car park they were building opposite the hospital, and she and Sadie changed clothes. Then Wing got hold of Ah Weng So and broke her neck and pushed her body down the lift shaft. We saw it all.'

Alfie switched on the tape recorder and made the opening declaration. Then he said, 'I am inviting Mr James Lee to make a full statement concerning the murder of the Chinese girl Ah Weng So. Please proceed, Mr Lee.'

I couldn't believe our luck. It had been so easy that I was sure that when it came to making a formal statement, he'd back out and deny what he'd admitted to us informally. But it was OK, he said it all again. And still didn't ask about the witness! I must have really panicked him.

Alfie told him he'd be required to sign this statement when it had been typed out, and he just nodded. But then I thought Alfie pushed it a bit too far, and I waited for it all to fizzle out.

While the tape was still running, Alfie asked him, 'Is Sadie Lee really your sister, Mr Lee?'

So when he just gave a straight 'Yes', I quickly closed the interview, copped the tape and hustled Alfie out of the interview room.

'What did you do that for?' I scolded him. 'What difference does it make if she's his sister or not? Once she hears that tape it'll be all over for the pair of them anyway.'

'Just I've got a horrible idea about those two,' Alfie said. 'I think they really are brother and sister, but they're, you know, living together like as if they're married, as well.'

Dear old Alfie, old-fashioned to the last. Who cared what kind of sex life those two were having, as long as we'd got some solid evidence from them. That pulled me up short. I'd been so over the moon about Lee's statement that I hadn't thought through all that it meant.

What if what he said was true, and it was Mr Wing who killed Ah Weng So? How should that affect how we thought about the rest of the case?

He couldn't have done it on orders, because like James Lee had said, there wasn't a chance for the instructions to come through. The timescale didn't work. So if Mr Wing had committed that murder, he hadn't done it because of a direct command from Mr Cheung. Who then? It had to be himself.

But that didn't make sense, either. If little Mr Wing was our Big Boss who we'd been looking for, who knocked him about? Who painted threats on his walls? Why did he take his wife and children to China for safety? And why did he write and tell us it was Mr Cheung who was responsible for all this?

By this time I was feeling as cheesed off as Derek had been looking. Instead of getting a statement from James Lee that would help us to solve our case, it had just made it even more difficult. And senseless. We'd got the answer to one crime, but the big picture was still a puzzle waiting to be solved.

Well, what with all the paperwork and having to get a corroborative statement from Sadie Lee when we'd played her the tape of her brother's confession, that was a whole day gone and not a lot achieved. But when I said as much to Derek, he was surprisingly upbeat.

'On the contrary,' he said, 'I think you and Alfie did a first-class job there, and I'm sure Mr Moon will say the same when we have our progress meeting tomorrow morning.'

'Progress meeting tomorrow morning?' Alfie said, sounding a bit faint and hollow, as if he was talking into an empty glass. 'What time would that be, Guv?'

'Seven sharp, Mr Moon's office, and I expect to have

debriefed Fred and Kevin about their day in Nasty by then,' Derek said, and we all parted without another word, friendly or other. Still, I was pleased he wasn't calling them Archer and Burton any more. It meant he'd relaxed a bit and taken the broom handle out of his trousers.

And I for one was well pleased to be alone for an evening for once.

*

Mr Moon asked Derek for his report first, which was a pity, because Alfie and I were busting to show off about James Lee's confession. Though we certainly weren't going to let on how we'd got it, which was why we hadn't taped the interview from the first. We'd learned that much from the time we'd had to get rid of a tape that showed how we'd tricked poor little Juan Garcia.

'PCs Archer and Burton did a good job in the village of Nasty,' Derek started. 'The turning point was apparently that before the peripatetic factory packed up and moved on, the manager gave some pet food to several of the villagers who had dogs. Of course this was in addition to the cash bribe given to every single one of the inhabitants to keep silent about the factory. But once all the dogs died, they felt differently. Not enough to contact us with information, but once they were asked, they were glad to make statements. I have the reports with me, but they mainly confirm what we already knew or suspected. The only additional information we have is a description of the manager of the factory, fortunately distinctive enough to be useful. Archer and Burton have gone back this morning with a sketch artist, and when his work is agreed by everyone, we'll get the picture on the computer and circulate it.'

'Hm, not bad I suppose,' Mr Moon said, not in a very encouraging way. 'And you yourself, what did you achieve?'

Meanwhile Alfie's eyes and mouth had gone round when Derek said 'peripatetic', and I saw him trying to write it down in his notebook. When I first met Derek, I used to be impressed by his vocabulary, so I could understand how Alfie felt. But I'd got over that.

Derek said, 'Forensics said it would take two weeks to give a report on the paper and envelopes of the letters from Victoria North and Mr Wing, but I impressed on them the urgency of the matter, and they said maybe they could manage in one week. Unfortunately no sooner. I got confirmation that there was no DNA on Ah Weng So's body other than from the nurses in the hospital, as we had already been informed. The forensic report on the Wing flat is inconclusive, but it appears that nothing shows apart from the prints and DNA of the family itself. There is nothing further on the disappearance of Charles North, the solicitor who represented Edward Franklin. Thomas Eagles, the supplier of human body parts from the hospital, has positively identified Edward Franklin as the person collecting from him. So it appears that Franklin not only sold the finished product, but was part of the chain of supply of what we might call raw materials.'

I glanced round and saw that everyone was looking as sick as I felt about this last bit of Derek's report. Meanwhile he was going on, sick or not.

'I intend to interview Franklin myself today,' he said.

'I'm not sure about that,' Mr Moon said. 'Don't do anything until I've given it some more thought. Now, Greta, I see you are anxious to give us some news. You'd better get on with it before you get too frustrated.'

I wondered why he'd chosen that particular word. He'd always been a shrewd old geezer, and he'd surprised me more than once by sussing out my feelings. But even he couldn't know what a mess my life had become recently. I dumped all those thoughts and gave my report, with Alfie beaming proudly as if he'd invented me himself. At the end, Mr Moon said he thought we'd done very well. This made Derek look even more fed up.

'Right,' Mr Moon said, 'this is what I want done today. Derek, I want you to go to the Chinese Embassy and ask for their help in trying to track down the Wing family. No need to tell you you'll have to be very diplomatic in how you approach them, but you can tell them we've uncovered a racket of smuggling illegal immigrants here from mainland China. See if they can give you any leads that we can follow up. Alfie, I want you and Greta to re-interview this Franklin fellow. But before you do, discuss it thoroughly with Derek to make sure you're on the right lines. Right, off you all go. Oh, by the way, I've decided to involve Scotland Yard. This is probably a national rather than a local problem, and we've got an appointment with the Deputy Assistant Commissioner this afternoon.'

'We?' Derek asked, and I could see a little faint hope on his face that meant he thought he might be included.

'Yes, of course,' Mr Moon said a bit testily, 'naturally Mr Goodison and I will be going together.'

Mr Goodison, a name we all said with indrawn breath, was our Chief Constable.

Derek's face clouded over again. It was clear to us all that he was well in the doghouse with Mr Moon, who'd taken over completely. Even if it hadn't been said officially, Derek was not in charge of this case any more.

Just the same, Alfie and I had a chat with him about interviewing Franklin. We still had to pretend he was the boss, because all said and done, so far he was still our superior officer. But it was very brief. Derek just advised that, since

Sadie Lee had folded and corroborated everything that her brother had given up about the murder of Ah Weng So, our best bet with Franklin was to play the tape to him as well.

'Can't tell if it'll get you anywhere,' Derek said, making it clear that he'd lost all confidence in his own opinions, 'but it's worth a try. Unless either of you has a better idea?'

We shook our heads and went off to follow his advice. I didn't have much faith in it, but as he said, neither of us had a better idea. As it happened, luck was on our side, and Franklin was struck all of a heap when he heard James Lee's statement. Then he got even worse when we played him the tape of Sadie's corroboration.

'Yes,' he said, all of a tremble, 'I know Wing and Cheung. I knew them both in Shanghai. I know what they can both do, and that's why I can't tell you anything about them. Whatever I'm accused of, I'll plead guilty and do whatever sentence I get. But you'll get no statement from me.'

Thank goodness, apart from a soft gasp, Alfie didn't react to Franklin linking Wing and Cheung together, but of course we were both gob-smacked. It was amazing enough to think that little Mr Wing might be our mysterious Big Boss, instead of Cheung as Alfie had thought, but none of us, even our clever Mr Moon, had thought they might be partners. So Mr Wing had written that letter just in case anyone pointed the finger at him, to shove all the blame on his other half, Mr Cheung. Not one or the other, but both! Alfie and I could hardly wait to get back to the office to write our joint report on this development.

*

My Gran had a collection of antique recordings of so-called comedians and comic sketches and plays and things, all about the police in the olden days. We still had an old-fashioned record player at that time, and she used to play them sometimes to remind herself of when she was a little girl. She said my Grandpa was very fond of them, too. I've still got them, though they're no use now, being those old black flat things that you can't use on a CD player.

Anyway, I remember one of them being of an old fool called Rob Wilton, who was supposed to be a typical bumbling bobby of the time. This woman was telling him she'd murdered her husband, and he was asking her to spell her name and give her date of birth and all that rubbish instead of taking the whole thing seriously.

Well, I was put in mind of all that crazy stuff when our Station Reception Officer phoned up to Derek's office that day, and when I answered, she asked me to come down to the front office because there was a woman there saying she'd shot her husband. And she was asking for me, by name. This has got to be a wind-up, I thought.

And that was another thing. I've never believed in coincidence, but I had to admit to myself there must be something in it after all when I saw who it was that our SRO had put in the front office interview room: Mrs Wing.

Gaping at her stupidly, the first thing I said to her was, 'I thought you were in China!'

She was as calm as ever.

'I know you did,' she said. 'That was what you were supposed to think.'

Chapter 21

Then suddenly we were in the middle of huge activity. No more sitting around asking each other what to do next. While I was doing the prelim interview with Annabel Wing, behind the scenes SO19 were being contacted, forensics were being lined up, and Alfie was trying frantically to get hold of Mr Moon at Scotland Yard.

Meanwhile, Mrs Wing was coolly telling me the tale of how, why, where and when she shot her husband.

'I had started to suspect him of living a double life some time ago,' she said, 'but of course in that trite *(trite? I thought, what the hell is a trite? but I wrote it down anyway)* way that we women do, I assumed it was another woman. Unaccountable absences, mysterious telephone calls, appearance of excitement for no obvious reason, and so forth. But against that, instead of our finances decreasing, we appeared to be getting richer all the time.'

'Excuse me, Mrs Wing,' I interrupted, scribbling furiously, 'if you wouldn't mind, it would be best if you left the explanations till later. Just tell me now where and when you killed Mr Wing, and how you happened to have a gun.'

'Oh certainly,' she said, still not seeming a bit bothered about it all, 'if you wish. This occurred at approximately nine forty-five this morning, just after I'd taken the children to school. If you give me your notebook, I'll write down the address for you to save spelling it out.'

'But this is in Chelsea,' I said when she handed me back

my notebook. 'Why did you come all the way to Watford to report it?'

'Because I know you, Sergeant Pusey, and I know I can trust you,' she said with a sweet smile. 'I thought it would be a feather in your cap to wind up this case. And we got on so well together, you remember.'

The cool nerve of the woman!

I was a bit numb by now, but still alert enough to notice the address was right near where James and Sadie Lee had lived. Also in the vicinity of the burglary we'd been told had mistakenly taken place in the home of a friend of the Big Boss. We'd come full circle from where this had all started, with Juan Garcia's 'little matey' being killed because he'd committed that error of breaking into the wrong house. I seemed to remember that the victim's name was Chang. I made a mental note to ask Annabel Wing if she knew Chang, but now wasn't a good time for that.

The woman's nuts, I thought as I rushed out of the room to get someone to call Derek's pal in Chelsea to meet us at the premises of the murder. I knew we should have handed the whole thing over to Chelsea to deal with, but I couldn't bear to let go of it when we might be so close to solving the whole thing. Of course she'd hit the nail on the head when she said it would be a feather in my cap, the shrewd bitch. What a pain if I owed it to her if I got promotion.

Derek would have to make it right with Rex Carothers so that we could handle this murder, even if only jointly with Chelsea.

The trouble was, I didn't know what to do with Annabel Wing in the meantime. I couldn't take her to the custody suite and charge her with murder until I'd checked that she was telling the truth. What if it was all some cock and bull story she was spinning for reasons I couldn't guess? And I couldn't really tell the custody sergeant to bang her up until she'd been charged. She wasn't even a suspect yet. Not that I didn't believe her, just that I'd learned that this case had so many twists and turns, it wasn't safe to believe anything without proof. Finally I decided the best thing was to take her with us to Chelsea. To what might or might not be the scene of the crime.

So off we all trooped in convoy, Mrs Wing and Alfie and me in the lead car, and Fred and Kevin behind with the forensics team, and SO19 somewhere on their way. Meanwhile Alfie was still trying to get hold of Derek at the Chinese Embassy, Mr Moon at Scotland Yard, and Derek's pal, DI Rex Carothers, at the Chelsea nick.

Alfie had agreed with me that it was best to get everyone to meet at the Wing's Chelsea home. This was a big deal and maybe with us just being sergeants we weren't qualified to handle it all. If Mr Wing was the Big Boss and he was dead, wouldn't that pretty well wind up the case?

Luckily Alfie got through to Mr Moon and Derek while we were shoving our way through the traffic, and Derek said he'd contact DI Carothers while he was on his way. Even with the sirens going and the lights flashing, we didn't make very good time, so I guessed we wouldn't get there before them.

Well, I don't know the Chelsea area very well, but everyone's heard of Cheyne Walk, so I shouldn't have been surprised when we finally drew up at this great mansion. One look and you could hear it screaming, 'Guess how many millions I cost!'

If it was the Wings' 'second home', it was enough to make anyone wonder how the humble little interpreter who lived above his shop in Watford could afford this palace as well. A good indication that Wing really was our master-crook.

I was relieved to see Mr Moon, Derek and DI Carothers had all managed to get there first and they were waiting for us outside. If anyone had told me I'd be afraid of new responsibilities, I'd never have believed them. But it was true, I absolutely didn't want to be in charge of this operation. I just wasn't ready for anything this big.

Mr Moon got the SO19 people deployed, then asked for the ram to break the door down. Mrs Wing pushed forward through the small crowd around him.

'Please don't do that,' she said, 'here's the key. Just let yourselves in. My – the body is in the largest bedroom on the second floor. Use the lift if you like,' she added in an offhand sort of way, as if of course everyone had a lift in their home.

That stumble when she'd nearly said 'my husband' instead of 'the body' was the first sign she'd given of not being as cool as I'd thought. If she was upset, she certainly was great at covering it up. It made me wonder how many husbands this woman had killed, anyway.

Even though it was such a big house, it didn't take long, with so many of us available, to search the whole place. There wasn't a living or a dead body anywhere. Except for us blundering about, in and out of all the rooms, there wasn't a sign of anyone. Nor could the forensic people, at first examination, find any blood stains or bullet-holes.

We all assembled in a large first-floor sitting room.

Mr Moon asked the commander of SO19 to stand by.

Then he asked Mrs Wing to sit down with us all and explain exactly where and how she had shot her husband, and what made her so certain that the shot had killed him. Also, where was the gun? That was the easiest part. She produced it from her handbag.

Gloved, Mr Moon handed it to one of the forensic team,

who seemed only too glad to have something to do. He peered and sniffed.

'Not loaded,' he reported, 'and if this gun's ever been fired, it certainly wasn't in the recent past. Not this week, I'd say,' he revised cautiously. Forensics always liked to be on the safe side. 'We'll check for fingerprints,' he went on, and then just stood there. After a bit, when nobody said anything, he asked Mr Moon, 'Is there anything else, sir?'

Mr Moon sighed.

'I suppose not,' he said, 'and on your way out, would you mind asking the SO19 commander to pop in?'

Always polite, Mr Moon, even with all this aggravation.

Helmeted, booted, body-armoured, the commander came clumping in.

'Looks as if we're not needed here, sir,' he said to Mr Moon, with just the smallest hint of sarcasm in his voice. And Mr Moon agreed, sighing again.

'Now, Mrs Wing,' he said, 'would you like to tell me what this is all about?'

'Well, as I was saying to Sergeant Pusey here,' she started, 'I became suspicious of my husband some time ago–'

'No, that's not what we need to hear,' Mr Moon interrupted, polite but firm, as ever. 'What we would like to know is why you say you have shot your husband when it is quite clear that you have done no such thing, at least not on these premises and not with the gun you claim to have used.'

She stood up and strolled to the window, as if she was thinking what to say next. We could see, as she pulled the curtain back, that all the support forces were driving away.

'I don't know what to say,' she said. 'I really did shoot my husband in this house, and I was certain he was dead when I left. I can't account for anything else. Who could have come into this house and removed him and cleaned up?'

'Not to speak of your gun not having been fired recently,'

I couldn't help blurting out. If this was all some sort of trick, I couldn't begin to work out what it was. And I could see that I wasn't the only one who was hacked off with the whole thing.

'Well,' Mr Moon said to me, 'you'd better take Mrs Wing back to Shady Lane for the time being. I have to go back to my meeting at Scotland Yard, and Inspector Michaelson has to return to the Chinese Embassy. When we are all back in Watford, we will discuss this matter further.'

So off Alfie and Mrs Wing and I went, with Alfie driving this time and me in the back with Mrs Wing. None of us seemed to fancy talking, so I passed the time by looking out of the window in a dreamy sort of way, not taking anything in. Mrs Wing kept looking behind us.

'I think we're being followed,' she said.

I had no time for any more of her nonsense.

'Alfie!' I said sharply, suddenly taking notice of where we were. 'Where do you think you're going? This isn't the way I told you to go–'

A car swerved in front of us and another one drew alongside. Suddenly we were surrounded by little Chinese men waving knives and guns.

I didn't even have time to say, 'What the f–' before they were all over us, two of them dragging Mrs Wing out of the car.

For once, she wasn't so calm.

'Sergeant!' she shrieked. 'I trusted you to keep me safe! I came to you to protect me from these–'

Alfie and I got out of the car, but there was nothing we could do. It was no good having a go, even with any of my karate moves. We were outnumbered and out-weaponed. We stood there like two dummies while they pushed Mrs Wing into one of their cars and it drove off at speed. The ones with the other car waited, and we waited, for about another five minutes. Then they jumped in and drove off in the opposite direction. No point in trying to follow them. What would we have done if we'd caught up with them? And what with Alfie having already lost our way, I wasn't even sure where we were. But I called for assistance anyway, useless or not. And with my ears burning, I called DI Carothers at Chelsea to ask if he could help. At least I had the reg numbers of the two cars, for whatever that was worth.

'I'm sorry, Greta,' Alfie mumbled. 'If I hadn't taken a wrong turning–'

'No, that wasn't it. They were following us anyway, looking for a likely place to spring on us. But who were they? What the hell do you think it was all about?'

What I was really dreading was telling Mr Moon we'd mucked things up again. It seemed as if every time we had some kind of lead, it slipped through our fingers.

As it turned out, he was back in his 'kind uncle' form, and didn't give us a hard time at all. He was as baffled as we were about whether or not Mrs Wing had actually shot her husband.

'I don't think so,' I offered. 'I think what it was all about was what she screamed at me as they dragged her off. She'd come to us for protection from some rival gang that she knew about, and she spun that yarn about killing her old man because she didn't want to just say to us, "Keep me safe, I'm in danger". If she'd said that,' I went on, by now getting all keen on my theory, 'we'd have asked questions she didn't want to answer. But she didn't reckon on our sussing out so quickly that she hadn't shot anyone.'

'Go on, then,' Mr Moon urged, 'see if you can develop your theory. Just let your imagination roam for a while.'

I wasn't sure if he was being sarcastic, but I thought, what the hell, give it a go anyway, what have I got to lose?

'Well, we've been saying to each other, maybe Cheung is the Big Boss, or maybe it's Wing, or maybe they're partners. But what if there's *two* gangs, and Cheung and Wing are rival bosses? If we're looking at as big an operation as it seems, why should it all be run by one lot? What do we know about the Triad Wars? Is all this part of that, whatever it is? And come to think of it, why should we be talking about two gangs? Who knows how many there might be?'

I shut up. I could see by their faces that I'd run on a bit too much. Alfie for one looked as if he was trying not to burst out laughing, Derek had his eyebrows up in his hairline, and Mr Moon – Mr Moon was nodding!

'According to what I heard at Scotland Yard today, you could be right,' he said. 'There's going to be a co-ordination of forces to try to get hold of this slippery lot once and for all.'

'You mean it's out of our hands now?' Derek asked.

I thought it was a bit tactless of him to sound so pleased at the idea.

'No,' Mr Moon said, at his sharpest, 'that's exactly what I don't mean. We're going to be part of a larger operation, and it has not yet been decided who will be the commanding officer.'

I really hoped it would be Mr Moon himself, but I knew it would sound too much like brown-nosing if I said so. For once I managed to hold my tongue.

Derek's mobile rang, and the prat actually looked at Mr Moon for permission before he answered it. Turned out it was the Chinese Embassy asking him to come back for a further meeting.

'Before you go, Derek, perhaps you'd like to tell us all if anything transpired from your previous meeting?' Mr Moon was still using his sharpest voice on him. He seemed to have gone right off poor Derek. I wondered why. Was it just because he thought Derek hadn't handled this case properly, or something I didn't know about?

'I'm afraid they weren't at all helpful,' Derek said, 'and I couldn't tell if it was they couldn't help or didn't want to. They had no way of tracing the Wings in this country, and all they could tell me was that they hadn't applied for visas to go to China, as they would have done being British subjects. The only other thing I got from the meeting was I noticed that all their correspondence is on the old quarto size paper that we used here years ago. And the letter we got from Wing was on normal A4 size. Those two points seemed to me to indicate that his letter was not written from China, but had been taken there to be posted back here to trick us into thinking that Wing and his family were all back in China.'

'If it was indeed from him at all,' Mr Moon added. 'What else we seem to have learned today is that Wing was certainly living a double life, and his wife was fully aware of it. Since we had been treating them as, so to speak, adjuncts to the police, they had opportunity to keep in touch with our progress and to mislead us from time to time if it suited their plans. The one-time Detective Constable Victoria North was correct when she wrote that she wasn't the only source of information for this gang, or Triad, whatever it is we're fighting. OK, Derek, off you go back to the Chinese Embassy and see what else you can pick up there.'

I couldn't speak for Alfie, but I didn't feel inclined to ask the Super what we should be doing next. Keeping shtum was my best bet at that moment, I thought. And as he didn't say any more to us, we just sort of smartly exited right behind Derek. My priority was to see if we could get a trace on those two reg numbers of the cars that had abducted Mrs Wing.

Alfie's was, as usual, to nip up to the canteen and have a bit of a nosh.

As I should have guessed, the cars weren't on the PNC (Police National Computer) for any offence, so I got the owners' names. Only one owner for the two, it turned out: a Mr Percy Chang with an address in Chelsea. I gave my forehead a smack – not three gang bosses, Lord help us! For the first time in my life, I felt that a bit of praying might help.

By then I felt I needed something a bit more restful in life. I started writing up my notes, and by the time Alfie got back from his tea, I was well into page four. He read what I'd written so far, and added a few remarks of his own, and in no time we'd got the whole sad story on paper. For what it was worth, which was about one old penny.

'Come on, Greta,' Alfie said, 'it's been a long day. Let's pack up. Come home with me for a spot of supper. You know my Betty's always glad to see you, and you haven't been round to us for weeks.'

'What about all this?' I asked, waving my sheaf of notes in his face.

'No, don't let's beat our brains out any more. Give it a rest, girl. Sleep on it. Maybe by the morning we'll have some fresh ideas, or something else will have turned up.'

He was right. We had a nice quiet family evening together, him and me and Betty and the twins and their loathsome pets, and we didn't speak or even think about the case the whole time. Then I went home and slept like a baby.

*

Sure enough, next morning something else did turn up. Nothing useful, of course. But a bit of a turn-up for the books.

Derek said, 'The Embassy people asked me to come back

because they had someone they wanted me to meet. Not that I could talk to him, because he didn't have a word of English. But it was mainly for his sake. God knows how he managed to make his way to them–'

'Start at the beginning,' Mr Moon said. 'Who was this person?'

Derek wasn't above putting a bit of drama into things.

'His name is Ah Wo-Pang,' he said, 'and he was the husband of the late Ah Weng So!'

Got to admit, he deserved the gasps we all gave at this. Then he got down to giving the facts, more in his usual reporting style.

'By chance, visiting in the next village to the one where he came from in China, he ran into the man who'd organised the journey for the people who'd ended up doing slave labour here in Hertfordshire. Ah Wo-Pang had wanted to be one of that group, but he'd broken his leg a month before, and it wasn't mended enough for the journey. Ah Weng So insisted on going in his place. She said when she got to the rich land of England and earned enough money, she'd send for him and they'd start a new life. Then they'd be able to repay all the villagers who had made a contribution to the cost of the journey for her. The organiser promised him he'd look after her and see that she came to no harm on that long voyage, and help her get a good job and somewhere to live. When Ah Wo-Pang saw this man again, he got hold of him and held a knife to his throat. "Tell me what happened to my wife," he said, "and why I haven't heard from her in all this time." When the man said he didn't know, Ah Wo-Pang made him bring him to England on the next journey without payment. How he made his way from Dover to the Chinese Embassy remains a mystery. And frankly, I think it's best that we don't enquire into that just now.'

Derek sat back while we all pondered this sad story. I

was really sorry for this poor man who'd gone through all that to find his wife, only to be told that she'd been murdered and none of us knew what had happened to their baby. Worse still, they couldn't have even known she was pregnant at that time, because surely he wouldn't have let her make that dangerous journey with a bun in the oven.

Well, yes, very heartbreaking. But as far as our case was concerned, my reaction was 'So what?' It didn't take us an inch forward, or make a splinter of difference to our fund of knowledge. I might have known that Mr Moon's point of view would be nothing like mine.

'Well, what a good thing the formal adoption hasn't gone through yet,' he said. 'It would have been a minefield to sort out if Mrs Perry had wanted to hang on to that poor little baby and her true father had wanted her too.'

'Mrs Perry?' Alfie asked.

'Yes, the nurse at the hospital where Ah Weng So had her baby. You remember she wanted to adopt the child from the start. Of course I've kept track of the little girl's progress.'

Of course. Just like Mr Moon. And he'd got the nurse's name right, too. I was only surprised he and Mrs Moon hadn't wanted to adopt the baby themselves. After all, they only had five of their own. Adding on a little Chinese one would have been their idea of fun, probably.

'I take it this unfortunate man has been informed of the situation?' he asked. 'How shattering for him, after all he must have been through to get here. And he probably didn't even know his wife was pregnant.'

And he shook his head sadly, sighed, and sat quiet for a minute, as if that was all he had to think about.

Derek said, 'Yes, of course he's been told everything, and the Embassy people are arranging for him to see his child. Although of course he *is* here illegally, I'm sure in the circumstance… Anyway, there's more. It emerged that he had managed, somehow, and we don't ask how, to take the organiser of the trip prisoner at some point. And he's left him in some deserted shed in the countryside between Dover and London.'

'My God, man, why didn't you say that at the beginning,' Mr Moon shouted, springing to his feet. 'Where is he? Did you get a location? Fetch him in. He could be the key to the whole case!'

Alfie and I jumped up too, all alert to rush off at Mr Moon's instruction. Derek stayed sitting where he was.

'I'm sorry,' he said, 'but you must understand that I was in the hands of the Embassy people who were translating everything Ah Wo-Pang told me. And when it came to that part, they just dried up. It was obvious they were intent on finding this man themselves. And there was nothing I could do about it. I made it clear to them that we badly needed to interview this person. But he is in all probability a Chinese national, and if they get him into their Embassy, as you know, sir–'

'We have no jurisdiction,' Mr Moon finished in chorus with him.

Well, I thought, *that was all very interesting. Even thrilling. But where does it get us? Just where we were before. Thank you, Derek.*

Chapter 22

Nobody gave me any instructions after that. Maybe even Mr Moon felt we'd come to a dead halt.

So I decided I was going to act on my own initiative, and do all kinds of things I knew I wouldn't get permission for. I took an unmarked car out of the yard and didn't log it out, and I drove to the Chinese Embassy, way out of our area of operation, and I parked right opposite, outside the Royal Institute of British Architects.

There's some international law or other that makes it illegal to park or demonstrate or stop to blow your nose actually outside the Chinese Embassy, so there I was, in amongst some sort of organised protest about Tibet.

Every now and then a security officer or a traffic warden would come by, and I'd give them all a different spiel, and that, backed up by my warrant card, seemed to keep me safely sitting there for a while. Those Tibetan protesters kicked up quite a racket, and I was surprised that the architects didn't ask them to move on. But that's British tolerance for you.

I knew what I was doing was nutty. My plan was to follow the Embassy car that took Ah Wo-Pang towards the Dover road. I was sure they'd take him to get his captive back from the shed where he'd left him. But there were problems. First of all, how was I to know Ah Wo-Pang if I saw him? Or they might have already gone and come back before I got there. Then, they might have tinted windows, so I wouldn't know who was in any car that took people out of their front door.

They might have cars picking people up from there all day, and I could easily choose the wrong one to follow. And anyway, if I did manage to get past those snags, how would I know if they weren't just taking him to meet the nurse who had his little daughter?

The fact was, the longer I sat there, the more I thought of all the reasons why this was a lousy idea. But I was just so bored of this whole case, and the way it was dragging on and taking up all of our time and thoughts, when we could be engaged in some interesting *solvable* case, I felt anything was worth a go.

On the other hand, sometimes luck is with the idiots of this world, and I was certainly one of those on that particular day. Not always, of course. A car stopped outside the Embassy, it didn't have tinted windows, and it had a uniformed driver with a uniformed security man next to him, and two deadpan Chinese gents got in the back. I had no idea what I was doing, but I followed it anyway.

From the start I was doing it just for the sake of something to do, but when it got clear that we were heading towards Dover, a little ray of hope shone through my gloom. (I never knew I was so poetic.) I'd never been trained in following a car in another car without being detected, so they probably knew from the off that I was on their tail. But what the hell, they didn't try to take any evasive action, so maybe they didn't mind this same car keeping right behind them all the way.

After a while they turned off onto a B road, then a minor road, then a little track, all with me close behind. They stopped at the gate to a field that looked completely empty (thank goodness, no cows), and all got out of their car. I did the same. One of the plain-clothes men made a sort of little bow to me. I gave him one back, with my best friendly smile. Wondered, show him my badge? Decided, no. They started to walk across the field, me following. Then they turned off to the right into a little clump of trees, and by this time I'd caught them up and was walking with them.

Blow me! That little bugger Ah Wo-Pang had said he'd left the illegal travel agent in a shed! But here was some poor sod tied to a tree! And as far as I could make out, what tied him was torn-up lengths of his own clothes. He looked in a bad way, too. I wondered how long he'd been there. The Chinese didn't seem to care, though, they just untied him enough to free him from the tree and then dragged him across the field and into their car. I was right beside them.

'Er, excuse me,' I began politely, 'I wonder if I could have a word.'

The security man said, 'I'm the only one who speaks English, you'll have to talk to me.'

'Is that gentleman called Ah Wo-Pang?'

'Yes.'

'And is the man who was tied to the tree–'

'Sorry. Can't tell you more,' he said, and got into the car.

This time the arrangement was different. The plain-clothes man drove, with Ah Wo-Pang beside him. In the back, the prisoner was sandwiched between the uniformed driver and the security man. The prisoner was looking more and more sorry for himself and I could see why. None of them spoke to each other, but I could see there were no feelings of mateyness between them.

So we all sped back to the Chinese Embassy. Outside, all got out, the driver got in the front and made off to wherever they kept their cars. I stopped outside the premises of the poor long-suffering British Architects, who must have been going deaf by this time, the Tibetan protesters making as much noise as ever. I dashed across the road just in time as the door was closing behind the other four.

'Excuse me,' I panted, planting an absolutely illegal foot in the doorway, 'could I possibly have a word with Ah Wo-Pang?'

My luck had run out. My foot was shoved back and the door slammed in my face without even a polite Chinese bow. But my blood was up by then, and I felt I was hot on the trail of something or other. So I stood there, ringing and ringing the bell until finally the door opened a crack and a very unfriendly Chinese eye looked out at me.

'Sorry,' the voice of the eye said, 'can't come in without appointment.'

I drove slowly back to Watford, turning over in my mind the different ways I could explain to Mr Moon what I'd done. The very least I could expect was disciplinary action, or it could be worse. But still I had to tell him what I'd found out. I was sure that this guy who Ah Wo-Pang had tied up was the key to our whole puzzle, if only we could get to him.

Turned out I could have saved myself a lot of brain-ache. When I went to see Mr Moon, he knew all about it. The Embassy people had been on to Scotland Yard, who'd passed the story on to him.

It seemed it was all for the best that they hadn't turned their prisoner over to us right away, because their methods of interrogation were a lot quicker and maybe more, let's say, intensive than ours were allowed to be. It was interesting that the prisoner absolutely swore that once he'd passed his 'passengers' on to whatever final destination he'd been given for each cargo, he had no idea what happened to them next.

But he knew alright who'd set the whole scheme up, and who he worked for. It was a partnership, but not one we'd expected.

The partners were Mr and Mrs Wing. *He* had the connections in the People's Republic of China, and *she* had a huge family link-up here in England.

'That's excellent,' Mr Moon told us, 'now all we have to

do is find Mr and Mrs Wing. We don't need to concern ourselves with Mr Cheung. He's currently having some difficulties with the Customs and Excise people. And it's clear that whatever his connection with illegal immigrants and slave labour, he won't be able to continue that line of business for some time.'

'And Mr Percy Chang?' I asked. 'He's the owner of the two cars they used to grab Mrs Wing.'

'Oh yes,' Mr Moon said airily, 'as I recall, Mr Percy Chang was the victim of the burglary committed by the late friend of your Juan Garcia – Charlie Hampson was his name, wasn't it?'

'You mean,' I asked, 'burgling the wrong house caused Charlie the Chump to be murdered? That must mean Chang is a friend of the Big Boss. But if Wing is the Big Boss, why would Chang kidnap his friend's wife?'

'I think we'll find it's a case of crooks falling out. After all, it wouldn't be the first time we've seen that kind of thing,' Mr Moon said, still not seeming bothered by the whole messy puzzle. 'Now you two,' he said to Alfie and Derek, who'd both been dead quiet during all this, 'I'd like to have a quiet word with Greta.'

They both seemed pleased to go and leave me on my tod to get a roasting. Friends! Who needs them?

'Now Greta,' Mr Moon said, still quite calm, 'you know one of the things I've always admired about you is the way you use your initiative. In fact, that was one of the factors that helped in your promotion to sergeant. But you really must curb your enthusiasm sometimes. We almost had a very sticky diplomatic incident with you trying to force your way into the Chinese Embassy. And if the Foreign Office had been involved, you know very well the repercussions could have been endless. In short, it would have been worse than embarrassing.'

And he frowned. But it wasn't very fierce, and it looked to me as if his heart wasn't in it. This was a man who could be quite scary when he was really angry, and this wasn't one of those times. And he hadn't said anything about my going off in a station car without logging it off, or watching the Embassy or following the Embassy car into the country, or any of that. Just the bit where I'd put my foot in the door.

I put on my most serious face.

'I'm really sorry, sir, if I caused any trouble. But I only asked–'

He waved his pudgy paw in the air.

'No, never mind. I've given you an unofficial reprimand, and let's say no more about it. The thing is, have you got any ideas about finding Mr and Mrs Wing? Naturally Mr Percy Chang has been questioned, and of course he claims to know nothing about two of his cars being used for an abduction. We've got people watching his house and all four of his restaurants.'

'Has he got any storage places, warehouses and things? Is anyone watching the Wings' house in Chelsea?'

'We haven't been able to find if Mr Chang has any storage places, and the Wings' house has been taped off with a uniformed officer guarding it. We've got people checking on all the schools in Watford and Chelsea to try to get a line on their children. The whole of Hertfordshire is being combed for more slave factories, and farmers are being questioned about gang-masters and their farm workers. Come on, Greta, you're the ideas person. What haven't we thought of?'

'Sir, wouldn't it be better if we had a brain-storming session with Alfie Partridge and Inspector Michaelson?'

His eyebrows shot up at the way I spoke about Derek so formally.

But he didn't say anything, just shook his head and muttered something about I could go now. I didn't need telling twice. I'd expected to get a severe reprimand, but in a way what I'd got was worse than that. I was being asked to get a brilliant idea when none of my superior officers could manage one. Goes without saying that when you're asked something like that, your brain empties out completely, and you can hardly remember your own name and number. Best thing I could do, I decided, was try not to do any thinking. Just sleep on it.

That evening I did all the relaxing things I could think of after my karate class. I put lovely smelly bubbly stuff in the bath and had a long soak with candles all round the bathroom and soothing music and a nice glass of plonk. I felt fine after that, except a bit randy, so I was more or less pleased when Ari turned up again, unexpectedly. He wasn't a bit put out about having been turned away with Jim a few nights previously. Instead he told me how gorgeous I was looking and smelling, and how much he loved me.

Well, I might be the brightest sergeant in Hertfordshire, but I'm human too. So, not much sleep that night, and not much chance for thinking about problems, either.

*

Course, it dawned on me next morning, while I was sipping the mug of coffee Ari had brought me in bed before he sloped off for early duty, what I should have done was talked it all over with him. Even though he's not the cleverest person I know, once in a while he comes up with a really good suggestion when you're least expecting it. And even when he doesn't, sometimes just telling him about a problem helps me to get my head straight. Anyway, too late for that, so I lay there and tried to concentrate. Nothing happened.

Not having an idea in my head, I couldn't figure out what I thought I was doing when instead of going to Shady Lane, I found myself driving towards what I had thought was the Wings' home in Watford. With all that had happened since we'd found those Chinese threats sprayed on the walls of that flat, it was obvious it was just somewhere they'd pretended to live. So what did I think I'd find there now? Standard answer: Buggered if I know.

With the usual method I let myself in, ready to discover absolutely nothing except that I was wasting my time again. Whatever I found would have been a surprise, so I shouldn't have been so shocked to find what I thought at first was a dead body. Course it wasn't dead, only half-dead. It was Mrs Wing, bound and gagged and hardly breathing. Now why should that surprise me?

I tried a bit of the old mouth-to-mouth while I was waiting for the ambulance, but it didn't seem to do her much good. And it sure as hell didn't make me feel any better.

Nor did the screaming Chinese geezer who jumped out at me from nowhere just as I straightened up to make another call to tell the ambulance people how urgent it was and they should get a move on. This feller came leaping at me making all this noise like one of those acrobats they call actors in the all-action Hong Kong films. None of my karate skills did me a bit of good.

That was all I remembered of that.

Turned out the ambulance people were amazed to find two bodies waiting for them instead of one body and a live police sergeant.

Still, they did a good job on us, and it was just bad luck that only one of the two of us survived. Guess which one.

True, I had a nasty knife wound. But poor Mrs Wing had worse than that.

She had all kinds of injuries, burns and knife-cuts, three fingers chopped off and the rest broken, as well as crushed ribs. I was told afterwards that the medics did their usual great job on her, revived her once, but then they lost her. The trouble was they couldn't give her the normal heart resuscitation because of the danger of the crushed ribs puncturing her lungs. But in the end, it was her heart that gave out, and she was gone.

You didn't need to be a doctor or a detective to work out that someone had been doing some brutal things to her. You'd think it was to get information. Or maybe not. With the people we were dealing with here, probably it was just plain viciousness, and not for any other reason.

Anyway, it did seem to all of us, when Mr Moon and Alfie and Derek gathered round my bed for a quick de-briefing, that what her captors had tried to find out from her was the very same thing we wanted to know ourselves: where was Mr Wing?

'Can we pull in Percy Chang?' was my next big question to Mr Moon.

But while he was considering his answer, I started to feel the anaesthetic kicking in again. I fought the waves of sleep to mumble out one more question.

'What about the children?'

Alfie told me much later that there'd been a bit of an argy-bargy about that. First of all, they weren't sure exactly what I'd been trying to say. Then when they'd decided I really did ask *what about the children?* they didn't know what children I meant. It was Alfie who worked out that I was trying to say, track down the Wing children and use them to locate their father. That's what they'd already been doing, but I'd forgotten Mr Moon had told me that.

With the help of their friendly neighbour, Mrs Patel, they found the school the Wing kids had gone to in Watford. Then with his usual cunning, Mr Moon used the Head to make a television appeal to them. She was so great at it, Mr Moon actually mentioned to her afterwards that she had the chance of an alternative career there, as an actress. I haven't got the exact text of what she said, but what it amounted to was that their mother had had a terrible accident and she needed to see them and their father, urgently. She asked for them to get in touch with her, personally, and not the police or the hospital.

She said something like, 'You know me, Carol and Keith, and you know you can trust me. I don't know why we can't find you, or why you stopped coming to school. But whatever problems or troubles you've got, you know I'll help you. So please give me a call or come and see me. If you don't want to come to the school, you know where I live, come to my home. You'll always be welcome there.'

And it was all done like with suppressed emotion and tears held back, and all that rubbish. Everyone thought it was most excellent. No wonder Mr Moon thought she was in the wrong job if her act was that good.

Sorry I missed it, but I wasn't feeling much like watching TV at the time. My knife wound wasn't exactly superficial, and I kept having to have scans and X-rays and stuff to find out how my internal organs were. I told the docs that I was tough and a good healer and would be fine, but for some reason they didn't take any notice. Just kept on wheeling me about and checking bits.

Well, it was my suspicion it was all their mucking about that made it take so long for me to recover. But whatever, it was weeks before they let me home, and even then I had strict instructions not to go back to work. And I was itching to be in at the end of this long drawn-out mess of a case.

But the fact was, it never had an end. Well, our bit of it did, in that the ploy worked and we got our mitts on Mr Wing through our use of the children.

As we'd hoped, the oldest child, Keith Wing, rang the Headmistress. And she persuaded him to tell her where his father was, easy-peasy. This time there were no glitches and Mr Wing was taken into custody without even a struggle. He'd been holed up with the children in a posh hotel in Bishops Stortford. I'd have loved to have been there when they stormed the place with all the SO19 characters stomping about and the place swarming with uniforms. Bet it was fun.

But finally, of course, the poor Wing kids had to be told that their mother hadn't just had a terrible accident but was dead. Mr Moon was quite upset that we'd had to use them in what he thought was a heartless way to get at their father, so he ended up trying to adopt them. I suppose if you've got five, a few more don't matter. But maybe he won't get them anyway, because I expect they've got hundreds of family members willing to take them.

Although we'd got our mitts on Mr Wing, we couldn't prove much of what we actually knew against him, but at least we got him on the murder of Ah Weng So. There was a bit of a puzzle about that. The DPS thought the case might be a bit dodgy, just depending on the statements of James and Sadie Lee. And then, miraculously, it turned out that there was forensic evidence after all!

I said to Mr Moon and Derek when they told me this latest news, 'But we were told quite clearly there was no forensic on or around Ah Weng So. And no DNA on her body. Or did I dream all that?'

'No, Greta,' Mr Moon told me, without a crimp of a smile,

'you didn't dream it. But you know, even forensic scientists have been known to make mistakes. And it turned out that they'd overlooked some little clue or other. But still,' and now he let go with a big grin, 'the important thing is, we got him, didn't we? He'll be found guilty and sentenced to life, you'll see.'

If I didn't know Mr Moon to be the soul of honesty, I might have suspected him of managing some kind of fiddle. Like getting a bit of DNA planted somehow. But he's not like me, ready to – as I've heard it said – push the envelope of truth occasionally. So it must all have been on the up and up. I'm sure.

And we really did get Mr Wing for murder. But all the other stuff, about the smuggling and enslaving the illegal Chinese immigrants, and the gang warfare, and the organised burgling, all that had to go by the board, because we simply couldn't find any way of proving he was in charge.

Still, the combined forces of Herts police did manage to locate all the factories and gang-masters and disband it all, and brought successful cases against the local little managers. And the guy that Ah Wo-Pang had captured turned out to be very helpful after all. No surprise that he changed his tune about not knowing the destinations of his 'passengers', after a bit of heavy questioning from those Chinese Embassy security men. They looked as if they knew their stuff. I certainly wouldn't want to be questioned by them.

We didn't proceed with action for obstruction against the villagers of Nasty.

Mr Percy Chang was never even arrested, never mind being charged with anything, even though it seemed clear to me that it was his gang that had kidnapped Mrs Wing and tortured her to death. And I was sure it was one of his lot who'd stuck a knife in me. But we couldn't prove any of it.

Mr Cheung went down for all kinds of offences against Customs and Excise, including evading paying his VAT – silly man. He had a good thing going, and spoiled it all just to save some amount that must have been like petty cash for him. Then it turned out he'd also been doing some financial shenanigans about not paying all sorts of other taxes – income tax, business tax, all that stuff that I don't know much about. So he got a severe sentence. Prison would soon knock some of the fat off him, I thought.

All the illegal Chinese immigrants were helped to apply for asylum, and most of their cases were still in the pipeline at the time that Mr Wing came up for trial. We could only hope they'd be given a fair deal after all they'd been through.

By the time Mr Wing was sentenced, I got permission to visit him. I felt strong enough by that time to face him.

'Ah, Sergeant Pusey,' he smiled when he saw me. How could he smile after all that had happened? I couldn't smile back at him.

I said, 'Mr Wing, you know who kidnapped your wife and caused her death, don't you?'

'No,' he said, the smile disappearing, 'how could I know such a thing? It was so terrible, I will never understand it. And now my poor children are orphans. Who do you think could have done this, Sergeant? And what reason could they have had? Can the police not discover anything?'

I could feel myself coming to the boil. OK, we knew by now that the woman had been as much a crook and a heartless dealer in people's lives as her husband. But she didn't deserve to be tortured and killed so brutally. And what a cheek, for him to turn it round as if it was our fault we didn't bring the perpetrators to justice.

'Mr Wing,' I said through gritted teeth, 'we know all about your people-smuggling and all the rest of your little empire of crime. Also that Percy Chang was your biggest rival. And we know he was responsible for your wife's horrible death. Give us evidence. Give us facts. If you help us bring him to justice, we'll put a stop to his activities and at the same time you'll get back at him for torturing and killing your wife.'

He stood up.

'I'm sorry, Sergeant, I'm afraid I have no idea what you are talking about. You seem to think that because I have been found guilty of the death of poor Ah Weng So, I am guilty of all sorts of other crimes. Let me take this opportunity to tell you, once and for all, I am innocent of all of this. I don't know who killed Ah Weng So or my dear wife. If I did I would be pleased to share my information with you. But I assure you I have done nothing wrong.'

So that was his last word. All that crime going unpunished. That was the worst of it. Everybody involved, from the Chief Constable of Hertfordshire to the Assistant Commissioner of Scotland Yard, knew that we hadn't really stopped anything. All the horrible trading in bodies and the rest of the racketeering would go on.

It left me feeling thoroughly depressed. Ari said that wasn't it; getting a knife stuck in your tender parts is what makes you depressed. Maybe he was right. He was always a great comfort, dear kind Ari.

And in his sensible way, Ari also pointed out to me that Mr Wing couldn't give evidence about Percy Chang without incriminating himself.

'He's got enough trouble,' Ari argued, 'without putting himself in deeper shit, innit.'

I had to agree. It made sense. But it didn't make me any happier.

Anyway, I cheered up a lot when Derek came to see me. Not because he came, but because of our conversation. I'd been looking forward to a private chat with him, but this turned out even better than I'd planned.

He said, 'My old Superintendent from Durham has asked me to go back there as soon as Mr Moon will agree.'

'Good idea,' I said. 'Nothing to keep you here. Unless you have the same opinion as those people who say that North of Watford, there's nothing.'

'Don't joke, Greta, I'm serious.'

'OK then, seriously. You didn't do very well here, did you? Maybe back there you'll make a better fist of things.'

'But what about us?'

'Us? What us? There's no us.'

He looked at me soulfully with those lovely chocolate brown eyes filling up.

'Look Greta, I know I've been inadequate in our personal relationship as well as in the Job,' he said, 'and I feel terrible about it.'

I didn't answer.

There was a lot I could have said.

My long struggle to get him had been won that evening in Chipperfield, after all that time when I'd been lusting after him.

Once I'd got him, there was a lot I understood that had been puzzling me.

Now I knew why all his relationships with women had failed.

I could have told him he was so hopeless in bed that there was no remedy for it. No amount of coaching could help someone so clueless.

I could have made mention of small men being small in all components.

I could even have told him he was worse at sex than Jim,

the Long-distance Lorry Driver had been before I'd taught him a few things.

But I didn't. I kept shtum.

Sounding a bit desperate by now, Derek said, 'Can't we give it another chance? That would give me a reason to stay in Watford. I know our first time wasn't marvellous, but won't you give me an opportunity to make things right between us?'

And I said, 'I don't think so.'

THE END